Do-Overs

A Time Travel Thriller of
Sudden Second Chances

By Jon Spoelstra

In 1905, Albert Einstein introduced the Theory of
Special Relativity. Einstein then spent ten years
finding that space and time were interwoven into a
single continuum known as space-time. It is here
where there are sudden second chances or
astonishing do-overs.

DO-OVERS

A Time Travel Thriller
of Sudden Second Chances

Roy Hobbs blew the cash windfall from his best-seller book. Gone was his money, and then his wife Rachel was murdered with the killer never found.

Roy chose to ride into his sunset as a crime reporter in a smaller market. Then a weird stranger made him a freaky offer. The stranger would pay Roy the same money as his best-seller book in return for Roy to write a book for the stranger. The subject of the book would be secret until after Roy makes a decision. Big payday or walk away?

Roy chose big money, and his life hurled into a dimension he could have never imagined. It was there that he faced the most savage do-over that would reconstruct his life in surprising ways.

Could he truly have a do-over on his biggest mistakes in life? Would he make those mistakes time and time again? Could a do-over allow him to rescue Rachel and put an end to the killings?

Roy Hobbs wouldn't be writing this strange new book, he would be *living* it, and the ending could kill him and kill Rachel again and again.

Yep, this is a trip you gotta take. You won't guess the twists and turns, and probably not even the final destination, but you'll certainly have fun. Take the trip today.

This novel is theory, conjecture
and fiction blended at the author's whim.

Chapter One

He looked like a homeless guy, except he was waving in my face a dollar bill that seemed to have way too many zeros on it.

He then raised his other hand to my face. I flinched a bit, not knowing what to expect.

There wasn't a rock or a gun in his hand. It was several more dollar bills with too many zeros pinched together by his thumb and forefinger.

These bills *looked* legit, but without my readers on, I had difficulty reading the bills' denominations. At the least, I could tell with certainty that the bills weren't one-dollar bills, nor were they tens and weren't hundreds. More zeros than two, that was for sure. I squinted and saw *four* zeros. That would be a ten-thousand-dollar bill! This nut case was fanning at least six or seven ten-thousand-dollar bills in front of my eyes. I stopped walking.

The homeless guy said, "I'll pay you exactly double what your advance was for *The Monster Among Us* if you sit down and have a cup of coffee with me." He flapped the greenbacks in front of my eyes as if they were little fans. "I'm buying," he said with a slight, crooked grin.

Hearing his reference to my book caught my attention.

I looked at him. I realized he looked more like an aging, sloppy hippie than a homeless person when I focused. I guess there's a distinction—mainly the smell. He didn't smell of cheap booze or cigarettes. And his face hadn't leathered as a homeless person would. But I could tell that he hadn't taken a big bubble bath recently.

He was tall, lanky, in his fifties, and his untended beard was a wild nest of gray. Strangely, he didn't look crazed or dangerous. He just looked like an old hippie. But who could tell if he was dangerous? After all, I had a best-selling book, *The Monster Among Us*, which chronicled the life of a nerd turned serial killer—murder-by-murder-by-murder. *He looked so harmless* were the words repeated by the serial killer's neighbors, work associates, the cops, jury members, and even the district attorney. If his sixteen victims could speak from the grave, they would probably say the same thing: *He looked so harmless*.

I should have kept on walking; the money had to be fake. This homeless guy probably bought them at a gift store for a buck. He's probably just another goofball that I seemed to attract. With the little bit of fame that had attached itself to me after my book hit the bestseller lists, I'd get goofy suggestions on what I should write next. I brought some of it on myself; my publisher told me not to put my email address in my book's dust jacket. I didn't listen. I wanted to hear from my readers. Most authors never get to talk to their readers. The author writes the book, the agent sells it, the publisher prints it, the bookstores stock it, the readers buy it. Some of them read it.

More people *saw* my book because it was turned into a blockbuster movie that grossed more than a hundred million dollars. At least I developed the sense not to have my email address plastered on the big screen. I had gotten smarter.

I listened to the first few wild ideas that came my way from my readers. After the fifth suggestion, I realized that a particular portion of my readers was stark raving nuts. That fifth suggestion was a detailed map giving the location of an alien killing field. The dead bodies had turned into mushrooms, poisonous mushrooms. If you ate one, you wouldn't die; you would become a reincarnated alien.

"The bills are real," the hippie nerd said, still holding one of the ten-thousand-dollar bills so I could get a better look at it. Instead of a George Washington or a Ben Franklin, a guy named Chase adorned the ten-thousand-dollar bill.

"Salmon P. Chase," the hippie said. "He was Abraham Lincoln's Secretary of the Treasury, and later became Chief Justice of the

Supreme Court." I nodded as if I knew. "If you took this bill into a bank, they'd give you ten-thousand dollars for it. If you took it to a collector, you could get thirty thousand, easy. They were taken off the market—all bills over a hundred were—in 1934. These seven bills are yours—on face value, exactly double what your advance was—if you have a cup of coffee with me."

That was a pretty impressive display. Seventy thousand dollars in that guy's fist. However, through collectors, the street value could be over two hundred thousand dollars that would pass from the hippie's fist to mine. But then a thought flashed in my brain: How would this weirdo know what my advance was for *The Monster Among Us*? Sure enough, my advance was thirty-five grand, less ten percent to my agent. This whack-job was going to give me seventy grand—without a deduction for the agent I presumed—just to *listen*? This had to be a scam. But those seven ten thousand dollar bills looked legit. Seventy grand to listen? I'm all ears.

Chapter Two

When I had received the advance for my book, I thought that had been a fortune.

I had been a newspaper reporter for over twenty years for the *Chicago Sun-Times,* and unless you were a big-time columnist, you got paid peanuts. My book, however, took off like crazy, made the *New York Times* Best Seller list, went back to the press thirty-one times, and sold over 260,000 hardbound copies. About two bucks per book came directly to my bank account, so I figured I was rich, and that was before the money from the paperback version and the movie rights rolled in.

When I look back at it, painfully, I still amaze myself at how fast I could spend it, or more accurately, lose it. A few years ago, there was a movie, *Boiler Room,* that seemed to be my financial life. *Boiler Room* was how these slick telemarketers conned hardworking stiffs— stiffs like me—into buying stocks that eventually ended up worthless.

When I first invested, my new-found boiler room buddy said I could turn fifty-thousand dollars into five-hundred thousand. Or more. However, I turned my initial fifty thousand into a *minus* two hundred thousand.

My boiler room buddy counseled me with a strategy that I wouldn't recommend—throw good money after bad. Unfortunately, it made sense at the time. That those boiler room boys eventually went to jail wasn't any consolation to me. I lost two hundred thousand dollars.

Then there were the pork bellies. A friend of mine was on the Chicago Board of Trade. He was making a fortune in pork bellies, which I found out was *bacon.* I gave my friend ten-thousand dollars to invest in bacon for me; six months later, he returned thirty thou to me. That was fun.

So, I gave him fifty thousand. I started to eat bacon as Elvis had, but bacon didn't fare too well. Not only did I lose my fifty thousand, but I was also on the legal hook for another one hundred and fifty thousand in what was called *Options*. I didn't know about Options, but the same Options that allowed me to make thirty thousand allowed me to lose one hundred and fifty thousand. I should have listened to my editor. He told me, "*Every* writer has a dead zone in their brain when it comes to money, to finances. Whatever you made off that book, put it under your mattress. It will be safer there."

"Let me introduce myself," the hippie nerd said. "I'm Allred Kosinski."

He smiled. It was not a Crest smile. You'd think that one of the world's richest men would have spent a tiny sliver of those riches with a dentist.

Of course, I knew the name Allred Kosinski, but not his face. Allred was the world's most famous recluse—next to chess champion Bobby Fischer.

The Mad Russian, that was Kosinski's nickname. I don't think the moniker came from his heritage, although clearly Kosinski could have been a Russian name, but it came from his first name, Allred. If I remember it right, Allred was born in the 1950s—the height of the cold war years—and his parents, dedicated peaceniks and devout socialists, believed that Communism was the answer to the world's ills. They commemorated their beliefs by naming their son, Allred, as in All Red. That must have been a helluva load for young Allred to carry in school in the Joe McCarthy era. It would have been better if they named him Sue.

Then in the 1970s, in Albuquerque, New Mexico, Allred met Bill Gates and Paul Allen. Gates and Allen and their merry band of computer code writers were writing the operating software for the world's first personal computer, the Altair. Allred wrote code like a maniac. He'd write code for six straight 22-hour days, crash for a day, then go back at it for another six consecutive days.

That was his pattern for *years*. Rumor had it that he would shower and shave just once a year, whether he needed it or not.

Gates and Allen never invited him to be an official part of Microsoft or its predecessor company Traf-O-Data. But they outsourced a lot of code writing to him before there was the word "outsource." I guess they wanted his code, but they didn't officially want him.

Along the way, however, Allred accumulated four million shares of Microsoft stock. That was peanuts to Gates and Allen, but when you considered all the stock splits and the vast leaps in value, those shares were now worth over one billion dollars.

There were stories about how he had invested some of that billion in pharmaceuticals and Intel and caught a few more great waves that doubled and then quadrupled his net worth.

That earned the Mad Russian twenty-second place in *Forbes* top five hundred richest Americans. His listing in *Forbes* was always short, never with a picture, that said: "Kosinski earned his fortune by writing computer code in the 1980s and then investing. An extremely private individual."

"Can I treat you to a cup of coffee?" the Mad Russian asked.

Treat? I looked at the wad of ten-thousand-dollar bills in his hand and said, "Sure."

It was three in the afternoon, rainy and cold in May, which could be nasty in downtown Portland, Oregon. It was no wonder there weren't many strollers on the sidewalk.

Kosinski pointed across the street. Even though it seemed that every other storefront in Portland was a Starbucks, we didn't go to one. Instead, we crossed 1st Avenue and walked into a Thai restaurant.

There were no customers there. We sat down at a table by the front window. He stacked the seven bills and placed them in the middle of the table. If a cop walked by and casually looked through the window, he'd know that he was seeing a drug deal going down. As if he had sensed what I was thinking about, Kosinski carefully placed a cloth napkin over the small pile.

A waitress came over to take our order. Kosinski laid his hand down on the napkin in the middle of the table. We both ordered tea.

"That's yours, of course," Kosinski said, lifting his hand and pointing at the napkin, "but first you must hear me out."

The Asian waitress delivered the tea.

I sipped the green tea. "I'm all ears," I said.

"I really enjoyed your book, *The Monster Among Us*," Allred said.

"Thank you," I said, sipping some tea.

"Not the story so much," he said, "but more the methodology."

"The methodology?"

"Yes, the methodology. You were very exact in your descriptions. Very exact. You have a keen eye for details, very keen. That's what impressed me. The keen eye for details is *exactly* what I'm looking for." Allred lifted the teacup to his lips and did a half-gulp that would have been embarrassing at a Japanese Tea Ceremony. But to me, I didn't mind the slurp.

"I want you to write a book for me," Allred said.

I was hoping that it wouldn't be the alien killing fields with the mushrooms and the reincarnation and all that crap.

"I will pay you exactly the same amount of money that you have earned from *The Monster Among Us*—*everything* you earned off the book. Hardbound sales, paperback, film rights, everything, every last nickel." Allred slurped the rest of his tea. He held up the cup to catch the waitress's eye, much like a drunk would hold up his empty beer glass to a bartender.

The waitress brought more tea.

"There will be much research that you will have to do with my book," Allred said. "At least two years of research, maybe more. However, if the research extends beyond two years, I'm willing to pay you more. You'll find that I'm a very fair man, very fair."

"May I ask what the book is about?" I asked.

Allred waved his hand like he was shooing a fly away. "Unimportant right now," he said, "unimportant. What is important is your interest."

How could I not be interested? I had blown the only fortune I had ever hoped to make, and this was a chance of a financial do-over.

Did the subject really matter? What if it was about mutant fruit flies? It didn't really make any difference; once a writer took a job solely for the money, it wasn't writing; it was whoring.

I'm no spring chicken anymore—fifty-one years old to be exact— so, as a fifty-one-year-old writing whore, I'd make a fortune writing about mutant fruit flies or whatever.

Allred's book would put me over the top financially, and if I made the same money off of Allred's book that I made off of *Monster* and didn't blow it on investments, I could live out the rest of my life with at least some financial wiggle room.

I looked at Allred. Already he was starting to look a little more legit. He was strange, yes, but I didn't think he was dangerous. Just a bit weird.

"Why me?" I asked. "There are plenty of authors you could get to write your book. I've only written one, you know."

Cops and reporters are born cynics, never trusting a deal that sounded too good to be true. And, besides, I wasn't a true book-writer; I was a *crime* writer.

For twenty years before coming to Portland, I had the crime beat at the *Chicago Sun-Times*. It was in Chicago, where I had written the true-crime bestseller, *The Monster Among Us*. Writing about crime was me; if I had been born to do anything, that was it.

With the money I made on the book and how beat-down I felt after finishing it, I thought it was a good time to walk away, so I had quit my job at *Sun-Times*. I didn't leave to write another book; I went to heal myself. I realized that I was inspired to write *The Monster Among Us* only because my ex-wife had been the monster's fourteenth victim.

I had still loved my wife, even after the divorce. I had never taken the divorce as *final*; I thought the divorce was just a temporary leave-of-absence type of thing until I could figure out a balance between my job and my marriage. Two years after Rachel divorced me, she became a notch on the Monster's belt. That's when I made the Monster my life. I had nothing to do in catching him, but after he was captured, I did do research so thoroughly it's as if I had crawled into his mind—and into his victims' souls.

"It's not because of just the descriptions of time and place and things in your book," Allred said. "It's the *emotions* in your book, the emotions of everybody that you interviewed, and how you were able to capture that in words on a page. I need that *type* of writing, not just reporting but capturing *emotions*. I'm a scientist. I deal in facts. I deal with formulas. In my book, I need *emotions*."

"Well, there was a price for those emotions," I said. "It was my *wife* who was murdered by that monster. I don't think I could do another book with that type of emotional weight."

"I've read almost everything you have written," Allred said. "Yes, I've read much of what you wrote at the *Chicago Sun-Times*. Your writing style is what I want, and since I'm paying the freight, that's all that counts."

"Well, you have piqued my interest," I said. I was able to choke back some of my own emotions when Allred was talking about my book. Writing that was an emotional roller-coaster ride that took me quite a long time to stabilize myself finally.

"There are some conditions, of course," Allred said.

"Like what?"

"You will work *exclusively* on the book—you will work on *nothing* else from the start to the end. I will pay you on a pro-rata basis. For instance, let's suppose that the book will take two years to research and one year to write. That's a total of thirty-six months that you will devote yourself to writing this book. I will pay you one thirty-sixth every month. Plus, I'll pay you a salary of exactly what you're making right now and all expenses, of course. Does that sound fair?"

"What about my job at the *Portland News*?" I asked.

"You'd have to quit or ask for a leave of absence," Allred said with an intensity that belied his appearance. No, Allred wasn't a jokester of any kind. "I'm making a major financial commitment to you, and I need you to make a major professional commitment to me."

I didn't say anything.

"Another condition is that I will own all copies of the manuscript," Allred said.

Own all copies? That didn't make sense. However, did I really mind that? Probably not. I was going to be paid the equivalent of another red-hot bestseller, and I felt, down in my bones, that I didn't have it in me to write another hot book.

"The last condition is that the book will probably not ever be published," Allred said.

"It wouldn't be published?" My face was the question mark.

"Most likely not," Allred said. "You're writing this book for *me*. For me. Most likely, I, and perhaps a few others, will be the only reader of your manuscript."

Did I mind *that*? This was writing-for-hire, plain and simple, but it was writing for big bucks. Once I accepted that this was writing-for-hire, did it matter that it wouldn't be published?

"What's the subject?" I asked.

"I won't tell you right now," Allred said, smiling, "but I will give you a peek."

"A peek?"

He nodded and then winked. Strangely, I felt that there was an odd charm about this geek.

"Yes, a peek."

He handed me a slip of paper with an address written on it. It was a street address in Astoria, Oregon.

Astoria was on the Oregon coast, about a two-hour drive from Portland. Steven Spielberg had done a movie based in Astoria, *The Goonies*. In the movie, there were secret caves, an old lighthouse, a lost treasure map, Sloth, all the things that were great fun on film.

"Come to my house tomorrow morning at eleven sharp," Allred said. "I'll *show* you what I want you to write about. After I show you, you'll have five minutes to make up your mind whether or not you want to take my offer or not."

Then Allred looked me squarely in the eye as penetrating as if he was a prosecuting attorney. "If you decide not to," Allred said, "then we have never had this conversation. I'll have something for you to sign tomorrow that guarantees your confidentiality. If you want to take my offer, I expect you to start the very same minute that you accept the offer."

Allred stood up and leaned over the table.

"Here, take your money," he said, pushing the napkin that hid the stack of ten-thousand-dollar bills towards me. "Think about this tonight. If the conditions meet your approval, meet me tomorrow at eleven at this address."

Allred dropped a five-dollar bill down on the table and walked out of the restaurant.

Chapter Three

I moved my hand over to the napkin on the table. I half expected that when I lifted the napkin nothing would be there. After all, Allred Kosinski had placed his palm on the napkin. Was this a Portland version of three-card monte? See the Queen of Hearts, see the Queen of Hearts, see the seventy grand, see the seventy grand, point to the Queen of Hearts, point to the seventy grand, oops, you lost. I lifted up the napkin. The money was still there. I picked up the seven ten-thousand-dollar bills. There wasn't a wrinkle in any one of them. Without folding them, I carefully put them in my shirt pocket, turned and walked out the door.

I felt nervous on the sidewalk. I was carrying what could be easily worth two hundred thousand dollars in *cash*. Heck, depending on collectors, this might be worth closer to three hundred thousand in cash. Even in my most affluent days I never had that much in cash. I reserved that type of money to send away to stupid investments. The most cash I used to carry was about a hundred bucks. Now, two hundred thou in my pocket felt like a pulsating neon target that could only be seen by a bad guy. It would be just my luck for some drugged out meth addict to come up to me with a Saturday Night Special and say, "Okay, pal, empty your pockets." I thought of that consequence: I'd throw him my wallet and run like hell holding onto my shirt pocket.

The two block walk to my car felt like the longest two blocks I had ever walked. Inside my car, I felt safer. Within ten minutes I was driving in my driveway. Within sixty seconds I was in my bedroom. Within five seconds I had placed the seven ten-thousand-dollar bills where my editor had told me would be the safest—under the mattress of my bed.

My breathing was heavy. It's not like I had sprinted to the bedroom. I must have just not breathed for the last mile to my house and then to the bedroom. I guess big amounts of cash would do that to you. I sat on the edge of the bed and caught my breath.

Here I was: a fifty-one-year-old man, a widower—we were divorced and then two years later Rachel had been murdered, which, I think, made me a widower—no kids and a blown-up fortune that forced me back to work, and now, because of a highly eccentric billionaire, I might get my fortune back.

It got me thinking whether my father was right when he named me.

Like Allred Kosinski's parents, my parents had been inspired when they named me. No, they didn't name me after any political motivations like Cap, as in capitalism. They named me after a character in a novel.

In 1952, my dad had picked up a book and he was moved by it. Two years later, he was able to act upon that inspiration when I was born. When I was growing up nobody connected the name in the book to me mainly because the book wasn't a big seller. It wasn't *Gone with the Wind* and I wasn't named Rhett. It was twenty-six years later when people finally connected the name in the book to me; that's when the book was made into a movie. All of a sudden, Robert Redford was playing my namesake in Bernard Malamud's *The Natural*. Roy Hobbs, that's me, and Robert Redford.

I don't look anything like Redford's Roy Hobbs. I'm taller—I'm about six-two and I always figured Redford to be five-ten or so. I don't have movie-star golden locks; my hair is more sandy brown and while I don't see it too often I'm growing a bit bald at the crown of my head. Like Redford, however, I'm not fat. It's not like I've got a personal trainer. I've just got the right DNA—there's no fatties sitting on the branches of my family tree.

I still have my dad's copy of *The Natural*. Although he had never said it, I figured he named me Roy because he wanted me to be a baseball player in the worst way. That he gave me a middle name of some long-lost uncle—Homer—cinched it. Yep, Roy Homer Hobbs. It sure didn't get me thinking I should be a pianist.

Roy Hobbs—at least Robert Redford's Roy Hobbs in *The Natural*—could throw bullets, hit huge home runs and had a magical bat named WonderBoy. I had none of those things. Little League was the end of my baseball career. So, if I was supposed to somehow be the alter ego of *The Natural*, I failed.

A couple of years ago it occurred to me that my dad didn't name me to be Roy Hobbs, the baseball player. I was at my father's deathbed, the cancer shrinking him down to about ninety pounds or so, when he said, "Something mystical, Roy, something magical will happen to you. I felt that since the day you were born." I could have just considered what he said a doped-out nonsensical muttering, but just that week I had been rereading *The Natural*. It's not like I thought a lot of it, but at least my name didn't represent something magical and mystical like Peter Pan. Peter Pan Hobbs wouldn't have been a fun name to grow up with. If I had been given that moniker, Allred and I could have been great pals trying to outrun the bullies.

A week after my dad died, I was cleaning out some of his stuff. In the top drawer of his dresser I found a well-thumbed book: *The Odyssey* by none other than Homer—the poet with my middle name. Finding that book did give me cause to think. Had I been wrong all these years, thinking that my dad had hoped I would become a great baseball player when he really hoped I would become a *mystical wanderer* that Homer wrote about?

The image of that mad-hatter Allred popped into my consciousness and made me plop down on my knees and pull back the mattress of my bed. Sure enough, the seven ten-thousand-dollar bills were lying exactly where I had tucked them in for the night. Meeting Allred had not been some strange hallucination. What confronted me now was a seemingly simple choice: go to Astoria, Oregon or not. Hah! Easy choice. No reporter could *not* go. Yes, money was a factor, but the curiosity of what in the world Allred was going to show me was an even bigger lure.

If I liked what I saw—if the subject matter was even more intriguing than the money—then quitting the *Portland News* wouldn't be difficult.

I enjoyed my job at the *News*. At the *News* I was doing what I had done at the *Chicago Sun-Times*—tracking down crime stories.

Being a crime reporter at *Chicago Sun-Times* was what caused my divorce. When I was after a big story, there were countless times that I didn't come home at night. I didn't even call home. I wasn't out drinking the night away or boffing my socks off. I just didn't come home; usually I was with cops on stakeouts. Other nights, I did come home—very late—after drinking the night away with cops. After all, cops were my lifeline into crime reporting. It was a never ending effort for me to cultivate insider sources. I was oblivious to any type of domestic responsibility.

Rachel and I had long drawn out conversations about this behavior leading me to swear that I would reform. I would reform, for a while, and I enjoyed those times, but then with the next big story I was a dog in heat. While I never used drugs, I knew what an addict must have felt like when he fell off the wagon; that was me, a new crime story and all my domestic resolve went out the window. Finally, Rachel had had enough. She divorced me. Two years after our divorce, she had been murdered.

Coming back to Portland was an effort of a lost boy coming home. I had been born and raised in Portland. At the time, my dad and two sisters still lived there. My mother had died a few years before that. Back in Portland, I spent hours wandering the Oregon coast. When the tide was out, I could walk for miles on the beach. Eventually, I caught on with the *Portland News*. The daily newspaper in Portland was *The Oregonian*. I knew a couple of writers there. The *Portland News* was rock-and-roll to the *Oregonian's* chamber music. The *News* had hired many of *The Oregonian's* best columnists. I met with the publisher. He wanted a rock-star crime reporter. That was me.

"We publish just two days a week, you know," the publisher said to me.

"So, you're not a daily and you're not a weekly," I said. "What are you?"

"The future," the publisher replied. "Fewer people each year are getting their daily news from the newspaper. Folks get their daily news from television and from the Internet. Each year, more and more will get their daily news from the Internet. Our job is to provide depth and dimension to their news. Publishing just two days a week gives us the time to develop that depth and dimension."

That made sense to me.

"I want you to work on stories with no deadlines," the publisher said. "I don't care if you submit one story every six months. But that one story should be a hum-dinger. If a Pulitzer comes our way it would be icing on the cake."

No deadlines. How sweet was that? I started at *The Portland News* and it was great getting back in the groove. I didn't have any contacts or inside sources, but I found out that getting sources was like riding a bike—just get on it and pedal. The money wasn't great at the *News*, but at this stage in my life I didn't really need a lot. What I needed was a job, and the *News* was the most acceptable to me at the time.

So, leaving *The News* would not be easy, but then again, a windfall was a windfall which shouldn't be easily dismissed.

I walked into my small home office and logged onto the Internet. The first thing I typed in was "ten-thousand-dollar bill."

Ten-thousand-dollar bills were real. They had indeed been taken off the market in 1934 as Allred had told me. The old guy on the bill was indeed Salmon P. Chase. The middle initial "P" in Chase's name was Portland.

Portland. What type of middle name was that? Was that some type of omen?

I then typed in Allred Kosinski. Amazingly, there were only six numbers at the bottom of the Google search pages. That was a startling low number. Each one of those numbers represented about ten links to *something* that had been written about Allred. To put it in perspective, I had almost fifty numbers at the bottom of Google. That meant that there were at least 500 links to something about me. Bill Gates had *thousands* of numbers at the bottom of Google, which would lead to tens of thousands of links.

The first link gave me a brief bio of Allred from *Forbes* magazine. He was the same age as me, fifty-one. He was born in Chicago, had attended the University of Chicago, dropped out, and made a fortune on Microsoft stock. Had also invested heavily in Intel. Was a recluse rumored to be living as a farmer in Washington or Oregon.

I looked at five more links. One of the links had a chapter in a book about how the young Allred had written code for Microsoft. Heck, I *remembered* more about Allred than what I could find on the Internet. I clicked through all of the links. The mosaic of Allred Kosinski was that he was rich and a recluse. Nobody knew exactly how rich he was, but the *Forbes* estimate slotted him at number twenty-two on their list, or worth about five billion. He didn't buy businesses like Microsoft cofounder Paul Allen had and if he had any pet charities they were anonymous. Here was the twenty-second richest guy in the country and he had as many Internet links as my barber would have.

The plan seemed pretty obvious to me.

I'd go see what Allred wanted me to write about. If it wasn't something really distasteful, I would do it. If it was something that made my guts roil, I'd thank him, walk out the door, drive back to Portland, treasure those seven ten-thousand-dollar bills and go to work at the *Portland News*.

If I had an old Beatles CD, I'd play Magical Mystery Tour right now, play it really loud, because tomorrow morning at eleven, Roy Homer Hobbs—the mystical and magical Roy Homer Hobbs—was going to meet with the very mystical and mysterious Allred Kosinski to see about joining a circus.

Chapter Four

I t was almost comical when Allred opened the door and said, "Welcome, Mr. Hobbs. Yes, welcome, welcome."

It's not that Allred was a funny guy. For just a microsecond I was reminded of a character in an old movie. It might have been the squeaky front door, or just Allred's big head peering out around the door or that he had lisped the 'Mister' part of the greeting. All of that made me think of Bela Lugosi in *Dracula*.

Allred was wearing exactly the same clothes as yesterday unless he had duplicate sets. In his closet he might have fifty denim shirts and fifty pairs of khakis. Was this how he started each day: Well, today I think I'll wear a denim shirt and a pair of khakis. Or he might just have this single set and wear it until it unravels around him. Billionaires that were reclusive could do a lot of funny things without anybody knowing it.

After a quick stop at my bank to put the seven ten-thousand-dollar bills into my safe deposit box, it had taken me a little less than two hours to get to the farmhouse door that Allred had just opened. The house was about a mile past Astoria Golf Club.

The road to Allred's house

Following my MapQuest directions, I turned right off of Highway 1 onto a gravel road. The road cut a field of wild grass and after about a half-mile on the right was a farmhouse. The mailbox at the side of the road matched the address that Allred had given me. The farmhouse was an old Victorian job with a couple of peaks on its roof. There was a large covered front porch. It needed some paint, and the grass needed tending. If this was where Allred lived, it was probably the most humble residence of any billionaire on the *Forbes* list.

I had parked my Taurus behind the late model Chevy Caprice that was parked on the gravel driveway in front of the house. I had walked up to the front door and looked for a doorbell. There wasn't any. I knocked on the screen door. That's when Allred opened the door and peered out like Dracula.

While driving to Astoria, I thought about the money and the writing. No matter how goofy the subject matter would be, I couldn't hurt myself professionally. After all, there was going to be just one solitary reader, Allred. If the book was about fruit flies, I'd just have to talk to a lot of folks that knew about fruit flies. Then I'd write one helluva book about fruit flies. The public wouldn't know I had veered off my crime writing path to write about fruit flies.

The money was the raison d'être, of course. I was crossing a line here since I had never written things for *the money*. Money didn't inspire me to write the *The Monster Among Us*. I never once thought about the financial rewards when writing it. I *had* to write that book; I *had* to research that book; not writing it was not optional; I *had* to do it.

So here I was: chasing the money. I could rationalize with myself and say it was the story and not the money. Any reporter loves a good story; any good reporter loves to go after a great story. The weirdness of this whole situation, however, was the story. Allred's book? Who knows if there was a story in the book? The story was in his *offer* to me. But, I felt I couldn't write about the offer, unless I returned the seventy grand. That wouldn't happen. So, it was for *the money*.

I concluded on my drive to Astoria that it wasn't bad going for the money. I was fifty-one and even though I had never once thought about retirement, I had a thought about it on the drive. If I continued at the *News* I would make a decent living. At the age of sixty-five I'd have to retire. There was no pension plan at the *News* and based on my woeful investments with the *Monster* money, I would be counting on Uncle Sam to provide me some help. Taking two years out of my life to put me financially over the top was a prudent thing to do. I didn't have to kill anybody; I didn't have to pollute rivers and streams; I just had to write a book that one billionaire whack-job would read. I remembered when guys used to go over to Saudi Arabia and work in the oilfields for two or three years and then come home with a pile of cash that could pay for a house or a boat or their kids education or whatever. Writing a book for Allred Kosinski was like my version of going to Saudi Arabia.

Allred invited me in his house. Inside, it was like I had walked into a time warp. I felt I had walked into one of those rooms at a museum that features a house from one hundred years ago. There was nothing in the room that resembled anything that used electricity. There was no television, no radio, no stereo. Gas lights were on the wall.

"May I get you some tea?" Allred asked, always ever so polite.

I nodded, "Yes, thank you." I could match politeness with anybody, if I wanted to.

Allred turned his head and said toward the back of the house, "Charles, tea please."

We sat there awkwardly, without speaking, like it was our first date.

In a minute, Charles brought tea to the room. On the lacquered wood tray was an ancient looking Chinese tea pot and three cups. It looked like Charles was going to join us.

Charles looked not like an aging hippie, but a severely aging nerd. There were white tufts of hair on his bald head and he had twirled those tufts to try to cover the rashes on his dome. The rashes were red, scaly patches that could have easily been the 'before' skin condition in a skin remedy ad. He wore dark framed glasses that had lenses that looked like magnifying glasses. He was clearly overweight; his stomach looked like he was eight months pregnant, but his shoulders were thin. His legs looked like they were stilts that had been cut way down. My nose told me that he hadn't just emerged from a shower. Maybe last month, but not today.

Allred formerly introduced us, "Roy, this is Charles Dombrowski. Charles, this is Roy Hobbs." I had a vague feeling that I had heard Charles' name before.

"Charles used to work at Intel," Allred said.

Of course, that's where I had heard the name. I remembered that Charles was one of the early scientists at Intel. He wasn't like cofounders Robert Noyce or Gordon Moore, but he was important enough for the market to speculate whether Intel could continue to grow after Charles left in the mid-1990s.

"Charles was never a public personality at Intel," Allred said. Charles looked down at his feet. "You've probably heard the analogy 'If the auto industry advanced as rapidly as the semiconductor industry, a Rolls Royce would get a half a million miles per gallon, and it would be cheaper to throw it away than to park it.'"

I nodded. Gordon Moore had said that. He also established Moore's Law, where the numbers of transistors in a semiconductor would double every couple of years.

"That Rolls analogy came in one of Charles' notes to Moore," Allred said. "I make that distinction because Charles understood the semiconductor better than any engineer ever has and didn't get much credit. He just wasn't political. But, he did get quite a few shares of Intel stock. Charles is a very rich man. Very."

fallen down the rabbit hole? I felt like asking something sarcastic like, "Where's Alice?"

"Charles, this isn't a quiz for Mr. Hobbs," Allred said. Then he turned to me and said, "Let me explain. Albert Einstein was the most brilliant physicist in the world—in the *history* of the world for that matter. Interestingly, for the last ten years of his life, or so, he tried to prove that there are parallel universes, parallel worlds."

"Time travel," I said.

"Not exactly," Allred said. "We all know about H. G. Wells' *Time Machine*. That is an interesting story. And to be frank, that captured my imagination when I was a boy. Yes, without H. G. Wells I don't think that you and I—and Charles—would be sitting at this table and talking today. But Einstein didn't believe in time travel, he believed in *parallel worlds*. However, he could never prove that parallel worlds existed. He knew it, he believed it, but he couldn't prove it."

"Would you care for something to drink before we go on?" Allred asked, always so polite.

I shook my head.

"Well, when I made all that money from Microsoft stock, I didn't know what to do," Allred said. "I had known Charles, of course, and a year or so after I made my money, Charles made his."

"And, those fellows in the work room?" Allred said, fanning his arm around to the work room. "Each is a brilliant scientist, each made a huge fortune by writing computer code or taking semiconductors to unbelievable levels. I think the *least* net worth of those five is in the five hundred million dollar range. While each was fabulously rich, each was like me and Charles in that they didn't know what to do with their riches. Could they be like Paul Allen and buy a basketball team and then buy an NFL team? No, none were interested in sports at all. Could they buy businesses like Paul Allen did? Paul spent over twenty billion dollars just buying businesses. Each one of those scientists has the financial ability to buy businesses, but each had an interest in business that was less than their interest in sports, which was nothing. So, what to do? What to do?"

Allred got up and walked the length of the boardroom, turned and walked back and sat down. He must have had to straighten his shorts.

"It's not that we all knew each other," Allred said. "We had *heard* of each other, of course. Interestingly, each guy knew another guy. For instance, I knew Charles, and Charles knew Robert McDougald— he's the one working at the far table, the one with the bushy hair."

I looked across the work room. The 'bushy hair' looked like an abandoned bee-hive. I'd hate to find out what's inside that mess.

"Anyways, I didn't know Robert, but Charles did. Robert knew Phil Lamparello—he's working at the table next to Robert—but Charles and I didn't know Phil. So, everybody knew at least one person and that's how this little group of seven got together. We decided to have a retreat, if you will, here at my farmhouse. That was ten years ago. We were all in the same boat. Each was brilliant in their own way, each was fabulously rich, each was entering their intellectual prime, each was courted by various corporations, each was not inspired by any of those corporations or what they wanted to do, and finally, each wanted to be inspired again, each wanted the *excitement* of breakthrough thinking, each wanted to reignite the *passion* of impossible research. Impossible research, that's what inspires each one of us. *Impossible research!* We sat in my farmhouse just talking for three straight days, just getting to know each other. We'd talk for twelve hours a day...then halfway through the third day..."

"Somebody mentioned H. G. Wells," Charles said, interrupting Allred. You could see that Charles was excited just by mentioning H. G. Wells. "When we looked back at it, nobody can remember who first brought up H. G. Wells."

"It's like we all had," Allred said. "We had all read *Time Machine* as kids. We, of course, knew of Einstein's quest, and we spent two more days just talking about Einstein's parallel worlds. We came to the unanimous—and enthusiastic—conclusion that we were destined to finish Einstein's work. It was *destiny* that had made us all rich, it was *destiny* that put us together in the same room, it was *destiny* that we solve Einstein's theories of parallel worlds. We did it."

"You did what?" I asked.

"We solved it. Mr. Hobbs, we have proved that there are parallel worlds," Allred said, smiling. "We want *you* to experience it first hand like we have, and that's what we want you to write about. Are you ready to take a trip, Mr. Hobbs?"

"Wait," I said, "wait. I have to go to the bathroom."

Allred laughed again, this time a big hyena laugh, heh-heh-heh-HEH-heh-heh. Charles smirked.

"Don't worry," Allred said, "you won't be gone for more than a few minutes. You can hold it."

Allred and Charles were gone. Standing on the 'x', I then noticed for the first time that there was a darkly tinted glass panel on the wall. On the other side Allred had put his face close to the glass. I could barely make out his face. Then he pulled his head back and gave me a thumbs up.

The entire room went black. There was no noise whatsoever. It was as if I was in a casket buried a mile underground. Buried alive. I felt like screaming. I felt a slight movement on my shirt as if there was a ghost of a breeze. I closed my eyes. I heard something move above me, or did I *feel* it? I *think* the top of the silo moved aside as I sensed, through my closed eyes, dim light above me. I imagined a tornado swooping down the silo and sucking me up. I stood there. I hoped I wouldn't piss in my pants. I must have stood there, at attention, for thirty minutes, but it could have been five. I was too frightened to count the minutes.

My eyelids sensed a bright light. I opened my eyes. I was in an alley that ran parallel to Ontario Street. I knew that alley because I used to use it as a shortcut to one of my favorites saloons, the Knight Cap on Ontario Street.

I blinked rapidly several times. How could it be possible that I was now in a parallel world? Was this some type of hallucination? Was there an exotic drug in that tea that I had been served; was I now unconscious and just dreaming all this? Had I been hypnotized?

I looked around. Whether I was dreaming or it was reality, I was in that alley behind the Knight Cap. I looked at my watch, well, Allred's watch. I had two minutes to get to the corner of Michigan Avenue and Ontario and I would, supposedly, see myself meet my wife more than twenty-five years ago.

Chapter Seven

I walked down the alley to Michigan Avenue. I took a left on the sidewalk. It was crowded. The cars were clearly 1970-ish. These cars didn't have the big fins like the predecessors of the late 1960s did. It was almost like the engineers had taken a saw and lopped off those big fins.

The men walking down the street had longer hair, some had very long sideburns. Almost every male was wearing a suit. Some of the women were wearing platform shoes. There was a newspaper rack on the corner. Inside was the *Chicago Sun-Times*, my former newspaper. Or, in 1978, the newspaper where I still worked. President Jimmy Carter's picture was on the front page. I considered stopping, dropping a dime in the slot, plucking out a *Sun-Times* and reading it right there. But, strangely, the words of that rabbit in Alice in Wonderland popped into my consciousness, 'Oh my ears and whiskers, how late it's getting!' I was on a timetable, and I walked briskly to the corner of Michigan Avenue and Ontario Street.

I crossed the street. I heard some music coming from an open window of a car waiting at the traffic light. *Lay Down Sally* by Eric Clapton. Standing next to me were two twenty-something guys dressed in Botany 500 suits talking about *Animal House*. They seemed like cocky young advertising guys; with their loud voices, they let all of us on that corner know they had seen a special screening of the whacky film. I remembered that Rachel and I had seen the movie right after its premiere, so that would have been in July 1978.

My position was across Ontario Street from where Rachel and my 1978 self would first meet on Wednesday, May tenth, 1978. I tried to remember where I had been coming from that day and couldn't. I looked at my watch. My 1978 self should be walking down the sidewalk on Michigan Avenue, coming from the north. Rachel should be walking down Ontario Street, coming from the east.

I spotted my 1978 self—there I was, twenty-four years old and walking like I didn't have a care in the world. I stared at my 1978 self. *How young I was!* Sure, we all can look at pictures of ourselves from twenty-five years ago and notice how young we looked. But, this wasn't a snapshot. This was seeing a living, breathing version of myself that was twenty-seven years younger. All that hair! Heck, my hair looked like it would fit in with those nerds in Allred's barn. On my upper lip was a drooping moustache—I remembered that my model for that had been Trapper John in the movie, *M*A*S*H*. Bad role model. I was wearing a nice dark suit with a tie. Those were the days when newspaper reporters dressed in suits or at least wore sport jackets. Nowadays, we dress like we're going to work on the engine of our cars. But, *everybody* I saw on that Michigan Avenue sidewalk was better dressed than folks walking down any sidewalk in the United States today. Heck, I remember that I used to dress up to take an airplane flight; today it looks like planes are filled with homeless people.

Rachel was like a beacon coming down Ontario Street. I don't think I have stared at anything harder than watching Rachel walk toward Michigan Avenue. She was dressed to beat the band. She was tall, about five-eight, but with the high heels of 1978 she was probably close to six feet tall. She was wearing an emerald green summer dress. Her shoulders were bare and deeply tanned. Her blond hair bounced in rhythm with her steps.

My 1978 self had already reached the corner and was waiting for the traffic light to change. Rachel stepped right next to my 1978 self. My 1978 self looked at her. This was a strange sensation: in my mind's eye, I could remember two visions of that first look. The first vision was etched in my memory; her face had that natural beauty look, clear complexion, no make-up or at least none that I could see, and a face that seemed to be smiling even when it wasn't. She didn't have that movie star look—she was wholesome, athletic, an Iowa corn bred look—but her face, that day, was the most beautiful face that I had ever seen. The second vision was the one I was experiencing right now, across the street from Rachel and my 1978 self. She was exactly as beautiful as I remembered her, but I had a little trouble juxtaposing the ages; here I was fifty-one years old and across the street was the love of my life at twenty-two. Staring at her, I felt like crying. Rachel was dead now. That beautiful vibrant woman I was staring at was dead at the monster's hand.

The traffic light was about to change. I quickly pulled the Kodak Instamatic Camera out of my pocket and placed it up to my right eye. I had Rachel and my 1978 self in the viewfinder. I snapped a picture. I snapped another one.

Rachel turned and said something to my 1978 self. I knew she was asking the time. I snapped another picture. My 1978 self answered her. I snapped another picture.

Rachel turned and looked straight at me. Did she sense something strange? I used the zoom lens. Rachel filled the viewfinder. I snapped another picture. The traffic light changed and both of them were walking toward me. I lowered the camera to my side and just stood there. An eddy of people went around me. Rachel and my 1978 self walked past me. They continued to walk up Michigan Avenue toward the *Sun-Times* building. I turned and followed them.

I didn't have to get close to them to hear what they were saying. I remembered the conversation almost word-for-word.

"I work at the *Chicago Tribune*," Rachel had answered me as we had walked. "Where do you work?"

"*Chicago Sun-Times*," I had said.

She had laughed. "We're competitors," she had said.

"Maybe," I had said, "but probably not. I'm working crime beat and I don't think you are."

"Nope, I'm an assistant in the women's section…"

I was following them, staying about fifteen feet back. I snapped off two more pictures. I particularly was enjoying the swishing of Rachel's walk. She had thin, athletic legs. When she walked her calves became more shapely—not muscular and bulky like a football player's, but strong like a runner's. Her legs used to turn me on; I found out they still did.

I didn't feel a jolt. I didn't feel yanked. I felt nothing, but with my next step I stepped into absolute blackness. It was as if somebody had turned the light off in the universe. I felt disoriented; I felt as if I were floating although I had the sensation that my feet were on solid ground; I felt dizzy; I thought I might throw up.

I felt several sets of hands holding on to me.

"Roy," a voice said. The voice was way off in the distance. It sounded like it was echoing.

"Roy," another voice said, this voice sounding a little closer.

The room started to lighten. In dim light, I could see Allred propping me up by my left elbow. Charles was propping me up by my right elbow. I was in the silo, where I had started.

They led me back to the anteroom and I sat down on one of the La-Z-Boy chairs.

"Here, take this," Allred said, handing me an open bottle of Gatorade. It was Gatorade Fierce, a blue liquid in the bottle. I took a big slug of it.

"We find that we are extraordinarily dehydrated when we come back," Allred said. "Gatorade seems to work. We prefer the grape flavor, Fierce."

I took another deep swallow of the grape Gatorade.

"Well, what do you think?" Allred asked.

"Wow," I said. "Wow, I think." The vision of what I had just experienced in 1978 was still at the forefront of my brain. While it was still vivid, there was a part of me that felt it couldn't be real. It was too fantastic to grasp in one experience, no matter how great that experience was.

Allred and Charles were standing there grinning.

"You might be a little stunned," Allred said. "We all were when we took our first trip. It's *natural* to doubt what you have just experienced. That's why we gave you the camera. So take a look at your pictures. You did take some pictures, didn't you?"

"Yes."

I pulled the Kodak Instamatic camera out of my pocket. Allred reached over, his hand outstretched. I put the camera in his palm. He snapped off the Instamatic cover and inside was a slim camera the thickness of three credit cards. Allred handed the camera back to me. "Take a look," he said.

I looked at the small screen. The last picture that I had taken was of Rachel's athletic legs. I had zoomed in, framing my 1978 self out of the picture, to just capture her from her ass down to the soles of her shoes. I guess I'll always be a leg man.

I pushed one of the directional buttons on the camera.

The next picture was of Rachel and my 1978 self walking down Michigan Avenue. Looking at the picture, my only thought was that we looked natural walking together.

I pushed the directional button again. Rachel's face was full frame staring at me. I had used the zoom. She had that look where it seemed like she was smiling, but she really wasn't. That was just the way she was; she always seemed happy. She had been happy with me until I let my career run out of control. To me, Rachel was the most beautiful woman in the world. I was stunned at her beauty; I felt a tremendous wave of remorse that over the years I had caused pain to that beautiful, smiling person.

I flipped through the rest of the snapshots. I didn't say anything as I looked at the pictures.

"We'll make prints for you, of course," said Allred.

"When can I go back?" I asked.

Allred laughed that hyena laugh heh-heh-heh-HEH-HEH-heh except it was louder, almost a barroom hyena laugh. Charles laughed hard too. He didn't put his hand over his mouth. He should have. It looked like moss was growing on his teeth.

"Yes, it's an interesting trip, isn't it?" Allred said. "I think tomorrow you'll be able to go back. We found that we can't go through white holes too frequently. We don't know the long range effect it has on us, but the short term effect with frequent visits is a tremendous case of jet lag."

"I feel pretty good right now," I said.

"Yes, you should," Allred said. "You went for just a few minutes, so your jet lag should be minimal if at all. If you went back now, and came back a few minutes later, you'd really feel it. That would ruin you for the next few days. So, we've got the time to fully explore these parallel worlds. There's no sense in rushing it."

I guess that made sense, but I could hardly wait to go back.

I absentmindedly looked at my watch. I stared at the hands on the watch. "It looks like my watch went haywire," I said. "This is almost an hour after I saw my 1978 self and Rachel. It couldn't be more than twenty minutes ago."

Allred chuckled. It wasn't his hyena laugh, more a little laugh reserved for little kids.

"Nothing is wrong with your watch," Allred said. "It might *look* like a Timex, but believe me, inside there's the best watch that has ever been created. We had to invent it because of the white hole. Once you're in the white hole, you lose all concept of time. For instance, Roy, how long did you think it took you to come back from 1978 Chicago?"

"Well, everything went dark," I said. "I presume that was when you had me programmed to travel in the white hole. I was in there for probably a minute. Two at the most…well, maybe five. Ah, I really don't know."

"Actually, we programmed the white hole to swoop you up," Allred said. "The Wayfarer Commander was the positioning beacon for the white hole. But your actual time in the white hole was more like thirty minutes. For some reason—and we don't exactly know why—all sense of time is lost in the white hole. But, think of it. The speed of light is one hundred and eighty six thousand miles *per second*. Reaching the end of our galaxy—where our parallel universes start—would take tens of thousands of years *at the speed of light*. You thought you did it in a couple of minutes, but it took about a half hour. That's where we scientists get confused. We think in terms of physics that we understand in this world. In a white hole, *it's a whole new set of physics*. It's a phenomenon we can't explain."

If Allred couldn't explain it, then I sure couldn't. Heck, I couldn't explain it if Allred explained it to me.

"We'll get you settled in this afternoon—we've got a suite for you right here at the site—and then you'll meet the rest of our group at dinner tonight."

I wondered if my cell phone would work in this fortress/barn. I needed to call the *News* and tell them that I was resigning.

Chapter Eight

After my little jaunt to 1978, Allred showed me a suite of rooms that I could use when on his book project. The suite was on Level One, the first floor below the ground floor of the barn, accessible by the elevator. This elevator was a *real* elevator, not like Allred's elevator between parallel worlds. Allred had, of course, programmed all my palm and finger digits to give me access to the barn and the elevator and floors that I would be using, one and seven.

If you imagined that living one floor underground would be like living in a basement, or a bunker, you would have imagined wrong. My suite was four spacious rooms: a living room, a den, a bedroom and a kitchen, plus a marvelous bathroom. The bathroom had all the normal stuff, plus a sauna, a large whirlpool tub and a large walk-in shower.

At least one wall in each room, including the bathroom, was a large picture window. This picture window didn't look out to a cement wall. In the picture window was the most astounding high definition TV screen that I had ever thought possible. For instance, I could choose a view of a beach in Maui or a view of New York City from a level of about thirty stories. The views were live—people, birds, cars, whatever was appropriate for the view. In the early morning, the imaged sun would slowly make the scene outside brighter. At sunset time, if I had chosen the Maui scene I would see spectacular sunsets. As I would find out, I never saw the same sunset twice.

In the first hour in my suite, I programmed each room. I tried an Antarctica landscape, Maui, New York City, Kansas plains, the Ginza in Tokyo. I was amazed how lifelike it was. Heck, it was so lifelike I really couldn't tell that it was just electronics. If I paraded one hundred people in front of my windows and asked them if it was real or fake, I think I would have fooled one hundred people. Everybody would have said it was real. I finally chose Maui for each room. Each room provided a different view of Maui. The living room and bedroom were beach views. The den was a mountain view. It was as if I was living in a fabulous beach house on Maui. The only thing missing was Maui trade winds.

The doorbell on my suite rang. A video screen next to the door showed that it was Charles. I opened the door.

"Your pictures," Charles said, handing me a large envelope. His eyes, as usual, were riveted towards his feet.

I sat down on the couch and slid out the photos. They were all eight-by-tens. The detail was tack sharp. That little digital camera I used had more power than any that I had used before. The detail was so sharp it almost seemed like 3-D.

I looked at each picture for about a minute each. Certainly I looked closely at Rachel. It's strange, but she looked better than I had remembered. But, I had also seen Rachel age over the years and each year etched itself into my memory banks covering the previous years. After Rachel had died, I tried to remember when she was young and in love and unburdened by the pain of my career. I didn't succeed; I kept coming back to the Rachel that I had hurt along the way. While we were having our troubles, she had lost that look of smiling when she wasn't, and I had, unfortunately, lost that view in my memory. The picture that I was looking at grabbed long lost memories and shoved them to the forefront of my consciousness.

I looked at my Timex—I had returned Allred's Timex to him. I had spent almost an hour looking at the pictures. I noticed that my cheeks were wet. I had been crying without noticing it.

Wiping my face, I walked to the den in my suite. The den had my laptop computer. Allred had retrieved it from my car. I turned it on and logged in to my Internet provider. My emails popped up. Several were from people at the *News* wondering where I was. If I had replied that I had taken a time machine gizmo and visited 1978 they would think I needed to go to a rehab center to get rid of whatever had addled my brain. I typed an email to my boss, Mike O'Bannon, the editor of the *News*. This was a chicken-shit way to do it, but I resigned from the *News* via an email.

I went back to the living room and picked up the pictures. I looked at them one at a time, but this time I didn't cry. Instead, my reporter's instincts started to kick in. One of the main instincts that a reporter has is skepticism. If a reporter wasn't born with a skeptic mind, it doesn't take too long on the job to develop one. Over the years, I had made skepticism an art form. My cop buddies had the same skepticism except they had taken it to an even higher level. When we were having a few beers together and talk drifted to the Chicago Cubs, there wasn't anybody who believed the Cubs could win a game, let alone a pennant. We cheered like crazy for the Cubbies to win—we even prayed that they would win—but deep down we knew that our prayers would not be answered and that the Cubbies would figure out a way to lose.

That skepticism jumped up full force. It's almost like having a second person inside you. I know that sounds like I'm describing a schizophrenic, and if that's the case then every reporter worth his salt is a schizo.

My skepticism was having trouble accepting that I had actually— really, really—traveled back to 1978. After all, the whole trip took less than an hour. Allred and his merry band of genius nerds were, of course, brilliant fellows. But, what if they had failed in their quest to prove parallel worlds? Along the way, however, they would have made certain scientific breakthroughs. Could one of those breakthroughs be a special digital camera that would record a picture of what a person had been *thinking*? What if that person had been hypnotized and then told *what* to think? This type of schizoid thinking was always within easy reach of a reporter. Now, however, my skepticism was weaving around loose and uncontrolled in my brain ready to get settled in.

A crime reporter always thinks: who would benefit? If this was indeed a scientific con game, who would benefit? It certainly couldn't be for *money*. Allred could burn half of his money in an incinerator just to watch the smoke and he wouldn't even feel that he'd lost half of his fortune.

The fame? If Allred's parallel worlds became public and he was able to prove it just as he had done with me, then certainly he would become famous. He might move a notch or two above Albert Einstein. Allred didn't seem to be the type to want that fame. After all, he had made a fortune and he could have spent much of that fortune publicly like Paul Allen had. He could have been on the cover of magazines. He could have bought *Rolling Stone* and done a cover story about himself.

If this was a scientific hoax, I thought, one of the props must be the digital camera. The camera had to be a space-age camera that the world wouldn't see for at least a decade or two. On my next little foray to a parallel world, I would need to bring my own digital camera. I knew that *my* own digital camera didn't take a picture of what I was thinking.

My doorbell rang again. It was Allred.

"May I come in?" He asked.

"Of course," I said.

Allred walked past me to the living room and sat down on the couch.

"We're going to have dinner over at the main house," Allred said. "I thought this would be a good time to explain some things before you meet the other scientists."

Allred got up and walked over to the kitchen. He opened the refrigerator, helped himself to a bottle of water, and returned to the couch.

"Ten years ago we set up a fund that we would use to extend Albert Einstein's work. There are so many more tools available to us today than what Einstein had in his day. Initially, we put in five hundred million dollars. We did this democratically—everybody contributed to the level they felt comfortable with. Just think, Mr. Hobbs, there's no research firm that has ever had the starting budget of five hundred million and a stable of clearly superior minds that were unencumbered by politicians or corporate suits."

I twirled that half-a-billion-dollar figure around in my mind. That was sure a lot more than just those computers in the big work room in the barn.

"Since that time," Allred said, "we had to replenish our fund. We have now invested more than two billion dollars. Those two billion dollars are *pure* dollars—they haven't been tainted by government waste or corporate profiteering. And, of course, that two billion dollars doesn't include any pay for us. We are all volunteers."

Two billion dollars chasing Einstein's ghost!

"But, every nickel we spent was worth it," Allred said. "We solved the problem. As you now know, there *are* parallel worlds!"

Allred got up and walked to the far wall. He opened a wood panel that hid the controls for the wall-size LED.

"Do you mind if I change your wall for a moment?" Allred asked.

"No," I said.

He typed in some instructions. My living room wall was now our universe—planets, stars, everything, in stark tack-sharp color.

"Hubble space telescope," Allred said. "Consider that our universe is duplicated. Thousands of times. Yes, *that* universe." Allred pointed at the wall.

"If you will, consider our universe like a floor on a very tall building. Each floor is a version of our universe, but in different time frames. This very tall building is surrounded by thousands of equally tall buildings."

I nodded thoughtfully. I was being the good student; I thought of the skyscrapers of New York City. Then I had a question, and like the good student I raised my hand.

"Yes, Mr. Hobbs," Allred said. He didn't seem bothered that I had interrupted his lecture. "You have a question. Good. What is it?"

"Why is our universe duplicated thousands of times?" I asked. "Why isn't there just one?"

"Good question, but only God can truly answer that," Allred said. "But, let's look at nature. For instance, we could also question why there are millions of duplicated atoms in this table? Or millions of duplicated atoms—different than the wood atoms—in the plastic arm of that dining room chair? It's all a part of nature—*duplication of*

49

atoms. I would say that it would be highly irregular in nature if there weren't thousands of our galaxies. It would be a phenomenal *fluke* if our universe was *not* duplicated. That's just not nature's way."

I guess that the only other person I could ask would be God. I didn't think that God would be as receptive as Allred in answering my question. He never had been before.

"So, let's go back to my analogy of the tall building," Allred said. "Each one of the floors in this very tall building is our universe. Each one is very much the same. Most modern physicists, or cosmologists as some like to call themselves nowadays, believe in the layering of the universes. The problem that scientists have is *not* whether universes are layered or not, but *how* do you get from one universe to the next? In my analogy of a tall building, how do you get from one floor to the next? All measurements known to us don't work. We think in terms of physics that *we know*—miles per hour, the speed of sound, the speed of light. In a span of fifty years in the middle 1900s, we went from a car going twenty miles an hour to a jet going the speed of sound. That's *huge* progress. While it is huge progress, it isn't enough to even consider going to another universe. We haven't yet developed a vehicle that can go the speed of light, but, *even if we did*, it wouldn't be fast enough to get to a parallel universe. So, if our universes are indeed *layered*, how do we get from one to another?"

I didn't know if I was supposed to answer, so I just kept my mouth shut. I pretended to be a great listener.

"You're probably not familiar with *white holes*," Allred said. "Black holes are more commonly known to the public."

I felt I had to answer this one; the great listener facade would last only so long. "Yes, I've read something about black holes," I said. "A star that had consumed itself, or something like that?"

"Close enough," Allred said. "The first black hole was discovered in 1963 by a New Zealand mathematician. It was thought at the time that was the only black hole in our universe. Now we know there are *hundreds* of black holes out in space. There is also a distant cousin to black holes—they're called wormholes. Have you heard of wormholes?"

I didn't think that Allred was referring to apples. "Vaguely," I said.

"The first person to identify wormholes was an interesting guy," Allred said. "His name was Charles Dodgson. Are you familiar with the name?"

"No," I said, "I don't think so."

Allred chuckled softly.

"Dodgson wrote under the pen name of Lewis Carroll. He wrote, of course, *Alice's Adventures in Wonderland,* or Alice in Wonderland. That was in 1865! Dodgson connected the countryside of Oxford to Wonderland using the looking glass as the wormhole. Then in 1935, Albert Einstein and his student Nathan Rosen introduced wormholes to the world of physics. Einstein believed that wormholes could be the gateway to parallel worlds. He also believed that wormholes existed naturally out in space, many of them, in fact."

I felt like saying what he had just told me confirmed that I had fallen down the rabbit hole, but it didn't seem that Allred wanted to hear wise-ass comments.

"Recently, there have been studies about *white holes*. These are the opposite of black holes. They do *not* consume and gobble up energy like black holes. Some physicists believe white holes are indeed the gateways to parallel universes and parallel worlds that Einstein was looking for. Physicists have theorized about white holes, but it's still speculation with them. We are, however, way past the speculation stage, *way* past it. We have discovered how to *manipulate* white holes. We have also found what Einstein believed, but couldn't prove: these holes in our universe do *not* conform to the physics that we know here on Earth. We're not dealing with miles per hour, speed of sound, speed of light—none of those measurements. Those measurements are obsolete concerning white holes."

Allred said, "We've got *full use* of white holes. We have the 'elevator' between parallel universes, between parallel worlds."

Allred stood up. "We don't have to use a white hole to go to dinner. We'll just walk." He headed for the door.

I stood there staring at the galaxy. I tried to picture a galaxy like that layered on top of an identical galaxy, and then on top of another like pancakes. Pancakes I understood. I didn't need to understand the physics stuff, however, pancakes or not. I just wanted to see Rachel again.

Chapter Nine

A llred and I took the elevator—not a white hole type of thing—up to the ground level of the barn.

"While we have dining facilities here in the barn," Allred said, "we occasionally like to eat in the main house."

Allred used the same security procedure to get out of the barn as he used getting into it. When he had used his various palms and fingers to get through the different security points, I had thought that there was a sequence to it. It wasn't a sequence, but you had to use any two different palms or fingers to open the security door. Left palm-right index finger, left pinkie finger-right thumb—any combination would work.

There was a large dining room in the farmhouse. Everybody was already seated, Charles and the five other scientists. I'd like to say that they had dressed up for the occasion, but they were wearing the same things that I had seen them wearing during the day. Looking at this group, *Alice in Wonderland* popped in my head again: A Mad Tea Party. The March Hare, the Mad Hatter, the Dormouse, and Alice. I hoped they couldn't take a picture of what I was thinking.

Allred sat at the head of the table; I sat in the empty chair to his right.

An elderly woman was putting large plates of food on the table.

"Mr. Hobbs, I would like you to meet my sister, Anna," Allred said.

Anna wiped her hands on her apron and curtsied. I'm not sure if I had ever seen an adult curtsy before, except perhaps in old black & white movies. She must be Allred's older sister. She looked to be in her sixties, was squat and thick, not so much fat as just built low to the ground. Somehow, this bowling ball of a woman had the same DNA as the string bean Allred.

The group of scientists didn't wait for Allred and me; they grabbed serving spoons and were shoveling food on their plates. Charles looked like he would like to bypass his plate and navigate the serving spoon directly to his mouth. Robert McDougald, the scientist who had hair like an unraveled beehive, probably should have been wearing a hair net to keep his hair out of the food.

Allred clinked the side of his water glass with his spoon. "I would like to introduce our guest," Allred said.

As they continued eating, I met each scientist one-by-one. Each one mumbled some sort of greeting.

Anna brought out another bottle of wine. On the table was Marcassin Pinot Noir. It was a spendy wine; I remembered buying a bottle in my steak-and-lobster days at about three hundred bucks. The scientists were drinking it like it was soda pop.

It didn't take them long to eat. The first one who pushed his plate away from him was Josef Landoski. In Allred's introduction, he had said that Josef was a refugee from Tektronics, the large firm in Oregon that had first pioneered oscilloscopes. I'm not sure what oscilloscopes do, but I assumed they had something to do with the monster computers that this crew had built.

Josef asked me, "So, Mr. Hobbs, what do you think of our parallel worlds?"

I took a couple of quick chews, then answered, "Please, call me Roy." I then took a swallow of the excellent Marcassin Pinot Noir. "Josef, to answer your question, I was totally amazed at my first experience."

There was chortling and chuckling around the table.

I should have answered, "No big deal." There wouldn't be any chortling or chuckling with that answer. But, these fellows seemed to be good guys; I didn't need to let my reporter's sick sense of humor invade this dinner table.

"You know what I find most interesting about parallel worlds?" Josef asked.

I shook my head.

"They're not dependent on each other," Josef said. "I mean the worlds are the same, but if you change one, it won't change the others."

I nodded my head like I knew what he was talking about.

"For instance, I understand that you went back to 1978 to see yourself first meet the woman you would eventually marry."

I nodded.

"Did you see your 1978 self?" Josef asked.

I nodded.

"Well, in time travel novels," Josef said, "they say you can never meet up with yourself. Obviously, you can because you're not really traveling through time, you're traveling to a parallel world."

I nodded again.

"This may sound gruesome," Josef said, "but if you would have had a gun and shot your 1978 self, you would have killed him in that world, but that would not have affected any of the other worlds."

Robert McDougald chimed in, "Right, er, Roy, I don't know if you've read any of the fiction about time travel, but characters are always warned not to do anything that would change history."

"Yes, I recall that," I said.

"Well, let's say you did indeed shoot your 1978 self," Robert continued, "you would only affect the history of that one parallel world. In all the other parallel worlds, nothing would be changed."

"What if I would go back to 1934 Germany and kill Adolph Hitler?" I asked.

"Well, you certainly would spare millions of lives in that *one* world," Josef said, "but, unfortunately, Adolph Hitler would continue to kill his millions in another million worlds."

Allred interjected, "Remember our little talk about atoms, Roy? Well, some atoms could become corrupt. For instance, the billions of atoms in this wood table are the same in atomic composition. However, what if there is one termite inside this table and that one termite starts chewing on the wood? Some of those atoms—because of the termite—would change, or cease to exist altogether. The same with somebody killing somebody. Let's say a parallel world traveler kills the president of the United States. That certainly would affect the

United States, but it wouldn't change the other parallel worlds in parallel galaxies."

I nodded my head. I was beginning to *start* to understand. It was just the *largeness* that made it so confusing. Sure, I could understand that parallel universes were layered like floors in a tall building. Or stacked like pancakes. The difficult part was the *size*. It's not easy for me to visualize our universe—something so large that we've never come close to reaching the end of it—was *just one floor* in this tall building.

"I don't particularly like this talk about killing," Allred said, "even if it is just to illustrate how these parallel worlds work. But, let me make this very clear to you, Roy. If you visited a parallel world, and *you* got shot and died on that world, you would be dead."

"Deader than a doornail," Charles said.

"Yes, there would be Roy Hobbs on other worlds," Allred said, "but this Roy Hobbs, the one sitting at this table, the one with this new knowledge of parallel worlds would be dead. You would be dead. Understand?"

"I think I do," I said. It was still a little confusing. The one thing I did understand, however, was that if I died on a parallel world that I would be dead. No recovery. No miracle cure. Dead is dead.

"Well, tomorrow, Roy," Allred said, "you get to go back."

"To the same meeting in 1978?" I asked.

"Yes, yes, I would like for you to go back to the same time frame. I'll explain why later, but for now, you be very aware of any changes. Major or subtle changes." Allred said. "You will be going back to twelve-oh-two on Wednesday, May tenth, 1978, but it will be in a different parallel world. Same time, different station."

"This time, however, I'll help you program your entry and exit," Charles said. Charles wasn't the most talkative type and he spoke when I least expected it. Behind that pregnant-looking stomach—it looked like he would be delivering twins tonight—he had beady, almost reptilian eyes. I almost expected him to spurt out his tongue, and it would be long, narrow, and forked. I think I preferred it when Charles was looking down at his weathered Nikes. If Charles decided

56

to look at faces instead of Nikes, he would probably unnerve everybody in the room.

"Yes, yes," said Allred. Allred reminded me fondly of Gyro Gearloose, the inventor duck that was the friend of Mickey Mouse and who worked for Uncle Scrooge. Allred was just a big, friendly guy, who happened to be brilliant and rich. "Once you get the hang of this, learn all the controls, learn how to program entries and exits, we'll want you to explore as thoroughly as you can as many parallel worlds as you can."

I nodded my head. I looked forward to going back to twelve-oh-two on May tenth, 1978. I wanted to live through that again. It went so fast last time. This time, I would take more time. Yes, since I would be learning the controls, I would spend more time on May tenth, 1978. And yes, this time, just to satisfy my reporter's skeptical mind—Gyro Gearloose or not—I would bring my own digital camera that I had in my briefcase.

Chapter Ten

T he alley behind the Knight Cap bar was *exactly* the same as yesterday. I looked at my watch. Eleven fifty-seven in the morning. I assumed it was Wednesday, May tenth, 1978. It seemed like I was in the exact position that I had been yesterday, but Allred had told me that would actually be on a different parallel world, a different parallel universe.

Something seemed different in this alley. I couldn't figure out what it was. I decided to take a picture from my digital camera so I could compare the alley with future trips. I brought out my own digital camera and took two pictures.

My camera wasn't disguised as a Kodak Instamatic camera, but it wouldn't attract attention. There weren't digital cameras in 1978, of course, but the camera itself looked like some miniature cameras of that era.

I decided to walk a different route to watch my 1978 self meet Rachel. I pushed open the back gate that led to the back patio of the Knight Cap. On warm summer nights, the Knight Cap's owner, Howard Jones, would grill cheeseburgers out there. He didn't have a kitchen inside, and I'm not sure if the city knew he had this makeshift kitchen in the back, but none of his customers complained.

I walked past the Weber grill and opened the back door of the Knight Cap and stepped in. It was a long, very narrow bar. It only had room for a long bar that a bunch of drinkers could lean on. There were no tables.

Howard was tending bar as I walked past.

I said, "Hi Howard."

Howard was a friendly guy, knowing the names of all his customers. He looked up and said, "Hi…"

I could tell he was searching his mind for a name. Because it wasn't a long walk from the *Sun-Times* building, I had become a semi-regular at the Knight Cap for the past couple of years. It was a place for mostly young professionals: Take some newspaper writers, add a bunch of ad people, sprinkle in some television folks from the nearby CBS television station and that mostly would be the Knight Cap clientele.

Even though I had been a semi-regular and Howard greeted me by name every time, he was stumped at seeing the 2005 me. There might have been some resemblance to my 1978 self, and if I would have given Howard more time, he might have connected the dots and come to a conclusion that I was the *father* of my 1978 self. Do people change much in twenty-seven years? Some change into entirely different people. Gain a hundred pounds and see how many people recognize you. I had pretty much stayed the same weight, but there were twenty-seven *years* of living that would change anybody.

At the end of the bar was a drinking pal of mine.

"Hey, Bud," I said.

Bud probably recognized my voice. Voices don't change as much as faces and bodies. He turned to say hello. My voice didn't belong to the face that he knew. He said, "Hi…"

Once out on the sidewalk in front of the Knight Cap, I laughed out loud. It was as if I had played a practical joke. But, I was the only one who knew the punch line. Still, it was funny to me.

I had taken the shortcut through the Knight Cap for one specific reason. That reason was walking down the sidewalk toward me. Rachel was coming from the east, down Ontario Street. I wanted to follow her when she met up with my 1978 self on Michigan Avenue and Ontario in just about a minute and a half. I watched her walk toward me. She was wearing the same emerald green dress. She walked with a bounce; her face gave an impression of a smile.

I stood in front of the Knight Cap and watched her walk toward me. She stopped right in front of me.

"Excuse me," she asked, "do you have the correct time?"

I was flustered. I hadn't felt this nervous in front of a woman since the seventh grade when I asked the best-looking girl in the class to dance. Since that time, I had never had a problem of introducing myself to beautiful women. But this was different, a lot different. I was a fifty-one-year-old man looking at a woman who I had been married to for almost twenty years. I had made love to this woman more than a thousand times, but now she was twenty-two years old. There was no way to assimilate that situation naturally. I could feel the sweat bead on my face.

Rachel's beautiful face peered at me. "Are you all right, sir?"

"Ah…yes," I said, "sorry…" I didn't know what I was apologizing for.

I looked at my watch. "Twelve-oh-one," I said.

"Oh, I'm late," Rachel said. Weren't those The Rabbit's words? Had I indeed fallen down some rabbit hole? I guess, when you figure in parallel worlds and white holes, that I had indeed fallen down an intergalactic rabbit hole.

"Thank you," Rachel said, "you should get something to eat." She smiled, gave a slight wave, turned and walked toward Michigan Avenue.

Perspiration slid down my face to my shirt collar. I watched her walk away, that bouncy walk in itself said 'happy.' I followed her down Ontario Street.

Sure enough, like clockwork, she met my 1978 self at the corner. I was probably fifty feet away. She said something to my 1978 self. I couldn't hear what she said, but I knew. She had asked for the time.

I took out my digital camera. This would not be the same angle as the previous day so I couldn't compare the details of the photos side-by-side, but it was my personal camera. I could at least verify whether Allred had developed some type of technology where his camera would photograph what a person was *thinking*. It sounds absurd to be even thinking that such a camera could exist, but which was more absurd: traveling the parallel worlds or an amazing camera that took pictures of what you were thinking?

I zoomed in and took three more pictures. At my different vantage point, I heard *We Are the Champions* on a radio in a car waiting for the light to turn. I couldn't remember who sang it. When the light turned green, my 1978 self and Rachel headed south on Michigan Avenue. I followed. I snapped a couple more pictures. Again, I snapped a close-up of Rachel from the waist down.

As I started to walk down the street, my mind was in a rush of questions.

Why had Rachel asked my 1978 self for the time? I had just told her the time less than thirty seconds before. Had she forgotten? Or had she asked *somebody* the correct time just before she had asked me twenty-seven years ago? Had that somebody—twenty- seven years ago—been *me*? These parallel worlds were confusing. But, this was something that I could check out, I think.

Rachel and my 1978 self crossed Michigan Avenue at the Marriott Hotel, and then headed south. They stopped in front of the *Chicago Tribune* building. They talked. I wracked my brain to try and remember the conversation. I couldn't. It was just small talk. What I do remember, however, was the feeling in 1978 that I was in love. That feeling had not happened frequently to me. Sure, it happened in junior high school all the time, but as a young adult in 1978 that feeling hadn't even brushed my side until I met Rachel. After Rachel and I had been divorced, I wanted that feeling one more time. Nothing, nothing came even close.

After that first accidental meeting on Wednesday, May tenth, 1978, I had come to believe in 'love at first sight.' I couldn't explain it, nor could anybody else for that matter. I could just *feel* it. I had surmised that it was electricity. For whatever reason, Rachel's personal electricity and my personal electricity meshed perfectly. This meshing doesn't happen very frequently, of course. But, it does happen with friends and lovers. Why do we become friends with certain people, and despise others? It's not always because of the same interests. I'm a Chicago Cubs fan and there are plenty of Cubbie fans that I know that I can't stand. With women, it's not always because of looks. Sure, looks help a lot, but there have been women that I would like to take to bed, but wouldn't want to have a cup of coffee with.

The feeling of falling in love was wonderful. That feeling, however, didn't usually last long. The electrical currents modified over time into something both partners felt comfortable with or came to despise. For the past few years when I was hoping to fall in love again, I marveled at Elizabeth Taylor. She had been married eight or nine times or more, I'm not sure. I presumed that she had fallen in love each time before she had married. What a great idea. She had taken the *feeling* of falling in love, used it, wallowed in it, and then discarded it when it was dissipating. She had the amazing ability to fall in love that frequently and then the brains to toss the marriage away when the electrical impulses started to short circuit. My plumbing wasn't constructed that way. I had loved one woman— Rachel—from Wednesday, May tenth, 1978 to our divorce to the day she was murdered to this very day.

After Rachel went inside the *Tribune* building, I followed my 1978 self, staying a half block away.

We walked over to State Street, past the *Chicago Sun-Times* building. I knew where he was going. After all: Been there done that. I followed him down State Street a couple of blocks to Illinois Street. On the southwest corner was a green three story building. The green was the color of puke. There was no sign on the outside, but even a stranger could figure out what type of establishment it was. It was a bar. Hobson's Oyster Bar.

My 1978 self was going to meet some buddies in there and then go out to a baseball game. I guess there wasn't going to be any crime committed that day, or at least none that needed me to report about. We were going to a White Sox game. As you know, I was a Cubs fan, but the Cubbies were in Houston; the White Sox were playing the Minnesota Twins at Comiskey Park on the south side of Chicago. I couldn't remember the final score, but I do remember three things: Lamar Johnson, the White Sox first baseman, hit a home run in the third inning and that proved enough to be the winner. The second thing was that I thought about Rachel all game long. The third thing was that I drank way too much beer at Comiskey.

While waiting across the street from Hobson's, I looked at the pictures in my digital camera. I had taken nine. Rachel was in each one except for the two that I had taken in the alley when I first arrived. It would be interesting to compare these with the photos taken yesterday. Except for the alley shots, the photos were the same subject matter, but they were from two different angles. One photo stood out. Rachel was at the corner of Michigan Avenue and Ontario Street. She had been talking to my 1978 self. What I hadn't noticed when I snapped the picture, Rachel had turned her head toward me. In the photo she was staring straight at me. I pushed the little button that could enlarge the picture inside the display. Rachel wasn't just looking down the street. She was looking at *me*.

I didn't follow my 1978 self to the White Sox game. I knew what was going to happen. After the game, my 1978 self and my buddies would take the 'L' back to Hobson's. I had told friends at Hobson's that I had met the girl that I was going to marry. At least that's what my friends told me a couple of days later. I had drank so much beer I didn't remember.

Most of the time drunks say stupid things; this time my drunken slobbering was perfectly accurate. The wonder of falling in love at first sight.

Maybe Allred could explain the electrical impulse of love at first sight. He wasn't the romantic genius, of course, but he knew strange things.

Chapter Eleven

My first landing back at the silo felt a little wobbly. The second landing felt like somebody had knocked the wind out of me.

Charles was in the silo and he handed me a bottle of Gatorade Fierce. I took two big slugs of it as if I had just wandered in off a desert.

Charles continued to look down at his feet. The top of his head was not a pretty sight with tufts of white hair failing to cover the scaling blotches of rashes. However, I preferred his downward glance because I couldn't get used to his eyes. His eyes were like a snake's. It's not that I had studied eyes of snakes, but the ones that I remembered seemed totally emotionless.

Eyes can be part of an optical illusion. After all, it's not the eyeballs that really show emotions—it's what's *around* the eyeballs that convey happiness or sadness or coldness. The perception is, of course, that it's the eyes that show emotion. The perception is wrong. It fools us. Think of a dog. Can a dog, bounding to greet you, have eyes that are happy? Of course, no doubt about it. How about a woman's eyes? By looking at her eyes, can you tell if she is happy or sad or angry or furious? Of course, no doubt about it. But, it's what surrounds the eyes that convey the emotion—the eyebrows, the eyelids, the corners of the eyes, the mouth, the nose. So, it was difficult looking at Charles' eyes because they never showed emotion, regardless of his eyelids, eyebrows, nose, mouth or any other body part. Even when he showed a slight grin, his eyes were flat, cold, peering—like a snake's eyes. I felt like giving Charles some cool sunglasses as a gift. And a baseball cap that he could wear inside.

"How do you feel?" Charles asked, his eyes looking at his Nikes.

"A little shaky," I said. I felt no worse than if I would have just briskly walked up a flight of stairs. Not bad for whisking through a white hole and sailing through only-God-knows-how-many-galaxies.

"Can you make some prints of these?" I asked Charles, handing him my camera.

He took the camera and looked at it. "This isn't one of ours," Charles said.

"It's my personal camera," I said. "I like the feel of it."

"Okay," Charles said, turned and walked away with my camera.

I went back to my suite and showered and then took the elevator to the main floor of the barn.

Allred spotted me as I got off the elevator.

"Roy!" Allred said, "How was your second trip?" He looked me squarely in the eyes and his eyes seemed to sparkle with emotion.

I briefly told him about the trip.

He ushered me to a room adjacent to the boardroom. It was a lounge with a great array of La-Z-Boy chairs. I didn't know that there was such a great variety. Allred must have bought out a whole store. We sat down in a corner. I was in a big La-Z-Boy model that was styled after a men's club with its tufted leather, nail head accents and turned wood legs. Allred sat in a red leather La-Z-Boy that didn't have the tufted leather or the nail head accents. It looked like it should be in a French whorehouse.

"You've visited 1978 twice in two days," Allred said. "We find that a person shouldn't go to parallel worlds three straight days."

"Really? What happens?" I asked.

"Nothing apparent, at least right away," Allred said. "When we first discovered how to travel to parallel worlds, we went quite frequently. You can understand the excitement. We kept copious records of any variations of our health. Nothing abnormal showed in the beginning. So, we continued to make more and more trips. Different disconcerting symptoms started to pop up."

"Like what?"

"Well, blotchy rashes, coughing spasms, dizziness, fainting spells, and a bizarre inability to bend joints," Allred said. "Some of us were walking around like the Tin Man, but with blotchy rashes. Those could all be symptoms of The Bends, what deep sea divers get when they come up too fast. We, of course, come up—if you will—a lot faster than any deep sea diver." Allred chuckled at his analogy.

"I guess Charles would be 'Exhibit A'," I said, "his rashes…"

"Yes, yes, I guess you could consider Charles as Exhibit A, but at times it has affected all of us. We now are far more conservative in our visits," Allred said. "We limit ourselves to no more than four visits per seven days. And instead of traveling on four straight days, we try to space it out. What I'm getting at is that we think you should cool it for a day or so. That will give you a chance to get caught up with your work."

"I would like to talk to you about that," I said.

"Yes?"

"I'm a little unclear on the direction."

"What do you mean?" Allred asked.

"Well, as you instructed, I picked a memorable and specific time in my life and have gone back to it," I said. "Those two trips were the most profound experiences I have ever had in my life. But, those are *my* experiences. Don't you want me to work with the other scientists, writing about their experiences? Do you want me to go back and verify some important facts about our history? Would we find that our history books covered things a little differently than the way they actually happened?"

Allred held up his hand as if he were a traffic cop. Then he laughed his hyena laugh, heh-heh-HEH-heh-heh.

"Roy, I only want you to write about *your* experiences," Allred said. "You have such a marvelous eye for detail. We all keep logs of our trips, but they read like abbreviated scientific papers, at least mine do. Boring! Boring! *You* are *not* writing a scientific book. I want yours to have the *emotion* that ours lacks; I want yours to be the *personal feelings* that ours lacks. You're writing this book for two people: me, of course, but also for yourself. You're living the book that you will write."

I nodded.

"You've got the complete run of the place," Allred said, "except the floors where the computers are. But, you don't need to be on those floors. You can come and go as you please. I just ask that you work full-time on this project."

"I can go to any parallel world I would want to?" I asked.

"Yes and no," Allred said. "You can go to any parallel world that involves *you*. We don't want you to go back and see if Christopher Columbus was the first one to discover America. We've already done that. And, he wasn't. Your goal is *you*. Also, there are some worlds that you aren't familiar with that you might think would be interesting to visit, but they are dangerous."

"Dangerous? How so?"

"Well, what if you went back to see General George Custer at Little Big Horn?" Allred said. "We don't really know the exact timing of that massacre. What if you went back and you were right in the middle of it? No, we want you to go back to timelines in your own life. This is a personal book about your personal feelings. Even then, you might run into some danger. It's happened to all of us at least once."

"What do you mean?" I asked.

Allred said, "Well, I went back to the Chicago of my teenage years and it was scorched earth. The tall buildings had crumbled; there was nobody alive that I could see. It looked like it could be the aftermath of a nuclear strike. Or it could have been a large meteor that caused that type of damage."

"When was this? What time frame?"

"In the 1980s," Allred said. "I quickly came back. We chart these different universes, of course, and when we see something like this we block it from our Wayfarer Commander so that somebody doesn't inadvertently go there. After that visit to nuclear Chicago, we created the 'Red Button' on the Wayfarer Commander. As you know, pushing the Red Button will immediately return you to where you came from. The Red Button will supersede any exit time that you had programmed. The point is: even in parallel worlds, there are things that are different. It's like small—very miniscule—inconsistencies in an atom. These inconsistencies don't *change* the atom, they don't even modify the atom. But, inconsistencies are occasionally there."

"Why would there have been a scorched earth in one parallel world, but not the others?" I asked.

"We don't know for sure. For instance, the Cuban missile crisis back with Kennedy and Khrushchev. That crisis happened in thousands of parallel worlds. What if—in *one* of those parallel worlds—an advisor to Kennedy or Khrushchev, it doesn't matter which one, convinced his leader to let fly with missiles? It would be an aberration, it would be an inconsistency, but in that one world it happened and the result was a scorched earth."

"So, Roy, let the scientists do their work," Allred said, "and you do yours. Yours is like—I guess—writing a very literate diary. I want you to write about subtle changes from one parallel world to another that *you* experience—not from a scientific point of view—but a personal, emotional point of view."

Allred stood up and as he walked to the door he said, "I've got to go, work to do, yes, work to do."

By the time I stood up, Allred was out the door.

Chapter Twelve

As I reached the door that Allred had just walked through, it came swinging in bumping to a stop at my feet.

It was Allred. He walked in and sat down in the same chair that looked like it came from a French whorehouse.

"I forgot something," Allred said, bringing out my camera from his jacket pocket.

"There are so many things that we don't know," Allred said, turning the camera around in his hand.

"I'll give you an example of what we don't know," Allred said. "White holes. What is the physics behind the white holes? We don't know. We've got arguably the brightest minds in the world with a virtually unlimited budget, and *we* can't figure out *the physics* of the white holes. We did figure out how to *access them*, but we can't figure out how they indeed work."

"How do you control white holes?" I asked, looking at my camera that rested in his palm like it was a frog. "In a way that I can understand."

Allred got up and walked over to a small refrigerator inset in the wall. He opened it and brought out two bottles of water. He walked back and handed me one. I guess I was going to get a quick lesson in physics. He twisted off the cap on his water bottle, clutching my camera in one hand.

"Below our barn, we built the largest magnet in the world," Allred said. "It spreads out over four acres. It's about thirty feet thick. We used many different crews to build this—one crew was not around when the next one came to build the next compartmentalized magnet.

With these huge magnets, *and* the electricity that we can pour into them, *and* our computers, we're able to focus a white hole into our silo."

"Where do these white holes come from?" I asked.

"They are a part of nature," Allred said. "As I mentioned before, there's usually a white hole floating around Sargasso Sea—the Bermuda Triangle. It's not always there, of course. We believe that there were white holes at one time around the pyramids. That might explain why they were built. The most convenient one for us is right around the corner. You've heard of Cape Disappointment?"

"Cape Disappointment?"

It sounded like Allred was tsk-tsking me like a teacher would, but he might have just been clearing his throat.

"Cape Disappointment is just a few miles from here—where the Columbia River flows into the Pacific Ocean. That area is called 'The Graveyard of the Pacific' because of all the shipwrecks that have happened in that general area. It's one of the most treacherous river bars in the world. The U.S. Navy practices out there because it's so rugged. That, my friend, is where we commandeer a white hole. We just pull it with our magnets over to our silo. Now, don't confuse a white hole with a tornado. Two different animals. The tornado is localized, it's dark, it's uncontrollable; the white hole is invisible and strangely controllable with our system."

"We all drink a lot of water here," Allred said. "We have to fight dehydration."

He opened the bottle of water and it seemed in one gulp drank half of it.

"Let me ask you one more question," I said.

"Sure, Roy, ask away."

"As you and I are here talking about Cape Disappointment and capturing white holes for our own use, are you and I having the same conversation on a thousand other parallel worlds?"

Allred laughed his barroom hyena laugh. Some water sprayed out of his mouth like it came from a spritzer.

"Very good question, Roy, *very* good question," Allred said. There was no tsk-tsk here. "The answer, however, is 'no.'"

"No? How can that be?"

"Well, with our heavy magnet below our feet, we are basically altering the activity on this *one* world," Allred said. "In the other parallel worlds, your life is going on as you were living it before you came here. My life is going on. This one experience that we're sharing together is indeed that: *one* isolated experience. This one experience is *not* happening on parallel worlds. We've checked. But, when thinking about this, we think that that is a good thing. We're keeping our knowledge contained. And safe."

"Safe?"

"Yes, safe. Consider this. What if somebody on any one of a million worlds stole what we know and then applied it for the wrong reasons? Mankind has a tendency to do those things, you know. For instance, what if that person went back to 1935 with the know-how on how to build an atomic bomb and with it helped Adolph Hitler win World War Two? What if that person then applied our knowledge for *total* domination and sent *an army* out to parallel worlds to change *all* of them for Adolph Hitler?"

It sounded far-fetched, but it did *seem* possible. Heck, from my two experiences, it *was* possible.

"So, we are extremely cautious with our knowledge," Allred said.

"How do you know that somebody isn't on to you?" I asked.

"Like who?"

"I don't know," I said, "but you've had a massive construction job in a remote area. Don't you think the government would be aware? How about NSA? Aren't they the government agency that has satellites that can read license plates?"

"We have considered that, of course," Allred said. "We are very protective. We have the greatest security system ever devised. While this looks like a barn, the walls are actually eight foot thick cement reinforced with titanium. It is earthquake proof, tank proof, bomb proof. There are seven sub floors, each with those eight foot reinforced walls."

"How did you build all of this?" I asked. I was astonished that such a structure could be built without it being the talk of Oregon.

"Good question, Mr. Hobbs," Allred said. "It's fortunate that people here in the northwest corner of Oregon think I'm a little daft. The story line was that I was building a bomb shelter, a very elaborate bomb shelter. It took two years to build, but because it was below the ground, it didn't create much interest. And, I spent a fortune—more than a quarter of a million dollars—with a public relations firm to keep it out of the press."

I found it interesting that Allred thought a quarter of a million was a fortune. With his wealth, he could have spent two hundred and fifty thousand dollars and not even known he had spent it.

"We imported many workers," Allred said, "and housed them right here on the site, much like the farmers do with migrant workers. Here, however, we set up *everything* these workers would need. There were stores, there were supplies. Workers signed on for one-month work duties and part of their deal was that they would never leave the grounds during that month. After a month, we'd rotate them home— mainly the south and the southwest—for one-month of paid liberty. By the way, have you ever seen the TV show, *Survivor*?" Allred asked.

"The *Survivor*?"

"Yes, yes, the TV show."

"Of course."

"Well, that show is shot months before it's aired on television," Allred said. "Did you ever wonder how the producers keep the results secret for all that time?"

"No, I hadn't thought about it," I said.

"Well, they set up a secret bonus structure," Allred said. "For instance, the winner of the show gets one million dollars. The participants that don't win are also paid a nice sum *if* no word gets out beforehand on who won."

"I didn't know that."

"And, of course, each participant signs an agreement that if they leak any information they would get their pants sued off," Allred said. "We followed those principles—the carrot and the stick. The carrot was bonuses; the stick was that we would sue them into oblivion. The carrot and the stick *and* our public relations firm kept this very secret."

Allred's strategy seemed to be a very expensive way to build a bunker, but if money wasn't an object, it had worked.

"There are seven floors here that can be reached by elevator," Allred said. "Five of the floors are essentially for computers. These computers are the most advanced computers in the history of the world. If you took all the mega computers that the government has— and our government has more powerful computers than anybody— they would represent, in computing power, one square foot of one floor in our building. We've constructed computers from scratch, and have made astounding advances in computing power. The world won't see that type of computing power for twenty-five or thirty years, if even then."

I sat there thinking about what Allred had said. It seemed possible to get that type of computing power if you'd take seven of the world's brightest minds, give them a project that they were insanely passionate about, then give them an unlimited budget and don't have any corporate suits or politicians breathing down their necks.

"Lastly, we're very careful allowing anybody to get a peek of what we are doing," Allred said. "We did in-depth research on you before you and I had that cup of tea."

"You did? Who did that? Not Charles or any of your other scientists."

"No, we're scientists, not private investigators," Allred said. "But, there are highly reputable companies that can do that. All it costs is money. We determined that you are safe for us. That wasn't a unanimous feeling among us, by the way, but I felt that you wouldn't betray us; you had never betrayed sources before."

If I had to bet, I'd bet that Charles was a dissenter.

"As for the government getting wind of this, we have our own sources inside government, and so far, we feel we haven't landed on any agency radar screen. But, we have to consider all possibilities. If the government wanted to take over our operations, we have a way of destroying all of information—and computers—in an instant."

That was scary. Nuclear explosions?

"Like Captain Nemo in *20,000 Leagues Under the Sea*," I said.

"Well, yes," said Allred. "He did it with explosions. Our method is much more civil. But more effective."

Allred stood up and dropped his empty water bottle in a recycle bin.

"Let me ask you another question," I said.

"You've far surpassed the one question you wanted to ask, but okay, one more."

"Why are you guys doing this?"

It was fortunate that Allred had finished his bottle of water. The barroom hyena laugh was larger than any I had heard and if he had just taken a big swig of water he could have plastered the wall with spray.

"I'll give you the best answer," Allred said and then paused.

I waited.

"Because we can!" Allred laughed again.

"Yes, we have the money *and* we have the brains," Allred said, "but mostly we have the motivation. Money, brains, motivation—with no corporate or government interference—that's a combination any scientist would kill for. This is what we do, Roy. We are *scientists*. We are in the discovery mode right now. We don't fully understand a lot of things in our discovery, but we are getting smarter. We don't even know what we will do with our discoveries. Give them to our government? I think not. We are doing this now as scientists—*pure* scientists—with no personal glory, no government peering over our shoulders. We're not trying to save the world—*any* world—we're not trying to save mankind. We're doing this because to each one of us this is the grandest challenge that we've ever faced, and we have the freedom to take that challenge on. Roy, ask me questions any time, but right now, I've got to get back to work."

Allred started to walk toward the door and then stopped.

"Oh, by the way, Charles gave me your digital camera," Allred said. My camera was still in his hand. He held it out to me.

"None of the pictures came out," he said.

"None?" I said, "But I looked at them all after I had taken them. They were perfect."

"It's in the camera," Allred said. "We've had to build special digital cameras for our traveling to parallel worlds. Your camera would presumably work perfectly here, but when it goes through a white hole, it wipes the digital imaging clean. So, when you travel to parallel worlds, take one of our especially adapted digital cameras. We'll print, of course, all the pictures you want."

I turned on the camera. Sure enough, there were no pictures in storage.

"Do film cameras work?" I asked.

"*Film* cameras? Those old-fashioned things?"

"Yes, film cameras," I said. "Suppose I was in 1978 and dropped and broke my digital camera, but wanted to take some more pictures. I could always buy a Kodak Instamatic."

"Yes, I suppose you could," Allred said. "I don't know if the film image would make it through a white hole. Some films don't make it through the security devices in airports. We've never tried it. We don't even have a way of developing film here. We're digital all the way. Film might work; you could try."

Allred wasn't very convincing. Or was it just my reporter's antennae receiving static? Allred had always been candid with me, I think, but how would I know? His eyes, however, *seemed* sincere.

Chapter Thirteen

With a day off, I decided to go shopping.

Where I was going to shop wasn't a typical store, nor was it a big box store like Wal-Mart. I was going to the 'Company Store.'

The Company Store wasn't very far away; it was right down the end of the hallway from my suite on the second floor.

This store was the most unique store I had ever been in. In square footage, it probably equaled the size of a small supermarket or a very big 7-11. Instead of food and soda and snacks, the Company Store had more old clothing than a Salvation Army outlet. The clothing wasn't shabby, by any means. Some of it was brand new. I don't know where they got brand new clothing for 1978, but they did. In fact, they had brand new clothing for many of the years.

The Company Store had its own manager, but they called this person a *librarian*. Unlike the normal librarian who catalogued books, this one catalogued clothes. She was also the clothing advisor.

Charles had picked me up to take me to the store. He introduced me to the librarian, Leona. She was tall, thin—think of a female version of Gyro Gearloose—except she specialized in old clothes, not inventions. Even from a distance, her body frame reminded me of Allred.

After Charles had introduced me to Leona, he wandered off into the stacks.

"Yes," Leona said to me, "I am related to Allred. I'm his twin sister. Unfortunately, he got the good looks." She laughed. I wasn't sure about the good looks, but she clearly got the good sense of humor.

Her size was about the same as Allred's. In fact, if the two were standing side-by-side, and wearing hats to cover their hair, I'd bet that from a distance I couldn't tell them apart. Up close, however, Leona didn't have the aging hippie look of Allred. She looked like a librarian. She was wearing a dark blue print dress that hemmed just below her knees. Her hair was tucked neatly in a bun. She wore thin wire frame glasses. What didn't fit the librarian stereotype were the dramatic streaks of white in her dark hair. I could tell that the white was not a dye job; I presumed that she had had those white streaks for many years. Being the twin of Allred, she got all the good looks; her face was beautiful. When she was younger, that face turned a lot of heads. Even now, in her early fifties, she had a face that could have belonged to a movie actress.

"In case you're wondering, my first name also had special meaning to my parents," Leona said. "Leona—in honor of Leon Trotsky."

She laughed. It was a good laugh—there was no hyena laugh in her. "At least I didn't have any problems with my name as a kid. Leona isn't that unusual, except when Leona Helmsley—the Queen of Mean—started to get all those headlines. But, poor Allred. He was always getting teased about his name."

Leona did a little pirouette. She had twirled on the ball of her foot as easy as a ballerina would. What was *that* move?

"You're looking for the late 1970s," she said as if nothing had happened.

I nodded. Leona had seemed so stable, then the pirouette. Pirouettes were not something that fifty-somethings normally did, at least in front of strangers. The rabbit hole beckons.

"I've been back to 1978 a couple of times," I said, "but just for a few minutes each time. The khakis I was wearing worked, but I think I'd like to stay a couple of days."

"And you need a wardrobe," she said, "and probably a couple of other things. Follow me."

We walked down a long aisle.

"Forty-two long?" Leona asked, guessing my suit size.

"Yes."

"Well, we have plenty in each size. Let's see what we have."

82

We walked a little further and stopped at a carefully painted sign: 1978. The sizes of sports jackets and suits started at thirty-four and ascended to forty-six long. There were about six items per size.

"How about this?" Leona said, pulling out a navy blue sports jacket. "It would go well with gray slacks, or khakis."

The navy blue sports jacket looked like the one I had in my closet back in Portland. Men's styles sure haven't changed much since 1978.

"Jogging suits?" Leona asked. "Jogging suits just started to become popular back in 1978. You look like you could wear one without looking foolish. What a crazy business, wouldn't you say?"

"Which business is that?"

"Jogging, of course," Leona said. "It really started around 1978. Do you realize that there were fifteen crazy souls who showed up for the first Hawaii Ironman Triathlon in 1978, and last year there were over fifteen hundred athletes who competed? There were thousands more who applied, but weren't accepted."

"How do you know this stuff?" I asked.

"Part of it is my job," Leona said. "Not only do I collect all this clothing, and match it with the eras, but I also need to know a lot about each era. We've got a lending library, which will give you a lot of information about each era. And, I was the second woman to participate in the Ironman in 1980."

"Do you still run?" I asked. Her body looked like she ran a triathlon every day.

She then did the splits. Her dress rose up past her knees displaying her thin, athletic legs. She bounced up as if she had been on a trampoline.

She laughed. It was a throaty laugh that sounded good.

"I hope I didn't scare you," she said, still laughing.

"Well, it was different," I said. "If nothing else, you've shown me that you have tremendous flexibility."

"You're familiar with Tourette Syndrome?" she asked.

"Of course."

"Well, I don't have that," Leona said, "but it's something *like* that. Instead of the twitching or the profane outbursts, I just get an

83

uncontrollable urge at times to do a pirouette or the splits or a cartwheel. It's strange, I admit, but down here, who cares?"

"Did you do a pirouette at the finish line of the Ironman?" I asked.

She laughed and playfully punched my arm, "You're funny, yep, you are funny."

I think that was a first for me: I got a librarian to laugh.

Leona outfitted me with 1978 versions of Calvin Klein slacks, Sears shirts, Jockey underwear, dark socks and Florsheim loafers. I had tried on some of the clothing, looked in the mirror and didn't see much difference from today. The biggest difference was the hair. Of the hair that I had, I didn't grow it as long as what was stylish in 1978. Donald Trump's hair would have fit better back then, but I was fifty-one years old and *not* a billionaire—long or short hair, it didn't make any difference.

"If you're going to stay a couple of days, you'll need some money," Leona said. She reached in a box below a table of shirts. It was filled with dollars. Just another prop, I guess.

"All of these bills were minted before 1978," Leona said. "I'd like to get you some credit cards, but that, of course, is impossible. We could do it if you were going to be there for a year—you'd just apply like anybody else. I *will* give you some fake I.D.—I'll need to take your picture for a 1978 Illinois driver's license before you leave. I'll also give you some fake credit cards. You can't use them, of course, but if you check-in to a reasonable hotel, they'll ask for a credit card. You can give them one that I give you, but it's bogus, so just tell them you're going to pay with cash. Most likely, they'll ask for an imprint of your credit card, and the cash upfront, but they won't bang the card unless you destroy the room. You won't be destroying any hotel rooms, will you, Roy?"

"Not likely," I said.

After about an hour, I was fully equipped for my next foray to 1978—new clothes, credit cards, Illinois driver's license, and five thousand dollars in cash.

With my shopping done for the day, I sat in my suite. I was restless. I didn't feel like doing a pirouette or a cartwheel, but I felt like doing *something*. I felt like going back to 1978, but I didn't want to risk it and end up looking like Charles.

Tomorrow would be the day for me to go back, setting the departure and return on my own.

Chapter Fourteen

The third time I returned to Wednesday, May tenth, 1978, I arrived an hour earlier than the two times before. This was, of course, a different parallel world than the previous two, but I couldn't tell the difference.

It did seem that the alley was different on the second trip, but the pictures I had taken from my own digital camera were wiped when I went through the white hole. At least, that was Allred's explanation.

This time the alley didn't *seem* different, but I took out Allred's digital camera and took a couple of shots for the record. In future trips I would be able to compare.

From the alley, I walked a couple of blocks north to a Walgreens on Michigan Avenue. I looked at the Polaroid cameras on display. I could spend almost fifty bucks on a Sonar model. Instead, thinking that Leona would like me to spend her Company Store dollars wisely, I chose the cheapo Polaroid One-Step for less than thirty dollars. A roll of film cost me another ten. The Polaroid was going to get me a little closer to solving my picture mystery. I wouldn't take the chance whether undeveloped film could make it back through the white hole; I would bring my own *print*. I might even wrap it in tin foil or something to help insulate it from whatever harmful rays were out there in the white hole. That was my scientific reasoning. I probably should have a photo encased in Lucite.

As usual, May tenth, 1978 was a terrific day—sunny, a little breeze, a type of day that you could make a fortune on if you could bottle it. Well, I guess parallel worlds were the closest thing to bottling it.

I didn't walk to the back alley of the Knight Cap. I walked directly to the position I had on the first trip—across the street from where my 1978 self would first meet Rachel on Michigan Avenue and Ontario Street. I got to my spot ten minutes before I had on my two previous trips.

I fiddled with the Polaroid. I wouldn't be able to take rapid fire pictures with it like I had with the digital cameras, but I just needed one good shot. I aimed the Polaroid to where my 1978 self and Rachel would be standing, and took a picture. Moments later, a little square piece of stiff paper popped out of the camera. Waiting in the shade of a tall building, I saw the picture come to life. In the picture, I saw several people standing where my 1978 self and Rachel would be. I was ready.

From my vantage point, I saw both Rachel and my 1978 self heading to the corner of Michigan Avenue and Ontario Street. I first spotted my 1978 self walking toward me. It was uncomfortable looking at my younger self. So young! So cocky! There I was, just barely past the fringe of adulthood with my whole world in front of me. In those days I never had really thought of the *journey* I was going to take; I just thought of that particular day, maybe tomorrow and, of course, the next story.

From the right side, I saw Rachel walking toward Michigan Avenue. I almost felt like crying. *She* was so young! Look at the bounce in her walk; she had so much *spirit*! Most of all, she was alive, not yet a victim of a maniac killer. As she walked toward Michigan Avenue, I wondered if she realized that she would be meeting the man of her life, the man she would marry, the man she would open her legs to make love to over a thousand times, the man she would divorce, the man who would squander her youth. If she did, would she turn on her heel right now and head for the hills?

Rachel stopped in front of a window of a small shop on Ontario Street. It looked like it was a dress shop. She held her gaze for about ten seconds and then continued on. This was different. I hadn't noticed her stopping at the window before. But, on my second visit to 1978, she had stopped and asked me the time when I was standing in front of the Knight Cap. The timing should work out then.

Those ten seconds, however, did make a difference. At the traffic light, another woman stepped next to my 1978 self in the spot where Rachel should have been. Rachel came up to the queue; she was about two people behind my 1978 self. The traffic light changed to green and my 1978 self was off like there had been a bang from a starter's pistol. Rachel lagged behind. She hadn't asked him what time it was; she wasn't even close enough unless she shouted out the question. This was a big inconsistency. Did this mean that in this parallel world my 1978 self and Rachel would never meet, never marry, never divorce? That gave me a moment of pleasure thinking that Rachel and I had never met. Perhaps she would meet somebody who would appreciate her more. Perhaps she would meet somebody and move to Keokuk, Iowa, out of the kill pattern of the serial killer who made her victim number fourteen. I had known what her life was like with me, and I was pleased that in this parallel world she had missed it.

As a rush of thoughts ran through me, my 1978 self went past me in a blur. I turned around to watch him walk down the street, thinking that he was creating a different destiny for himself. I wondered if he would ruin some other woman's life while he chased crime stories. As a crime reporter, I had covered mafia trials and corruption scandals, notorious murders, and government inquiries. I hadn't won a Pulitzer, but I had a best-selling book. Was it all worth it? I wouldn't be honest if I didn't admit that the chase of the story was exhilarating. Was that exhilaration a fair price for losing Rachel? Now that I was older, I realized that I didn't have to make the trade. I could have got the stories *and* kept Rachel if I hadn't been such a maniac in chasing crime. That was this old man's perspective. George Bernard Shaw had indeed been right: Youth was wasted on the young.

"Excuse me," I heard Rachel's voice. I turned around. Rachel was standing next to me.

"Do you have the correct time?"

This time I wasn't as clumsy or flustered. Practice, I guess.

I could just tell her the time—twelve-oh-three—but I looked at my watch. "Twelve-oh-three," I said, looking her squarely in the eyes.

"Have you and I met?" she asked, pushing her blond hair back with her hand. "You seem so familiar."

No longer was she late for something. That's what she had told me the other day when I told her the time—that she was late. Had there been something instinctive for her to reach that corner of Michigan Avenue and Ontario Street by twelve-oh-two to meet my 1978 self and she thought at the time that she was late? Once she missed that first rendezvous with my 1978 self, did the urgency evaporate?

"I'm relatively new to Chicago," I said, not exactly lying. I'd spent my adult life in Chicago, but I had been away from her Chicago of 1978 for twenty-seven years. "Maybe we met traveling?"

"Do you travel a lot?" Rachel asked.

Why wasn't she walking away? She kept the conversation going when there was no reason to. Was she trying to pick me up? That made no sense at all: she was a startling twenty-two-year-old beauty and I was a fifty-one year old with a Polaroid camera in my hand.

"Way too much," I said.

"What do you do?" She asked, smiling. It wasn't actually a smile like you'd see on another person. Her mouth was straight; her *face* and *aura* exuded a smile.

I couldn't say that I worked at the *Chicago Sun-Times*. My 1978 self did. I couldn't even use my own name, Roy Hobbs. Young Roy Hobbs was getting occasional bylines at the *Sun-Times*. I was a stranger in 1978.

"Investor," I said. That's always a safe answer; that's an answer that could support a lot of bullshit.

We chatted some more, standing there on Michigan Avenue. My 1978 self was probably already at Hobson's Oyster Bar. He didn't know that his destiny was being altered. He would just be slurping beer thinking about what he normally thought about—today, the next beer and the next story.

"If you've got the time," I said, "would you want to catch a quick bite to eat?"

"Sure," she said, "I would enjoy that. It's not every day I get to meet an 'investor.'"

I couldn't take her to Hobson's Oyster Bar, that was for sure. It would be a cute play walking up to my 1978 self and saying, "Hey, Roy, I'm you twenty-seven years later." It might be black comedy to me to see his expression, but it would have been a lame joke. Nor could I take her to the Knight Cap. I didn't want people there that I knew well to try to connect the dots by asking if I was related to Roy Hobbs. "Yes, I am Roy Hobbs, twenty-seven years in the future." That would go over like a turd on a table.

We exchanged names. I used my middle name as my first name: Homer. She thought the name 'Homer' was cute.

"How about a hot dog?" Rachel asked, laughing, touching my hand. "It's not much, but it's quick and I need to get back to work."

The proposal of having a hot dog lunch caused me to blink. It's not that I was thinking of a more gourmet meal. I hadn't had a hot dog for lunch in probably twenty years, unless I counted the hot dogs out at Wrigley Field during a day game, but what caused me to blink was memory. The second time I had met Rachel in 1978 we had a hot dog lunch. We had run into each other again at the corner of Michigan Avenue and Ontario and this time we had a hot dog lunch.

I knew exactly where we were going to go for the hot dog lunch. "Let's go," I said.

We walked back the way Rachel had come, toward Lake Michigan on Ontario Street. On the corner of the next block was a parking lot. On the corner of that parking lot was a trailer with a walk-in porch—the hot dog stand. The porch was where we stepped in to order what we wanted. That hot dog stand brought back memories.

Rachel fixed her hot dog just as I remembered—she loaded it up with relish, onions, mustard, and ketchup. I, of course, limited my fixings to mustard. The two hot dogs and two Cokes cost less than five bucks. We hauled our hot dogs and sodas in a paper sack down to a small park just a block away. On the bench in the shade, we attacked our hot dogs. After the first bite, Rachel couldn't talk because she loaded an un-dainty-like portion of the hot dog in her mouth. I set down my hot dog, picked up the Polaroid One-Step and snapped off a picture. Rachel had tried to block the lens of the camera with her hand but was too late. The picture rolled out of the camera. She took a big swallow and laughed as she watched the picture slowly crystallize before our eyes.

She grabbed the Polaroid and snapped off a picture of me.

She reloaded another large bite in her mouth and chewed. The picture of me wasn't as funny as the one of Rachel, but she laughed anyway. She stuck the picture of me in her purse.

I was falling in love with Rachel *again*. There was no Polaroid camera and picture taking the first time we fell in love, but there were hot dogs, Cokes and this park. Unlike the first time, I was fifty-one years old; Rachel was the same age as before, twenty-two. Yes, I had fallen in love with Rachel the first time I had met her twenty-seven years ago, but these emotions were accelerated. My emotions were a runaway freight train. I think I could understand it. After all, I was falling in love with a woman who I thought I had lost forever. My feelings for Rachel, smoldering for so long, were rekindled in a roaring flash fire. Allred had never told me about these wild time warps.

I felt that wonderful euphoria that touches people who were falling in love. I didn't want the hot dog lunch to end. Everything was wrong with this, of course: I came from a different age, a different parallel world; I would be leaving to go to another parallel world. This was wrong for Rachel, just as falling in love with me was wrong for her the first time. Yes, this time I was more mature, I would be able to love her better, respect her more, but this time warp made it wrong. Even though it was wrong, it didn't stop me from savoring each *moment* of falling in love with Rachel again.

Rachel stopped a young mother who was pushing a baby in a carriage and asked her if she'd take our picture with the Polaroid camera. The woman looked at us; she must have figured that I was Rachel's father. But, when the woman put her eye up to the viewfinder of the Polaroid, and looked at how Rachel and I were looking at each other, she would have clearly dismissed the father-daughter thought. The young mother snapped a picture and when the camera was spitting out its picture, she handed the camera back to Rachel. Holding the print, Rachel asked for one more and the woman agreed. Rachel snuggled under my arm and the second picture came slipping out of the camera. We thanked the young mother and she strolled on.

We watched the pictures take life. I couldn't help but think that those pictures were like me traveling in parallel worlds. The Polaroid pictures added color, took definition, much like I had when I appeared in the alley behind the Knight Cap. I, of course, would disappear as if it was a reverse process of the Polaroid picture. However, these pictures that Rachel and I were looking at would last.

If I were fourteen years old, I would think of what happened between Rachel and me as puppy love. In high school it might be considered an infatuation. As adults, it might be considered love at first sight. Considering that I had already fallen in love with Rachel twenty-seven years ago, this might be considered love at *second* sight.

Whatever sight it was, knowing what I had already actually lived, I knew it was love. If I wouldn't have screwed it up, it was a love that was destined to last as long as we lived.

There must be some kind of cosmic connection—*something* that somehow linked Rachel and me. I would have to ask Allred about it.

"You're thinking deep thoughts," Rachel said.

I looked at her. I wanted to kiss her. I nodded my head instead.

"So, what're you thinking about?" Rachel asked.

"Time," I said.

"Time?"

I nodded. "This is so corny," I said, "so, so corny, but we just don't appreciate time—times like this. I guess it comes with age—the appreciation of time, I mean."

Rachel laughed. "This isn't so corny," Rachel said. "Speaking of time, I've got to run. I've got to get to work."

She got up; she seemed embarrassed. Was she embarrassed because she had just fallen in love with a fifty-one-year-old man? Or was she embarrassed that a fifty-one-year-old man had fallen in love with her?

"Will we see each other again?" she asked. Then she answered herself, "No, I don't think so. You do a lot of traveling, right?"

I nodded. I didn't know what to say.

"Here," she said, handing me her business card. "If you're in town again, give me a call. Let's have a hot dog lunch again." She leaned over, kissed me on the cheek and briskly walked out of the park.

I watched her walk out of the park. I wanted to run after her, grab her by her shoulders and say, "Yes, yes, we will see each other again. How about tonight for dinner, how about a lifetime of tomorrows?" That's what I wanted to do, but I sat there almost numb from the experience.

I took out the small digital camera from my pocket. The only pictures I had taken from that camera on this trip were two shots in the alley. I snapped off two shots of Rachel walking away. She didn't turn to wave; she was gone.

I sat there just staring out into the park.

Finally, I looked down at the two Polaroid pictures. The first one was of Rachel with her mouth stuffed with the hot dog; the second one was of Rachel and me standing in the park. If I didn't pay attention to the age difference, it was a picture of two people in love.

Chapter Fifteen

My reentry was rough. My legs were wobbly and I thought I was going to keel over. Charles held on to me. He led me over to a chair and I plopped down in it. He handed me the bottle of Gatorade Fierce. I took two quick gulps, breathed deeply, and then took two more large swallows.

"I feel like I crash landed. What happened?" I asked Charles.

"Not every entry is easy," Charles said. "By the way, did you have any alcohol yesterday?"

"No, why?" I said. "That's not right—I had maybe two glasses of wine last night."

"Well, a little bit of alcohol seems to be okay," Charles said. "But, like at dinner two nights ago with the wine? That would have been too much to travel the next day."

The amount of wine that I had drank that night was a thimble compared to the two large glasses I had last night, just sitting around my apartment watching a Maui sunset.

"Alcohol and traveling to parallel worlds have one thing in common," Charles said. "Dehydration. So, we find it best not to drink *any alcohol* for at least twenty-four hours before traveling, and to always drink lots of water. In fact, I think it's better to totally abstain from alcohol."

"Don't drink and drive, eh?" I said.

"Huh?"

"A joke, Charles," I said.

"Oh…yeah…hah…"

The one-liner wasn't meant to be a gut-buster. Pointing it out as a bit of humor made the line worse.

Two lessons learned: don't drink before traveling to parallel worlds, and don't try any light humor with Charles.

"I'd like to see Allred when he's got the time," I said.

"I'll tell him. In the meantime, I recommend that you get some rest," Charles said. "You don't look so good." I felt like laughing. Charles *never* looked good with his sprouts of white hair, his rashes, his reptilian eyes. But, if *he* thought I didn't look so hot, he was the expert and I should follow his advice and get some rest.

I walked down the hallway back to my suite of rooms.

Instead of taking a shower, I felt like a bath. The bathtub was industrial size—it could easily fit two people. I turned on the water and it was like turning on jets—the water rushed out in a torrent and was filling the tub quickly. I stripped down. The digital camera in my pants pocket clunked on the floor. I pulled it out and looked at it. It didn't look broken. I turned it on and looked at the little screen. There were four pictures—the two in the alley and the two of Rachel walking out of the park. As the bathtub was filling, I took a closer look at the two of Rachel. Then I thought of the Polaroids. In a low-tech way to protect them from the white hole I had wrapped them in aluminum foil. Remember, I was a crime reporter, not a scientist. The Polaroids were in my back pocket. I pulled out the little aluminum foil package and unwrapped it. The two Polaroid pictures were inside. I looked at them. The backs of the pictures were facing me. I turned them over. I was anxious to see that picture of Rachel stuffing her mouth with a hot dog and the picture of Rachel and an old Roy Hobbs. Both pictures were black. Not blank, but *black*. There was no detail in the pictures whatsoever, just pitch blackness.

In the park, I had *seen* those two pictures. I had *held* those pictures in my hand. I had personally wrapped aluminum foil around them.

I looked back at the digital camera. Those pictures inside were *exactly* as I remembered seeing them in a Chicago park in the parallel world of 1978. No distortion, no subtle changes, *exactly* the same.

I added the Polaroid pictures to the list of questions I had for Allred. For now, I just had wonderful memories of my hot dog lunch with Rachel.

As I sat in the tub, I thought about what I had just experienced with Rachel. I wondered what would happen if another guy had the chance to take a trip like mine to a parallel world. If he met his first love, would he feel the same way about his first love as I did about Rachel? Would he fall in love all over again? Or, if the marriage turned into an ugly mess, would the anger carry over to the parallel world? How would he react if he traveled to a parallel world and saw the woman he fell in love with—the woman that was twenty-seven years younger, thinner waistline, thinner thighs, full of youth and vitality and fun? Would he buy her a hot dog lunch? Or, would he just walk on by and pretend not to see her?

I typed in some notes of my trips into my computer. There weren't many; at this point it was mostly first impressions about seeing Rachel each time. I fell asleep on the couch and didn't wake until the morning. Although I was in a bunker, my high-definition windows showed Maui in all of its wonder. Through the windows of my suite, I could see the low-level dawn start to brighten up the ocean outside my windows. I laid there on the couch just watching the ocean. Through the glass windows, I could *hear* the ocean lap up onto the beach. There was a small window that was open and fresh salt air wafted inside. Allred's scientists were geniuses! If I had been a stranger to this suite, I would have been convinced that somehow I had woken up in a beach house in Maui. I would want to go outside and take a quick swim in the ocean. Beyond the glass wasn't an ocean, however, it was just reinforced cement that would put a federal bomb shelter to shame.

My kitchen was better stocked than any kitchen I had owned, including those that Rachel and I had shared. This kitchen could supply a small restaurant. Who knows how long I could feed myself without ever leaving the suite? Well, I guess Allred would know. A month? Longer?

A full breakfast was a necessity of mine. I prepared a full one, laying out the whole thing on a dinette that was positioned in front of a large floor-to-ceiling window overlooking a Maui beach. On the table was a five egg-white cheese omelet with some sliced jalapeños tossed in along with a couple of squirts of Tabasco, a bowl of sliced cantaloupe, a bowl of red grapes, and a large glass of orange juice. I was about halfway finished when the doorbell rang.

It was Allred. I invited him to join me. He chose to have a glass of orange juice and to finish off the cantaloupe.

"Wonderful place, isn't it?" Allred said, pointing out the window.

I'm not sure what he was referring to. Was he referring to the *real* Maui or to the genius of the simulation? So, I agreed; either choice would work. It was indeed wonderful.

"You wanted to see me?" Allred asked.

I finished the last bite of my omelet.

"Yes, I had a strange experience yesterday," I said.

Allred's face brightened. "Really? Tell me about it."

I told him about the major inconsistencies that I had seen and experienced.

"Lives would change, lives would be completely different," I added. "If I had never met Rachel, how would my life have changed? If Rachel had never met me, how would her life have changed? That, in turn, would affect other people's lives—people that Rachel and I probably didn't know at the time."

Allred had his hand on his chin. His forefinger arched up and he scratched his nose without moving his hand which still held his chin. I guess that was his thinking stance.

"As I've mentioned before, we have had some inconsistencies," Allred said. "This one is important. This is wonderful! This is *exactly* what I want you to follow up on. You're not doing a scientific paper; you're doing a journal, if you will, of one man finding his way through parallel worlds." He said all that without moving his hand from his chin or his forefinger from his nose.

"Are you going back?" he asked.

"Yes, I'd like to go back to the same parallel world a week later—maybe a month later—and see what happened," I said.

"If you wanted to do that, you could, but you'd have to wait a week—or a month," Allred said.

"Why? I don't understand."

"That world you visited progresses at the same timetable as this world—its clock is just twenty-seven years before the time that you and I are living. You can't turn that world's clock ahead," Allred said, dropping his hand to his waist and standing. He was in the professorial mode right now. "If you wanted to jump ahead a week, you could do that right now, but it wouldn't be the same universe. It would be a different universe, and I doubt if you could pick up with Rachel where you left off. So, if you wanted to visit Rachel in the same universe but a week later, then you'd have to wait a week."

Allred stood close to the window and looked out.

"I think I see some whales way out there in the ocean," he said, pointing. I got up and looked. Sure enough there were at least two whales way out on the ocean's horizon. For the moment, I think both Allred and I felt like we were in Maui.

"If you want to see what happens in the parallel world you visited, you have to wait, then go," Allred said, "but it's probably not a bad idea that you wait at least a couple of days before you travel again. Charles told me you had a rough entry. Everybody responds a little differently to the white holes, and it's better to be conservative than to push it. You have plenty of time to explore different possibilities."

As much as I wanted to go back right now, I had to agree with Allred.

"Yeah," I said, "I'll wait a couple of days at least. In the meantime, let me ask you something."

"Sure, fire away."

"Is there some cosmic connection between the parallel worlds?" I asked. "I mean, it seems that in three different parallel worlds I visited there was something special between Rachel and me. In the first visit, she just stared at me; in the second visit she initiated contact; in the last visit, she missed meeting my 1978 self, but really sidled up to me as a fifty-one-year-old guy. That didn't happen with the other people who were also in that same sequence. It seemed there was a cosmic connection between us. I don't understand how that could happen."

"I don't quite understand it either," Allred said. "One explanation could be that you and Rachel have that certain chemistry. That would be an easy answer. And, it is probably the correct one. You see, we all have auras. We can't see them, of course, but we have them. I believe that people who are charismatic—you can see this with certain athletes and movie stars—their auras extend far wider than ordinary people. And, their auras blend more comfortably with a large amount of people. We haven't done a study of auras—that's on our list, if I can ever get to it—but I would bet that your aura and Rachel's aura are totally complementary."

"Electricity," I said.

"Yes, exactly," Allred said, "but auras can change. I believe that when most people fall in love their auras are highly complementary, but as the auras change over a period of time, they can become far less complementary, even hostile to each other. What's interesting about you and Rachel in your third visit was that her aura, as a twenty-two-year-old woman, seems to have been highly complementary to yours, a fifty-one-year-old man. I would think that is highly unusual, but I don't have a study to prove it."

"The auras don't necessarily explain a cosmic connection, but we do believe there is some type of cosmic connection. It could be like dancers in the chorus line at Radio City Music Hall. The fifty dancers all kick their left legs at the same time, then they all kick their right legs at the same time. Their kicks are the same height, the same movement, everything is the same. Is there something like that with parallel worlds? What happens when one of the dancers doesn't kick with her right leg as everyone else does on the chorus line? What happens if she kicks with her left leg? That, we believe, would be an inconsistency in the parallel worlds."

Allred lost me there with the chorus line analogy, but I didn't want him to further explain. I would accept that there are inconsistencies. But, there was one inconsistency that I couldn't accept. The inability to bring back pictures from any camera except Allred's digital camera.

"One last question," I said.

"You're like a little kid with one last question," Allred said, laughing. "But that's good, I'm delighted you're getting into this. Fire away."

I got up and retrieved the two Polaroid pictures. I showed them to Allred.

"What about them?" Allred asked.

"I bought a Polaroid camera in Chicago in 1978 and took some pictures," I said. "They came out perfectly—I looked at them in Chicago 1978. I wrapped the pictures in aluminum foil to help protect them on my journey back. This is what I ended up with. What's going on?"

Allred laughed, a full hyena laugh heh-heh-HEH-heh-HEH-heh-heh.

"You really find this question funny?" I asked.

"Roy, Roy, a Polaroid picture will fade just by itself," Allred said. "Heck, if you did *nothing* but expose it to the atmosphere for twenty-seven years, it might look *exactly* like this. But, you didn't expose it *just* to the atmosphere; you took it through a white hole and there was *no chance* that a picture as fragile as a Polaroid could make it. Why not just rely on the digital camera we gave you?"

Allred turned and again looked out at the ocean behind my picture window.

"You don't trust us, do you, Roy?" Allred asked. "Is that part of being an investigative reporter, trust?" Allred wasn't laughing now. He was as serious as an axe.

"It's not a question of trust, Allred," I said, "it's a question of *questions*. I have questions; sometimes I have nagging questions. That's just the way good reporters are. To answer some questions, I want to take my own pictures with my own camera..."

"Something that you can *trust*."

"Okay, yes, something that I can trust," I said. "It's just another building block in the foundation. Without this one building block it doesn't mean that the house will fall down, but with the building block, it's really solid. I don't want you to take offense, Allred, it's just the way I think."

"I don't take offense," Allred said. "You have an inquiring mind, much like I do. There are certain things that *I* needed to prove to myself; there are things that *you* have to prove to yourself. I can understand that. Let me do some tinkering to see if we can come up with a *film* camera that you can use and will withstand the travel of the white hole. You want snapshots, Roy, we'll give you snapshots."

Chapter Sixteen

I was standing outside the *Chicago Tribune* building, leaning against a street light pole, when Rachel first spotted me.

It was five-thirty in the afternoon five days after I had last seen her in the park.

The five-day wait had been agony. I would have liked to have spent the time writing Allred's book, but I hardly had enough information even to dent the first chapter. More trips were needed.

Thinking of Allred's analogy—where one dancer was out of step with the rest of the chorus line—I considered my last visit one of those errant kicks. Rachel had missed the connection with my 1978 self. I considered that the first missed kick. Then she connected with the fifty-one-year-old me; that was the second errant kick. Even Allred would have to consider this more than just an inconsistency.

Rachel was streaming out of the building with a bunch of other people when she spotted me. It was the end of her work day. When she saw me she stopped like she was flash frozen. A woman behind her bumped her, but Rachel kept eye contact with me. Rachel smiled—this time it was a full-fledged ear-to-ear smile. Rachel had certain facial expressions that she couldn't fake. For instance, if a photographer told her to smile for a picture, she would smile. It would be a nice smile. If my grandmother saw that smile, she would have said, "Oh, such nice teeth." The smile that she flashed at me, however, wasn't a posed one. On demand she couldn't replicate this smile. Believe me; I've tried to coax that smile out of her in the past. But, on certain special occasions, her facial muscles produced a smile that would etch itself in the memories of whoever the smile was pointed at.

She walked briskly over to me. We didn't kiss; we didn't hug. We hardly knew each other here in this world, and yet, we both felt some sort of cosmic connection. Somehow, the twenty-one years that we had known and loved each other in a different world wafted around us and spiked the air we breathed.

"You're back," she said, still smiling.

"I'm back," I said smiling.

She reached in her purse and pulled out the Polaroid picture that had been taken in the park. She showed it to me. The picture wasn't black; it was perfect.

"I didn't think I'd see you again," she said, "I thought that it was just a moment in time."

That was an interesting observation of hers—*just a moment in time.*

"I knew I'd see you again," I said.

"How did you?"

"I traveled a long way to see you again," I said.

"That's right," Rachel said, "you travel a lot."

We stood there smiling at each other. Everything seemed so right, but we didn't know what the next words would be.

"Drink?" I asked.

"Absolutely," she said.

I wracked my memory for what nice little bar would be right for us. I knew the drinking holes where I had gone—those didn't leave my memory banks—but I felt that Hobson's or the Knight Cap was off-limits.

"There's a new boutique hotel near where we had that hot dog in the park," Rachel said, probably sensing that I didn't know the bars in the area. "There's a neat little bar there. You can tell me about yourself there."

We spent about an hour at the bar, then we found a cozy little restaurant in the near north and had dinner.

Over dinner, Rachel told me a little about herself. She told me her history exactly as I had remembered it.

I could have preempted her and said, "You were born in Milwaukee in 1956. Your father worked at Pabst Brewing, as his father had. Your mother was a housewife. You got a scholarship at Northwestern

University and graduated with honors. You were married—to me—in 1981 and divorced in 1997. You were killed by a serial killer in 1999 when you were forty-three years old. The killer preyed on divorcees. In fact, *every* woman of the sixteen that he had killed had been divorced." Yes, I could have told her all those things, but I listened to this beautiful twenty-two year old tell me about all the things that she wanted to do in this wonderful world.

There were others at that time that didn't make the world so wonderful. There was still the hangover of Vietnam, the disgrace of Richard Nixon, the inability of President Jimmy Carter in getting American hostages out of Iran and the eighteen percent inflation that made us feel like a South American country. While each issue could boil passions instantly, Rachel just considered those things as bumps in life.

She had asked about me, of course. I had to add large portions of fabrication. My history was pretty accurate until my first job. Born in Detroit. Graduated from the University of Michigan. I didn't say when I was born; 1954 would have been accurate, but that would have made me twenty-four years old. At fifty-one, I didn't think I could pass even a decade over twenty-four even on my best days and looking in a distorted mirror. I never mentioned that I had been a newspaper reporter. I had said that I was in investments. I knew the investment language because several years before I had done a long crime story on how some investment bankers had conned and stolen their way to millions of dollars. I did such great research that I could talk the lingo, use jargon like an insider. So, in talking about my vague past in the financial world, I was able to sprinkle the conversation with words that sounded like I had really known what I was talking about. While I knew the words, I certainly hadn't grasped the concepts enough to not have lost a fortune on investing when the dollars flowed in from my best-seller.

If people had watched us, nobody would have mistaken us for father-daughter. We clearly looked like May-December—you know, old guy and young chick. This May-December thing was, of course, a new experience for me. I never had pictured myself in this type of relationship, except this was *Rachel*, not just some young chick that I had picked up.

For the whole evening, I had trouble taking my eyes off of Rachel's face. Her skin was so beautiful. She had been blessed with perfect skin. Her facial skin was as soft and clear as the underside of her breasts. She had told me years ago that she never had a pimple in high school. In fact, for the twenty-one years that I had known her, her face was blemish free except for three exceptions; two of those exceptions were when our marriage was heading for the rocks, the last exception was when we officially got divorced. Even the DNA that somehow provided protection for her skin couldn't ward off pimples that I think had my initials imbedded in them.

After dinner we waltzed down Rush Street, hand in hand. There were other couples out on this fine spring night hop-scotching from bar to bar. We walked toward Division Street. That was where my 1978 self had met Rachel for the second time. It was in a singles bar, Butch McGuire's.

We walked inside Butch's. Rachel had to show her I.D.; I didn't. There were no sit-down tables in the bar, just a few stand-up tables where the drinkers could put their drinks. The crowd of drinkers was so dense that it looked as if they had swallowed the tables. We wormed our way through the crowd toward the back, found an empty stool at the bar and I offered it to Rachel. I stood in front of her, and hollered over her shoulder to get two beers. I had to be the oldest person in the bar by at least a dozen years, maybe even two dozen. The mix of sound—music, laughter, shouting—was like standing near a jet plane ready to take off. We tried to talk to each other, but it was reduced to me leaning over and speaking loudly in her ear, then Rachel responding by cupping my ear and raising her voice volume to almost a shout. I could tell her everything about parallel worlds and most likely she would cup my ear and yell, "What? I didn't hear you." When I was in my twenties, I thought Butch McGuire's was a terrific place; in my fifties, I just wanted to get out. So did Rachel. We finished our beers and snaked our way toward the entrance, single file with Rachel being the pathfinder.

About ten feet from the door, she bumped into a guy. He smiled at her and leaned over and said something in her ear. There was no chance that I could hear what he said. Rachel laughed and touched his forearm and then pointed at me. I looked at him; he looked at me. He was my 1978 self.

He didn't see me as himself twenty-seven years later. There was no way anybody could see themselves at that advanced age. He just saw me as an old man, an old man who somehow had a beautiful, young woman in tow.

My 1978 self laughed and leaned over, put his hand on Rachel's shoulder and said something else. I couldn't hear, but I felt like punching him.

Rachel turned to me, smiling, and kissed me hard on the lips. She put her hand on my neck and held the kiss. I guess that was her answer to whatever my 1978 self had said to her. It worked better than a punch and we squeezed out of the bar.

Chapter Seventeen

Out on the street, we started to walk toward Lake Michigan, just a couple of blocks away.

I heard a voice calling after us to wait. I turned. It was my 1978 self. He ran up to us.

"I would like to apologize," my 1978 self said to Rachel, "for what I said."

Rachel held my arm tightly.

"Apologies accepted," Rachel said.

"I'm Roy Hobbs," he said, holding out his hand for Rachel to shake.

She shook his hand. "I'm Rachel Strong," she said. "Do you work at the *Sun-Times*? I think I've seen your byline."

Reporters were always sensitive to bylines, far more receptive than the normal reader of newspapers.

"Yep, the crime beat," my 1978 self said. He fished out a business card and handed it to Rachel. "Have you read my stuff?"

Rachel laughed. "I'm in the business too. I'm with the *Tribune*."

She then proceeded to introduce us.

"Roy, this is my friend, Homer," Rachel said. "Homer, this is Roy, a fellow newspaper reporter, except he works for the bad guys—the *Sun-Times*."

"Nice to meet you," my 1978 self said. "My middle name is Homer. I don't run into too many Homers."

We shook hands. As preposterous as this was—me meeting myself—I found it stranger that I didn't feel some type of cosmic connection to him like I had with Rachel. In fact, I felt a little bit of jealousy; right now I didn't like the guy. Freud would have had a field day analyzing relationships in parallel worlds.

I was getting confused with the twists of this 1978. It was now like *two* dancers in Allred's chorus line let fly with errant kicks. I certainly would have to ask Allred about this inconsistency. Rachel, my 1978 self and I were going on uncharted waters right now.

"What do you do for a living, Homer?" Roy asked. I could tell he really wasn't interested; he just wanted to prolong his time near Rachel.

"Investments," I said.

"Really?" my 1978 self said with genuine interest. I knew it was genuine—I knew how that guy thought. "I'm working on a story about corruption in a certain bank on LaSalle Street. Mind if I give you a call and pick your brain?"

"I travel a lot," I said, "but, if you give me your phone number, I could call and we could set up a time." That was one phone call I would never make. I didn't want to meet with my 1978 self, now or any time. I just wanted to get rid of him.

He handed me his business card. I looked at it. It brought back a rush of memories.

"We gotta go," I said to my 1978 self. "I'll give you a call."

We walked down Division Street toward the lake.

"Pretty brash guy, eh?" Rachel said.

"Uh…yeah," I said. I had been thinking about my 1978 self. I think it's part of nature that as we get older we sometimes reflect on our youth. It might be a song that pries open a long past memory; it might be reading an obituary of somebody we knew. But, here, tonight, I was *face-to-face* with my younger self. This wasn't just a fleeting reflection; I had shaken hands with my youth! I wasn't sure I liked what I saw. Sure, I saw the brashness. Others would characterize it as cocky. My editors would phrase it differently: bulldog. They considered me a *bulldog* because I really went after a story. In fact, one of my editors thought of me more as a pit bull, the dog that was famous for its bite.

"I want you guys to be like a pit bull. For instance, if Hobbs bit you on the ass like a pit bull," that editor had said to some other young reporters like me, "and you turned around and shot him dead, you'd be carrying Hobbs on your ass for the rest of your life. He doesn't let go."

I liked the looks of my 1978 self. I was more handsome as a young guy than I had ever imagined. But, I also looked *so* young.

As we walked, I thought about Allred's chorus line of errant kicks and cosmic connections. Obviously, there was a cosmic connection— an *accelerated* cosmic connection—between Rachel and me. We both could feel it right from the beginning. Did my presence in 1978 pre-empt the cosmic connection between Rachel and my 1978 self? Why, I thought, how could that be? My mind raced with possibilities. In 1978 I was quite self-centered, which was quite natural for a young immature male forging a career. Today I was probably as mature as I would ever get. I thought less of what I wanted and more of being accommodating. I was more capable of loving somebody for who they were than for what they could do for me. So, did that maturity—that sense of being able to love in a more fulfilling way—pre-empt my brash, take-no-prisoners 1978 self? I didn't know the answers, of course, and I doubted if Allred did. This was new, uncharted territory.

"Do you want to stop at my place for a cup of coffee?" Rachel asked. We had walked about a block, each to our own thoughts.

"Yes, that sounds good," I said. "Do you live around here?" I knew, of course, that we were exactly a block away from her apartment.

"Just a block away," Rachel said.

I also remembered that Rachel had a roommate. I had met her twenty-seven years before. Janet *something*...Janet Emerson, that was it. Rachel and her roommate, Janet, however, had some type of signal where if one wanted some privacy the other would go visit a friend for the night.

"My roommate is out tonight," Rachel said. Rachel must have sent out the signal by using the pay phone when she went to the restroom in the restaurant.

We quickened our pace a bit. We weren't *running*, of course, but I think we both felt a surge of excitement that quickened our pace.

111

Rachel's apartment was on the third floor of a Brownstone apartment. We kissed in the small elevator that ascended slower than a drunk walking up the stairs.

Inside the apartment, Rachel excused herself and went to the bathroom. I looked around; her apartment was like walking into a memory. It was exactly as I had remembered it from twenty-seven years ago.

Rachel came out of the bathroom and went to the small kitchen on the left to make coffee. I joined her. As she was pouring water in a kettle, I reached around her and kissed her neck. She put the kettle down in the sink, turned and kissed me on the lips.

This wasn't like when we first met. We had dated about six months before we ended up in bed. Here we groped each other like we were trying to make up for twenty-seven years.

She led me to her bedroom. Although I didn't stop to take in the details, it was generally exactly as I had remembered it.

Rachel unbuttoned her blouse, took it off and tossed it on the floor. I kissed her and unhooked her bra; she unbuttoned my shirt and both ended up on the floor. Then she started to unbuckle my belt. I undid her belt.

"I can't get your belt," she breathed. "What is that, a cowboy belt?"

There was a little trick in unlocking the belt. Rachel would not have been able to un-cinch the belt no matter how hard, or desperate, she would have tried. There was a fake ruby implanted in the large belt buckle. It worked like the security pads in the barn. I needed to press any two fingers on the ruby. That allowed me to un-cinch the belt. I quickly went through the security procedure. The belt was undone and Rachel pulled my pants down. The pants hit the floor with a thud. I hoped that the Wayfarer Commander wasn't damaged, but the thought evaporated as Rachel took my extended cock and pulled me to the bed.

Afterwards, we laid on the bed, Rachel in my arms. It seemed like she was purring like a cat. There were so many curious and extraordinary thoughts going through my mind.

The first thought was that I had enjoyed sex with Rachel more than ever before. I had remembered the first time we had sex. I shot my wad almost as soon as I had entered her. This time, I was older—twenty-seven years older—and even though we both had a powerful sense of urgency I was able to control the tempo until I knew that she was on the brink of a climax.

The second thought was what did Rachel think? It's not that she could compare my 1978 self with me—at least not yet—but, what was it like for her to make love to a fifty-one-year-old man? Fortunately, my body hadn't ballooned over the years, but I sure wasn't some young stud.

Her body seemed strong, supple, and soft at the same time. I probably enjoyed the *feel* of it better than the first time. I thought I could still *feel* the touch of her skin on my fingertips. That residual effect had never happened before.

Rachel started to fondle my penis again. It didn't take too much to make it stand up. As I kissed her, I had a weird thought. What if the Wayfarer Commander got scrambled when it hit the floor and instead of responding to the programmed exit time—which was tomorrow—flew away by itself into the white hole? My pants would arrive in the silo. And, here I would be, stuck in 1978 with a woman that I had loved in two lives.

Chapter Eighteen

"What is this?" Rachel asked.

"What do you mean?" I said.

"This! You and me, here in this bed," she said.

We were on our sides lying in bed the next morning. Her leg was hoisted over my hip. We had made love twice that night. Judging by the height of the sun streaming in, she would be late for work. She stroked my shoulder.

"I've never done this before," she said, "never just taken a guy home after he bought me dinner."

I felt like saying, 'I know.' I didn't say anything. I thought: *I* hadn't done anything like this before either. It's not like I was a dirty old man that tried to rejuvenate my life by dating young chicks. After Rachel and I divorced, I had not had sex with anyone. Shame on me, but that's just the way it was. I hadn't gone to bed with a twenty-two year old since I had gone to bed with Rachel twenty-seven years ago. You'd think that a best-selling author would have some groupies. Not so. I wasn't a rock star or a baseball player. I wrote about crime. Sure, like any other guy I enjoyed the *Sports Illustrated* swimsuit issue, but that was like looking at artwork at a museum. Nice picture, but don't touch. I didn't really have the desire to bed a twenty-two year old. They seemed *so* young. It would be like boffing a daughter that I didn't have. But, I didn't feel like I was robbing the cradle by sleeping with Rachel. It was *Rachel*—the Rachel who I had fallen in love with—not some strange young chick. If I would have seen an old guy with a young chick behaving in public like Rachel and I had, I would have thought *gold digger* or *dirty old man* or something else that wasn't complimentary. But, Rachel wasn't a gold digger and I didn't have the traits of a dirty old man.

"And besides," Rachel said, "I don't know anything about you. Yeah, yeah, I know you were born in Detroit, I know you went to Michigan State…"

"Michigan," I corrected her, "University of Michigan."

"See! See what I mean!" Rachel said. "I don't know anything about you. I don't even know how old you are. I'm afraid to ask."

"Fifty-one," I said.

"Aggghhhh!" she said, laughing. "I would have never guessed fifty-one. I was thinking you were in your sixties at best." She laughed some more.

I laughed.

"You're four years older than my father," Rachel said.

I knew that, too. "Does it bother you?"

"No," she said. "For some strange reason it doesn't. It seems *right*. It *seems* that this was meant to be. How foolish is that? How terribly foolish is that?"

It didn't make any difference to Rachel that night, but my mind played the 'age game.' For instance, when I would be a genuine relic at sixty-five—retirement age for most folks—Rachel would be just thirty-six or so. She would be on the cusp of entering her prime. Her prime was something else: I had known her all my adult life and she had aged more gracefully than anybody I had known. She maintained her weight over the years, and mostly her skin remained soft and pure without her having to resort to an arsenal of creams, lotions, and potions. Sure, I had personally caused some wrinkles to etch their way onto her face, but she carried those wrinkles well. Rachel had aged like Sophia Loren—each successive decade she had become more appealing. There would be, of course, eventually a decade of diminishing returns, which happens to all of us, but, sadly, Rachel would never see that decade. So, in fifteen years she would be a startling thirty-six year old puttering around with this dirty old man. There was no other way to slice it; this wouldn't work.

"So, Homer, what is *this*? This is all so powerful, so strange, so…I don't know…what is *this*?"

I pulled her close to me. I didn't answer her; I kissed her ear.

I think she wanted me to use the 'love' word. Believe me, I had no problem saying 'I love you' to Rachel. I always have loved her, from Wednesday, May tenth, 1978 to her death in 1999 to now in this parallel world. It didn't make any difference to me when it was: I loved Rachel.

"When are you traveling again?" she asked.

"Today," I said. "Noon."

"Out at O'Hare airport?" she asked.

I had to be careful with my answer. If my lie was O'Hare, then she might just want to see me off at the airport. In those days, there was no security at airports and she could go right to the gate and wave me onto the plane.

"No, I've got a rental car and will drive downstate," I said. "Then I fly out of St. Louis the next day for Japan."

"What's in Japan," she asked, "they can't even make good cars. My roommate has a Toyota Corolla and I think our toaster is more solidly built."

Wait a couple of decades, I thought, and the Japanese will make the best cars in the United States. I could try to explain it to her, but that would be like telling her that there would be this little store in the sticks in Arkansas with an unlikely name of Wal-Mart that would grow to be the biggest retailer in the world. Bigger than Sears, Penney's and K-Mart combined.

"There are some good investment opportunities in Japan," I said.

"We aren't going to see each other again, are we?" she asked.

"I don't know," I said. I *did* know. I could control it, I could control that I would see her. I just didn't know if I should come back. It would be terrific for me to spend a year with Rachel. It would be like a dream come true. But, it wouldn't be fair to her. In my younger years, I just might say, *so let it be*. Now that I had become an older guy, I couldn't sweep fairness in the gutter, particularly with Rachel.

"Your 'I don't know' means 'no,'" Rachel said. "I can tell. Hold me." She trembled in my arms. Somehow—and this was difficult for me to understand—she accepted the finality as if it had been written in the stars.

We held each other close. I could feel her tears slide onto my neck. I stroked her hair. I kissed her face. I never wanted to lose the sensation of that feel, but, I knew that I would. She quietly inserted me into her and we made love so slowly that it seemed we didn't want it to end.

Chapter Nineteen

When I arrived back at the silo, Charles was waiting for me. He handed me the Gatorade Fierce, but I didn't think it would cure what ailed me. I had not expected what had happened on the trip. I'm not referring to the night with Rachel, although that was totally unexpected. I couldn't have predicted that in a thousand years.

What I had not expected nor anticipated was that I had fallen in love again with Rachel. It's not like I had ever fallen out of love with Rachel, even during our divorce, but this was so unexpected that I felt my love had deepened to levels that I didn't know could exist. I had experienced an entirely different experience with her, and now, if I was honest with myself, I had lost her again, it being my fault *again*. I couldn't let this love extend itself; it wouldn't be fair to Rachel. Forget the Gatorade Fierce, I felt like asking Charles if he had any Gatorade Cyanide.

Unlike my previous entry this entry was pretty easy.

"You look pretty good," Charles said. Getting the approval of my appearance from Charles didn't make my day, but it was better than his previous observation. "How're you feeling?"

"Pretty good," I lied. I felt shitty, but not from traveling through a white hole.

"Good," Charles said. "Physical time."

"What do you mean?" I said. I didn't know if he wanted me to beat up a punching bag or what.

"You need to take a complete physical."

"Why? I haven't taken one before," I said.

"We should have had you take this physical the first day," Charles said. "However, we have found that traveling to parallel worlds is safe. It's safer than riding in a car. The purpose of these tests is to monitor any changes that might occur. You have to take them after every eight trips."

"Have you seen changes in yourself or anybody else?" I asked, "Like did livers turn into stone, or hearts into marshmallows?"

Charles looked at me. I had violated one of my lessons learned. Charles didn't have a sense of humor and even throwaway lines meant to be slightly humorous would confuse him.

"Just kidding, Charles," I said. "Seriously, have you seen any changes?"

"Yes, we have, but nothing serious," Charles said. "However, sometimes, we have to ground a person for a week, sometimes more. Once, I had to be grounded for over a month."

"What for?"

"Nothing too serious," Charles said. "For instance, my hair fell out. You can see it's just growing back in."

I didn't know if I should ask why it was growing back in tufts. Was that the way it was before? Did he comb the tufts before or just let them grow like weeds like he did now? I didn't ask.

"Plus, my blood pressure dropped quite significantly," Charles said. "In fact, the doctor said that I had the blood pressure of a dead man. I didn't feel dead, of course, just a little tired. So, I didn't travel for a month."

I didn't have to make an appointment to see the doctor. The doctor came to us. The 'clinic' was down the hallway from the silo.

When I saw the doctor, it seemed I was going further down the rabbit hole. The doctor didn't really look like a doctor. I don't mean that you can stereotype the look of a doctor, but this guy looked like he could have been one of Allred's long lost buddies dressed up like a doctor. His hair was long and all over the place. He certainly was a candidate for a hair net. His glasses were so thick I thought if I put them between the sun and a chicken that in moments I'd have chicken barbeque. I felt that he was play acting, but it wasn't because of what he said or did that betrayed him. It was just a feeling.

The doctor didn't introduce himself; he just shuffled some papers onto a clipboard. I could tell his bedside manner wasn't going to endear him to any patients.

"I'm Roy Hobbs," I said.

"Yes, yes, I know," the doctor said.

"And you are?"

"I'm your doctor for this physical," he said, looking at his clipboard. I wondered if there were some nudie pictures on the clipboard that captivated his interest.

"Doctor…Doctor who?" I said.

"Eh, yes, exactly," he said, "Doctor Who." I now knew for sure that I had fallen down through the rabbit hole. I wanted to scream for Alice.

"Really? That's your name?"

"Of course, of course, Doctor Julius Wu," he said, "W. U. Who."

"That's how you pronounce it? Who?"

Dr. Wu nodded.

It sounded like a Chinese name, but the doctor looked full-blooded American weird.

"Is that a Chinese name?" I asked.

"Polish," Dr. Wu said. "When my grandparents arrived from the old country, they shortened the name at Ellis Island. Wujokowski."

That was the end of our conversation, unless you considered an extension of that conversation when he told me, "Now turn over," or "Very still now, very still," as the machines peered inside my body.

My physical was more than taking some blood and seeing what my cholesterol level was. The industrial strength monitoring machines in Allred's underground clinic would make a full-blown hospital jealous.

The full day of tests was exhausting. It's not like I had to exert myself. Most of the time I just sat there, or laid there, and the machines measured different things. It was tiresome doing nothing or maybe it was the residue of a fifty-one year old guy tumbling in bed all night with a twenty-two year old woman.

There was rest time between visits to machines. While I did all this sitting and laying down, I, of course, thought of Rachel. I thought of my previous life with Rachel, our meeting, our marriage, our divorce; I thought of the Rachel of 1978. On a couple of occasions, my thoughts of Rachel caused my hospital gown to tent with an erection. That hadn't happened spontaneously like that in at least a decade or so.

There were two others that I thought of while the machines calibrated different parts of my body. The first one was Abel Burrard. Burrard was, of course, the monster in my best-selling book *The Monster Among Us*.

Even though I had written a book about him, I hadn't thought about him in years. This time I thought: In a parallel world, I could do something that the police couldn't do until Burrard had murdered sixteen women. I could *stop* Burrard. I could actually *save* Rachel.

I thought about this at length: *How* could I stop Abel Burrard? I knew *everything* about Burrard. There was no human that knew more about Burrard than I did. I had all my notes, all my files, all my drafts and the final copy of my book in my laptop computer. I had the chronology of his life. It all took up five gigabytes. There weren't too many people in this world that would require five gigabytes to store information about them.

In a parallel world, could I stop Burrard from making Rachel his next victim? Yes, I thought, I could. I could do it two ways. Firstly, I could just go back and shoot him dead. Or secondly, I could direct the cops to the evidence that would lead them to Burrard and they would arrest him. The cops would probably ask how I knew about such evidence. Okay, I would provide it anonymously. I would never give away information anonymously when I was a reporter. After all, I wanted the story. Anonymous doesn't get the front page story. But, in this case, I didn't want the story; I wanted to save Rachel.

Yes, I could save Rachel, one way or the other.

After a full day of letting the doctor test the machines out on me, I went to my suite. In the early evening I sat on a couch, beer in hand, watching the sun go down over the Pacific Ocean. I sat there in front of that ocean—ersatz as it may be, it fooled me after my first beer— and thought about the second person. Adolph Hitler.

I didn't think of Hitler as a person—I had thought about what Allred had told me about the danger of parallel worlds and how he had used Hitler as an example. Allred had hypothesized that a person with the power to travel to parallel worlds could take the know-how of building an atomic bomb, go back to 1935 and help Hitler win World War Two. That person then could get an army to do the same thing in *thousands* of parallel worlds and help Hitler dominate them all.

That was a wild premise, but with the knowledge of parallel worlds, a madman with big money—let's say money like Allred and his gang—could do it. So, twisting that premise to my scenario, with an army and a fortune and Allred's cooperation, I might be able to save Rachel in a thousand parallel worlds. I thought about that for a long time.

There were problems, of course, with that scenario.

The biggest one was Allred. He wouldn't go for it. He and his merry band didn't spend billions to save Rachel. Without Allred, this plan was dead.

However, I could save her in at least one. That wouldn't be difficult at all. Rachel would live. Yes, Rachel would live.

The scenario of providing tips to the cops to collar Burrard bothered me. It would work, but it would be in a parallel world where he had killed at least one woman. I couldn't make it work in the parallel world I had just visited. Burrard hadn't killed anybody at that time. He was just twenty-one years old, and while he tortured, killed, and mutilated animals before it was legal for him to drink a beer, he hadn't killed a person yet. He wouldn't kill a person for another eleven years. I would just have to go to a different parallel world. According to Allred, I had thousands or millions to choose from.

Suppose I went back to a parallel world where Rachel was forty-two? That would be one year before she was killed by Burrard. I could then easily drop enough clues to the cops for them to nab Burrard before he got to Rachel. But, what about the thirteen victims who preceded Rachel? Would it be right for me to allow Burrard to extinguish their lives and just save Rachel? That brought some serious questions—questions that I have never asked myself.

I could save *all* of Burrard's victims—every one of them. To save all of Burrard's victims in one world I would have to kill him. At that point, before he had killed sixteen women, he was an *innocent* man.

123

He was just an innocent nerd before he started his killing spree of divorcees.

What if I killed Burrard in a parallel world where his destiny had changed, just like Rachel's destiny had changed in the last parallel world that I visited? What if—in that parallel world—Burrard would have gone on to live a peaceful long life? If that was the case, I would have killed an innocent man.

Yes, I had some serious questions. One of the last questions I had was: can I kill a man? I, of course, had never killed a man. Had never come close. Had never thought about it before today.

I had all these questions. I had no answers.

Chapter Twenty

"Have we met before?" Abel Burrard asked me.

Standing in front of me, behind the check-out counter at a hardware store, was Abel Burrard. He was just twenty-one years old and looked like he'd probably have to wait six months to be eligible for his driver's license.

Burrard was not an evil-looking guy like Charles Manson. I had seen pictures of Manson when he was in his twenties and he looked evil then. Burrard, in 1978 was a budding nerd. He was about six feet tall, maybe one-hundred and thirty pounds, his dark blond hair combed down good, a few pimples and a disarming smile. He needed the world of personal computers to blossom into a full-fledged nerd, but the computer world would pass him by. He was destined to be a hardware store guy. If personal computers had never been invented, if that paradigm had somehow never happened, I could see Allred and Charles working their lives in a hardware store alongside Abel Burrard. Heck, they might have been working side-by-side with Bill Gates and Paul Allen.

Burrard was, of course, just as evil as Manson. He just didn't gather a bunch of misfits to be his family of slaves. Burrard had worked solo. If body count was the measurement of evil, Burrard would far surpass Manson. Burrard just didn't *look* evil.

I was surprised by Burrard's question. I had indeed met him once before. It was about a month before he would be electrocuted. He had known that I was doing a book about him and he finally agreed for me to meet with him.

"I don't think so," I said. I had, of course, come back to the world of 1978 just two days after I had left it. I hadn't gone to see Rachel. I had come for one reason: to see Abel Burrard. I wasn't going to kill him, at least not yet; I just wanted to *see* him. I had written a book about him and knew every facet of his life, but had met him just once, on death row.

Throughout the trial, he had looked so innocent. If any of the jurors had pictured Burrard in their minds as a kid, they would have seen Opie, from the old *Andy Griffith Show*. When Burrard was eventually caught, he looked like a grown up Opie—not the bald Ron Howard who played Opie—but a tousle head forty-two year old that looked like an adult Opie should have looked. When the evidence was parceled out day-by-day in gory shovelfuls, Burrard *still* looked innocent. It was difficult to connect that man's appearance with the brutality of the murders. When I visited him on death row, and saw him up close, he had a harder look, but living in solitary confinement could probably do that. Still, he didn't have that Charles Manson look that would make you think you wouldn't be safe from him even if he was dead.

The hardware store where Burrard worked was on North Clark Street in Rogers Park, a community north of downtown Chicago. I had taken the white hole 'elevator' to the alley behind the Knight Cap. Then I had taken the elevated train to Rogers Park. I had been there before when I researched my book and was familiar with the area. The owner of the hardware store, Darrell Rutter, had told me at the time about Burrard, "I've never had a better employee. Never. He knew every tool in the store, knew which tool was right for which customer, for which job. He was a true genius in hardware. Our customers loved him. Quiet, really quiet, he was, but always polite, helpful. He never, and I mean *never*, missed a day of work. Worked for me for fifteen years. Now we get folks that stop by just to see where he had worked. They usually buy something, but I wish he wouldn't have done all that killing. This may sound strange to you, but I miss him."

If Burrard had been an accountant, Rutter should have been nervous about the employee never missing a day of work. But, a hardware store employee? What damage could Burrard have done? Stolen a bunch of hammers?

"I never, *never* expected Abel to hurt a fly, let alone become a serial killer," Rutter told me when I was researching the book. Rutter's assessment wasn't unusual. Nobody had thought that Burrard was dangerous. It was like the Anthony Perkins character in *Psycho*. He wouldn't hurt a fly.

"I'm sure we have met," Burrard said, smiling. He did look so harmless.

"Maybe," I said, "but I do a lot of traveling."

"I bet you do," Burrard said. His grin turned to a quiet smirk.

What type of comment was *that*? What did he mean?

I put the roll of masking tape down on the counter and two one-dollar bills. I didn't need masking tape, but I did want to meet Burrard face to face. I didn't just want to stroll into Rutter Hardware Store, introduce myself to Burrard and tell him that one day I was going to write a book about how he killed sixteen divorcees, including my ex-wife.

Burrard took my money, put the masking tape in a paper bag, gave me change and said, "That's a real dandy belt you got there."

I said, "Thanks."

"Can I see it?" Burrard asked, with a small lopsided grin sneaking onto his face pushing away his smirk. "I mean, can you take it off and let me look at it real good?"

It didn't take alarm bells to make me wary. Allred had, of course, impressed upon me never to let go of the belt and the Wayfarer Commander. If Allred had known, he probably wouldn't be too pleased that I let it clank on the floor when Rachel had undone my pants. And here, in 1978, a serial killer wanted me to take off my belt and *hand* it to him?

"Can't," I said, "I gotta go."

What was that all about with the belt? The belt buckle wasn't fancy at all. It wasn't like the big belt buckle that the World Heavyweight Champion would brandish upon winning a title fight.

Why did Burrard ask about the belt? Or was I just getting paranoid? Reporters are a great lot: they don't believe people and they're paranoid as hell.

But, *why the belt*? Was there a *cosmic connection*, a *cosmic consciousness* of some sort? Allred thought there might be, but he didn't know. If Allred didn't know, I didn't either, except here I could *feel* it.

"Okay, see you around," Burrard said as I walked out of the store.

I hoped not. However, if there was a next time, I thought that I would kill him. I just had to figure out which parallel world.

Chapter Twenty-One

"Have we met before?" Abel Burrard asked me.

Standing in front of me, behind the check-out counter at Rutter Hardware Store, was Abel Burrard. This time he was thirty-five years old. Just a month before, he had killed his first divorcee and then used a variety of saws—from Rutter Hardware Store—to slice and dice the victim, carefully putting the internal organs in different jars of formaldehyde. Those he would save in a locked storeroom in his basement. The bigger body parts he incinerated.

When I was back at Allred's barn, I had programmed two legs of this trip to parallel worlds. The first leg was to visit Burrard in the 1978 that I had visited before. I just wanted to see what Burrard was like before he had started his killing. I had hoped to see a madman in his eyes like I would have by looking at Charles Manson. That was the first time he had asked me if we had met before.

The second leg of the trip was tricky programming, at least for me. It was the first time I had attempted two legs in one trip. When Charles had taught me how to program my trips he showed me all types of whiz-bang tricks. One of those tricks was to program multiple trips before heading back to the silo. So, instead of returning to the silo after seeing young Burrard, I went directly from 1978 to 1992. This was an entirely different world and universe than the trips I had taken to see Rachel.

This trip was as easy as any that I had taken before. I had just gone into an alley in Rogers Park, confirmed my departure on the preset coordinates on my Wayfarer Commander, and *voilà*, I skipped fourteen years ahead. I made it a little easier for myself by programming in May tenth—the day that Rachel and I first met—but in the year 1992.

I wore the same clothes, but khakis were khakis whether it be 1978 or 1992 or 2006. And, my pre-1978 money was just as good in 1992.

My mission here was the same as the first leg; I wanted to personally take a look at Abel Burrard. If I was going to kill Burrard—and it seemed that if I was going to save Rachel *once* that I had to kill Burrard *once*—then I just wanted see for myself if there were any signs that the crazy gene had missed him in a different parallel world. Missing the crazy gene could have been one of those inconsistencies that Allred talked about. I doubted it, but had nominated myself as Burrard's sole judge and jury and executioner. So, these two trips were to gather evidence, if I could call it that, in my mind's eye whether this bastard was sane in that parallel world or not.

"Have we met before?" Abel Burrard asked me in the same innocent voice as in 1978.

"I don't think so," I said, saying the very same thing I had said in 1978. I did *not* expect Burrard to ask me that question. While I had waited in the small line, he did not seem to know those customers and he had not asked that question to them. Why me?

"You wouldn't lie to me, would you?" Burrard said. His eyes seemed to bug out a bit. If he was trying to give me his best Charles Manson look, he had achieved it. I had never seen that evil face on him before. He still looked like a nerd—he was still slim, hair cut short and carefully combed, large glasses, khakis—but his face betrayed his appearance. Standing there, he didn't look so harmless anymore.

"Pardon me?" I said, with a wisp of an anger tone. Burrard visibly shrunk back.

"I just want this roll of masking tape," I said. I dropped the roll of tape and two dollars on the counter.

"My apologies, sir, if I offended you," Burrard said, "I thought you were somebody that I used to know." He looked harmless again. Did I really see that quick snap of venom that had curled his face just a moment ago or was I imagining it? I didn't think that I imagined it, but it appeared so quickly and then dissolved like it had been a mirage.

"No problem," I said. I wasn't trying to create a scene here. Heck, I might be coming back to kill him and I didn't want to call attention to myself.

To kill him would be an easy thing to do, and an easy thing to get away with. I would just waltz in to Rutter Hardware Store with a gun in a small paper bag. My hand would be in the bag on the trigger of the gun. I would walk up to the counter, point the bag at Burrard and pull the trigger as many times as I felt was necessary so there would be no chance that he would survive. I would then reach down with my left hand to the Wayfarer Commander on my belt and push the Red Button. The Red Button was the emergency exit that Allred had invented after he had visited Chicago in a parallel world that was scorched earth and rubble. The Red Button would supersede any pre-programmed instructions. Even if I was surrounded by cops, I would instantly be back at Allred's barn, still with a smoking gun in my hand. If Bonnie and Clyde had had that escape route they would have lived to a ripe old age tending a garden in southern Missouri.

"That's a pretty fancy belt you've got there," Burrard said, reaching over the counter to touch it. His fingers grazed the belt buckle. I was slow in reacting, but as I jumped back, I swiped at his arm like I was shooing away a snake. I hit his arm and he recoiled it back behind the counter.

"Hey!" Burrard said. That Charles Manson glare burst onto his face and held for just a micro-second. It held long enough, however, for me to confirm that the first time I had seen it wasn't just my imagination.

"Take it easy," he said, Mr. Harmless again. "I just wanted to see that belt buckle."

He had rung up the roll of tape, put it in a paper bag and handed me my change.

I turned and started to walk out the store.

"See you around, Mr. Hobbs," Burrard said.

I whirled around and said, "What did you say?"

"Uh…see you around," Burrard said, stepping back away from the counter.

"Did you say my name?"

"Your *name*? Why no, I don't even know your name," Burrard said, looking as innocent as he did during his trial.

I stared at Burrard. He looked down at the floor.

I turned and walked out of the store. I heard Burrard laugh. It wasn't the type of laugh I'd expect out of Mr. Harmless. I had never heard Charles Manson laugh before, nor had I ever read a description of what his laugh sounded like, but it occurred to me that Burrard's laugh was something that would seem logical coming out of Manson's mouth. Evil.

Chapter Twenty-Two

"See you around, *Mr. Hobbs*." That's what I heard; I had no doubts about it. *Mr. Hobbs*. How did Burrard know my name? I had paid for my roll of masking tape with cash. I did have a fake driver's license and phony credit cards in my wallet, but I had not taken out my wallet and even if I had, I had used a fake name on my fake I.D. I had chosen my alias to be Homer Murphy; Homer was, of course, my real middle name, and Murphy was the name of the dog that Rachel and I had. Heck, not too many people are named after a dog. The phony I.D. was a masterpiece; the forger was Leona Kosinski, Allred's twin sister.

I was so shaken by the experience that I practically staggered down North Clark Street to the 'L' train station. I had one more stop to make before I headed back to Allred's barn.

It was 1992 and I should have been married to Rachel for eleven years. We would be divorced just five years later in 1997. She was killed two years after that. I wanted to see if we were married in this particular parallel world, or if another inconsistency had happened. If we had missed each other again and weren't married, then my mission with Abel Burrard wasn't necessary. Not being married to Rachel didn't make Burrard a harmless guy, but my goal was to save *Rachel*. If we weren't married in this parallel world, then we couldn't, of course, been divorced. Since Burrard had killed only divorcees, Rachel wouldn't have been a target.

Rachel and my 1992 self should be living in Evanston, Illinois. Evanston was just a short train ride north from Rogers Park. I hopped on the train and tried to calm myself. I had so many questions about my two visits to see Burrard, but I pushed those away for the moment. I would have time to think all this through when I got back to Allred's barn. I might not get any answers, but I could do the thinking, staring out at the Maui beach from my bunker suite.

I had two missions in going back to 1992. One was to determine if Rachel and I had married and were still together. The second mission was to find out if Burrard had indeed taken his first victim. So, I had to do some research. The first step would be the library at Northwestern University.

I'd start with newspapers. The first newspaper I looked at was the *Chicago Sun-Times*. In this parallel world was I still a crime reporter with the *Sun-Times?* I couldn't remember what stories I had worked on during that time frame, so I just started to leaf through the paper. I didn't have a story on the front page, but then I thought back and tried to remember my front page scoops. I didn't think that I had any front page stories in 1992. The front page story was an unusual thing for a beat writer. I'd had only a dozen or so in my career. I turned the pages. On page five, I found a story with my byline. A story about a corrupt alderman. He hadn't stolen enough to warrant the front page. Well, at least I knew that I still worked at the *Sun-Times* and lived in Chicago. That's one of the things I needed to know.

I pulled the latest *Chicago Tribune* from the rack. I started looking for Rachel's byline in the Living Section. Her byline would tell me what I needed to know. Since we married, she had gone by Rachel Hobbs. I didn't see a byline. That by itself wasn't unusual. When you're a reporter, you don't get stories every day. I looked in the previous day's *Tribune*. Nothing. I looked through the previous month. Nothing. Then I remembered. It was June of 1992. I stressed my memory, groping for details that had smudged during the years. Sometime in the early 1990s, Rachel had a miscarriage. It had been her second one. I remember she had taken the second one like she had fallen off a cliff. Instead of broken bones, she had a psyche that needed mending. Yes, it was in 1992, it was in the summer. She had taken the month off and worked like a maniac in our garden. I could look back several months in the *Tribune*, but I decided that I would visit the old house. First, however, I needed to find out if Burrard had killed his first divorcee.

Before I had taken off to these parallel worlds, I had gone over my notes from *The Monster Among Us*. Marcia Kinnear disappeared from her Skokie, Illinois house in May, 1992. She was never found as Marcia Kinnear; one lonely fingertip was found in a formaldehyde jar in Burrard's basement vault. That was enough to put her on the list of victims. I had researched each victim—talked to neighbors, relatives, co-workers, former husbands. What had happened with Marcia Kinnear was that she had just disappeared. There was no sign of violence, no sign of flight, no sign of anything. She had just disappeared. In my notes, I had the names, addresses and phone numbers of everybody who I had interviewed about Marcia.

I went over to a pay phone in the library. I dialed the first name on my list, a neighbor, Hilda Stern. It would have been better if I had gone to visit Mrs. Stern in Skokie, but I wasn't getting material for a book, I just wanted to know if Marcia Kinnear was still missing. That would be good enough for me that Burrard was the same monster in this parallel world that he had been in mine. My chances were good that Hilda would be at home; she was an old spinster who rarely left her house.

The phone rang only three times. Hilda said, "Hello?"

"Mrs. Stern, I'm a reporter for the *Chicago Sun-Times*. My name is Roy Hobbs," I said.

I got the answer I was expecting. Hilda was a great reader. "Oh, Mr. Hobbs, I read your stories all the time," she said. "You're always writing about those crooked politicians…"

"Yes, Mrs. Stern," I said, interrupting her. If I didn't interrupt, I knew she could itemize at least ten of my past stories. Hilda didn't think too kindly of politicians. She thought that *all* of them were crooked.

"I understand that Marcia Kinnear is missing," I said.

"*Well*, it's about time some paper is looking into this," Hilda said. "She's been gone for a month. The police have been out here asking questions, but I haven't seen anything in the papers."

"That's why I'm calling, Mrs. Stern," I said. "I'm looking into it now."

I had what I needed, but it took me about two minutes to extricate myself from Mrs. Stern.

I then pulled out an envelope from my pocket. Inside was a single sheet of paper. This was the tip that I was going to give my 1992 self. There was enough substance in this to let him know that it was not a crank accusation. It was a synopsis of the disappearance of Marcia Kinnear that I had written the day before. From my notes, I itemized everything that a reporter would need to go after a story: Marcia's disappearance, the cop's name who had taken the report, Hilda Stern's address and phone number, Abel Burrard's work and home address, details of where his vault in the basement was, and the formaldehyde jar with Marcia's fingertips. I also included the name and address of Burrard's next potential victim. That woman would die in about two months if my 1992 self thought that this tip was bogus or couldn't get the cops interested.

The envelope was addressed to Roy Hobbs at the *Chicago Sun-Times*. I had never got a tip that had such all-inclusive information, but I knew that my 1992 self had the wherewithal to find out if the tip was phony or not. My 1992 self would find out pretty quickly if there was a real story in this tip or not. The only question would be whether this one tip-sheet was enough for the cops to get a search warrant to get in Burrard's vault. I bought a 29-cent stamp, put it on the envelope, sealed the envelope, and dropped it in the mailbox at the library.

I might be helping the fifteen other victims of Burrard and I might be helping my 1992 reporter self.

Now on to my second mission. Was I indeed married to Rachel in 1992?

Chapter Twenty-Three

I wanted to arrive at the Hobbs house in Evanston around six at night, which gave me the best chance to see if Rachel and I were living there. I had some time to kill and stopped at a bookstore, browsed awhile and eventually bought *Stephen Hawking, A Life in Science*. I remembered that it was a big seller and that Hawking was the scientist who, among other things, explained black holes. He would have loved to have spent some time with Allred Kosinski and his merry band of thinkers. I read some of the book over a cup of coffee in downtown Evanston, but I was thinking about my former house.

The house we had lived in was in the south end of Evanston, a couple of miles from Northwestern. There was a large park across the street. Swings, slides, a basketball court, lots of trees, and park benches. My plan was to just sit in the park around dinner time and see if both Rachel and my 1992 self arrived at the house. If Rachel and my 1978 self were there that was all I needed to find out. I didn't want to meet them; I didn't want them to see me; I just wanted to see if they were together.

At about five-thirty, I started to walk from the library to my 1992 house. It would take only a half hour or so. When I got to the park across from my house on Forest Avenue, I sat down on a bench at the far corner. I would be able to see any movement at the house, but they would never be able to distinguish a solitary person reading on a park bench. I hoped I looked like a nice guy reading a book on a fine summer evening and not some predator scoping out kids on the swings.

Rachel's house in Evanston

I spotted Rachel right away. She was working on the flower bed at the front of the house. She had the green thumb in the family. She could make a twig grow. She was wearing her favorite jeans and a t-shirt that she used for gardening. I used to kid her that it was her gardening uniform. She used to kid me back that I didn't need a gardening uniform because I didn't know we had a garden. This time, I marveled at the garden and all the work she had done. I hadn't noticed those things before. From my position from across the park, the garden looked like it should be featured in *Better Homes and Gardens*.

At about six-thirty, I saw my 1992 self come from around the side of the house. Our garage couldn't be reached by the street, only the alley. So, I had driven in the alley, pulled in the garage, and now I was greeting Rachel. Since it was six-thirty and I was home, it was a sure-fire sign that I wasn't working on a big crime story. My 1992 self and Rachel walked in the house.

I sat on the park bench pretending to read. I don't think I read three words in the whole time that I sat there. Eventually, I knew I'd have to go, but I just sat there. In 1992, our marriage was not on the rocks. There were some rough edges, yes, but it didn't need the emergency room. It just needed some real attention by me. I sat there thinking how stupid I had been. As I sat there, I noticed the light being turned on at the front door. A few seconds later, the light went on in the back. That was our ritual if we were going out at night. I got up from the park bench and walked so that I would have a better perspective toward our backyard. Yep, Rachel and my 1992 self were going out, probably to dinner. I saw the car start to drive down the alley then I lost sight of it. I looked toward the corner. In a moment, our car crossed the street toward Sheridan Avenue. That was the path we would take to go to downtown Chicago.

I went back to the park bench and pretended to read for another twenty minutes. I then closed my book, stretched, got up and walked toward my old house. From across the street, I walked past it. Then I took a right, walked down the alley and took a right into the alley. I didn't really know my neighbors too well, but I hoped I wouldn't accidentally bump into one. I doubted it. In that neighborhood, we didn't hang out in the alley. I reached my former garage. I looked inside through the side window. Rachel's car was in the garage; mine was gone. I smelled stale cigarette smoke. Over in the corner of the garage was a chair, my smoking chair. In the early nineties, Rachel had banned smoking from the house. She had quit smoking a few years before and had told me it was my turn, but in the meantime, no smoking in the house. So, this intrepid crime reporter would mull over things—come rain, sleet, hail or snow—firing down a couple of quick cigarettes in the garage.

I opened the little door on the picket fence and walked through to the back door. The house was an old one; it still had a milk chute. I had hoped that the milk chute would be my avenue to get inside. The milk chute was, of course, where the milkman would deliver milk, when there were such things as milk men. We had never had a milkman in Evanston in the years we had lived there. The milk chute was metal, and it stuck out from the house by about three inches. The milk chute was, of course, too small for me to slip through. Besides, the door had been permanently bolted shut from inside. But, I wasn't trying to pull a Houdini. I reached at the bottom of the outside ledge of the chute, and sure enough, the house key was stuck to a magnet. I pulled the house key away from the magnet, walked over to the back door, inserted the key in the lock, and I was inside.

It had been thirteen years since I had been inside that house. I marveled at the surge of memories that flowed through my mind in a torrent.

I heard a pattering on the hardwood floor. Coming toward me was Murph. Murph had been our Irish Terrier dog. Irish Terriers are a strange breed. When Murph was glad to see you, she would bare her teeth. To most folks, they would think that the baring of the teeth would be followed with a bite. With Murph, however, her baring of her teeth was a *smile*. Irish Terriers were the only dogs that I knew that *smiled*. Because she had crinkled up her nose to make the smile, she would sneeze. Then she would smile again, sneeze again, smile again. For family, this could go on for a dozen or so smiles and sneezes. I got the full treatment of smiles and sneezes. Strangers didn't get any smiles or sneezes. Neighbors would get a tail wag. Murph was greeting me like it was the 1992 me. She was probably wondering if Rachel was going to come in the back door. I knelt down and petted Murph on the head. I reached in a kitchen cabinet and got her a Milk-Bone.

I walked down the hallway. This was our version of Memory Lane. Rachel had hung probably fifty pictures of her and me. I looked at each one as if I was in an art gallery. The early pictures were fun; we were indeed so young. But, of course, I had personally revisited that youth in my travels to 1978.

The pictures were on the wall in chronological order. One wall was about two-thirds full. The other wall was empty. "That's for our fifties, sixties, and seventies," she had said. "Then the wall will be filled and we won't take pictures of two old people holding on to each other to keep the other from falling."

I felt some moisture around my eyes. I didn't have tears, but my eyes were watering up a bit. We had had such great times.

I noticed the most recent pictures that had been put up in our Memory Lane. Now that I had the perspective of *time* and of knowing how things turned out, the pictures told me that things were not going as well as the early years. Our body language in the pictures was different, subtly different. Did I see it *then*? I doubt that I did. I could see the next big crime story, but I couldn't see the story that was being revealed on my own hallway wall. Did this happen to other people who had let their careers consume them—people like lawyers or investment bankers or doctors or anybody who put their career first, second, and third priority, and if they chose to count some more that it would be fourth and fifth? There were no little kids in those pictures, and that probably hurt us, but there was no guarantee that kids would have changed my focus. Yes, kids would have helped, I think, but there were no guarantees of a man possessed by his career.

I felt like taking one of the pictures. When we got divorced, everything was divvied up. Somehow, most of the pictures went with Rachel. When she was murdered, not all the pictures on the wall had been recovered from her belongings. It's not that Burrard took them; the pictures—the memories on this wall—just disappeared. Had Rachel burned them? I didn't know, but there was one picture of Rachel and me that had been my favorite. I thought I had the image of that picture etched in my mind, but standing in front of it, looking at it, I realized that my memory was just a hazy version of that picture. I left the picture in its place.

Twenty minutes had passed and it seemed like seconds. I needed to move on. I had proved what I needed to prove that this was a similar parallel world I had lived in. There weren't any major inconsistencies.

Murph was at my feet. She nudged my leg. Murph slept on a pillow on the floor in our bedroom. When she wanted to go to bed, she didn't want to wander upstairs alone. She wanted company. Nudging either Rachel or me was Murph's way of saying that it was bedtime. I walked upstairs with Murph. She went right for her pillow on the floor.

I looked at the bed. I went over to Rachel's side of the bed and sniffed the pillow. I then walked to her closet, opened it, and sniffed there. Murph watched me.

"You wondering about me, Murph?" I asked.

Murph just stared.

"Well, I'm wondering about me."

I walked over to Murph, reached down and petted her head.

"I gotta go now. Don't tell anybody that I was here."

I turned and walked out of the bedroom, down the stairs, past the pictures and out of the house.

By the side of garage, I fiddled with the Wayfarer Commander. With one push of the Red Button, I would be back in the silo.

Chapter Twenty-Four

Allred came to my suite when I was halfway through breakfast.

"It looks like a storm is brewing out on the ocean," Allred said. "See the rain way out there on the horizon?"

I looked. I had been watching two young twenty-somethings stroll down the beach. They wore practically nothing; between the two girls, they didn't have enough clothes for one. I took my eyes off the beach and looked way out on the horizon. I did see some rain.

"It all depends on which way the wind is blowing," I said. "I don't think the rain will come in to shore. Right now we have some slight trade winds." The fronds on the palm trees ruffled slightly in the wind.

"I brought something for you," Allred said. He handed it to me. In his hand was a small Minolta camera. "This is a real film camera. Thirty-five millimeter. It even has a built-in three-to-one optical zoom. You can take pictures in whatever parallel world you're in, bring the camera back, and we'll develop the pictures here."

I took the camera and carefully looked at it. It looked like a typical thirty-five millimeter camera. It was heavier than I remembered them to be.

"If you tore that camera apart," Allred said, "you'd find a Titanium lining. We think that will protect the unexposed film as you re-enter through a white hole. We haven't tested it, but in theory we think it will work."

"What if I want to have the film developed wherever I am?" I asked.

"You can do that, yes, it would work," Allred said. "You'd get nice pictures. What we're not sure of is whether those pictures would be affected in your reentry. We think that whatever happened to your Polaroids would happen—at least to a degree—to any snapshots from this camera. You can try, however."

I asked Allred to join me for breakfast. "I can fix you an egg-white omelet," I said, "or if you'd prefer we've got some waffles in the refrigerator."

"No, thank you," Allred said, sitting down, "but I wouldn't mind finishing your cantaloupe, if you don't mind."

I got him a fork and Allred went to work on the cantaloupe pieces while I told him about my latest experience with cosmic connections. As I described my meetings with Abel Burrard, Allred didn't say anything nor did he even nod. He just polished off the cantaloupe and then reached over and ate the English muffin that was on my plate.

When I finished my story and Allred had finished the English muffin and poured himself a cup of tea, he said, "Interesting."

The word 'Interesting' I have found is an uninteresting word. I think people use it when they don't know what to say. I guess when they say, "Interesting," it's better than saying "I don't care" or "So?"

Allred stared out at the ocean. I tried to see what he thought was so interesting out in the ocean. He didn't say anything.

"What do you mean by 'interesting'?" I finally asked Allred.

"You actually saw and met Abel Burrard?" Allred asked.

"Yes," I said, "how could I not? I wrote a book about the guy."

"I suppose so," Allred said. "Did you find him like the person you wrote about in your book?"

"Yes…and…no," I said. "On the surface, he did seem like a harmless sort. I could see how people could get fooled by him. If I didn't know what I know, I probably would have trusted him. But, I saw flashes, Allred, just flashes—I think just *microseconds*—where I saw evil in his face. It was as if his face couldn't hold back the evilness all the time and there were just a few microseconds where his true self showed through."

"You're probably wondering about 'cosmic connection'," Allred said.

I nodded.

"You and I have briefly discussed 'cosmic connection' before, mainly in regards to your ex-wife Rachel," Allred said. "But, this thing with Burrard, this is uncharted territory for us. We think a cosmic connection is indeed possible, but we haven't even figured out how to test that phenomenon. But think, Roy, think of all the electric impulses that pass by us every day—I'm talking about cell phones, radio stations, television stations. There has to be a sending device—like a cell phone or a TV tower—and a receiving device—like a cell phone or a television set. If each one of those signals were not invisible—let's say they looked like red laser beams—then we'd be absolutely surrounded by red laser beams all day long. We wouldn't be able to see the person in front of us because of all the red laser beams. We now take it for granted that there is an unlimited space— *unlimited*—for us to send and receive various signals."

I nodded.

"Are there invisible electric impulses that travel from one parallel world to the next?" Allred asked. I didn't think he needed an answer. "Without thinking it through, we would say that those electrical impulses were impossible. But, Roy, we could say the same thing about traveling to parallel universes that it was impossible, and yet, we are doing it as easy as it is to walk around the block."

Allred got up and walked to the floor-to-ceiling window overlooking a Maui beach. The two women who had showed almost all of their skin had walked to the far end of the beach. Allred was looking out toward the rain cloud way off on the horizon.

"Déjà vu," Allred said.

"What?" I asked.

"Déjà vu," Allred answered. "Everybody has experienced moments of déjà vu. I once heard a psychologist explain it. He said it was all in our head." Allred laughed at what he had said.

"*All in our head*, that psychologist had said," Allred said. "Where else would it be? In our arm? In our toes? Anyways, that psychologist explained that when we see something that *seems* familiar, but that we *know* we had never seen it before that it's just a quirk in our brain translating that information to our conscious mind.

But what if, indeed, déjà vu is a *cosmic connection*? Suppose it was possible. Suppose there is a greater cosmic connection than we ever imagined. Suppose that some people have more intense *receptors* to this cosmic connection. Would that explain *psychics*? Or Nostradamus? Or Edgar Cayce? There is, of course, precedence in that regard. For instance, idiot savants have a tremendous ability to remember numbers. Suppose that Nostradamus or Cayce had freakishly highly developed receptors. Was that how they could make predictions for centuries in the future? Suppose that Burrard—maybe because he is crazy, maybe because he is a monster—has a freakishly highly developed internal receptor that rings these cosmic impulses in as clear as a bell. Suppose that Burrard easily interprets déjà vu. I should like to meet with our little group and discuss this. How can we test it? How can we confirm it?"

The two women on the beach were walking back toward our view. Both looked like they had walked off the pages of a *Sports Illustrated* Swim Suit Issue. They could have been carrying a sign that said, "Allred—we want to blow you" and he wouldn't have seen it. He was looking way out to the horizon. Somewhere out there, way out there, there might be answers to his questions.

"*If* there is such a thing as a cosmic connection," Allred said, "I think you should be careful."

"What do you mean?" I asked.

"From your exhaustive research of Burrard, did you ever find that he had a high interest, or even a low interest, in belts?" Allred asked.

"No," I said.

"Assume for the moment that there is indeed a cosmic connection," Allred said. "That cosmic connection somehow alerted Abel Burrard to *you*. As you told me, he gave signs that he knew who you were, just as Rachel did. How could that be, except for this unknown cosmic connection concept? But, that could have been *coincidence* with Burrard; he might have just mistaken you for somebody else and you were too sensitive about it. But, he gave signs that he knew about *your belt*, the Wayfarer Commander. The belt buckle isn't that unusual to draw attention, to get somebody to want to see it up close. In fact, we specifically designed it to be boring. Yes, we needed some bulk to fit all the micro-instrumentation in it, but we didn't want it to be like some fancy cowboy belt. If Burrard has a feeling—some type of *cosmic feeling*—that that belt can do something unusual for him then he might try to steal that belt from you. To do that, he might feel like he has to kill you."

"I'm not sure if he connected the dots that well," I said. "There might have been a slight, hazy recognition—like déjà vu—but nothing more."

"We really don't know that," Allred said. "I find it remarkable that he even mentioned your belt let alone *reached* for your belt. I've lived over fifty years and never once has anybody ever asked me about my belt. How many times have people asked you about *your* belt?"

"Nobody," I said, "except Burrard."

"So between us there is one hundred years of living and nobody—except Burrard—has ever asked us about our belts. Don't you find that more than coincidental?"

"I have to agree even if I don't understand how it could happen," I said.

"*I* don't know how it could happen either," Allred said. "*We*—our group— don't know either. We're scientists—we figured out what Einstein was trying to prove—but we're not psychiatrists nor social scientists like anthropologists, archaeologists, geographers, historians, political scientists, and sociologists. In a word, we're scientific dreamers. As a dreamer, I think we have to assume that there is a cosmic connection. We already know that Burrard was dangerous—*is* dangerous—and from what you have told me, he has been consistent in the parallel worlds that you visited. Do you realize how infinitely more dangerous Burrard would be if he had the Wayfarer Commander at his beck and call?"

It didn't take a lot of thinking to visualize how much more dangerous Burrard would be.

"My feeling is that you should not revisit any of the parallel worlds you have gone to," Allred said.

"Why?" I asked.

"The cosmic connection may have altered his thinking in that parallel world," Allred said. "I might sound extraordinarily paranoid, but what if he wanted to trap you? For instance, what if you went back to visit the twenty-two-year-old Rachel in 1978? I would probably want to, if I were you. Well, what if Burrard staked out Rachel's apartment, followed her everywhere, just waiting for you to show up? If I was Burrard, that's what I would do."

I laughed. "You are getting a little paranoid," I said.

"Am I?" Allred said, "am I?"

Chapter Twenty-Five

A llred asked me to follow him.
"I want us to go on a little field trip," Allred said.
"Where to?" I asked. I wondered if he was angry because I had said he was getting paranoid.

"Just follow," Allred said, "I think you'll find this interesting."

That word 'interesting' again. This time I felt I would indeed find it interesting.

Allred and I left my suite, walked down the hall to the elevator and stepped in. Allred pushed a button. The elevator stopped on the third floor. Allred had to press two body parts on the security pad to open the door. We walked out onto the floor. An alarm bell went off.

"On this floor, you have to pass security too," Allred said, almost yelling in my ear. "Go back and press some fingers to the security pad."

The sound of the alarm bell was piercing, seemingly jumping my heartbeat past the point any of those machines in the clinic could measure. I felt like I staggered over to the security pad. I quickly placed my two thumbs on the pad. The alarm bell stopped. Because it had been so loud, the sound echoed in my head.

When I turned to walk back to Allred, there were two machine pistols pointed toward my face. They were being held by two large men, dressed like some type of special soldiers. Both had the black boots, black pants, black shirt and even a black beret. Unlike the military or the police, they had no insignia or medals. When they saw that my two thumbs had been approved by the security pad, they stepped back.

Allred said, "Good, good." He was looking at his watch. "Five seconds."

The two soldiers stepped back quickly and quietly. Although they were big—about six-feet-four or so—they were quick and agile. They walked out of the lobby of the third floor and disappeared around a corner.

"By the way, if you wanted to come to this floor on your own," Allred said, "the elevator doors wouldn't have opened. But, when you accompanied me, the sensors sensed that there was another person with me, somebody who had not coded themselves in. *That* caused the alarm, in case somebody had...er...kidnapped me...and forced me down here to the computers."

Allred started to walk down the hallway.

"You might think I'm getting paranoid, but believe me, I have already arrived at that state," Allred said. "I'm as paranoid as hell. I'm a full-fledged member of the paranoid club—I might even be president of it. But, I like to think that paranoia is a blessing, not a curse. Paranoia allows me to freely think: *what could go wrong*? This has helped tremendously in building the capability of traveling to parallel universes. So, am I afraid for you if you went back to a parallel world where you had met Burrard? Yes. Am I paranoid about Burrard somehow confiscating your Wayfarer Commander? Yes. Am I afraid that if he did that we would be in danger here at the barn? Not so much. Even if Burrard got a hold of your Wayfarer Commander and decided to come back here, we have an ample amount of security. I wanted to show you that security."

"Except for those two guys dressed in black, I hadn't seen any security in the barn at all," I said.

"Of course not," Allred said. "We like to keep everything as low profile as we can. You'll *never* see our security outside on the grounds, unless, of course, there was an emergency. If outsiders saw security on the grounds, they might figure there is something valuable in the barn. So, we're secure, but you would not have seen this security if I didn't take you on this little field trip."

Allred walked to a steel door. He put two body parts on the panel. "You'd better do the same," Allred said, "or you're going to summon those two gentlemen again."

"Why haven't I had to do that upstairs?" I asked. "I mean several of us have gone through doors together where only one person did the security procedure."

"These floors are the most secure floors we have," Allred said. "This is where the computers are."

I pressed both thumbs against the pad by the steel door. The steel door snapped open an inch. Allred opened the door.

"Welcome, Dr. Kosinski," a man said. He was about six-feet tall, built close to the ground, short graying hair, about fifty years old or maybe in his early sixties. Whatever age he was, he looked in great shape. I had dealt with cops and other types of military authority to know that this guy's background was FBI or Special Forces. He looked like he would sprinkle nails on his Wheaties to give him fiber.

"I came to give Mr. Hobbs a tour," Allred said. "Roy, this is Captain Kilburne."

We shook hands. My impression was that Kilburne's name was appropriate for this aging warrior. His middle name was probably Slash or Pillage. If I said something to him, I felt like I should say, "Permission to talk, *sir*."

The room behind Kilburne looked like a television station control room. On the wall were over fifty television monitors. There were six guys, all dressed in black, viewing the monitors.

"Everyplace you go on the compound," Kilburne said, hardly moving his lips, "we can see you. There are also motion sensors that will alert us to look at certain screens."

I looked at all the screens. It did seem that in every hallway and in every inch of the outside that a camera had been viewing the activity.

"The suites are, of course, private," Kilburne said. I quickly scanned the monitors. I didn't see any monitors that looked like they were viewing anybody's suite.

"If you went looking for our cameras," Kilburne said, "you wouldn't find them. The camera lens is smaller than the period on a page of a book."

On one of the monitors, I saw Charles in the silo. He looked as if he was going to go to some parallel world. I thought that Charles should go to some really strange parallel world to blend in. Anything else and he would really stand out. As I watched the monitor, Charles disappeared. He was on his way to wherever.

"Happy travels," I said, referring to Charles.

"What?" Allred said.

"Charles," I said, pointing to the monitor that looked in at the silo, "he just left for somewhere."

"He did?" Allred said. "I wonder where he's off to?"

As far as I could tell, each scientist—and myself—had complete freedom in choosing where to go. I didn't have to register destination plans like an airline would. I just decided where to go and then program it in to my Wayfarer Commander. Programming the Wayfarer Commander wasn't difficult at all. It was as difficult as programming TIVO. The first step was to type in the date and the city. If I had an address where I would like to enter, I would type in that address. Because of the white hole, it was better to have an address that was not indoors. I was told that the white hole could sometimes create havoc on interiors. If I didn't know the exact address, the Wayfarer Commander could be used like Google Map, type in an address and just scroll to where I would like to enter. I didn't see where Charles had programmed himself to go; he was just gone.

We left the control room and walked the third floor. The entire room was comprised of huge computers. Row after row after row.

"I could try to explain these computers to you," Allred said, "but, no offense intended, you wouldn't understand. What Einstein needed years ago was the computing power that we have now. He had himself—the most brilliant physicist ever—but he needed *massive* computing power. Part of that computing power was needed to identify all those parallel universes and parallel worlds. There is an order to it all, just like there's an order to all the atoms in a wood chair. For example, you wanted to go back to Wednesday, May tenth, 1978. Our enormous computing power was able to identify where that parallel world was and *voilà*, you arrived there. We also needed the computing power to figure out how to control the white holes. You could take all the massive computers that the United States government owns, combine them all, and it would be a small fraction of our computing power. That may sound preposterous that seven guys—seven really rich guys—could build such a system, but we didn't have any politicians—or executives--approving what we do. There was nobody here to hold us back, except ourselves, and believe me, we're not here to hold ourselves back. Because of this type of focus, our semiconductors are at least forty years ahead of the most sophisticated semiconductors of today."

I wasn't thinking about the massive computing power that Allred and his crew had created. Heck, I had *lived* their computing power by going to parallel worlds in 1978 and 1992. I was thinking more paranoid thoughts. Reporters were charter members of the paranoia club. Allred felt that he was the president of the Paranoids Club; if he was, I was the CEO.

Allred and I left the security room and walked down a hallway.

"Who's guarding the guards?" I asked.

"What do you mean?" Allred asked.

"Well, Allred, you have built this barn like a fortress," I said. "You have the most elaborate security system known to mankind. Heck, NSA or the FBI would love to have your security system. But, what about the guards?"

"So, what do you mean?" Allred said again.

"If left alone to think about it," I said, "I could come up with a couple of nasty possibilities. The guards that I saw all looked like former military. As many countries around the world could attest to, military were sometimes subject to a thing call coups, as in *coup d'état*.

Allred laughed that hyena laugh, heh-heh-HEH-heh-heh-HEH-heh. He actually thought what I said was funny.

"I like the way you think, Roy," Allred said, "a true paranoiac. Wonderful! Wonderful! But, not to worry. The head of security, Captain Isaac Kilburne, is my brother-in-law."

"Oh, he's married to Leona?" I asked.

"Oh no, Ike's married to Anna," Allred said. "You met her when we had dinner at the main house."

I remembered her. She was squat and heavy, unlike Allred and his twin sister Leona. Allred sure believed in nepotism, but with his money and his project who could blame him?

"I suppose your guards are your nephews," I said.

Allred laughed again. Heh-HEH-heh-heh-HEH-heh. "Not quite, but three of them are. Just to let your paranoid mind rest a little, we ran background checks on everybody—including my sisters, brother-in-law, nephews—everybody. For the guards, each is paid as good as some pro athletes. There are restrictions so they can't spend like pro athletes can, but there are certain financial trusts that are set up so each of the guards can retire at forty and be well taken care of for the rest of their days. If you eliminate greed as motivation, you've eliminated most of the problems. None of the guards live in Astoria. They come to work here for two weeks at a time, live on the compound, and then go home for two weeks. Out of state. It's somewhat similar to those workers at Area 51 in Nevada. In their case, they are flown in daily from Las Vegas on a private plane, work the day, and then are flown back. We don't need to fly our guards in daily."

We walked to the elevator and both of us pressed body parts to the pad. The elevator door closed. Allred dropped me off on my floor and then proceeded up to the barn.

I wasn't thinking about security when I walked down the hall toward my suite. I was thinking I was going to have to do something in the parallel worlds that I had visited. *Something*. I wasn't sure what that something was, but I had some general ideas. The first something that I would have to do was go shopping. I walked down the hall, past my suite and went to the Company Store.

Chapter Twenty-Six

Leona Kosinski was at a desk near the front of the room. She was reading a book.

"Oh, Mr. Hobbs," Leona said, "how're you doing?"

She put her book down on the desk, splaying it out so that the cover and the back were facing us. It was *My Gun Is Quick*, a Mickey Spillane book.

"I just love Mickey Spillane," she said. "I've read all of his books, of course. I would like to do that parallel world travel thing of Allred's just to meet Mr. Spillane back when he wrote *My Gun Is Quick*."

"Why don't you?" I asked.

"Someday I will, but I'm too busy, way too busy," Leona said. "How can I help you?"

"Do you have weapons?" I asked.

"Of course," Leona said, "follow me."

We walked down a long aisle. Clothing was on racks and tables for each year. The years weren't in chronological order. We walked past 1995 and then the next table was 1939, then 1951, then 1984.

"You're probably wondering why the clothes aren't in chronological order," she said.

"Now that you mention it, yes," I said.

"Organized chaos," Leona said. "Isn't that what the world is? Isn't that what the universe is? Isn't that what your parallel worlds are? Organized chaos?"

"I guess," I said.

She then did the splits in front of me. Her skirt rose up above her thighs; I saw that she was wearing black panties. She then rolled and did a perfect backflip, solidly landing on her two feet. She might have what she thinks is a strange version of Tourette Syndrome, but if nothing else, she was tremendously flexible for a woman in her fifties.

"Ah, here we are," Leona said. "We don't have a lot."

On the table in front of us were all sorts of weapons. There were three hand grenades, an Uzi machine gun, an old Winchester rifle, several Saturday Night Specials, a box of four Berettas, a couple of modern assault weapons and some Eastern European weapons.

I wasn't a big fan of weapons. As a crime reporter, I had seen too many times how weapons had not been used for self-defense, but to take something from someone. In many cases, what was taken was a life. However, along the way I had taken some lessons and I at least had a useable knowledge on how to shoot a hand gun.

I picked up a Beretta and felt its heft. The best thing about a Beretta was that it had stopping power and it was relatively small.

"Do you have ammo for this one?" I asked.

"Of course," Leona said. She did a full pivot and as she turned she grabbed a box of ammo. When her pivot was complete, she handed me the box of bullets.

"Anything more?" she asked.

"I don't think so."

"How about this," Leona asked, pulling a small black box off of the table. It was the size of a pack of cigarettes.

"What's that?"

"It's called a Small Fry Stun Gun," Leona said.

"I don't see the gun part," I said. "It looks like a small black box."

"There is no gun barrel on the Small Fry Stun Gun," Leona said. "You don't shoot it. You just turn it on, *touch* somebody with it. The electrical charge will disrupt the brain messages to the muscles and after three to five seconds that person will lose muscle control. Recovery takes about five to ten minutes."

Leona touched the Small Fry Stun Gun to my arm. I jumped back.

"Silly," she said, laughing. "I haven't even turned it on. I was just showing you what you have to do. *Touch* somebody."

She did a pirouette and grabbed something else off the table.

"This works the same way," she said. She held up what looked like a marking pen. "This works the same way as the Small Fry Stun Gun, but it looks like a fat pen. You can put it in your shirt pocket. It takes just two triple-A batteries."

"Okay, Leona, I'll take both."

Leona did another pirouette and grabbed something else off the table. If K-Mart sales people had ever put on a show like this they wouldn't have gone broke; they would have beat Wal-Mart.

"Pepper spray," Leona said, holding a tube the size of a lipstick case with a key chain on it. "A one-second shot of this stuff in a person's face will cause temporary blindness, coughing, choking, and they might even barf. Oleoresin Capsicum is the active ingredient in this spray, which if you ask what Oleoresin Capsicum is, it's red pepper."

"Okay, I'll take a couple of those too."

"Do you want these gift wrapped?" Leona asked, laughing, and then did a backward somersault.

Back at my suite, I sat and watched the sun slowly work its way to the horizon. Before the sun plunged into the ocean, the two girls I had seen this morning came walking by. It wasn't like the scene had been rewound. This time, the two girls had changed what they were wearing. It's not like they added clothes; they just subbed skimpy for scant. The two girls looked so real it seemed like I could just walk out the door, bound down to the beach and join them on their little stroll. But, they weren't real—they were part of a high-definition video tape of somebody's view of a Maui beach. Beyond the windows in my suite there was no sandy beach. There was just a reinforced cement wall.

The girls passed and waved at me. I waved back. This was an amazing optical illusion. I didn't allow my eyes to follow them as they walked down the beach. Instead, I watched the descending sun, continuing to think about what had plagued my mind most of the day. It was Allred's paranoia speculation about Burrard. I didn't like the speculation that I might have been the cause of awakening the cosmic connection abilities in Abel Burrard. I didn't like the speculation that I might have altered Burrard's thinking in the parallel world of 1978. But, I thought about it. For instance, if Burrard's thinking had been scrambled a bit by the intrusion of a cosmic connection, could Rachel jump from being victim number fourteen to victim number one?

I was dealing with two Burrards: the first was in 1978 before he had started his killing spree, the second Burrard was in 1992 when he had just claimed his first victim. Both were dangerous, both would eventually murder Rachel. In fact, in thousands of universes, Burrard probably murdered Rachel. But, for the moment, Rachel should be safe in both 1978 and 1992. I knew then that I would have to do something to the Burrards in 1978 and 1992. I had to at least save Rachel in those two universes. I would have to either somehow disable Burrard. Or just flat out kill him in 1978 and 1992.

Since Burrard-92 had already murdered his first victim, I could probably expose his crime by using my 1992 self. 1978 was another story. I would probably have to kill him. I still felt uneasy about that. Burrard hadn't killed anybody yet. And, there was no evidence that he would. Burrard-78 might be the one inconsistency in a world of parallel universes. One thing would tell me that. When Burrard-78 was a young man, he had started grabbing neighborhood pets, torturing them, killing them and then keeping body parts in formaldehyde jars in a locked room in the Rutter Hardware basement. If I somehow got into that room, and if the animal parts were there, then I felt comfortable that Burrard-78 would indeed turn into the monster I had written about.

There was one way to confirm this. I would go back to 1978. I had two purposes. One was not to murder him, yet. First I needed to somehow alert Rachel about the danger of Burrard in case cosmic connection caused Burrard to alter his targets and move her up the list. The second purpose was to get into Burrard's locked basement room in Rutter Hardware Store. If Burrard's collection of animal parts were there, then I would have to kill him.

This time, I would take my newest acquisitions from the Company Store with me.

Chapter Twenty-Seven

I entered 1978 in an alley in Rogers Park, Illinois. It was the same alley that was close to Rutter Hardware Store. This was the same 1978 universe where Rachel and I had made love.

It was eleven in the morning, a bright spring day in May. I was dressed as usual—khaki pants, navy blue sport coat, tie—but this time I carried a small gym bag. Bringing this bag was like taking carry-on luggage on an airplane except I didn't store it in the overhead compartment or put it under the seat in front of me. I had to hold onto that bag when going through the white hole as if the family jewels were in there. After I had arrived in the Rogers Park alley, I checked through the bag. Everything seemed to be in order.

I walked to a small coffee shop across the street from Rutter Hardware Store on North Clark Street. There was a nice little clump of neighborhood stores in this area. Besides Rutter Hardware Store and this coffee shop, there was a drug store, a dry cleaners, a hobby shop, a women's clothing store, and a newsstand. This was a nice friendly street.

I sat in a booth by the window. I ordered a cup of coffee. Thirty cents, unlimited refills the menu said.

"Sorry," the waitress told me, "we just raised our coffee prices last week."

"What was it last week?" I asked.

"Twenty-five cents," she said. "We've had folks stop drinking coffee because of that price increase. I told my boss—the owner—that people wouldn't stand for it. A nickel is a nickel and you just can't raise prices like that for working folks."

I doubt that she would have believed me if I told her that in about fifteen years there would be a coffee shop called Starbucks where customers would stand in line to pay three bucks for a cup of coffee. No refills either. You want another cup of coffee? Fork over another three bucks. And that Starbucks coffee shop would most likely put this coffee shop out of business.

There was a *Chicago Sun-Times* on the next table. I reached over and grabbed it. I leafed through the paper and didn't find my byline. That wasn't unusual at this point in my career. On the second page, I saw a story about Larry Flynt, the publisher of *Hustler* magazine. The story was about his recovery of being shot in March. He had recuperated, and yesterday had fired the guy he had named as acting publisher. He was resuming the duties himself, this time in a wheelchair that he would never leave.

The waitress delivered the coffee. I took a sip. Tasted like Starbucks to me, but I wasn't a coffee connoisseur so how would I know the difference?

I took out the Minolta thirty-five millimeter camera and put it on the table. This was the film camera that Allred had given me. I was going to take some photos of Burrard, have the film developed while in Chicago, and use them to alert Rachel of the danger of Burrard. This was just a short-range plan to keep Rachel alert while I figured out how to get into Burrard's locked basement room at the store. The locked basement room would tell me what I needed to do. If the animal parts were there, I would then plan to kill Burrard.

Instead of just walking into Rutter Hardware Store, telling Burrard to say cheese and then snapping a couple of pictures, I thought I'd be a little more discreet. I'd sit here for a while and using the three-to-one zoom lens, I hoped to get a decent shot of him. I hoped he would walk outside the store.

Waiting, I flipped to the back of the *Sun-Times*. The Cubs had lost the night before in San Francisco. Dave Kingman had hit his eighth homer for the Cubs in just thirty-two games. He was on pace to get forty homers this year, but my recollections said that he didn't. As I read the sports page, I would look up occasionally to see if Burrard would show his face. The White Sox got beat by the Yankees at

Comiskey Park. Bobby Bonds had hit two homers for the Sox. Which person in the city of Chicago could ever imagine that Bobby Bonds' son, Barry, would become the greatest single-season home run hitter ever, just waltzing past Roger Maris' sixty-one? Not even Bobby Bonds.

The waitress gave me my third refill. No charge, of course, for that refill. I felt like somebody was looking at me, and I looked up and saw Burrard standing in front of the hardware store. He was staring right at me. I lifted the Minolta to my eye and pointed it at him. I didn't think he could see me through the glass. I swiveled the zoom lens to get tighter. I snapped two quick pictures. Burrard looked left, then right, waiting for the traffic to pass. When the traffic cleared, he crossed the street. He looked as harmless as a schoolboy. I took pictures of him every step of the way. I must have snapped off ten shots. The thought occurred to me that I should have been firing bullets instead of snapshots.

Burrard came in to the coffee shop.

"Hello, Abel," the waitress said, smiling. I could tell that she thought Burrard was a nice guy.

"Hi, Janine," Burrard said, his most harmless face smiling at her. "How's business?"

"Thirty-cent coffee, what can I tell you?" Janine said.

"I'll have one to go," Burrard said.

"I'll have to brew a new pot, Hon," Janine said. "It'll just take a minute." Janine walked to the kitchen in the back.

Burrard stood at the front of the shop. He noticed me. "Why, hello," he said, as friendly as an evangelist.

"Hello," I said, like I would to a stranger on a plane.

"I sold you some masking tape," Burrard said, playing the adult Opie role all the way.

"Good memory," I said.

"Yeah, I've always had a good memory," Burrard said. He sat down at a table near the booth I was sitting in.

We didn't say anything for a few moments.

"You're the one with the fancy belt," Burrard said.

"Not so fancy," I said.

"Can I see it?" he asked.

"Not today," I said.

"I know who you are," Burrard said, lowering his voice to a slight decibel above a whisper. "I know who you are."

"What do you mean by that?" I said.

"I see things in my dreams," Burrard said. "I used to get nightmares, almost every night—awful nightmares—but now I get strange dreams. I know who you are."

"Who am I then?"

"You're Roy Hobbs," Burrard said, still speaking in low tones. "You're here to disrupt my life. I can't let you do that, you know."

"How do you know my name?" I said. The Abel Burrard of 1992 had also known my name. It's not like I had my name printed on a card and pinned to my shirt like some conventioneer. Yes, Allred definitely should do more research into cosmic connections.

"My dreams are strange," Burrard said, "very strange. I see you in my dreams. You're going to try to harm me."

The waitress came over with Burrard's cup of coffee in a white Styrofoam cup and handed it to him.

"You can pay me later, Abel," the waitress said and then walked back to the counter.

"Well, see you around," Burrard said to me, winking. Burrard walked out the door.

The waitress came over with a pot of coffee. "Want another cup?"

"No thanks, this is fine," I said. I was still shaken by what Burrard had said. "What do I owe you?

"Thirty cents," she said. "That boy sure is a nice boy, isn't he?"

I nodded. Yep, they all said that. Nice boy; he looked so harmless.

"Sorta shy," the waitress said, "but he's gonna make some woman happy someday."

I nodded. I knew of sixteen women who he would eventually murder. Each murder was tremendously horrible. Each victim was mutilated beyond imagination. Each murdered woman had a mother. I didn't think that Abel Burrard would make any woman happy in his whole life in *any* parallel world.

"Such a likeable young man," the waitress said, "not like those hippies, down further on Clark Street. It's too bad about his mother."

"What happened to his mother?" I asked. I, of course, knew the whole sordid story about Abel Burrard's mother. In fact, I would have interviewed this waitress for my book, but this restaurant was long gone by then.

"God rest her soul," the waitress said. "She was the daughter of a preacher. Married a guy from the neighborhood. He was a quiet guy, sorta a loner. She had Abel, then was divorced. Haven't seen that no-good husband since. There were stories about how she had mistreated young Abel, but how bad could that have been? Look at him now, just a picture of a fine young man. A couple of years ago though, Abel's mother committed suicide. I went to high school with her; I always thought she was a little tetched in the head, you know, crazy."

I put down fifty cents on the table.

"Keep the change," I said and walked out of the coffee shop.

Across the street, Burrard was watching me. He waved. Just for a moment—no more than a microsecond—he gave me that Charles Manson glare. I wish I had taken a picture of that.

Chapter Twenty-Eight

After I had met Rachel during my second visit to 1978, I was hoping for some type of sign that made me feel she would be safe from Burrard in that parallel universe. After all, she hadn't met my 1978 self on my second trip to Wednesday, May tenth, 1978 so maybe her future had been changed and she would have avoided Burrard altogether. At the time, I thought there was plenty of time to figure out the various options. But now, with Burrard being fully aware of me, I had to take immediate precautions. I didn't know if cosmic connection created a new timetable for Burrard, some massive tumble of destiny. Was Burrard's timetable revved up to warp speed? I would have to get into that locked basement room at Rutter Hardware to see for myself if he was following his own destiny. That would have to be soon, very soon.

In the meantime, I needed to alert Rachel. I would show her the pictures that I had taken of Burrard. I would also arm her with some defensive equipment. She would have to be on alert for two or three days until I could get into Rutter Hardware.

Then the choices were easy: if there were animal parts stored down there in formaldehyde jars then I would kill Burrard. Almost immediately.

If there was *nothing* down there—no signs whatsoever of any aberrant behavior by Burrard—then I might not have to kill him. I didn't think there was any chance of that. I had seen the evil in Burrard's eyes. But, I'd never killed before. I needed proof—not proof for a judge and jury, but proof for *me*. If the verdict was death to Burrard, I could do it. Yes, even though I've never killed, or even previously thought of violently hurting anybody, I could kill a serial killer. Yes, I could do that. If Burrard was indeed evil in this parallel universe of 1978, I knew that if I didn't kill Burrard he would murder Rachel. Burrard had killed her in my world, and he probably murdered Rachel in a thousand other parallel worlds, and his cosmic connection would probably drive him to kill her in this parallel universe of 1978. I couldn't stop him back in 1999, I can't stop him in thousands of parallel worlds, but I could stop him here. I had to stop Burrard at least once.

The next step would be to show Rachel the pictures of Burrard. In 1978, there weren't, of course, digital cameras. If it was like today, I could just walk in to Walgreen's, take out the memory card in my digital camera, pop it in the photo kiosk and print some pictures. However, this was 1978 and there weren't digital cameras and I was using film. In 1978 there weren't any one-hour photo finishers. It was drop your roll of film off at Walgreen's and come back a few days later to see if the prints were in. I didn't want to take three or four days to wait for the prints. Not knowing the cosmic connection effects on Abel Burrard, I wanted to set up a defense for Rachel right away.

I took the 'L' down toward downtown Chicago. I got off at State and Kinzie. At the time, this area was the printing capital of the world. Besides two major daily newspapers being printed nearby—the *Sun-Times* and the *Tribune*—R. G. Donnelly printed the phone books, White and Yellow Pages for most of the Midwest. Because of the density of printing companies, there were a ton of companies that provided services like paper, metal printing press plates, inks, and of course, film. The companies that developed film weren't in the consumer snapshot business. They developed certain color films for professional photographers. The black and white pictures were easier to develop and they were usually developed by the photographer himself. As a writer at the *Sun-Times* I had not used one of these professional photo finishers, but I knew where they were.

I stepped in to Willard Color. I actually stepped *down*. If this was an apartment building, Willard Color would be located in the 'garden apartment.' There was a large counter that separated the workers from the customers. Standing at the other side of the counter was a skinny guy who had a fat face and a beer belly. It's amazing how fat could isolate in certain parts of the body. His arms were rails, his chest and shoulders belonged to a cadaver; his stomach and face belonged to a medieval king.

"Yeah, what can I do for yuh?"

I held up the roll of 35-millimeter color film. "I need this developed," I said.

"We don't do snapshots, fella," the skinny guy with fat face and gut said. "Go down to Walgreen's or something."

"I want you to do it," I said. "How much would it cost if I wanted prints in an hour?"

"An hour! Whadya think I'm Flash Gordon or something?"

I put a twenty dollar bill down on the counter. Then I put another one on top of it.

"You gotta have an account with us," the skinny-fat guy said. "There's a minimum, you know."

I put down two more twenties. This reminded me of Allred, except he had flashed ten *thousand* dollar bills in my face, not twenties.

I put down another twenty on the pile. I then picked up the pile, straightened the bills and handed them to the guy.

"That probably covers your minimum, and I probably just opened an account," I said. "But I'll double that if you finish this within an hour."

"An hour?"

I nodded. "An hour."

"What size prints you want?" the skinny-fat guy asked, looking at his watch.

"Four by fives would be good."

"You got 'em," the skinny-fat guy said. "Be back in less than an hour." He turned and walked through the curtain behind the counter.

I sat in the one-chair lobby and read *Field & Stream* magazine. My reading was as intense as it was when I was reading the book about Stephen Hawking—about three words every half hour. My eyes stared at the printed page, but my mind was a runaway freight train.

"Here they are, bud," the skinny-fat guy said. He checked his watch, "Fifty-four minutes." He handed me a batch of color prints.

"Nice looking young guy," skinny-fat said. "He your son?"

"No, not at all, no relation," I said, shuffling through the pictures to look at each one. What if I told skinny-fat that this nice looking young guy was destined to go on to slaughter sixteen women? What if I told him that the only way I knew to stop him was to kill him?

Chapter Twenty-Nine

I put the pictures in the envelope and walked out of Willard Color. I loaded another roll of film into the camera. I looked at my watch. Even though she wasn't expecting me, I might be able to catch Rachel leaving work. I was just a couple of blocks away from the *Tribune* building.

I positioned myself outside by the streetlight as I had done before. I stood there with my athletic bag at my feet. The Burrard pictures were in the athletic bag. It seemed that everybody that passed by me was smoking. With that much carefree smoking around me I too felt like smoking. But, I resisted buying a pack. It had been too tough to quit before. I didn't want to come back from 1978 with a nicotine habit: "Hey, Charles," I could say upon re-entering the silo, "instead of that Gatorade Fierce, how about a Marlboro or a Winston?"

Rachel came out of the *Tribune* building and spotted me right away. I wondered if she had looked for me every day since we had last been together. She smiled, a big smile that lit up her face and then waved as if it was a reflex action to the smile. I snapped a picture of that perfect smile. I snapped off another four or five shots as she walked toward me, each step a smile unto itself.

She walked quickly over to me. Like the last time we met, we didn't hug or kiss. We just smiled at each other. I marveled again at her complexion; it was so clear of any blemishes or moles or wrinkles. I had seen her face mature, of course. I had seen it age up to the age of forty-three when she had been murdered. If Leonardo da Vinci would have painted her face at forty-three—a face that aged with such comfort and ease—it would have been another classic treasure at the Louvre.

"You have come back," she said, and then she laughed. "Is that always going to be my opening line to you? That you've come back?"

I laughed. "Yes, and I'm saying the same thing, I think. I'm back," I said.

"From Japan?"

"From a long, long way from here," I said.

"That's right. You travel a lot," she said and laughed. "This sure sounds like déjà vu, all over again," she said, laughing.

I laughed too, but I was uncomfortable about déjà vu. It reminded me of Abel Burrard.

"So, let me try something new," Rachel said. "How was your day?"

"Terrific," I said. "I got to see you."

"So, are you going to buy a hardworking cub reporter a drink?"

"Absolutely."

The cosmic connection we had felt before was just as strong. I felt it; I knew Rachel felt it. While the cosmic connection was perfectly right, there were two things that were perfectly wrong with us meeting: I was from a different parallel world, and I was old enough to be her father. Other couples had overcome the latter. I don't think any couple had ever overcome the former.

We walked to the same small restaurant just a couple of blocks away.

"Do you remember that guy at Butch McGuire's?" Rachel asked as we walked. "You know, Roy Hobbs, works at the *Sun-Times?* He said his middle name was Homer."

"Vaguely," I said. "Why?"

"Well, he called," Rachel said. "He wants to go out."

"Are you gonna go?" I asked.

"I don't know," she said. "But, it's funny, he reminds me of you."

I laughed.

"A *younger* you, of course," Rachel said, poking me in the ribs. "Seriously, you both are about the same height—tall. You both sorta walk the same. You both have the same head shape. You are older, of

171

course, but he reminds me of you. Since you pop in and out of my life, maybe I should see Roy as a substitute for those times when you've popped out of my life."

Rachel laughed. She didn't know how close to the truth she was. If she got to know Roy Hobbs more intimately, she'd find out that we both would have second toes that were longer than our big toes. She'd also notice Roy's birthmark on the back of his right shoulder was identical to my birthmark. And, she would notice that our penises were exactly the same shape, the same length.

"I see you're traveling heavy this time," Rachel said, pointing to my gym bag. "Whatcha got in there?"

"Gym stuff," I said. I didn't think it would be appropriate that I bring out my arsenal—the Beretta, bullets, an assortment of stun guns, pepper spray, and the pictures—in the restaurant.

We ate dinner quickly. It seemed both of us were in a rush to get to her apartment. While we had coffee, Rachel excused herself to go to the rest room. She was probably calling ahead to her roommate, Janet Emerson, to give her the signal to get out. I paid for the dinner and once outside we jumped in a cab.

We held hands in the back seat. Rachel's fingers were long and supple. If she had wanted to, she could have been a *hand model*. Procter & Gamble would have loved to have featured her hands in an ad for Oil of Olay hand cream. As we held hands, an awful memory forced its way into my consciousness. Abel Burrard. Burrard mutilated his victims beyond anything that the police had ever experienced. With some victims, he would take their heart, with others he would take their kidney; with all of them he took at least one fingertip. With Rachel, he had taken *all* of her fingertips. I didn't know if that was his sick way of appreciating Rachel's hands; he would never say. I thought of her fingertips being in formaldehyde jars, and I clenched her hand a little tighter. She leaned over and kissed me on the cheek.

If I would have ordered up a white hole we could have made it to her apartment quicker, but we would have caught Rachel's roommate scrambling to pick up the apartment. As it was, we saw Janet just getting into a car, overnight bag in hand, as the cab pulled up. What a wonderful roommate Janet was.

This time there wasn't any foreplay. We were at each other as soon as we got in the apartment. While I had been in my suite looking at the Maui sunset, I had thought of another evening with Rachel, but had dismissed it. Even though I had dismissed it, I hadn't dismissed some daydreaming. I thought if there was ever another evening in Rachel's bed that I would take it slow, be the perfect gentleman, be the perfect lover. My daydream was wrong. I was all over Rachel like I was a teenager. Rachel, tall and athletic, showed every ounce of surpassing my energy. We both shot off like firecrackers with short fuses.

We must have slept a bit because the next thing I noticed was that I was alone in bed. I got up, buck naked and self consciously sucking in my gut a bit, and walked toward the kitchen.

Rachel was sitting naked at the kitchen table. She had a shot of whiskey in front of her. She was smoking a cigarette. She had quit years ago—during her first pregnancy—and I hadn't seen her smoking until now.

"Hey," I said.

She turned to me. Her face was moist; she had been crying. "Hey," she said.

I walked over to her, squatted down and put my arm around her.

"What's the matter?" I asked. How many times had I asked her that during our marriage? Too many times; too many times.

She stubbed out the Virginia Slims cigarette after only a couple of puffs. The ashtray had three of those long cigarettes in it; each one stubbed out after just a couple of puffs. When we were young and married and both smoking, I used to scavenge those beautiful cigarette butts when all I had was an empty pack and then I would smoke them down to the filter.

"Nothing," Rachel said. How many times had she given me that answer? Too many times.

I took her by the elbow and raised her up to standing and then held her. Our naked bodies pressed against each other.

"I love you," I said, kissing her forehead.

173

"I know you do," she said. "I have *never* felt that feeling from a guy before, that he *really* loved me, that it just wasn't the sex. With you, Homer, I *know* that you love me. It's crazy, I know, but I know that you love me. And, Homer, I love you."

"I know you do," I said. "If there were ever any two people made for each other, you and I are it. So, why the crying?"

"I'm just so happy," Rachel said, "but I feel that this has just been a dream, that this will go away like a puff of smoke. I don't want it to go away. I know you're way too old for me, but that's okay, I love you."

She craned her neck and reached up and kissed me on the lips. Her lips were salty.

I cupped her buttocks with my hands, like I used to do. She held me tight, like she used to do. It didn't take us too long to edge back toward the bedroom. This time we were slow, like I had daydreamed watching the Maui surf.

After we had made love the second time, and then watched a bit of Johnny Carson, I said, "Rachel, you know I'm going to have to leave again, tomorrow."

"I know," she said, "I expected it. If I told my roommate Janet about all of this, she would think I was crazy, putting out for you—an old *old* man—and then just waving you good-bye. But, I *know* there is no other woman, I know that you love me, I know that I love you, but everything is so strange, and why I accept it, I don't know. Does that make any sense to you, Homer?"

Surprisingly, it made all the sense in the world to me if you believed in cosmic connection, so I said, "Yes, it makes all the sense in the world." I didn't identify which parallel world, but if I went to a thousand of them I think the love would be there in each one of them.

Chapter Thirty

Over coffee and an English muffin, I was thinking how I was going to get into the Rutter Hardware basement. I had walked down the stairs to that locked room before. It had been after Burrard had been caught and I was researching my book.

I'd have to somehow get Burrard out of the store for a half-hour or so. I wasn't concerned about the store's owner. When I interviewed him for the book, he had told me he hadn't been downstairs in years. The stairs were way too steep for his wobbly legs.

Rachel joined me at the breakfast table. She was just about ready to go to work.

"I need to show you something," I said, "something that you promise me you will do." I was going to show her those personal safety devices, and I felt that she would show reluctance to carrying them.

"What is it?"

"You have to promise first," I said.

"So this is a blind promise?"

"Yep. Promise?"

"Okay," Rachel said, "I promise to do what you ask me to do. What is it?"

I walked over to my gym bag and pulled out an envelope. I took out the pictures. I handed her one.

"Have you ever seen this guy before?" I asked.

Rachel glanced at the picture.

"Yes, I have," Rachel said.

"*You have!*" I said, the loudness of my voice even surprising me. "Where?"

"He's a friend of my roommate Janet," Rachel said. "She introduced me. In fact, I think that's where Janet was going when we got here in the cab. Why do you want to know?"

"Did Janet leave a phone number," I asked. I tried to be as calm as I could be. Inside I was almost hysterical; I didn't want Rachel to mimic that. While Burrard had not killed any single women back in my world that didn't mean Janet was safe. Could the cosmic connection caused by me visiting Burrard in 1978 have caused him to tilt his internal gyroscope? It seemed possible. Instead of systematically murdering divorcees could he be on tilt and killing women that were loosely associated with me? I didn't know, but I knew I'd have to find Janet.

"I don't think so," Rachel said. "Let me look." She got up and walked to the kitchen, looking at the pieces of paper that were stuck to the door by magnets. She then went to Janet's bedroom. She came back twenty seconds later. "Nope, no phone number," she said.

I, of course, knew where Burrard lived. I had written a book about the bastard, but I knew the house where he lived when he was doing the killings. *I* had even visited the house he had lived in before it was torn down. I had gone down to the basement and seen his killing room. When he was younger, however, he had lived in a series of dumpy apartments—that's why he used the locked room in the Rutter Hardware Store basement to keep his animal parts—but I didn't know the locations of those places off-hand.

"How long has Janet known this guy?" I asked.

"Oh, not very long," Rachel said, "it's been a whirlwind romance, sorta like ours, except Abel doesn't leave town."

"Abel Burrard?"

"Yes, that's his name, how did you know?" Rachel said.

I looked at my watch. Seven thirty-five in the morning. I knew that this was a little before Burrard would open up Rutter Hardware Store. I might not know which seedy apartment he was living in, but I knew exactly where to find him.

"I've got to go," I said. "Janet may be in danger."

"In danger? From Abel? I don't think so," Rachel said. "He's so harmless. I never knew what Janet saw in him. He's a wimp."

"Trust me," I said, "he's *very* dangerous."

I thought of my options. There weren't many. I couldn't go to the cops. At this point in Abel Burrard's life he had not been a murderer. He was a twenty-year-old guy who everybody thought was harmless. *I* didn't even know for sure if Burrard was a killer in this parallel world. I felt that he was, but there certainly wasn't any proof. The only option I had was to confront Burrard at Rutter Hardware Store.

I tried being calm. I faked it as good as I could.

I slowly opened up my gym bag and put it on the kitchen table and I took out the Small Fry Stun Gun, the Pen Stun Gun, and the pepper spray.

"What are those?" Rachel asked.

"This is what I wanted you to promise to do," I said. "I want you to carry one of each." I picked up the Pen Stun Gun. "If I turned this on, and then held it to your body—anyplace on your body—for about three to five seconds, you would be incapacitated."

"What do you mean 'incapacitated'? Knocked out?" Rachel asked.

"Not knocked out cold," I said, "but you would just be laying there, not able to move your muscles. It lasts for just five to ten minutes, just enough time for you to either tie the attacker up or get the hell to safety."

Rachel pushed the button to turn it on. She then held it to her thigh. "Oh my God!" she said and quickly pulled the Pen Stun Gun away.

"I've never seen products like these," Rachel said. The pepper spray she might have seen, but yes, she had never seen these miniature stun guns. They wouldn't become mainstream until after she had been killed in 1999.

"I got them in Japan," I lied. "You know those Japanese have always got these little gadgets—you know, like their little cars."

That lie made sense to Rachel. I didn't like to lie to Rachel, but the alternative—the truth—was silly. Could I really tell Rachel about Leona Kosinski's Company Store in a bunker in a parallel world in a parallel universe?

"Now listen to me, Rachel," I said, "I can't give you all the details, but you have to believe me: Abel Burrard is the most dangerous man you will ever meet. If he has the chance, he will *kill you*. Do you understand? He will kill you." I didn't tell her that Burrard had succeeded in killing her—and then mutilating her into hundreds of pieces—in countless numbers of parallel worlds. *This* one world—the one where she and I were sitting—was now the important one.

I felt that she did *not* want to believe me. It was too fantastic. That wimpy guy Burrard a murderer? But, I could tell she did trust me. Whether it was the seriousness of my words, or an underlying trust from the cosmic connection, Rachel believed that Burrard was dangerous.

"Who are you?" Rachel asked as calmly as if she had asked me the time.

"Homer Murphy," I said. "Want to see some I.D.?"

"Yes, if you don't mind."

I took out my wallet and extracted my Michigan driver's license. Leona was a master forger, but she felt that since I had been visiting Illinois I should have an out-of-state driver's license.

Rachel scrutinized the driver's license like she was a bouncer at a bar looking for underage kids trying to get in. Leona could have made a fortune making up phony I.D.s for kids.

Rachel handed the driver's license back to me.

"You are fifty-one!" Rachel said.

I nodded.

"Okay, I know your name, Homer Murphy, but that could be faked," Rachel said. "I had a fake I.D. in college. So, *who* are you? Are you an undercover cop? Are you FBI? Are you CIA? Who are you?"

"There are some things I can't tell you," I said. "I can tell you, however, that Abel Burrard is a murderer. I can tell you that I will catch him. I can tell you that I genuinely love you. I can tell you that nobody in this world will love you as much as I do."

Rachel put her hand on mine. "Undercover," she said, "undercover *something*."

I nodded. I guess I was undercover, but the 'something' might be better classified as vigilante. Undercover vigilante.

"When Janet stays the night at somebody's place, does she come back here in the morning?" I asked, hopefully.

"If she's not here now, she probably won't," Rachel said. "She was carrying an overnight case, so she probably has what she needs and she'll just go straight to work."

"Where does she work?" I asked.

"Marshall Field's, the main office."

"What time will you get to work?" I asked.

Rachel looked at her watch. "About eight-thirty," she said, "maybe a few minutes earlier than that."

"Well, once you get to work, call Janet at Marshall Field's first thing," I said. "I'm going to meet Burrard at the hardware store where he works."

"I'll call you from a pay phone before I go into the store in case Janet does indeed show up for work."

"What are you going to do to Abel?" She asked.

"If Janet shows up for work, I'll do nothing, I'll just leave," I said. "If she doesn't show up, I don't know."

Chapter Thirty-One

T he front door to Rutter Hardware was locked.
I had taken the 'L' up to Rogers Park and had made good time going opposite of rush hour traffic.

It was eight-fifteen in the morning; the store was scheduled to open at nine. I had hoped that Burrard would open the store early so I could get him alone.

I knocked on the door. No movement. I knocked harder. Nothing.

I walked around to the alley behind the store. The back entrance to Rutter Hardware was a steel door. It was locked. I pounded on it. No answer. I pounded on it some more. Nothing. The door was solid and there were no windows to the store from the alley. It would take a howitzer to get through that door.

I walked to the coffee shop across the street from the front entrance to Rutter Hardware Store.

I ordered a thirty-cent cup of coffee. Janine, the waitress, remembered me from the day before.

"Abel usually come in for his morning coffee?" I asked.

"Yep, and he's usually here by now," Janine said, looking at her watch. "He's late. I don't ever remember him being late. He usually stops here at eight on the dot for his coffee to go and a donut before he opens the store. He likes the Bavarian Crème the best. The crème is vanilla and the donut is topped with chocolate frosting. Want to try one?"

"No thanks," I said. "That young man opens the store every day?"

"Oh yes, he's a sweetheart," Janine said. "He opens up every morning like clockwork. Old man Rutter usually doesn't get in until nine or so. But Abel, you can count on him being the early bird, that's for sure."

I leafed through the *Chicago Sun-Times*. Again I didn't have a byline. In the sports page, I read that the White Sox lost again to the Yankees, three to nothing. Reggie Jackson went hitless for the Yanks. The Cubs got beat again by the San Francisco Giants, this time nine to five. Dave Kingman didn't get any homers.

After I finished my coffee, it was close to the time that I had to use the pay phone.

At eight thirty, Rachel was going to phone Janet Emerson at Marshall Field's. According to Rachel, Janet was almost always at work before that time. Then at about eight thirty-five or so, I was going to call Rachel at the Tribune. We wanted to know if Janet was safe. If she was safe, it simplified what I was going to do. I had told Rachel that I would not confront Burrard, that I would just walk away. I lied; I didn't want her to somehow become an accessory to murder. If Janet was safe, and Burrard was in the store, I was going to just walk into Rutter Hardware Store carrying a small paper bag—the size that winos used to hide their cheap wine bottle. The bag would be covering my right hand which held the Beretta. I would just walk up to Burrard and shoot him dead. No conversation, no nothing, just bang, bang, bang. I would then push the Red Button on the Wayfarer Commander and get the hell out of 1978.

Rachel, of course, didn't know of my plan. But, she didn't need to know. What was important was that Burrard would be dead and that at least in this one parallel world, Rachel could live her life.

There was a pay phone at the back of the coffee shop. At eight thirty-five I walked over to it and dialed Rachel's number. She picked it up on the first ring.

"Hello?" she said with an urgency that pushed her voice to squeak a bit.

"Rachel," I said, "any word?"

"No," she said. "I've called twice and left a message twice. I said that it was an emergency."

"Okay," I said, "I'll try to find out something this morning. I'll call you back in an hour." I sure missed cell phones in 1978. It had been years since I had used a pay phone and I forgot how inconvenient pay phones were.

I went back to my booth by the window. Janine had refilled my cup of coffee. I waited for the store to be opened. I would call Rachel again before I went to Rutter Hardware in case Janet happened to just be late for work. In my gut, however, my feeling was that she was dead.

In the past when he had snatched a woman, Burrard didn't dillydally. Every time the woman was dead within sixty minutes of her capture. According to police testimony, the victims were sliced and diced—completely—within thirty minutes after they were killed. If Burrard was true to form then Janet was dead. Still, I couldn't take the chance and just go into Rutter Hardware Store and plug Burrard. Janet might be tied and bound in some forgotten closet. A dead Burrard could mean death by starvation for Janet. I needed to find Janet—dead or alive—*before* I shot Burrard.

The chances of Burrard just telling me where Janet was were not good. The Cubs had a better chance of winning the pennant than Burrard telling me where the girl was. The only way was through intimidation. I had the intimidation in the paper bag. The Beretta. I would have to use it to get Burrard out of Rutter Hardware Store.

I made another call to Rachel on the pay phone.

She picked up on the first ring.

"Hello, this is Rachel," she said.

"Any word?" I asked.

"No," Rachel said, lowering her voice. "I've called over there twice more. They haven't heard from her. I think all my phone calls are making them really worry."

I was disappointed that Janet wasn't at work. That cinched it for me. I would have to snatch Burrard and threaten the information out of him.

I saw an older man walk up to the Rutter Hardware Store at a little after nine and try to open the front door. He tugged at the door. It didn't open. He peered through the door window. He then reached into his pocket, retrieving something. That something was a key and he inserted a key into the door, opened it and walked in.

Several cars passed and then I walked across the street. I opened the door to Rutter Hardware Store.

Burrard was not at the front counter, the big older guy that opened the front door was. I recognized him from the time I interviewed him for *The Monster Among Us*. I interviewed him in 2002, or about fourteen years from now. He didn't look much different now. Maybe a few pounds less, maybe a little more hair. I remembered him to be a friendly guy.

"Hi," I said, "Abel in?"

"Nope," Rutter said. "He always opens up, but not today."

"Heard from him?" I asked, friendly-like. One thing about reporters, we have a tremendous ability to get on the same page with a person that we are interviewing. We might blast the shit out of him in the story, but when we're talking we're the best of friends. Every good reporter I know has this ability to connect—really connect—with the person they are interviewing. Mike Wallace on *60 Minutes* gets guys to confide in him, and then he absolutely skewers them on national TV.

"Nope, every day the kid opens up my store, and has never missed," Rutter said. "He's like a son to me. Never misses a day of work. Never complains. But today, I try to walk in and the store's locked up tighter than a drum. I get out my key, open the door, and nothing. Abel hadn't opened up the store."

"That sure doesn't sound like Abel," I said. "I wonder if he's sick?"

"You know Abel?" Mr. Rutter asked.

"Sure do," I said. "I've been helping him in night school."

My research for the book told me that Burrard had tried night school for several years. He wanted to learn computers. He wasn't trying to learn the things we have today; he was trying to learn mainframes. Who knows, if he would have stuck with it, he might have changed his entire life and he would be one of the rich scientists in Allred's barn.

"I'm Homer Murphy," I said, extending my hand over the counter. Introducing yourself always works better for a reporter. It's like we have nothing to hide.

"I'm Darrell Rutter, I own the place. So how's Abel doing in night school?"

"He's got some real talent," I said, which he did. Burrard was not a dumb guy. In many respects, he was brilliant. That brilliance, unfortunately, allowed him to kill far more women that he should have been able to.

"I hope he does well, but I don't want to lose him," Rutter said. "He's the most reliable employee I've ever had."

"I've got some papers for Abel to sign," I said. "If you want me to drop by where he lives, I'd be glad to check up on him, see if he's sick or something."

"That sure would be nice of you Mr. Murphy," Rutter said, "being that I'm short-handed here right now. Do you know where he lives?"

"No, I don't," I said, "around Rogers Park?"

"Well, he just moved about a week ago. Let me see if I can find the address, it's around here someplace," Rutter said, looking through a stack of notes behind the counter. "Yeah, here it is. It's over by Wrigley Field. I don't know why he moved down there. I think he told me it was some girl or something."

Rutter gave me the address. I thanked him and told him if I saw Burrard that I would tell him to call in to the store.

I jumped on the 'L' in Rogers Park and it took me right to the area where Burrard was supposed to be living. It was only about four miles away.

When I got off the 'L' I called Rachel again from a pay phone.

She again answered on the first ring, "Hello, this is Rachel."

"Any word?" I asked.

"Nothing, Homer, nothing. I'm really worried now," Rachel said. "Where are you?"

"Well, Burrard didn't come in to work either. I've got his address. I'm going over there."

"Be careful," Rachel said. Her voice had the same concern in it as when I was working on a story about the mob years ago.

"I will," I said. I always told her that and I meant it.

I looked at the address on the sheet of paper. It was just a block away. Wayne Avenue was just three blocks away from Wrigley Field.

In 1978, there were some rough areas around Wrigley. I walked down Wayne Avenue looking at addresses. I found it. It was a four story brownstone that looked like it should be demolished. Even the wonders of gentrification couldn't save this building.

I still had my gym bag. There was nothing in it except the Beretta and Allred's thirty-five millimeter camera. I tucked the Beretta under my belt. I wrapped the strap of the camera through my belt and tossed the bag.

It looked like there were four apartments per floor. There was a directory by the main entrance. Most of the slots for names were empty. A few names looked like they had been placed in the slots a century ago. There was one that was new. The name said, in neatly printed letters: Roy H. Hobbs.

Chapter Thirty-Two

I stared at the nameplate. Roy H. Hobbs.

It was apartment 4B.

The front door to the apartment building was ajar. It did have a buzzer entry system, but that probably hadn't been working since Franklin Roosevelt was President..

Inside the small vestibule, the first sense that was pricked was *smell*. The place smelled like an outhouse. The floor hadn't been washed in at least a decade. There was a large turd in the corner. Somebody had to pay rent to live here? This was not the type of place that Abel Burrard would live in. He had always been as neat and tidy as a nun. Even the formaldehyde jars of body parts had been lined up in his secret vault like soldiers at attention.

There was no elevator, and even if there had been and it somehow was working, I wouldn't have taken it. An elevator in this building would be like a vertical coffin.

The stairs were just off to the left. I pulled out my Beretta, keeping the paper bag covering it. If I wanted to look like one of the residents, I figured I would careen off the walls clutching my paper bag. Instead I climbed the stairs on full alert.

The smell didn't get worse as I climbed the stairs. There were actually wafts of cooking food that sliced through the smell of urine and stale cigarette smoke. I didn't see anybody as I made it to the fourth floor.

Apartment 4B was at the end of the hall. I didn't knock; I just tried the door knob first. It's strange what goes through a person's mind when there is stress. A sequence of the movie *Psycho* jumped into my head. It was the part where the detective was climbing the stairs of the old house and once he got to the top, Norman Bates—dressed like his invalid mother—jumped out and stabbed him.

The door knob turned when I squeezed it to the right.

I pushed it open and jumped back. Old lady Bates wasn't going to jump me.

I was met with a smell that was worse than the lobby.

I didn't know what I was expecting when I pushed open the door, but I didn't think I would find Abel Burrard in this wreck of an apartment sitting there watching TV, munching on a bowl of popcorn. With my name on the apartment's directory and going to an apartment that Abel Burrard would *not* live in, I felt that this was one thing: a kill zone.

When nothing jumped out at me, I carefully stepped into the apartment. I had been at enough crime scenes as a reporter to recognize the smell that was gagging me. A dead body.

It looked like a one bedroom apartment. These apartments were built along the lines of a train, each room following the next down the line. The first room was the living room. Down the hallway would be the bedroom, then the bathroom, and lastly the kitchen.

The living room's furniture was basically Salvation Army rejects. There was a couch with broken legs, a chair, and a small TV sitting on the floor. It looked like an old black and white TV; nobody was sitting there yucking it up watching *Happy Days*.

The bedroom was worse. There was just a skimpy weathered mattress on the floor with old stains like a jumble of Rorschach tests for crazy people. While the bedroom smelled, it wasn't the source that was leading me room-by-room.

The light from the bathroom illuminated part of the hallway. I felt that this was going to be it. Burrard had left the light on just for special effect.

I carefully stepped in the light in the hallway, facing the open bathroom door. In my right hand I had the Beretta out of the paper bag ready to shoot; my forefinger on my left hand was resting on the Red

Button of the opened Wayfarer Commander. I was ready for anything, except what I saw.

Janet Emerson's face—*just the skin*, not the whole head—was hanging by clothes pins on a rope over the bathtub. As Burrard had been killing and mutilating sixteen women, he had become an expert at removing body parts and skinning. After they had caught Burrard, the police found a February 10, 1958 *Life Magazine* in his house. That issue of *Life Magazine* included a pictorial story of the serial killings of Charlie Starkweather. Starkweather had carefully skinned his victims, and used their skin to cover chairs and lampshades. Burrard had been born just a year before 1958, but somehow, later on in life, Charles Starkweather had become one of his idols.

Janet's heart was left in the sink. Her body was not in the bathroom—just her face and her heart.

I staggered back out of the bathroom. The crime scene has never been one of my favorite places to visit, and there were times when I felt like throwing up, but this scene hit me like an axe handle in the belly. I fell down to my knees and threw up in the hallway. With my last retch, I realized I was vulnerable in that position. If Burrard had been in the kitchen waiting for his horrible tableau to have its effect on me, he could have jumped me and I would have been a dead man with barf in my mouth.

I got up quickly, repositioning my forefinger on the Red Button. I walked toward the kitchen. There was a trail of blood stains to what looked like a small pantry. Inside the pantry was the rest of Janet Emerson. She hung on the wall as if she were on a meat hook. I backed away.

Off in the distance I heard sirens, but what caught my attention were some envelopes on the kitchen table. The envelopes were new and fresh. I picked one up. It was addressed to me, Roy Hobbs. It had my 1978 address. It was a bill from Diners Club credit card. Most guys my age had Diners Club instead of the more prestigious American Express because Diners Club was willing to extend credit to young professionals. American Express wanted you to make it first before they would give you their prestige.

The next envelope was my phone bill for April, 1978. The sirens were getting louder, but they wouldn't be coming here; I knew from experience that the cops didn't bust their asses to get to a rundown building like this.

There were two glasses on the table. They were beer mugs from Butch McGuire's. I didn't touch them. I didn't need to. If I had them dusted for prints, I would bet a fortune that my prints—from my 1978 self—were on at least one of those beer glasses.

If I tracked down who the landlord of the building was, I would make another bet that the deposit for this wreck of an apartment came from a guy named Roy H. Hobbs.

The frame-up was pretty transparent with a lot of holes, but if my 1978 self didn't have a rock-solid alibi for last night, he would be spending a lot of uncomfortable time in a small room at the police station answering and re-answering questions from tough Chicago cops. To me, the evidence seemed highly circumstantial and sloppily planted. But, I knew all about Abel Burrard. I knew how cunning and vicious he was. Even if I had tipped off the cops about Burrard, they would look at Burrard as a harmless clerk at a hardware store. As trumped up as I thought the evidence was in the kitchen, there were guys serving life sentences in Joliet State Prison with evidence that was even less convincing. I know, I had written about some of them. I hoped that my 1978 self was out drinking last night with some of his cop buddies.

The sirens now sounded like they were inside my eardrum they were so loud. I looked out the window. There were three cop cars, lights flashing, cops running, this was the real deal. Whoever had tipped them off—if I had one hundred guesses, all the guesses would be Abel Burrard—had been convincing enough to get that bevy of cops to respond with such force to this neighborhood.

There was a back door leading out of the kitchen. It was unlocked. I opened the door and started down the stairs. Cops were in the alley. They saw me. I didn't know what to do so I held up my hands to let them know I wasn't dangerous. However, my gun was still in my right hand.

"Drop it!" a voice yelled from the alley.

"Don't shoot," I yelled back.

"Put your gun down!" the voice yelled back.

With my left hand, I felt the Wayfarer Commander for the Red Button.

"Put the gun down!" the voice yelled. *"Right now! Or you're a dead man! Put...the...gun...down...now!"*

I put the Beretta on the stairs. Surprisingly, I started to think clearer. What a fool I had been to try to run. I could have just calmly pushed the Red Button and *voilà*, I'm safely and seamlessly out of 1978 and back in the silo with Charles handing me a Gatorade Fierce. I don't think I was meant to be a Rambo-type or even an Indiana Jones-type; I was meant to write about cops and robbers and deviants and scam artists—not be any of them. As I stood there with my hands up, I wondered how much fingerprints change. I had left some of my fingerprints on the front and back doors, I was sure of that. I was also sure that my 1978 self's fingerprints were on the beer glasses. I had my prints on the Beretta. Would they all match? Probably yes. Crooks had used acid to get rid of fingerprints, so I guessed that they didn't change much over three decades. Heck, when I visited 1992, *my dog* thought I was my 1992 self. Dogs don't make mistakes like that. If scents don't change, I figured that fingerprints didn't either. So, my prints were there—on the doors, on the glasses, on the gun. Somehow I would have to help my 1978 self. I would figure that out later.

I heard one cop barreling through the kitchen. Two more were coming up the back stairs, their guns pointed at me. My left forefinger was on the Red Button.

"Get your hand off your belt! Get both of those fucking hands up in the air!" the cop yelled.

I heard a gun fire; I pressed the Red Button.

Chapter Thirty-Three

The entry into the silo was pretty even. Allred was there, not Charles as usual.

"You're bleeding," Allred said.

"What? I'm bleeding? *Where?*" I quickly glanced at my body. When I spotted some wet blood on my right shoulder, I felt the sting.

Allred went right to work. He unbuttoned my shirt and pulled it back. The wound was not deep. In fact, the blood had already started to coagulate. The white hole must have the healing touch of a saint.

"Come with me," Allred said, "we'll get you properly fixed up."

He handed me a bottle of Gatorade Fierce. I gulped at it.

"What's this tied onto your waist?" Allred asked. "Oh, it's my camera. Here, let me take that." He unwound the strap from my belt.

"Where's Charles?" I asked Allred. Every time I had re-entered Charles had been there.

"We don't know," Allred said.

"Charles is missing? Where?" I asked.

"Here, here, Roy," Allred said, "not so many questions right now. Let's get you fixed."

We took the elevator to the first sub-floor. My suite and the clinic were on that floor. We walked into my suite.

"Go over there and sit down," Allred motioned toward the couch in front of the big picture window. "You look awful." I saw myself in the reflection of the glass window. I was sweating like a fat man running for a train in July. I guessed that the white hole might coagulate slight wounds, but it didn't cool you down as you flew billions of miles in seconds.

Allred pulled out a cell phone and pushed one number and mumbled into the phone. He then walked over to the kitchen, took some ice out of the refrigerator and wrapped it in a towel. He handed the towel to me.

"The doctor will be here in about fifteen minutes," Allred said.

"What happened to Charles?" I asked.

"Tell me first what happened to you," Allred said, "then we'll talk about Charles. It doesn't look like you came from a good experience." Allred was the master of the understatement.

I slurped some more Gatorade Fierce. The scientists had been right: this was terrific stuff after traveling a billion or so miles. As I took frequent swallows of the Gatorade, I told Allred the whole story—really a continuation of where I had left off the last time we had talked. In our last meeting, Allred had warned me, of course, not to go back to parallel worlds where I had met Burrard. He feared that this unknown thing we called cosmic connection could somehow put Burrard on tilt. Allred's fears were right; Burrard had detoured into bloody uncharted waters.

"Why did you go back to 1978?" Allred asked.

I didn't want to say that I went back to kill a man. Allred said it for me.

"Did you go back to kill Burrard?" Allred asked.

"Maybe," I said. "I don't want to sound evasive, but my sole goal was to go back and try to make sure that Rachel, my ex-wife, would not be killed by Burrard. She's probably been murdered by Burrard a thousand times in a thousand parallel worlds—maybe ten thousand times, a million—but *in this one world*, I wanted her to live."

Allred was in his familiar pose; his thumb was propping up his chin, his forefinger stretched over his nose.

"That's why you got the stun guns from Leona," Allred said.

I was surprised that he knew, but why shouldn't he? He knew everything that went on in Allred's barn. His relatives were his key employees.

"Yes," I said, "I gave those stun guns to Rachel."

"You know that technology hadn't arrived yet in 1978," Allred said.

"Of course," I said, "I told Rachel that I had come from Japan and they had all these new gadgets."

"The Beretta?" Allred asked. "That was for self defense?"

I put my thumb up to my chin. "No," I said, "I brought the Beretta in case I felt that Rachel wouldn't be safe from Burrard. I brought the Beretta to kill him."

"Have you ever killed a man before?" Allred asked.

"Never even close," I said, "I've never tried; I've never had the chance. As a crime reporter, I've covered plenty of murders, but I'm not a violent person. As an adult, I've never even been in a fight. Heck, I think the last fight I was in was in the seventh grade. It was such an inconsequential event in my life I don't even remember who won."

Allred nodded. He didn't show any signs of disapproving what my intentions had been, nor did he show any signs of approval. He was just listening.

"Could you have killed another human being?" Allred asked. "Could you have killed a terrible human being like Abel Burrard?"

"Yes, I *think* so," I said. "I think *any* human is capable of killing another if there is serious motivation—like defending your family, or self defense—and this would have been the case of me protecting the only woman I have ever loved, a woman that has been killed *thousands of times* by the same guy. This time, *this one time*, I wanted to step in and save her. So, yes, Allred, once I determined that Burrard had not changed in that parallel world, I think I could have killed him. This may make me sound like a psychotic, but I don't think I would have lost any sleep after I killed him. I would not have grieved for that man's soul."

"Well this cosmic connection thing is something that we had never anticipated," Allred said. "We've never seen this before. It had never come up in our travels. The scientists here were going back and basically charting the historical similarities between the parallel universes. We had various checkpoints in verifying history from one parallel world to the next. For instance, one of the checkpoints was the Boston Red Sox."

"The Red Sox? The baseball team?"

Allred nodded and said, "Do you realize that in our travels the Boston Red Sox *never* won the pennant after 1918, except 2004, of course."

"How many trips did you guys take?" I asked.

"Verifying the Red Sox checkpoint, we probably took trips to over three hundred parallel worlds," Allred said.

"So the Red Sox were oh-for-three hundred?"

"Multiply that by *eighty-six years*," Allred said, chuckling, "and that would give them zero-for-twenty eight thousand eight hundred." Allred laughed, a little bit of the hyena heh-heh-HEH-heh punctuating his laugh.

"Even though they lost every year for eighty-six straight years," Allred said, "there were some inconsistencies."

"How do you mean?"

"Well, remember Bill Buckner's error?" Allred asked.

"Sure," I said, "it might be the most famous error in the history of baseball. It lost the 1986 World Series for them."

"Not really," Allred said. "In the same game in a dozen different parallel universes, Buckner *made* the play. He did *not* make an error."

"So how did the Red Sox *not* win the Series then?" I asked.

"Before Buckner made the error in our world, the Red Sox had allowed the Mets to tie the game in the bottom of the tenth. In the dozen games that I mentioned, where Buckner makes the play—end of inning. In each of those cases, the Red Sox lost the game in the twelfth inning. Most people forget that the 'Buckner Game' only tied up the Series for the Mets. In every case the Mets won the seventh game."

"Destiny?" I said.

"Maybe," Allred said, "maybe. Maybe it's that cosmic connection."

Allred got up and stretched, looked out at the Pacific Ocean and stood there and just stared. Maybe he was letting the concept of little inconsistencies settle in my brain.

"The point I was trying to make, Roy, was that we just compared points of history from different parallel worlds in parallel universes," Allred said. "There were very little variations. However, there were some occasional inconsistencies. There was only one major inconsistency. You may remember I mentioned to you that I visited Chicago one time and it was nuclear rubble. That was the biggest inconsistency we ever found. Out of over one thousand trips that was the only major inconsistency. However, your mission—as I described it to you—was *not* to do a scientific paper, to not do a statistical analysis or historical comparisons, but to do *exactly* as you have done. By doing what you have done, you have exposed something that none of us would have ever dreamed of—this cosmic connection thing. It also seems far, *far* more dangerous than I had first thought when you brought it up. I thought it was *nice* that there was this cosmic connection between you and Rachel. I never even imagined that it had its evil darker side. Even if we brought in a team of psychiatrists and psychologists, what could they tell us? They've had absolutely no experience in parallel worlds and its effects on people on these planets. What we're learning is that we have to very careful—very, *very* careful—when we make contact in parallel worlds."

Allred walked over to the refrigerator and pulled out a bottle of water. "Want one?" he asked me.

"Is there any Gatorade Fierce left in there?" I asked.

"Sure," Allred said and grabbed a bottle. The stuff sorta grows on you.

The doorbell to my suite rang. Allred went and opened up the door. It was Doctor Who, otherwise known as Doctor Julius Wu. He walked into my suite, looking at his clipboard. If Doctor Who and Charles were in a small room together, they'd see a lot of their own feet and could go days without seeing the other guy.

Doctor Who walked over and looked at my shoulder.

"Not bad," he said to Allred. "It looks like something seared the skin."

"A bullet," I said.

"Oh, yes, then, well, we should clean it thoroughly and I probably should put in a couple of stitches," Doctor Who said.

For the next ten minutes, Doctor Who cleaned my wound and put in four stitches. The whole time, he didn't say a word. Allred busied himself making cell phone calls. I sat there like a warrior and watched folks frolic on a Maui beach.

Doctor Who slapped a bandage on my wound and said to Allred, "All set."

"Good, Julius," Allred said. "Thank you."

Doctor Julius Wu, one of the strangest in Allred's merry band then picked up his small medical bag and left.

"While Julius was working on you," Allred said, "I was thinking of cosmic connection. Even now, it's difficult for me to grasp how powerful this cosmic connection is," Allred said. He took a long slug of water. "You've literally turned Burrard's mind upside down and inside out *by just being there*. Remarkable, quite remarkable. Just by you meeting with him seems to have thrown him completely off his destiny in that parallel world. That could be considered good since he was destined to go on and kill sixteen women, but now his mind is barreling out of control with the potential of killing even more."

"I have to stop that, you know," I said. "At least in that one parallel world, I can't let Burrard start a rampage of killings."

"Yes, yes, I understand that," Allred said. "I'm uncomfortable with it, but I don't see an alternative. It's something that *we* have caused. I think we should talk to Captain Ike Kilburne, our security chief. You've met him. He's had a lot of experience with violence; yes, a lot of experience. While you were getting stitched up I called him. He should be here any moment."

It sounded like Allred was calling in the Seventh Calvary.

Chapter Thirty-Four

Almost as if on cue, my doorbell rang again. Allred opened it and Captain Ike Kilburne walked in. Kilburne wasn't weird at all. He looked like a Special Forces lifer that would get antsy if his life wasn't regularly threatened.

Allred quickly asked, "Before we get into this situation with Roy, any word about Charles?"

I could tell that Allred was very anxious. This Gyro Gearloose of a guy, who was basically unflappable, seemed very nervous about Charles.

"Nothing," Kilburne said. "We've checked all the video. He did not leave the barn; he did not leave the grounds; we know that for sure. The last video we have of him is when he went into the silo. We just don't know where he was going."

Allred shook his head. "I don't like the sound of this, Ike. We'll wait five more hours. If he hasn't come back by then, I want you to call an emergency meeting among the scientists up in the boardroom."

"Yes sir," Kilburne said, "will do."

"Now, Roy," Allred said, "tell Captain Kilburne about your problems with Abel Burrard."

In just a few minutes I gave Captain Kilburne a pretty good summary of Abel Burrard and how he had gone haywire.

"You want to go back, right?" Captain Kilburne said.

"Yes," I said, nodding. "I need to."

"Un-unh," Captain Kilburne said. "No way do you go back alone. I'll go back with you but not until we get a better read on what's happened to Charles. He is our first priority."

"How long would that be?" I asked.

"Just a matter of hours," Kilburne said. "Then you and I and one of my men will go back to 1978. Fair enough?"

I would have liked to have gone back right away, but I understood. I just hoped that Rachel was carrying the weapons that I had given her.

After a few moments of silence, Kilburne said he had to go and walked out of my suite. He sure walked the part—his back was as straight as if a crow bar was his spine.

"What happened to Charles?" I asked Allred.

"We don't know precisely," Allred said. "He took off for a parallel world, and he didn't return when we expected him to. He's normally exceptionally punctual."

"So, can't you send somebody to find him?"

"Therein lies the problem," Allred said. "As you know, we give our scientists—and you, too—complete freedom in traveling. We don't monitor where each guy is going. We, of course, have many, many coordinated trips like when we were doing statistical analysis about the Red Sox and other historical comparisons, but each scientist is able to take what we call 'extracurricular' trips. The fact of the matter is: we don't know where Charles went."

"Don't you have some whiz-bang technical GPS system to track him?" I asked.

Allred laughed. "Global Positioning System? Hah! That only works on Earth. Where would you put the satellite to measure movement in thousands of parallel universes?"

If Allred didn't have an answer, I surely didn't.

"What about the computers? Couldn't you get a read-out from the computers to at least see what he had programmed in his Wayfarer Commander?" I asked.

"Yes, theoretically we could," Allred said, "but we never built the algorithms necessary to do that. It might sound fantastic that we didn't do that. You have to understand that these scientists—myself included—have lived in a corporate world where Big Brother Executive was always looking over our shoulders. The scientists—again me included—wanted *total* freedom on our extracurricular trips. Thus, we did *not* build the algorithms to track our travel. We *can* do that, of course, and all the information is in the computers and all of us could pitch in and write the algorithms. We'll decide whether we need to in five hours if Charles isn't back."

I got up off the sofa and stretched. My shoulder didn't feel bad at all. I needed to go back to 1978. More than ever, I felt that I needed to go back right away. Writing code to track where Charles had gone could take *days*. I needed to be in 1978 *now*.

"He could have gone to Easter Island," Allred said.

"What?" My mind was a billion miles away. Allred, of course, was still thinking about Charles. I was thinking I would need to stop down and see Leona at the Company Store to get a new supply of weapons.

"Easter Island. Charles has always had an interest in some of the mysteries of our planet," Allred said. "He's taken quite a few trips— perhaps fifty—to find out what Stonehenge was. You should ask him about it someday. Fascinating. Easter Island has become his latest preoccupation. He wanted to know—really know—how those monoliths were built and why. My guess is that he somehow got delayed at Easter Island."

"Well, I hope that's it," I said, "but, Allred, I need to go back to 1978 right now."

"Right now?" Allred said, "we've discussed that with Captain Kilburne. And besides, you should take at least one day off before you head back."

"I just need to go back for a few hours," I said. "Rachel probably knows about her roommate now. My 1978 self might be in jail. I just need to get back to just warn Rachel."

"Yes, yes, I understand," Allred said. "But, you should take Captain Kilburne with you."

"Maybe," I said, "but he's needed here because of Charles. Believe me, Allred, I'm not going to do one thing that could even remotely be considered dangerous. No way am I going anywhere near Burrard." I was pleading with Allred like a teenager pleading with his father to use to family car.

"Yes, yes, I understand," Allred said. I could see that he was clearly preoccupied with Charles. I could have said to Allred that I was going to go fly a kite to 1978 and he would have said, "Yes, yes, I understand." Charles missing somewhere out in hyperspace was far more serious than Allred was showing.

"I'll go see Leona now," I said, inching toward the door. I was somewhat reluctant to leave Allred. He seemed so preoccupied; his thinking took him so far away.

"Yes, yes," he said.

I turned to walk out of the suite. Allred was staring off into the Pacific Ocean.

"Roy," Allred said.

I turned. "Yes?"

"Roy, pack a bottle of that Gatorade Fierce with you," Allred said. "You're really pressing some of the limits of travel. It will help you, take some with you."

I almost said, "Yes, yes, I understand," but caught myself and said, "Good idea, thank you, Allred."

"And, Roy," Allred said, "be careful." He told me to be careful the last time we had met and I didn't exactly follow his intentions. Rachel also told me to be careful, and while I thought I was being careful, a cop shot me.

"I will," I said, and this time I made a personal resolve to not try to find Burrard, but to protect Rachel. I would leave Burrard to Captain Ike Kilburne. He looked like he would like to take out Burrard just for the pure fun of it.

Chapter Thirty-Five

J ust a few hours after I had arrived in the silo I went back to 1978. It was late afternoon on the same day that Janet Emerson had been found mutilated in a dreary apartment near Wrigley Field.

I reentered in the alley behind the Knight Cap and walked down to the same park where Rachel and I had enjoyed a hot dog lunch just two weeks before.

I sat on the same park bench. I was feeling a little woozy. And why not? Earlier in the day, I had traveled a billion or so miles back to Allred's barn, got my gunshot wound patched up, went to Leona's Company Store, watched her do some singularly spectacular pirouettes as she outfitted me again, and then, finally, was whisked a billion or so miles back to the alley behind the Knight Cap. I didn't want to land in that alley in Rogers Park. It was too close to where Abel Burrard might be. Before deciding what to do about Burrard, I needed to make sure that Rachel was safe. So, I chose the alley behind the Knight Cap as my familiar—and presumably safe—landing ground.

The landing wasn't easy. It's not like I went tumbling down the alley as if I had been thrown off of a truck. Like always, I landed on my feet without much more than a severe jiggle; my brain just *felt* like it had been between a cement wall and a crashing truck. After landing, I just sat down on the cement and tried to gather my equilibrium. If anybody had walked down the alley they could easily have mistaken me for a fried wino.

It took me a few minutes to gather myself and walk to the park. I had brought a new gym bag. My other gym bag was at the grungy apartment where Rachel's roommate had been found. That gym bag had nothing incriminating except for one Small Fry Stun Gun that I had kept for myself. I bet the cops would puzzle over that.

From my new gym bag, I pulled out a plastic bottle of Gatorade Fierce. I took a swig that would satisfy a rhino. I took another rhino swig. Amazingly, my head started to stabilize. I then reached in the bag and took out the Beretta. Leona had wrapped it in a Rolling Stones 2003 Tour t-shirt. While the stun gun was clearly of a different era, amazingly the Rolling Stones Tour t-shirt was still very current, except for the date. I stood up, unrolled the t-shirt, gripped the gun and inserted it under my blue blazer sport coat under my belt in back. I had seen cops do that in real life and in the movies, of course, but I never realized how uncomfortable it was. It felt like I had a five-iron back there.

I had positioned the gun at an easy reach as pure precaution in case I was surprised by Burrard. I didn't expect to see him, but if I did I didn't want to fumble through the bag and unwrap it from the Rolling Stones.

Walking to the park gave me my sea legs back. Just a block away was the hot dog stand where Rachel and I had ordered our lunch. In front of the hot dog stand was a pay phone. I sure missed cell phones. I walked down to the pay phone, dropped in a dime and dialed Rachel at the *News*.

She answered on the first ring.

"This is Rachel," she said. I could tell right away that she had been crying; it sounded the same way when we were in the midst of a divorce fifteen years from now.

"Rachel," I said.

"Homer!" she said. The modulation of her voice changed as dramatically as turning on a light in a dark room. From her voice I could tell she was glad to hear from me. "Where are you?" she said in a breathless whisper.

"At the hot dog stand right now," I said, "I'll be in the park where we had lunch in five minutes. Can you come over right away?" I didn't want to meet Rachel outside the *Tribune* building like I had before. I didn't know where Burrard was; I didn't want to be like a beacon standing out there by the light pole. I felt that Rachel would be safer if she just got in a cab and came to me. From there, we could plan the next step.

"Haven't you heard?" she asked, and then catching her breath, she said, "Janet is dead. Oh, Homer, Janet is dead. The police just left about an hour ago. They told me. I just got back from the ladies room—I've been crying for the last hour. It's so awful. But, they caught the killer."

"They did? They caught Abel Burrard?"

"No, not him. This is where it really gets scary," Rachel said. "The police didn't tell me. They just asked about Janet. Remember that Roy Hobbs? You know, the one at Butch McGuire's? The one who I said looks like a younger you? Well, the word flew through the news room here—he's been arrested by the police for murdering Janet. Nothing travels faster than when one of our own gets in trouble."

Shit.

"They asked me about him, the police did," Rachel said, "I told them I had only met him once, well twice."

"I told them about Abel Burrard," Rachel said. "I told them that Janet was going to spend the night with him."

"What did they say?"

"They took notes," Rachel said, "they asked if I knew Burrard's address. I told them that I didn't. I told them that I hardly knew the guy. I had just met him once with Janet. Excuse me for a moment, Homer."

Rachel had put down the phone. I heard her blow her nose. I heard her take a deep sigh. She got back on the line.

"Did you tell them about me?"

"No, of course not," she said. "I couldn't just blurt out that this older man—you, by the way—told me that Burrard was the killer. They think they caught the killer. Roy Hobbs."

"Rachel, I do know this for a fact: The cops have the wrong guy. Hobbs didn't do it. Burrard did. Burrard is still at large and that makes me really concerned. Can you leave work *right now*; take a cab directly to the park where we had lunch? Don't walk, take a cab."

"Yes, I can leave right now," Rachel said. "My boss told me to go home right after the police left."

"Do you still have that little stun gun I gave you?" I asked.

"Of course, it's in my purse."

"Okay, follow my instructions exactly," I said. "Take the stun gun out of your purse, turn it on, leave it in your hand, walk out of the *Tribune* building, and then get in a cab and get over here to the park. Got it? Tell me that you will do that exactly."

"Homer, you're scaring me now."

"Good, I want you scared," I said. "There is a reason to be scared. But come over here, and follow my instructions *exactly*."

There were mostly mothers and kids in the park. If I just watched them, one mother might consider me a possible predator. I didn't want that so I picked up a *Chicago Sun-Times* that was in a trash barrel. I quickly thumbed through the paper. Still no byline by my 1978 self. I couldn't remember back, but it sure seemed like an off-week for the 1978 Roy Hobbs. That would change in tomorrow's edition. Instead of getting a byline on the front page, the 1978 Roy Hobbs might be the front page story. Above the fold.

Chapter Thirty-Six

I pretended to read the rest of the paper, but behind my sunglasses my eyes focused on the different park entrances. I was looking for Rachel. It seemed that I looked at my watch every sixty seconds or so, more out of nervousness than actually noting the time.

I saw Rachel get out of the cab. I scanned the street around her. No Abel Burrard. I waved my hand up high to signal her. I didn't get the big smile that was so natural to Rachel. It's difficult for people to give the big smile when they're scared down to their toenails.

Rachel practically trotted toward me. I stepped toward her. Unlike our meetings before, this time we hugged as if we wanted to crush the air out of each other's lungs. Rachel held me extremely tight; I had forgotten how strong she was. I kissed her cheek. Her cheek was moist with tears that had sprung up after we had grabbed each other.

"It's okay," I said, whispering in her ear, "it's okay, it's okay."

Rachel trembled. I held her tighter. With my fingertips, I caressed her temple. I kissed her on the cheek and repeated my 'it's okay' mantra.

Her hand on my back slid down until it reached the Beretta underneath my jacket.

She pulled her head back and with wide unblinking eyes, still moist from tears, she asked, "You've got a gun?"

"Yes, don't worry," I said. I separated us. "Sit down here with me," I said, pointing to the park bench.

"Can you take some time off work?" I asked.

"I don't have any vacation time coming," Rachel said, "but I think my boss would let me take a few days off, considering everything. Why?"

"Burrard is extremely dangerous. I think you would be his next target."

"Why me?" Rachel said, almost squealing. "I never did anything to him. I hardly even know him."

"Burrard is *crazy*," I said. "When a person is as crazy as that, logic doesn't fit into the equation. So, I think we need to get you away from Chicago for at least a few days. I've got some resources—not the police—that could bring him in." Captain Ike Kilburne was my *resource*. That tough bastard wouldn't bring Burrard in for justice. He would just eliminate him from that parallel world.

"But, we've got to get you away from here," I said. "Is there a place that you could go—some long lost friend in another city?"

"My parents up in Milwaukee?"

"I would prefer not," I said. "It should be somebody that would be difficult for a guy like Burrard to trace."

"You think *my parents* are in danger?" Rachel asked, putting her hand up to her mouth.

"No, I don't think so," I said, "not unless you're around them. To keep them safe, I think you have to stay away until Burrard is captured. Give me somebody else."

"I've got an old boyfriend who moved to Indianapolis," Rachel said, with a wry smile on her face, "I'm sure he would let me bunk in with him." She reached over and pinched my ribs. I was delighted to see that she still retained at least part of her sense of humor.

"Is there somebody else?" I asked. "I'd hate to put you in an uncompromising position."

"Sure you would," Rachel said, "you've put me in an uncompromising position every night we've spent together. Which gives me an idea. How about *you*, Homer? You and I could go off somewhere. Florida? Hawaii? Paris?" Rachel's face brightened about a thousand kilowatts at her suggestion. "You can have your 'resource' take care of Burrard while you're chasing me around some deserted beach."

The mental picture of Rachel and me on a beach was instant. It made me smile. Another thought edged that image aside. The safest place for Rachel would not be here in 1978; the safest place would be back in the world that I had come from. I thought about this. I was able to bring things with me when I traveled through the white hole. I had brought my clothes, of course, but I also brought a gym bag. It seemed that anything that I held traveled safely with me. What if I held Rachel? Would both of us be able to travel back seamlessly to the world that I came from? This 'bicycle-built-for-two' concept had never come up in my conversations with Allred or Charles. But, shouldn't it work? Or, would it overload the system?

This led me to another thought. In all my travels, and all the travels that Allred talked about, they were all going to the *past*. Heck, Charles had traveled back over one thousand years to check out Stonehenge. There was never any talk about traveling to the *future*. Allred had never said, "Wow, you should see what happens in 2040 or 2240 or 4240." All the conversations were about the past. If, indeed, it was possible that the bicycle-built-for-two concept would work, would Rachel blow a fuse because *she* had traveled to the *future*?

Florida or the Bahamas or Hawaii seemed far less risky than Rachel and I trying the bicycle-built-for-two concept to the future. I would, however, have to ask Allred about the bicycle concept and why I hadn't heard any talk about traveling to parallel worlds in the future.

I wasn't sure if I could leave with Rachel to some exotic place. It would be wonderful, sort of like an exotic dream that had come true for an old man. While I might be able to delegate the rough stuff to Captain Kilburne, I'm sure I would be needed to draw Burrard out. The only solution that I could come up with was to *take* Rachel to some exotic place, get her settled in, hit the Wayfarer Commander to come back home to fetch Ike Kilburne, drink a gallon of Gatorade Fierce and then head back to 1978 Chicago to kill Burrard. Kilburne would go after Burrard like a mongoose after a snake. All that parallel world traveling might whack me out, but after Kilburne nailed Burrard, I could recover chasing Rachel on some grand beach.

Chapter Thirty-Seven

As much as I would have liked to have spirited Rachel away to Hawaii or the Bahamas or some other exotic port, I didn't. I didn't have the time. I didn't feel comfortable just putting Rachel on a plane by herself and if I would have escorted her, it would have taken too much time.

My solution was simple. We walked over to the South Shore train station near the Standard Oil Building. From there, I used cash to buy two tickets to South Bend, Indiana. I was going to stash Rachel at the Morris Inn, the hotel on the University of Notre Dame campus.

It was about a two-hour train ride to South Bend. When we arrived, we took a cab over to the Morris Inn. I checked Rachel in under a phony name. I pretended to be her father. The young clerk at the front desk, probably a student, looked at Rachel like he had breathed in some pixie dust and was instantly in love. Even though I paid cash for four days, they still had to run my credit card through their machine. There was no credit on that card, of course, it being a terrific forgery by Leona Kosinski. They wouldn't find that out by just taking an imprint of the card. They would need to try to run it through the bank, which they wouldn't do unless there was damage to the room.

"I don't want to pay by credit card," I said to the clerk.

He snapped his eyes away from Rachel. "I know," he said, "it's just something we have to do with every check-in."

I took Rachel up to her room.

"I think you'll be safe here," I said. "You'll fit in nicely. Notre Dame went co-ed five or six years ago, so you can walk around the campus and not be gawked at because you're a woman. You might have to spend three or four days here, so don't just lock yourself in your room. Go over to the Huddle—it's an on-campus snack bar. Go to the library. Burrard doesn't know you're here, you're checked in under an alias, so you will be safe."

I knew she would be safe from Burrard. She might, however, draw some attention from some football players. In fact, I thought Joe Montana was still a student at Notre Dame in 1978. At this time, he didn't know he was going to go on and win four Superbowls and enter the NFL's Hall of Fame. As I remember, I think Montana had married three times, so he did have a roving eye. I hoped his eyes wouldn't rove toward Rachel.

"You have two stun guns," I said, "the Small Fry Stun Gun and the Pen Stun Gun. Carry both with you at all times."

Rachel hugged me. "You'll be careful?"

"Of course," I said. "I'll be back in a couple of days. If it's longer than that, I'll call. How're you doing for cash?"

Rachel looked in her purse. I saw the Small Fry Stun Gun in there. She had a couple of twenties and several ones. In 1978 that would be enough for meals and sundries, but I took about ten twenties from my roll and placed them in her purse.

We kissed and I was then on my way.

I walked past the kid at the front desk who still had visions of Rachel in his head and felt like saying, "Don't even think it," but I waved instead.

I didn't even bother to take a cab back to the South Shore station. I walked behind the Morris Inn. Across the parking lot was a golf course. Standing close to the Morris Inn, out of sight of any golfers, I pressed the Red Button. Somehow, like before, the white hole found me and I was back in the silo in Allred's barn.

Allred was standing there with a bottle of Gatorade Fierce.

I reached for it and fell on my face. My fall wasn't a slow wobble and down; I fell forward as if I had been tripped and then pushed. Allred had tried to catch me, but while his mind was agile, his hands were slow and un-athletic. He was probably always the last one picked for kickball in grade school.

My face was bloody. Allred got me to sit up. He pressed a clean handkerchief against my nose.

"I don't know if you fell on your nose, or if it was an effect from the white hole," he said. "Let's get some ice on it."

We walked back to my suite. I had my head tilted back and it felt like the blood was just draining down my throat. Inside my suite, I sat on the couch. Allred got me a towel with some ice wrapped inside. This was becoming a habit, walking in to my suite bleeding somewhere and Allred being a medic.

Allred asked me to roll up the right sleeve of my shirt.

"What for?" I asked.

"I'm going to give you a little shot of this," Allred said.

"What is it?"

"It's something that Doctor Who came up with," Allred said, "for frequent parallel world travelers. It's sort of intravenous Gatorade Fierce. All the scientists swear by it. Without it, we would have to ground you for probably a week."

"I can't be grounded," I said, "not for a week, not for a day."

"I know," Allred said, "thus, I've got this for you." He held up the syringe. "The only problem with this is that you can't take this frequently—like no more than once a month or so, and absolutely no more than three times a year."

It sounded like powerful stuff. I didn't want to know what would happen if a person took this intravenous Gatorade Fierce twice in a month, or three times. I turned as Allred stuck the inside of my right elbow.

I put my head back on the couch and just rested. Allred put away the syringe. We both sat there looking at the Pacific Ocean.

"Any word about Charles?" I asked.

"None," Allred said. "However, we had a meeting among the scientists. They all agreed that we should write the algorithms where we can track each trip. They're all concerned about Charles."

"How long will it take to write those algorithms?" I asked.

"They're working on it right now," Allred said. "It shouldn't take long—these guys are very, very bright—but then we will have to de-bug it. Maybe a day, maybe two or three. It's a little complicated in that we have to work backwards. If it was just to track future trips, no problem, but we had taken such precautions for privacy for our 'extracurricular trips' that it's more difficult going backwards."

"I need to go back right away," I said. I brought Allred up to date on what was happening in 1978.

"I'll call Captain Kilburne right now," Allred said. He pulled out a tiny cell phone and pushed a button. He said, "We're ready, Ike."

"I've filled in Ike with all the details of your previous trips," Allred said. "I had him read parts of your *Monster Among Us* book, particularly some segments that dealt with Burrard's habits. It sounds like those habits have been severely disrupted by the cosmic connection, but you never know when he could revert."

Allred reached in his lab coat pocket. "I almost forgot," he said. "These are yours—your pictures—we had them developed."

"Pictures? What pictures?"

"Roy, remember when you came back with that bullet wound in your shoulder?" Allred asked. "You had my film camera strapped to your belt. I took it off you, and then I had the film developed. The old fashioned way—film, negatives, prints. Here they are."

I opened the envelope. There were six pictures of Rachel. The first one was when she was walking out of the *Tribune* building. I had caught her smile just perfectly. The remaining pictures were of Rachel walking toward me, each one revealing a smile that made me smile.

I looked at the negatives and held them up to the light. Like most color film negatives, they looked like a swirl of muted colors. I looked back at the pictures of Rachel.

"This is real," I muttered, "this is actually real."

"What are you mumbling about?" Allred asked.

"The pictures, they made it through the white hole," I said. "This is all *real*."

"Of course it's real," Allred said, "what did you think it was?"

"Oh, I don't know," I said, "it's just a paranoid mind, sometimes out of control. In the back of my mind, I thought strange things. I thought, *perhaps*, I actually wasn't traveling to parallel worlds, which somehow you guys had developed a process where you could take pictures of what a person was *thinking*. You would hypnotize me, and in that hypnotized state would feed my brain with suggestions. Your digital camera would somehow pick up those images."

Allred's hyena laugh was almost an explosion, HEH-HEH-HEH-heh-HEH-HEH!

"You actually thought that?" Allred asked, holding his side.

"Not thought it," I said, "it was just a question I needed to answer."

"The bullet wound to your shoulder wasn't the answer?"

"Actually, Allred, I forgot my doubts quite awhile ago," I said. "These pictures just reminded me of those doubts. Believe me, I haven't doubted anything for quite awhile."

There was a knock on my door. Allred walked over and opened the door.

Ike Kilburne stepped in. He looked like a senior executive from 1978. Gray slacks, navy blue sport coat, light blue shirt, rep tie, black loafers. I noticed that he had a belt like mine. Leona had done another good job at the Company Store. Ike carried a large briefcase—the type that salesmen would carry with samples of their products.

"I'm ready," Ike said, hooking his belt buckle with his thumb. "Where to?"

"There's a little alley behind the Knight Cap bar that I would like you to visit," I said.

"Just give me the coordinates," Ike said.

I chuckled to myself. Ike was at least ten years older than me. His body looked twenty years younger than mine. But the fact was: here we were—two old men—strapping on our twin Wayfarer Commanders, straightening our shoulders, ready to go off and kill a man. If we didn't kill him we knew that man would kill dozens more.

I told Ike the coordinates. We synchronized our belts. We walked down to the silo. We pushed the 'go' button.

Chapter Thirty-Eight

"So, this is your old landing pad?" Ike asked me as we stood in the alley behind the Knight Cap.

"Yep," I said, "it almost feels like home." I was feeling terrific. Whatever Allred shot in my arm, it gave me an energy lift where I felt like I was twenty-two. It could have been dog piss in that syringe, and if it was, shoot it in me again. But, not until next month, heeding Allred's warning.

"Let's start where Burrard works, Rutter Hardware Store," Ike said. No chit chat for him. He was ready for business. "I'm sure he's not there, but it's a place to start. Show me the way."

We jumped on the 'L' heading north. It would be quicker than taking a cab. It would take only ten or fifteen minutes to Rogers Park. The train rambled and clanked through neighborhoods on its elevated position, sometimes passing apartment buildings so close that I thought I could spit on them. I thought of the people who lived there. If they had lived before in Beirut, they probably thought their apartment was nice and quiet.

Nearing Rogers Park, the train rambled over the center of North Clark Street. I sat staring out the windows watching the shops pass on by.

"*Look!*" I said, almost yelping. I pointed toward the sidewalk. "I think I saw *Charles!*"

Ike craned his head closer to the window. It was too late; he didn't see who I was pointing at.

"You saw *Charles?*" Ike asked.

"I did," I said. "I'm sure it was him. Let's get off here." The train was pulling up to a stop.

We both got up quickly and walked out of the train, about four or five blocks from Rutter Hardware Store.

I had seen Charles about two blocks back. We backtracked down North Clark Street, going away from Rutter Hardware. After briskly walking for a block, we both spotted a figure not too many humans would have: oversize belly, stilt-like legs, thin shoulders, and tufts of white hair flowing like crabgrass from his head.

We picked up our pace to a trot. When we were about twenty feet behind Charles, I yelled, "Charles."

The man kept walking in a weaving, staggering pattern. When I saw him stagger, it crossed my mind—and probably Ike's—that this wasn't Charles; it was probably a North Clark Street derelict. We had been fooled by the white crabgrass hair that only a nerd or a wino could have.

We approached the guy we thought was Charles. I was a little winded, Ike wasn't. We stepped in front of the man.

It *was* Charles. Ike took him by the shoulders, held him steady and asked, "Charles, are you all right?"

Charles didn't respond.

Ike asked him again, "Charles, are you okay?" Clearly he wasn't.

"What?" Charles said. He squinted at us. Charles had beady eyes to begin with and when he squinted his eyes he looked feral, like he was sizing up his prey. He then looked straight at me, his eyes opening wider than I had ever seen before. "*Roy?*" he said, almost gargling my name.

Charles collapsed in Ike's arms. Ike sat him down on the sidewalk. A passerby would think that we were Salvation Army helpers attending to an old wino. Ike reached in his large briefcase. Inside the flap was a small vial. He cracked it open and held it under Charles' nose.

"Is that something like Allred shot me up with?" I asked.

"Nothing so exotic," Ike said. "Smelling salts. Good old fashioned smelling salts."

Charles whiffed the acrid stuff and his eyes popped open to the uncharacteristic bulging position. He blinked several times, seemingly trying to focus.

"Ike," he said, then, "Roy." The gargle was becoming a gurgle.

He pushed the smelling salts to the side.

"Help me up," Charles said, "help me up."

We walked over to a coffee shop. This coffee shop was just about four or five blocks away from the coffee shop that was across the street from Rutter Hardware Store. We sat down in a booth. Charles slumped against the wall. He looked awful. It's not like Charles ever had a *CoverGirl* complexion, but now it was whiter than a sheet of bleached paper.

"You want some Gatorade Fierce?" I asked Charles.

Charles blinked his eyes. "You have some?"

Gatorade Fierce was Charles' favorite drink. He was the one who had discovered it as the best elixir for reentry in the silo. I think he liked it better than any milk, coffee, beer, wine, soda, anything.

I reached in my gym bag and pulled out a quart jug of Gatorade Fierce. We didn't wait for a glass. I handed it to him; he tilted his head back and poured about one-fifth of it down his throat. He wiped his mouth with the back of his hand.

The waitress came over. Ike and I ordered coffee. We ordered some ice water for Charles.

Charles took another large swig of Gatorade Fierce. I don't know if the stuff really worked that well for dehydration, but Charles *believed* it could cure all ills. If Charles had cancer, he'd ask for Gatorade Fierce.

When we had our drinks in front of us, Ike said, "Charles, you know Allred has been looking for you—we all have. Allred is really concerned."

"I didn't think that I would still be here," Charles said, sipping his ice water as if it were hot.

"What happened? What are you doing here in 1978?" I asked.

"I've followed you before," Charles said to me.

"You've *followed* me? Why?"

"I was concerned," Charles said. "Allred felt comfortable just turning you loose, but I didn't. I really like the project that you're working on. In fact, *I* was the one who suggested it to the board—us scientists. I felt that we had to get somebody else besides us nerds—us scientists—to experience parallel universes. Sometimes we just can't see the forest because of the trees. I just wanted to make sure nothing went wrong on your early trips, so I followed you."

I nodded my head. "It's funny," I said. "A couple of times, I felt like I was being watched, but I could never pinpoint that feeling. I just shrugged it off as part of the experience of traveling to parallel universes."

Charles smiled. It would have been a prettier sight if he hadn't. "That was me," Charles said. "I wore disguises."

I know it must have been running through Ike's head just as it had been with mine: What type of disguise could Charles wear that would actually disguise his appearance? I didn't let my imagination wander trying to visualize it.

"What happened this time?" Ike said.

"I was concerned about Abel Burrard and all this cosmic connection stuff," Charles said. "I just came here to keep a look-out on Burrard. I hung out in a coffee shop across the street from Rutter Hardware."

"I know it well," I said.

"Anyways, yesterday I didn't see him at all in the morning," Charles said, "so I left the coffee shop. I just started to walk around and pretended like I was window shopping. I didn't notice Burrard come up from behind me. He had a knife cupped in his hand and then he held it tight to my ribs. He forced me into an alley. He looked like a madman. I thought he was going to kill me. In fact, as I was pulled into the alley I was thinking that I had worked like crazy at Intel, made a fortune, and then worked like crazy with Allred and the other guys where we had the greatest breakthrough in the history of mankind, and I, *I*, was going to catch my lunch by a madman in an alley in 1978. It seemed so unfair. But, Burrard didn't want to kill me. He wanted my belt."

Both Ike and I looked at Charles' waist. We hadn't noticed it before, but sure enough, Charles was beltless. His fat stomach mostly bulged over the waistband of his pants, but it was crystal clear that Charles wasn't wearing a belt.

"You gave him your belt?" Ike asked. "The Wayfarer Commander belt?"

Charles nodded. "I didn't have a choice. He held a knife right up to my Adam's apple."

I saw a small dot where a scab had formed at the base of Charles' throat.

"Did he try to make it work?" Ike asked.

Charles nodded again. "As you know, Roy, it's not that difficult to work. It's highly intuitive. We made it *so* simple. Roy, you were able to operate it right off the bat, remember? Nobody would consider you a computer genius. But, Burrard had had some computer training. He fiddled with it and asked me some questions."

"Did you help him?" Ike asked.

"No, of course not," Charles said, "but I could tell by his questions that he understood how it worked."

"Did he tell you where he was going?" I asked. I was thinking about Allred back at the barn. Allred wouldn't have been any more match for Burrard than Charles was, and Ike—Allred's muscle—was here with me.

"I asked him where he was going," Charles said. "When I asked him, he started to laugh. He *really* laughed. He was laughing so hard I thought he might stick me with his knife by accident. It was like my question was the funniest thing he had ever heard in his life. He said he was going to 1992. He said he had some unfinished business with Mr. and Mrs. Roy Hobbs."

"Do you know which parallel world in 1992?" Ike asked Charles.

Charles nodded and said, "I had followed Roy on his trip back to May tenth, 1992. Its navigational points are saved on my Wayfarer Commander."

"In 1992 Rachel and I were married," I said. "At that time Burrard had killed only once."

"Well, if his 1978 self joins him, I bet that number will jump pretty quickly," Ike said.

I was trying to grasp the possibilities. If Charles' story was right, there would be *two* Abel Burrards in 1992—the 1978 Burrard and the 1992 Burrard. I shouldn't find that too crazy. After all, I had shaken hands with my 1978 self on a sidewalk outside Butch McGuire's. I remembered that I didn't have that cosmic connection with myself, but I did with Rachel, and somehow it had stirred up Burrard. The cosmic connection in 1978 had tilted Burrard's internal gyroscope and the result was that he killed Rachel's roommate. In 1992, the cosmic connection was working again as Burrard recognized me somehow.

There were now two Burrards loose in 1992, and both were crazier than a loon. Most likely, because the cosmic connection had tilted their internal gyroscope, both Burrards would be highly unpredictable. I, however, could make one prediction: both Burrards were headed toward my 1992 self and Rachel.

"Let's go." I said.

Chapter Thirty-Nine

C aptain Ike Kilburne and I arrived within seconds of each
other in 1992 in the alley in Rogers Park behind Rutter
Hardware Store.

Before we had programmed our Wayfarer Commanders, Ike and I
had discussed our strategy.

"You know I've got certain priorities," Ike had said.

"Yes?"

"First and foremost is the safety of Charles," Ike said. I agreed.
The safest place for Charles wasn't to go with us to 1992 even if he
had his Wayfarer Commander. He was weak right now and needed
plenty of rest. We took him to the Marriott and checked him in to a
suite. It was similar to the suite Rachel and I had shared just the night
before. I put one room key on the dresser; I pocketed the other one.
There was no Gatorade Fierce in 1978 so I had stopped at a grocery
store and bought a couple quarts of regular Gatorade, the old lime
stuff. Charles would have to adjust.

"Getting the Wayfarer Commander back is, of course, my second
priority," Ike had said. Once we retrieved Charles' Wayfarer
Commander from Abel Burrard, then we would retrieve Charles and
escort him back to our world. It was unsaid that to get the Wayfarer
Commander back from Burrard we would have to kill him. Killing
Burrard wasn't even a spoken priority; it was just a given. We both
understood it; we both knew that there was no other alternative. Both
Burrards—the 1978 Burrard who had stolen Charles' Wayfarer
Commander and the 1992 Burrard—would have to die.

"How're you feeling?" Ike asked me.

"I feel good," I said. That shot that Allred gave me was like getting a snort of the fountain of youth.

"I feel a little shaky," Ike said. I figured that two legs on the same trip could slow a guy down, even Ike who looked so fit that only death would make him walk a step slower. We stood there in the alley while Ike caught his breath.

"Okay," Ike said, "let's go to where Burrard works—the hardware store."

Rutter Hardware Store was just around the corner.

By the time we got close to the store, Ike was back to his normal steely self. I pointed to the coffee shop. "That's where I sat one morning trying to observe Burrard."

"Fuck that," Ike said, "let's 'observe' him up close."

Ike walked down the sidewalk like he was a professional walker—a forceful stride, erect as a bamboo tree. I followed as quickly as I could.

Ike stopped outside the front entrance of the hardware store and saw that I was right behind him. He stepped inside the store. I followed close behind, trying not to step on his heels.

The owner, Darrell Rutter, was at the front counter, just as he was in 1978 when I went looking for Burrard the second time.

I stepped in front of Ike and said the same thing as I did in 1978, "Hi, we're looking for Abel."

"You just missed him," Rutter said. He was as friendly in 1992 as he was in 1978 and as he was when I interviewed him for my book in 2001. I guess there are just some folks that are friendly to the core.

"Abel's nephew came here to the store," Rutter said. "Amazing likeness, he was, of Abel. Amazing likeness."

You don't know the half of it, I felt like saying. Instead I said, "Do you know where we can find them?"

"I gave Abel the afternoon off," Rutter said. "He's such a good worker—such an *excellent* worker. He rarely takes any time off, so I had to practically shove him and his nephew out the door. They mighta gone to see the Cubs play."

I doubted that.

"Abel still live on Jarvis Street?" I asked. I knew the house well. That house was where he had sliced and diced his victims and kept various body parts in jars of formaldehyde in a fortress-like room in his basement.

"Yep, Abel's still there," Rutter said, "still got trouble with the plumbing—still stinks because of the sewers, I guess. I've told him a thousand times he should sell that house, get a better one. I'd help him out."

John Wayne Gacy, the serial killer from Des Plaines, Illinois, who had killed thirty-three young men in the 1970s had a similar problem with a smelly house. Gacy, however, had buried his victims in the crawl space below his house. Burrard's house didn't stink like Gacy's because Burrard had purchased an industrial strength incinerator, but witnesses afterwards talked about the strange smells around Burrard's house.

We thanked Rutter and walked out on North Clark Street.

"I don't think Burrard is going to his house," I said. "I'd bet that he's going to the house on Forest Avenue in Evanston where Rachel and I lived in 1992."

"Let's check out both," Ike said. "First, however, we have to get some wheels. I'm not going to traipse all over Chicago on your elevated trains."

"How do we rent a car without a valid credit card?" I asked.

"We don't," Ike said, "we just borrow a car. C'mon, let's find some lonely car that wants to give us a ride today."

"You know how to hot-wire a car?" I asked.

Ike nodded and walked briskly down North Clark Street. I followed.

We turned at the next corner. It was a residential street of mostly apartments. Both sides of the street had cars parked bumper-to-bumper along the curbs.

"I figure most of these cars are parked here for the day," Ike said.

"How about that one, you like it?" Ike said, pointing to a Chevy, a late 1980s edition of the Malibu. It was dusty and looked like it had been parked in that spot for several days.

Before I could answer, Ike had popped the door with a long thin piece of metal he had taken from his briefcase.

"Get in," he said.

He sat in the driver's seat. He placed his hands under the steering column. His eyes scanned the street; he wasn't even watching what his hands were doing. He could hot-wire a car blindfolded. I watched his hands whirl and curl. He pulled a couple of things and within moments the engine started to turn over. Ike brought his hands to the steering wheel, then shifted in reverse, backed up a few inches, put the car in drive and we were gone. That simple.

"Where to?" he asked.

"Let's drive by my former house first," I said. "It should be quiet this time of day. If we don't see anything, then let's check out Burrard's house." I was concerned about Rachel. I thought that Rachel was still at home recuperating from her miscarriage, but I wasn't exactly sure. Three days ago when I had visited 1992, Rachel had been home gardening. I hoped that she was back at work.

"Okay, you navigate. Where do I turn?"

I guided us to my old neighborhood in Evanston.

We drove slowly past my house. Rachel was not in the yard gardening.

"Turn right," I said, "then turn right at the alley."

Ike drove slowly down the alley.

"Stop here," I said. "I want to see if Rachel's car is in the garage."

I jumped out of the stolen Malibu and peered through the garage window. Both cars were gone. When Rachel was working, she usually drove because sometimes she needed her car to track down a story. I hoped that was the case today. If she was at work, she was safe, at least for now.

"I need to make a phone call," I told Ike. "There's a pay phone up a couple of blocks at a magazine store by the train station."

"Who're you calling?" Ike asked.

"I'm gonna call Rachel at work," I said. "If she's there, I don't think we have to worry about her with the Burrards right now."

Ike nodded. At the magazine store, I got out of the car.

Ike honked the horn. I looked back. He motioned me to come back.

"While you're making that phone call," Ike said, "I've got another one you can call."

"Who?"

"Do you remember Abel Burrard's phone number?" Ike asked. "His place is our next stop. It would be nice to know if he's home or not."

"Good idea," I said. I got back in the car.

"What's going on?" Ike asked. "What about the phone calls?"

"Just a minute," I said, opening up my gym bag. "I don't know Burrard's phone number, but I'm sure I have it in here." I pulled out a Sony Vaio laptop computer. Ike looked surprised that I had brought my computer. He shouldn't have. He brought his tools—guns—and I brought mine, a computer.

In 1992 there were laptop computers, but nothing as slim as the two and a half pound Sony Vaio. Compaq made a so-called portable, but you probably could fit four or five Vaios inside the Compaq. If anybody had seen me and asked me about the Sony Vaio, I'd just say, "Japan." People would nod knowingly.

I had stored everything about *The Monster Among Us* on my laptop—manuscript, notes, articles, *everything*. I know I didn't print his phone number in my book, but I most likely had it in my notes.

My notes were carefully filed using Windows Explorer. One of the headings was *Burrard House*; there were thirty-seven files under it. I looked at the title of each file. The file 'Stats' most likely would have Burrard's phone number. I opened the file. Ike craned his neck to look at the screen.

"It looks like you got more shit on that house than a real estate broker," Ike said.

I nodded. I found the phone number. I took out a pen and wrote it down on a piece of paper from my shirt pocket.

I handed Ike the laptop, got out of the car and walked into the magazine store. The pay phone at the back of the store was not being used.

I dropped a quarter in the slot and called Rachel at the *News* first. On the second ring, Rachel answered the phone, "Hello, this is Rachel Hobbs." I didn't say anything. I had accomplished my mission—I had established that she was at work. But, I didn't want to hang up; I just wanted to keep hearing her voice. "Hello," Rachel said again, "Helllllooooo." When nobody answered, she hung up.

I dropped another quarter in the slot and dialed the number of Abel Burrard. If he answered, I didn't know what I was going to say, even if I was going to say anything at all. It might just be like my call to Rachel. A mute calling.

Burrard's phone rang seven times. Eight. Nine. Ten. I remembered that he didn't have an answering machine. When the phone had rung fifteen times, I hung up. He either wasn't there, or he was busy down in his basement showing his 'nephew' his secret rooms, his personal Hall of Horror.

I got back in the car.

"No answer from Burrard's house," I said.

"That's okay," Ike said. "Let's think this through. Where can he be? He's not at the store; he's not at your old house; he's not at his house. Eventually, however, he'll come to his own house. So, let's go over to his house and wait for him."

Ike put the Malibu in gear. "Point the way," he said.

We got on Sheridan Road and headed south toward Chicago. It would take less than ten minutes to get to Burrard's house.

"I looked through some stuff on your computer," Ike said. "I can't believe how much shit you got on Burrard. Where'd you get the architectural drawings of his house?"

"The cops," I said. "They had an architect draw it up, all the hidden rooms and stuff."

"You know how to get into those hidden rooms, I take it?" Ike said.

"I do," I said.

"Let's go there and wait for our boy…I mean, our *boys*."

Chapter Forty

W e were at the back door of Burrard's house.
We had found a parking spot about four houses down
the street from Burrard's. If I had a cell phone, I would
have called his house again from where we parked. There were cell
phones in 1992, but they were the size of bricks. And, those brick
phones weren't easily accessible to buy. I couldn't just walk in a
Walgreens and buy a cell phone like I could in my own world. Instead
of calling, we walked up to the front door like two Jehovah Witnesses
dressed in nice sport coats looking for converts, and rang the doorbell.
We stood there waiting. Unlike two disciples of Jehovah Witness, we
had no bibles, we had weapons; Ike had two guns on his body, I had
my Beretta tucked under my belt in back under my sport coat. Nobody
answered the doorbell; we saw no sign of life when we looked through
the window in the front door.

After nobody came to the front door, we walked around the back.
First we checked Burrard's garage. It wasn't attached to the house;
entrance to it came from the alley. There were no cars in the garage.

We had already checked the street for Burrard's car. On our way
over here, Ike had asked me what type of car Burrard drove.

"1982 Pontiac Firebird," I said. "He bought it used, but kept it in
cherry shape. The '82 Firebird was really popular. Do you remember
the TV series *Knight Rider*?"

"No, not really," Ike said. He didn't look the type to watch
mindless shows on television.

"Well, the '82 Firebird had a speaking part."

"Speaking part? The *car* talked?"

"The '82 Firebird's name was K.I.T.T.—it was a *talking* Firebird Trans Am. Funny part was that the car out-acted David Hasselhoff, the star of the show," I said. "The Firebird was sorta the poor man's Corvette. But, that car became an accessory in Burrard capturing his victims."

"How do you mean?"

"Well, as you know, Burrard looks like a choir boy," I said. "He *looks* like the son every woman would want. He could practically walk up to a woman, give that shit eating little grin, stammer a word or two and say, 'Hi, I'm a serial killer and you're my next victim,' and the woman would say, 'Hi, my name is...' He just seemed so *friendly*. When Burrard picked out his next victim—always a divorcee—he couldn't just jump her and haul her off the street. He *befriended* her in various ways, and eventually he got her in his Firebird. The Firebird was a cool car back then, and here was this altar boy offering a ride in his cool car. Once inside the car, it was pretty easy for him to chloroform her. She'd wake up in his basement."

Ike peered through the back door. "No alarms in this house, right?" Ike asked.

"Nope," I said. "Burrard didn't leave anything incriminating lying around the house. It was down in the basement in his secret rooms where all the evidence was. He could have left his doors unlocked and wide open and burglars would have never figured out his secret rooms, and even if they did find out where the rooms were in the basement, they'd never be able to get past the locks."

"You can, of course?"

"Of course," I said. "After all, I wrote the book." I had gathered all that information after the fact, after Burrard was convicted. But, now, I had all the arcane info that became our version of *open sesame* to Burrard's secret basement rooms.

There wasn't any secret in opening the back door—Ike popped it with his bogus Shell Oil credit card.

Ike stepped in. I noticed that his Beretta was in his right hand. His snub-nose .38 Smith & Wesson was holstered on his ankle. I pulled out my Beretta and followed Ike inside.

The house was small. We quickly walked through the kitchen, into the dining room and then into the living room. Each room was a little more bland than the previous one. If the furniture could talk, they would say *Sears,* and then *used.* But, the furniture would also say *neat.* The forensic cops could attest to the neatness. They could not find one piece of evidence—not even one tiny sliver of anything—that would connect Burrard to his serial killings, except for his secret rooms in the basement. Burrard lived as cleanly as only a mother could love.

"I can smell the insanity," Ike said.

"You can?" I said. I sniffed. My nose just told me that the air was stale. I couldn't even pick up some of that smell that Rutter had talked about. Maybe Rutter was right that it was a sewer that sometimes backed-up and occasionally needed to be fixed. As a young buck reporter, I had been to John Wayne Gacy's house just once. There was an undeniable rotting smell to that house. That was clearly understandable. There were thirty-some corpses buried in his crawl space. As much as he had tried to burn away the smell with mountains of lime, it wasn't enough. So, I didn't smell insanity at Burrard's house, as much as I tried. I thought it smelled like the house needed airing out.

"Madness," Ike said walking around the living room.

The house was extraordinarily neat. Transparent plastic covers stretched over the couch and chairs to keep the fabric clean. Just think, in twenty years, Burrard could take off the plastic covers and his furniture would look pristine used. Dimly in my memory, I remembered I had bought similar clear plastic seat coverings for my first new car in the 1970s. Made those seats hotter than hell in a Chicago summer.

Ike checked behind the couch, I checked the front closet.

We checked the upstairs. Three bedrooms and a bath. All as neat as anybody could make it.

Ike was satisfied that nobody was lurking in the house. "Okay, let's check out the basement," Ike said. "I don't think he's in his basement hideaway, but we sure gotta check to find out."

He let me lead the way. The door to the basement was in the kitchen. That door was always locked, but it was so easy to get open I could have opened it with my credit card. Ike, however, did the honors.

We stepped down the stairs one at a time. I let my Beretta lead the way. At the bottom of the stairs was an old basement. Over to the side was an old Kenmore washing machine with matching dryer. There was an old sink. Across from the Kenmore's was a large oil furnace. Its vents stretched across the basement ceiling like a large metal octopus.

"So where are the secret rooms?" Ike asked.

"If you could spot them easily," I said, "would they be secret?"

I walked over to the wall between the Kenmore's and the oil furnace. There was a stack of metal shelves that held old paint cans, some towels, a couple of cardboard boxes filled with rags, and old engine parts. I stepped up to the shelf, pushed one of the cardboard boxes to the side, reached toward the back of the shelf, and gently tugged the shelf toward me. Ike took a step back—he probably thought I was trying to topple the shelves right onto us.

The shelves didn't topple. The shelves pivoted out exactly as it should have—it was actually a door.

"Well, I'll be damned," Ike said. He examined the hinges. "I woulda never spotted it."

Behind the shelves was not an opening. There was another door, this one a steel one. It had a combination lock built into it. No combination, no entry.

"This guy was like Jack Benny," Ike said. I nodded at the grim joke. I had said a similar thing to Allred when he was showing me the security of his barn. Allred didn't react like he knew who Jack Benny was.

Part of Jack Benny's comedy was that he had a vault in his basement—complete with moat and alligators—to guard his money. Burrard wasn't guarding money. He was guarding body parts of the sixteen women he had killed and mutilated.

"I knew what the combination was after he had been captured," I said, tucking my Beretta in my pants so I could work the combination.

"We don't know if he had changed it, but there was no reason to. Still, you never know."

I tried the combination that I knew.

I turned the handle and the lock thunked open. I pushed the metal door inward.

We stepped in a small vestibule. There was a door to the left, a door straight away, a door to the right.

"The door over here," I said, pointing to my left, "was where he kept his victims until he killed them."

"How long would he keep them?" Ike asked.

"We don't really know for sure," I said. "Burrard never gave extensive details. And the prosecutor didn't need all the details—he had plenty of evidence to fry Burrard. The best guess is that Burrard kept most of his victims for just a few hours. Some, however, the police think he kept for a day, some for maybe up to a week."

There was a small window in the door. I knew what that one window would show us—a small room, dimly lit. There would be no furniture. The walls would be covered by hundreds of egg cartons that were glued to thick Styrofoam. The loudest screams would be muffled to a low hum. Rachel had been in that room, and as I stood there, I thought of how frightened she must have been.

Ike leaned over and took a quick glance through the window. He stared and then pulled his head back.

"There's somebody in there," he said, "a woman, curled up against the wall."

I looked inside. The woman was naked. I could barely see the side of her face. She hadn't noticed us looking in.

I thought of Burrard's victims in 1992. This was not Burrard's first victim, Marcia Kinnear. Marcia had been a natural red-head. At this time frame in Burrard's murders, he had not yet killed his second divorcee. If he followed the same timeline in this parallel world, that murder would happen in about a week. But, the woman curled up in that room was not the second victim. I remembered the description of the second victim. She was Judith Halkett, a chubby brunette of thirty-five or so. The naked woman on the floor was a thin blond. I stared at her. I would have to confirm it with my notes in my computer, but this woman looked like victim number nine or ten, a perky blond, Melinda Uline.

Burrard was way out of sequence with what he had done in my world. Had he killed eight or nine women already in this parallel world? Or, had the cosmic connection scrambled his sick brain to take women in a different sequence?

"Leave her there, for the moment," Ike said.

"Why? We can get her out right now," I said.

"We *will* get her out," Ike said, "but first we need to get Burrard. She doesn't know we're here. It looks like she's resting, so let's let her rest while we get Burrard—or should I say both Burrards. We better look at the two other rooms."

I led Ike over to the middle door.

"This is the incinerator room," I said. I opened the door. Ike held his Beretta aimed at the entrance. Nobody was inside. Inside were two large metal incinerators.

"Wow," Ike said, looking at the dual incinerators. "These look like something you'd find in a factory."

"They are industrial incinerators," I said. "You can see that one is attached to another. He'd burn body parts in the one on the left, but the smoke and the fumes would be fed in the incinerator on the right. That incinerator—at very high temperatures—would *burn the fumes*. He'd cart the ashes off and dump them in Lake Michigan."

"I can still smell something," Ike said.

"Yeah, ashes," I said. "I thought that Burrard had only killed once up to this point, so the smell wouldn't be too bad. But, I don't know, seeing that women in the room, there may have been more that have been incinerated." I explained to Ike that I thought that the woman, Melinda Uline, was thought to be Burrard's ninth or tenth victim. I didn't speculate on the effects that cosmic connection had on Burrard.

"Madness," Ike said. He didn't need for me to agree with him—we both knew that we were wandering through insanity.

I saw a *Time Magazine* on the floor to the left of the incinerators. I leaned over and picked it up. It was an old one. It featured the Olympian Marion Jones on the cover. The question on the cover was whether she could win five gold medals in the Olympics.

"This is all wrong," I said.

"What's all wrong?" Ike asked.

"This," I said, holding up *Time Magazine*.

"Marion Jones? I remember that cover," Ike said. "I remember how good looking she was. What's wrong about that?"

"The *date*," I said. "The date on this *Time* is September 11, 2000."

"A year before the terrorist attacks?"

"Not that. Ike, right now, you and I are standing in a parallel world where the date is *1992*. This magazine is dated September 11, *2000*. This magazine could not be in this basement unless somebody traveled to a parallel world and brought it back."

"Charles' Wayfarer Commander," Ike said.

"What makes this even worse is the date. Abel Burrard was caught on September 19, 2000. So, this magazine was published one week *before* Burrard was caught."

Ike nodded. "You're thinking that Burrard used Charles' Wayfarer Commander to go to a parallel world to warn off another—ah …ah…another Burrard—in the year two thousand?"

"Absolutely," I said. In my quest to save Rachel from Burrard *one time*, I had, of course, fantasized about going to a hundred parallel worlds and saving Rachel a hundred times. A thousand worlds? Yes, saving her a thousand times had occurred to me. What had occurred to me was what Burrard was now doing in reverse in a twisted demented way. It seems that he had gone back to a parallel world in mid-September of 2000 and warned off a Burrard that he was about to get nailed. Along the way, he had picked up a *Time Magazine* and brought it back with him. Was he going to use Charles' Wayfarer Commander to go back to a thousand parallel worlds and keep a thousand Burrards out there killing and mutilating?

"The last room?" Ike asked. "Let's get through this house and then wait for that bastard—*those* bastards—to come back."

I dropped the *Time Magazine* where we found it.

"The last room is the killing room," I said. "He butchered the women in there. Saved some body parts in formaldehyde jars."

We walked over to the third door. As usual, it wasn't locked. I started to open the door but it shot open like it was spring loaded. The door slammed against my face and I fell backwards. Burrard leaped out like he was a jack-in-the-box on amphetamines. With a swift hammering move, he knocked the gun out of Ike's hand and just as quickly Burrard recoiled and hit Ike in his jaw with the barrel of his gun. Ike went down on the floor like a sack of potatoes.

My Beretta was still tucked in my pants. I stood there staring at Burrard. The Burrard that I was staring at wasn't the younger version that had come from 1978. This was the thirty-five-year-old version of 1992.

"I want your belts," Burrard said, pointing his gun at us.

Chapter Forty-One

My nose was bleeding in a red stream. I wiped it with the back of my hand and it looked as if I had painted it red. The door that Burrard had propelled so savagely had hit my nose square, probably breaking it.

"Let it fucking bleed, asshole," Burrard said. This was not the gentle-as-a-field-mouse altar boy Burrard of 1978. His eyes were large and wild; his upper lip was snarled; his hair, usually so neatly combed, was disheveled like he had been in a wind tunnel. Every demented cell in his body had risen to the surface like a parallel world's Mr. Hyde. This was a psychotic who had proved in countless other parallel worlds to be a killing machine, but here, due probably to an infusion of cosmic connection he was more fucked out of his wits than even he could imagine.

Ike lay on the ground moaning. For the first time, he looked his age. His gray hair before had looked like steel wire, now it looked like an old man's that needed a trim.

This was a different Burrard than I had written about. The Burrard I had written about had always been charming to men. He was charming to his court appointed defense attorney, he was charming to the male prosecutor, he was charming to the judge, he was charming to his jailors. Heck, he was charming to me. He didn't kill men; he didn't mutilate men. Women were his prey. But, now, Burrard pointed a gun at us, two men that he had disabled in a flash of amazing adrenaline.

"You," he said, pointing his gun at me. "Stand up, stand up."

I stood up. Blood was dripping from my nose like a leaky faucet that badly needed a new washer.

"Put your hands in the air, you know, just like in the movies," Burrard said.

I put my hands up in the air.

"You know that Red Button on the belt?"

I nodded.

"If you reach for it, I will shoot you dead before your finger even gets close," Burrard said. "Yes, Roy, I know what the Red Button does. That's how I got back here. I was fiddling around with it in 2000, talking to Abel-2000, and I ended up here in a blink of an eye. So, don't think that you're gonna escape by pushing that button."

I tried to follow what had happened. It seemed obvious that Abel-1978 had jumped Charles, stolen his Wayfarer Commander and went to 1992. Then somehow Abel-1992 went to 2000. It was like passing a baton, but it seemed that they were *all* still in the race.

Then Abel-2000's face slightly softened. "Look, Roy," he said, like we were long lost buddies, "I don't want to kill you. I just want your belts. Once I have them, I'll just lock you in with Melinda. Then, man, I'm outta here. Trust me, somebody will find you. They just won't find me."

I had been right—the naked girl in the room was his tenth victim, Melinda Uline.

"How many have you killed?" I asked Burrard.

"What?" he asked. "How many? I don't know. I don't know."

"You don't know?" I asked. Burrard had always known before. He knew who his eighth victim was; he knew who his fourteenth victim— Rachel—was. His victims weren't nameless faceless women to him. He kept track just like a Cubbies fan kept track of how many home runs Sammy Sosa had hit.

"I just got here," Burrard said. "From 1978."

"You're from *1978*?" I asked. It didn't seem possible that this guy in front of me was the young Abel Burrard who I had met in 1978.

"I stole the belt off of that weird old man," Burrard-1978 said without answering my question. He was too intent on telling his story. "I didn't know what to do with the belt, but it's relatively easy to figure out. In that little viewfinder on the belt, I saw some previous trips that the old guy had taken and somehow—I really don't know how—but *somehow* I knew that an Abel Burrard in July of 1992 had started to do what I had always been *dreaming* about. *My dreams were coming true!* Every one of them! I pushed a button and like magic went to 1992 and right nearby was Rutter Hardware Store. I went inside and Abel Burrard of 1992 *knew* me, said that he was *expecting* me. We came to this house. I *knew* this house as if I had been living here, but I had never seen this house before in my life. Abel and I talked all through the night. It was strange—we were like identical twin brothers. We were thinking alike."

"But, you look different than you did in 1978," I said. I was pressing my fingers firmly against the side of my nose trying to stanch the blood. It seemed to be working; the blood was slowing to less than a trickle.

"I *am* different. I've aged," Burrard said. He was talking softly. I could see the gentler Burrard surface occasionally like a branch floating down a river. "I aged right in front of Abel when we talked all night long. He told me to look in the mirror. I *had* aged. I was starting to look like his younger brother. But, then I went to 2000. When I came back, I looked in the mirror and it was so weird—I looked *exactly* like Abel-1992, *exactly*. I had aged fourteen years in the matter of just a couple of days."

I guess that answered the question I was going to ask Allred: why was all traveling to past parallel worlds and *not* to the future? It seemed that traveling to parallel worlds was a one-way street. You could go back in time—heck, Charles had even gone back to the beginnings of Stonehenge—and it was like a walk in the park. But travel to the future and you would age like you had put your biological clock on fast forward. Burrard-1978 had aged more than the *fourteen years in just a couple of days.* If he didn't travel to the future again would he age normally or had his travel to the future triggered a hyper-aging event?

Ike groaned loudly. He was starting to gain consciousness.

"Stand him up," Burrard said. I helped Ike get to his feet. He didn't look his normal vibrant self; he still looked like an old man who had played too many shuffleboard games down in the sun of St. Petersburg, Florida.

"Hold up your hands, old man," Burrard said.

Ike glared at him, but did raise his hands.

"So where is Abel-1992?" I asked, referring to the 1992 version.

"I don't know," Burrard said. "We decided that I should try to go to another world just as I had done here and see if I could save another Abel Burrard. Together we chose 2000. It seemed to us the right year. I went to 2000. I met Abel-2000. He, too, *knew* that I was coming. He said he had been *waiting* for me. Abel-2000 had taken from the world sixteen women that should not have been living; he took them *before* they could have children. They would not have been good mothers. *I know*."

Burrard's mother had, of course, been divorced. That, by itself, surely didn't create the Abel Burrard that was standing in front of us. She had, however, blamed her divorce entirely and fully on Abel. The blame wasn't personified just verbally; the physical manifestation of blame was just as great. For instance, Abel's mother *never* touched Abel except in beatings. If he wanted a hug, he got a slap. 'You don't deserve a hug,' Abel's mother would say. '*You* caused your father to leave; *you* caused us to get a divorce.' Kisses, of course, were out of the question. Once when Abel was just ten or eleven, they were watching television and they saw a mother kiss her young son. Abel's mother yelled that it was sinful, that the son was going to hell. To make the point more dramatic, Abel's mother took a jalapeño, sliced it open and spread the juices over Abel's lips. 'This is what your lips will feel like in hell. Burn! Feel it burn!'

I had written two full chapters on the hell Abel had lived in as a boy. It was the toughest two chapters I had to write. I wasn't trying to make the readers feel sympathetic to him—how could anybody feel sympathetic to a serial killer—but I had to at least try to show where his evil had germinated from. How his mother had treated him was, of course, inhumane, but to make it even worse the psychologists I had

241

interviewed felt that Abel's mother was clinically insane. They felt, without much reservation, that her insanity could easily have been passed along to Abel genetically. Abel was probably insane from the get-go, then toss in his mother's continual abuse and Abel Burrard was the finished product.

"Okay, enough of this," Burrard said. "It's time I take control of your belts. Take off your shirts first," Burrard said.

"Our shirts?" I asked.

"*Your shirts*", Burrard said, his voice was a scream, but without the volume. "When your hands reach the bottom button, be very careful. If I think you're going for that Red Button—even just *think* it—I'll shoot."

Ike and I unbuttoned our shirts.

"Now take your shirt off and drop it daintily to the floor."

We dropped our shirts as if they were hankies.

Ike's torso belied his age. His skin looked old and textured, but it covered muscles that looked like they had a lifetime of workouts.

"Now your shoes, take them off," Burrard said.

I looked at Ike. He nodded as if he was acquiescing.

I bent down to untie my shoe laces. Ike did the same.

I *felt* the bullet whiz by my leg. The noise was as if somebody had dropped a cherry bomb next to my ear.

Because I was a half step in front of Ike, Burrard's view of Ike's hands was partially blocked and he couldn't see Ike take his snub-nose .38 Smith & Wesson from his ankle holster. Ike took out his gun, aimed it between my legs and fired. Who knows which body part I would have lost if I would have moved a fraction of an inch.

The bullet hit Burrard-1978 hard on his left side, close to where his heart should have been. He fell against the wall. Burrard-1978 was hardly conscious, holding his side, his groan more of a whisper. He was bleeding from the side like I had been bleeding from the nose. I, however, had been able to stop my bleeding by pressing firmly against it; fingers weren't going to stop Burrard's wound from bleeding. The bleeding would stop when there wasn't any blood left to bleed.

Burrard dropped his gun on the floor. Ike picked it up. He leaned over Burrard and pressed his fingers against Burrard's neck.

"His pulse is really weak," Ike said.

I saw Ike's lips moving, but I hardly heard what he was saying. The gunshot was still echoing in my ears. "What?" I asked, pointing to my ears.

Ike leaned over and spoke loudly in my ear, "He'll be dead in two minutes." Then he calmly said, "Well, one piece of shit down and two to go."

While watching Burrard-1978 die, Ike put his gun back in the ankle holster. He reached over and tested Burrard's pulse again.

"He's dead," Ike said loudly. "Yep, he's dead. Let's get this guy out of the way. The other Burrard might show up any time."

Ike grabbed Burrard's shirt collar; and started to drag him toward the killing room.

"Grab something and help out," Ike said, pointing at Burrard. I hardly heard his words, but I figured out his gesturing. I grabbed hold of Burrard's waist and started pulling in synchronization with Ike's pulling.

We felt it before we saw it.

There was a small whoosh—sort of like walking down a sidewalk in New York when the subway rumbles below. You don't see the train, but you feel the air moving around you. With Burrard, the air moved, and then he disappeared. When I grabbed Burrard to move him, I didn't realize that I had my hand on his belt buckle. Burrard had been wearing his shirt untucked. I had—inadvertently and stupidly—pushed the Red Button on his belt. The white hole had snatched him from our grasp.

"Shit," Ike said. I could tell he was angry at my oversight.

"Where'd he go, do you think?" I asked.

"Probably back to his last stop. Was it 2000? We could follow him, but we don't know the coordinates. Maybe Allred and his boys have worked out the algorithms now, and we could catch up to Burrard, but for now, one dead fuckhead will arrive to another fuckhead who is running for his life from the law. I'd like to be there to see that reunion."

Chapter Forty-Two

"I want your belt," Ike said to me.

"What?" I said. I was still having trouble hearing because of the gun shot between my legs. It sounded like, however, Ike had told me the same thing that Burrard had. He wanted my belt, my Wayfarer Commander.

"I want your belt," Ike said, leaning toward my ear and speaking louder. "We need to get Charles back home. God knows how long he'll stay at the Marriott. He might be wandering the street right now. I've got to go back to 1978, get Charles and then head back home. Understand?"

I nodded. My hearing was spotty; listening to Ike was like listening on a cell phone that was on the borderline of its range. However, I caught most of his words.

"And, we need reinforcements," Ike said. "I need to take Charles back home, get reinforcements and come back. In the meantime, you stay here and wait for Burrard to come back. He will. Burrard-1978—the *dead* Burrard—told us that he hadn't seen Burrard since he got back from 2000. He probably came back right in the killing room. Burrard-1992 is probably bringing back another trophy. You've got a gun, and I'll leave my Beretta. You'll now have two guns, and if he comes back before I do, empty both of those guns in him. Remember, he doesn't know we're here—you'll have the element of surprise."

I didn't want to wait in Burrard's basement, but it didn't sound like a bad plan. We did need reinforcements. Ike was an impressive guy, but he was old, and it showed when Burrard had jumped us. We needed a couple of those studs that were part of the security team at

Allred's barn. I knew that I was certainly overmatched. I'm a writer, not a soldier-of-fortune. I might be able to handle myself in a bar fight—*might* being the operative word—but going toe-to-toe with a crazed serial killer was a mismatch that would yield one result: one dead writer. Allred had hired me to write one book, not chase multiple versions of a serial killer around various galaxies. So, as much as I didn't want to wait in Burrard's basement, I might not have to wait very long until Ike played the role of John Wayne and rode back in with the seventh cavalry.

"What about the girl, Melinda Uline?" I asked.

"Leave her be," Ike said. "She needs medical help, but she didn't look like she was in a critical situation. Just sit tight here, guard the fort, shoot Burrard-1992 if he shows up, and I'll be back in a couple of hours at most."

That seemed easy enough. Ike handed me his Beretta. "I'll keep my snub-nose .38 Smith & Wesson, just in case *I* run into Burrard getting out of here."

There wasn't much to say. The plan was set. I thought of Ike's return trip with reinforcements. He'd really be whacked out by the travel. "If Charles has any Gatorade left you should take a couple slugs of it," I said. "And, as soon as you get back, have Allred give you a shot of that stuff that Dr. Who concocted. It really helps with the jet lag, or I guess I should say, 'white hole lag.'"

Ike and I shook hands. He gripped my shoulder and squeezed. He had a grip like a vice; he was one tough old bastard.

I followed Ike up the stairs. We looked out to see if there was any activity. The street looked as innocent as a main street in a small town. Ike slipped out the back door, walked to the alley and was gone. I stood there looking through the back door window waiting to see if Ike changed his mind and came back. He didn't. He was on his way with my Wayfarer Commander to pick up Charles and take him home. I saw my reflection in the window. In that distorted glass, I *looked* like I had some soldier-of-fortune blood in me—I had one Beretta in my right hand; the other one was tucked into my pants. I may have looked the part, but I wasn't feeling the part.

I would have liked to have called Rachel at the Morris Inn at Notre Dame. Rachel, however, was safe back in 1978; I was in 1992 in a different distant universe. I could at least feel comfortable that she was safe. Of the Burrard's that I knew from the different parallel worlds, they were all accounted for. The 1978 Burrard was dead and sent to the year 2000; the Burrard of 2000 was hiding out from the law; the 1992 Burrard would probably be coming to this house within the next few hours. Rachel, in 1978, was safe.

The doorbell rang. It was a loud chime and it startled me. I jumped when it chimed, almost pulling the trigger and plugging the floor.

I stood as if I was flash-frozen.

The doorbell chimed again. Even when I was expecting it, the chiming made me jump a little.

It was the front door. I walked through the kitchen and the dining room. From the dining room, I could see the front door, but I couldn't see who was pushing the door bell. I stepped quickly to the living room, eluding the line of sight that a person at the front door would have if he looked through the window.

The front window gauze curtains were pulled closed. I could make out the silhouette of a man at the front steps. I inched over to the curtain, and pulled the gauze back to allow a sliver of a look.

Standing on the porch was *me*. It was Roy Hobbs of 1992. What the hell was he doing here? I then remembered that I had tipped him off in 1992 about Abel Burrard, but I didn't want him to traipse up the steps and interview the maniac. I wanted him to bring the cops.

The doorbell rang again. Typical me, I thought, just waltz in to a potentially dangerous situation and keep on ringing that damned doorbell. I thought what my 1992 self would do. My 1992 self would have first tried to bring in one of his cop buddies, I was sure, but at this point, there weren't a lot of divorcees missing. So, my 1992 self must have had a spare hour to come and looksee for himself. Instinctively I knew what his next step would be. He would come to the back door. He wouldn't break in like Ike and I did, but I knew he'd come around to the back.

I retraced my steps through the living room, dining room, and then the kitchen. A minute later, there was a knock on the back door. I didn't know if Burrard was watching from the alley or some other spot, but if he was, he might get spooked with my 1992 self hanging around the house. I'd have to get him on his way.

My Beretta was still in my hand. I couldn't tuck another gun into my pants—I had Ike's Beretta there—so I opened a drawer by the sink and put the gun there. I then opened the door.

"Hi, I'm Roy Hobbs of the *Chicago Sun-Times*," my 1992 self said. "Are you Abel Burrard?"

"No," I said. "He's not here."

"Mind if I come in?"

It was strange seeing my younger self. What a pushy bastard I was. "No, you can't come in."

"Do I know you?" my 1992 self asked. He might have seen some likeness—like height, weight, and maybe even hair style—but he could never connect the dots that I was him more than a dozen years in the future. If I told him that I was his future self, he couldn't believe me. Nobody could believe that type of story. I might be able to try to prove it with the Wayfarer Commander, but hopefully Charles was now using it to go back home with Ike.

"I do know you," my 1992 self said. Obviously he was feeling the cosmic connection. Of course he knew me; he just didn't know that he was me.

I was getting nervous about my 1992 self hanging around the back door. I didn't want him to scare off Burrard. Knowing myself, I didn't think that my 1992 self would just walk away. The only other option then was to bring him inside. That, by itself, wasn't a bad idea. After all, I had tipped him off about Burrard. I had wanted him to break the story about Burrard. It might as well be right now. And maybe, *just maybe*, in the process I could save Rachel's marriage to this brash, pushy reporter.

"C'mon in," I said, and stepped away from the door.

My 1992 self stepped in the kitchen. I could tell he was on edge. He didn't know if he should trust me. If I would have said 'boo,' he would have jumped.

"Who are you?" my 1992 self asked.

"I'm the one who gave you the tip," I said. "I will give you the biggest story of your career, but there is one condition."

"And that is?"

"I'm left out of the story altogether."

"Why the anonymity? Who are you?"

I could have said that I worked for a secret government organization and that I had been on the trail of Burrard for quite some time. If I would have said that, I knew he wouldn't believe me. I decided to tell him something that would be far more difficult to believe.

"I need to be left out of the story because nobody would believe you," I said. "Not in a thousand years. My name is Roy Hobbs. I am you, thirteen years from now, from a parallel world in a parallel universe."

Chapter Forty-Three

My 1992 self laughed. It wasn't a big barroom laugh. It was more like a laugh where you'd say 'sure' at the same time. I could tell, however, that he was on full alert. He probably thought he was in the midst of a madman—maybe Abel Burrard himself—and he was ready for any quick violence.

"I've got proof," I said.

"You've got proof that you are me?" the 1992 Roy Hobbs asked. "Be my guest. What's your proof?"

"Let's take likeness for the first step," I said. "Look in the mirror behind me, see any real likeness between you and me?"

I turned to face the mirror. He took two steps toward me so that we both faced the mirror.

The likeness was, of course, remarkable. I think that if I ran into somebody on the street that looked *exactly* like me, it wouldn't register. I would maybe see somebody that has the same size body, same weight, and coloring, but I wouldn't be jolted by seeing somebody that looked exactly like me. Somebody else would see the likeness for sure. But, if I stood next to that person and saw our likenesses in the mirror, I would be convinced.

When I had traveled to 1978 and compared my fifty-one-year-old self to my twenty-four-year-old self, there was a likeness—maybe like a cousin. Most people's appearance changes quite dramatically over twenty-seven years. But, compare my fifty-one-year-old appearance to my thirty-eight-year-old appearance, and it was a lot closer, particularly since I weighed about the same. If I had gained twenty or thirty pounds that would have distorted the comparison. We eyed our images in the mirror.

"You've got a mole on your right forearm, by your elbow," I said, rolling up my right shirt sleeve. I pointed to my mole on my right forearm near my elbow.

He looked at his. They looked identical.

"How about the small birthmark on your left calf?" I asked. "It looks like a teardrop. Want to compare?"

I pulled up my pant leg and let him see the birthmark. He didn't roll up his pantleg—he knew both birthmarks were exactly the same.

"If I dropped my pants," I said, "I could show you an indentation on my left buttocks. It was from a pellet gun, shot by Billy Bramlett, over by the railroad tracks. I was—*we* were—nine years old. He shot me—and you, of course—in the ass. It got imbedded, bled like a bastard, and we had to be taken to the hospital to have somebody dig it out. Five stitches, I think."

"Six," my 1992 self said. He stared at me like I was a ghost or something.

"What type of trick is this?" he asked.

"No tricks, I am from a parallel world in a distant universe," I said.

"You can read minds or something. This is some kind of trick?"

"Want to know the first time you jacked off?" I asked.

"No, I don't need for you to tell me that. And, you don't need to drop your drawers and show me your ass. So, if you are me—from a parallel world—how'd you get here?"

I told him about Allred. He, of course, knew about Allred. In 1992, Bill Gates, Paul Allen, and Allred were starting to get some press about their wealth. I told him about Allred's crew of scientists. I didn't talk to him about the physics on how this stuff worked mainly because *I* didn't understand it. If I had tried explaining it I would have just blabbered on like a crazy man. I told him that because his reporting career was so important to him that Rachel would divorce him in 1997.

"Bullshit," 1992 Roy said. "Rachel and I won't get divorced."

"You *will* get divorced," I said, "and just two years later, Abel Burrard will kill and mutilate Rachel. You eventually will do a book

252

about Burrard titled *The Monster Among Us* and it will be a best seller."

I told him about Abel Burrard. I told him about the 1978 Abel Burrard who had come here on a stolen Wayfarer Commander. I told him about Ike. I told him that Ike had shot and killed the 1978 Burrard.

"I've got proof on Abel Burrard," I said. "Down in the basement."

"You want me to go down in the basement with you?" he asked. The story that I had told him was, of course, the wildest story that he had ever heard. I thought of myself: would I believe such a wild-ass story? With the evidence provided, I think I would have to suspend my disbelief and accept the story, at least for the time being. But, crime reporters are half-man half-skeptics. I was hoping that the cosmic connection would somehow negate the skeptic half.

I reached in a kitchen drawer and withdrew Ike's Beretta. Roy took a step back. I turned the gun in my hand, holding onto the barrel. I held the gun out to him.

"Take it," I said. He hesitated. "You have some doubts about me. I understand that. But, I don't want you to *fear* me. I want you to fear Abel Burrard. I came here—with Ike—to kill him. I wanted to kill him for just one reason and one reason only—I wanted to save Rachel's life. She will die in a thousand other parallel worlds. In this world I wanted to save her. With you here, *I* don't have to kill Burrard. There's evidence in the basement that would put him in the electric chair. That's good enough for me. I would have achieved the one thing that I wanted to achieve—Rachel would live."

My 1992 self took the Beretta.

"Okay," my 1992 self said, "let's take a look downstairs."

"I don't want to alarm you too much," I said, "but because of the Wayfarer Commander, people can appear just out of nowhere. If Burrard shows up, use that gun in your hand."

"I don't even know what he looks like."

"You'll know when you see him," I said. "He looks like he's one crazy bastard."

"You could have just been describing yourself, pal," 1992 Roy said, "and me for believing all this shit."

Chapter Forty-Four

"Who's that?" 1992 Roy asked. He was looking through the window of the door of the first room. He saw a naked women scrunched up on the floor.

"In my world, that was Burrard's ninth victim, Melinda Uline," I said. "In this world, his internal gyroscope was put on tilt—I think by me—and I think that she was going to be the third victim."

"You have proof that Burrard killed two women?"

"This way," I said, tilting my head for us to move on. I felt awful about leaving Melinda in that room, but assistance would have to wait for a few hours or so. I thought of Rachel being in that room and my instincts were to help that woman right now. Still, we had to get Burrard first.

We walked over toward the third room, the killing room.

"This is where Ike shot the 1978 Burrard," I said. We had to step over the drying blood. I watched 1992 Roy. As preposterous as time travel was, he seemed to have accepted that he too had fallen into the Rabbit Hole and was believing it more with each step he took.

I was cautious when I approached the third door. This was where Burrard had jumped out like he had been jet-propelled. I stepped over to the side, out of the way of an opening door, and pushed the ajar door open with my fingers. It swung open; nobody jumped out. I stepped in the room.

It was a small room. The room was dominated by a large steel workbench. The top was black, but I could see some brownish red stains. In my book, police were able to trace seven different victims to those blood stains. As neat as Burrard was in the rest of his house, he was a sloppy workman down here. Over to the left, mounted on the wall, were tools for sawing. There was a large 7¼ inch circular saw. This could take off an arm in seconds. Off to the corner of the table was a large woodworking bandsaw. With this saw, Burrard could cut a body in half like he was slicing cheese. For finer work, like around hearts, Burrard had a variable speed scroll saw. Each of the saws he had taken from Rutter Hardware Store.

On the opposite wall were floor-to-ceiling shelves. On three of the shelves were seven jars of various sizes. The smallest jar was a Ball canning jar. Inside was an ear, floating in formaldehyde. A larger jar had a heart.

"Holy shit," my 1992 self said looking at the jars.

I had seen these same jars ten years later. At that time, however, the shelves had been expanded and there were over one hundred jars.

"There are some body parts of Marcia Kinnear," I said. "I don't know which ones, but they're there. This is where parts of Rachel ended up."

Whatever shred of disbelief that hid in the crevices of 1992 Roy's brain evaporated on the thought of Rachel becoming part of the collection.

"We need for Burrard to return," I said. "Ike is bringing back reinforcements, but that could be several hours. In the meantime, you and I will wait here for Burrard."

"How about waiting upstairs?" Roy asked.

"I know what you mean," I said, "I don't like these rooms any better than you. But, we can't be seen down here by Burrard until he steps in these rooms. If we're upstairs, he could see us through a window."

Roy nodded.

"Remember, as impossible as this may seem, *two* Burrards could show up. One would come back using the Wayfarer Commander to the exact spot where that blood on the floor is. That would be the Burrard from 2000—he would have taken the Wayfarer Commander off of the dead Burrard and come back. Or, Burrard of 1992 could just come in through the door in the kitchen and down the stairs. Or, I guess, both could come down here together. You and I just have to be ready for *anything*."

"We just wait here?" 1992 Roy asked.

"We don't have to wait in this room," I said. "Let's go over by the main door. We'll be able to hear him coming down the stairs."

There were two stools in the killing room and we brought them with us. We sat in the small anteroom and waited.

My 1992 self saw the *Time Magazine* on the floor. He picked it up.

"Is this real?" my 1992 self asked of the September 11, 2000 edition of *Time*.

"It's real," I said.

He turned the cover page and leafed through the pages. He pointed to a picture of George W. Bush. "This is the son of George Bush, our president?"

"It is," I said. "You won't know this, but the father lost to Bill Clinton. Clinton won re-election and the economy had never been better."

"No shit," my 1992 self said.

"In the late 1990s, fortunes were made in technology, huge fortunes," I said.

"What else happened? Did the Cubbies win anything?"

"Nope, the Cubs didn't win a pennant and they didn't make it to the World Series. The Red Sox, however, won the World Series in 2004."

"So, Rachel and I really got divorced?"

"You did," I said. "Or at least *I* did. Allred's scientists have found some inconsistencies from one parallel world to the other, but I have found it fairly consistent, by and large. I would bet a fortune that you and Rachel would get divorced. And, if you and I don't do something about Burrard, she will end up getting murdered and mutilated by him."

I thought of the body parts in jars in the killing room and I knew that my 1992 self was thinking the same thing.

"Can I avoid getting divorced?" my 1992 self asked. "You know I love her."

"Yes, I do know you love her, but you love the big story better," I said. "Remember, pal, I've been there, done that."

I've had talks with myself over the years—plenty of talks. I imagine that is pretty much a human condition—talking to yourself. I have had long talks with myself the morning after drinking too much. Those talks weren't too helpful for me the next time I was out with my cop buddies. We still drank like drunken sailors. I had, of course, long talks to myself about Rachel and our marriage. Sometimes those talks had an effect. I would improve. But, then the next big story would come along and I was off to the races, leaving Rachel not in the starting blocks, but back in the pasture somewhere. Now I was having a talk with myself, but it was with myself sitting just two feet away from me. I was looking at myself—thirteen years younger—and trying to give him advice that he had already tried to give himself.

"So, what do I have to do?" my 1992 self asked. "Quit my fucking job?"

"Don't get defensive on me, pal," I said. "You know what you have to do. You don't have to quit your job. You might want to quit drinking instead."

"I'm not an alkie," he said.

"Yeah, yeah, how many times have we said that to ourselves when we were hung-over the next day? I don't know if we are clinical alcoholics, but I do know this—you drink too much with your cop buddies."

"Those are my sources, man."

I laughed.

"What's so funny?"

"That's what I told myself," I said, "that the drinking was needed for my sources. I found out after Rachel was killed—and I cut down on my drinking a lot—that I didn't need to drink to get information. I wrote the whole book *The Monster Among Us* without drinking and I had a zillion sources."

"You wrote a book?" he asked. "*I'm* going to write a book? I never saw myself as a writer of books."

"Yeah, I wrote a book. In fact, it was a best seller. But, it was about Abel Burrard and the women he had killed. Including Rachel. I hope you never get to write that book."

"So, if I cut back on drinking, you think I've got a shot at saving my marriage," my 1992 self asked.

"Yeah, I do," I said. "Rachel still loves you. Heck, when she divorced me, she still loved me. She just needed to get away from me until I grew up. I always—and let me underscore this, Roy—I *always* thought I could go back to Rachel. Like an idiot I had looked at our divorce as a timeout, or maybe halftime. But, I never saw it as final. I know the way you're thinking—you're thinking the same fucking way I did—that after the next big story you'll change. I bet you've been thinking about this story, the one that we are living right now, and how it's gonna be above the fold on the *Sun-Times* for probably at least a week."

Roy nodded his head and a smile curled out of the side of his mouth. I knew the look well. It was the look that I had when I had been caught with my hand in the cookie jar. "Give up drinking, eh?" he said.

"That's what I would do, if I could do-over my life," I said. "I can't do-over my life, of course, but you can change yours."

"So, er...Roy...can you give me some big tips on some stories?" my 1992 self asked. "You know, like you gave me here. Like which big political scandal could I get the scoop on?"

I laughed. "You're such a 'scoop animal,' but forget the scoops for a minute," I said. "Answer me this: are you going to quit drinking and save your marriage to Rachel? Give me a yes, no, or maybe right now."

Roy hesitated while he thought.

"Times up," I said. "You aren't gonna give up the scoops for Rachel. If you gotta think about it, you aren't gonna do it." I felt bad for myself. This wasn't a do-over for me—to help save the marriage of Roy and Rachel—but it was close enough. I wanted to see that marriage work.

"No, you're wrong," he said. "I was thinking about it. I was thinking could I do my job without drinking? I felt that I could. I love Rachel, and if nothing else, this goofy time travel with you has got me refocusing on what I need to do. So, Mr. Time Travel hot-shot guy,

I'm gonna quit drinking, and quit chasing scoops as if my life depended on it. Rachel will think we're newlyweds."

"Well, in that case, I will give you one scoop of the future," I said.

"Yeah? Okay, let me hear it."

"Microsoft."

"Microsoft what?"

"Buy every share you can," I said. "You know that three grand you got in that emergency fund in the bank?" Roy nodded. "Take it and buy Microsoft. Let's see, Microsoft in 1992 was probably selling for five dollars. If I count the splits, that one five-dollar share would be worth probably two hundred dollars in ten years. With the three grand in the bank, that would translate to over a hundred thousand dollars. Roy, that's over a hundred thousand! You and Rachel will never have that type of money. Knowing your finances, you probably could get a hold of another ten grand. That ten grand would escalate to over four hundred thousand. And you could buy on margin. If you bought another ten grand or twenty grand on margin, you'd be worth over a million in a decade. So, my advice to you: quit drinking and buy Microsoft."

A voice sounding like it came from the top of the basement stairs interrupted me.

"Oh, Roy," the voice said, "oh, Roy, yoo hoo, yoo hoo, this is Abel, Abel Burrard."

My 1992 self and I looked at each other. I clearly felt the terror. I could tell that he didn't. He was still after a story.

"I've got something for you, Roy," Abel Burrard said.

I clenched my Beretta so tightly I thought I could dent the steel.

"Yoo hoo, Roy, listen carefully."

I heard Rachel scream. It was a horrible scream, filled with more terror than I had ever heard before.

Rachel then screamed my name in a long screech that made my heart thump as if it was going to explode, "Rooooyyyyy."

Her scream echoed down the stairwell, "Roooooooyyyyyyyyy…"

Chapter Forty-Five

Rachel was standing naked at the top of the stairs.
Her ankles were tied together.
Her arms were pinned behind her back.
Blood was running freely from a cut that started at her belly button and ended somewhere in her pubic hair.

Even from where I was standing at the bottom of the stairs, I could tell that the cut was deep. It looked like there was a flap of skin loose near her belly button.

A knife was being held to her neck.

The knife was held by Abel Burrard.

"Come up, gentlemen," Burrard said. "Yes, come on up. And, oh yes, leave those nasty guns down there."

My 1992 self looked at me. I nodded and we both put our guns down on the floor.

While my 1992 self and I were getting to know each other in the basement, Abel Burrard had waltzed into his house with Rachel in tow. I assumed she wasn't brought in naked. He then stripped her, held her at the top of the basement stairs and sliced a deep cut in her abdomen for the sole purpose of catching our attention. It worked. I was terrified for Rachel.

As we climbed the stairs, another person standing behind Rachel emerged. It was another Abel Burrard, possibly a few years younger.

As we got to the top of the stairs, Burrard pulled Rachel back and the other Burrard resumed the position of holding a knife to her throat. Her bleeding edged past her pubic mound and started to stream down her legs. The first Burrard aimed a gun at us.

"Mr. Hobbs, so good to see you again," Burrard said. He clearly was speaking to me and not my 1992 self. "I never thought I would see you again, but I do appreciate the time you spent with me in regards to your book."

Burrard was acting as if it was him that I interviewed. This wasn't the same Burrard. He looked *exactly* like the Burrard that I had interviewed in prison. How could this be possible? The Abel Burrard that I knew had been electrocuted in 2003. I had been asked to be a witness at the execution, and I gladly accepted the invitation. I saw Burrard eat electricity until his eyes popped out.

Burrard laughed. "Yes, it's me," he said. "I'm the very same guy you interviewed. You're wondering how it's possible. Easy. You interviewed me in a different parallel world than the interview you were thinking about. You're forgetting, Roy, you interviewed me in *hundreds* of parallel worlds. You're probably confusing me with the Abel Burrard that you interviewed in your particular world, who unfortunately, was electrocuted. In all of these parallel worlds, I was destined to die, but I was saved just this week from the 2002 parallel world. If I wouldn't have been rescued by Abel here, I too would have been electrocuted. He *saved* me! Wonderful thing, this time travel is, isn't it?"

We were now upstairs in the kitchen. It looked like Rachel was in a state of shock. She was crying, but it was quiet; her eyes had glassed over. The other Burrard had wrapped a blanket around her. They had probably had her in that blanket when they brought her in the house.

"Take her downstairs," the first Burrard said to the other one. "Put her in with Melinda."

I stepped in front of the other Burrard. "She needs medical attention," I said. I don't remember getting an answer. Everything had gone to black. When I regained consciousness, my hands were tied behind my back and I was trussed to a kitchen chair. It didn't take me too long to figure out what had happened. It was obvious that the first Burrard hadn't taken kindly to my concern for Rachel's condition, and had slammed his gun into the back of my head, knocking me out. Even though I couldn't touch it with my hands, I could feel a large bump at the back of my head pulsate.

At the table were two Burrards and two Hobbses. The Hobbses were tied up. The Burrards were not and they had the guns.

"Ah, you've rejoined us, Roy," the Abel Burrard-2002 said.

"You're probably wondering so many things, aren't you?" Burrard-2002 asked. That innocent altar boy look was still there in the general view of his face, but the years of torment had etched lines that hardened his look. If he lived to be fifty—which he wouldn't in most parallel worlds—the evil would have turned his face into something that would have scared off puppy dogs.

"Well, I'll explain, and then I'll want you to do me a favor, okay?"

I didn't respond. There wouldn't be a favor that I would do for this whack-job.

"My friend here," he said, nodding to the other Burrard, "is the Burrard of 1992. He is who your 1978 Abel Burrard had come to visit using his magical belt. Abel, here, fiddled around with that belt and was able to program it to go to the year 2002. What did he find out? He found out that I, Abel Burrard, was going to die for the sole reason of killing those wanton divorcees. Pretending to be my cousin, he came to visit me at the jail. He wore the magical belt. He found out that the magical belt buckle was *not* made out of metal. As you know, all visitors to maximum security prisons have to take off their belts *and* then go through a metal detector. Abel did that. He took off the magical belt, cinched it under his shirt, and because the belt buckle is not metal, just waltzed in, clean as a whistle. During our meeting, he told me about the belt and how to use it. He then handed it to me. I pushed the right buttons, and here I was, out of jail and safe in 1992. Abel, here, played his part well when I had just disappeared—he looked as mystified as everybody else including the guards—and eventually was able to just walk out of the jail. To bring *him* back to 1992—where he had come from—we needed another one of those magical belts so I could go rescue him. That's when your old man friend helped."

"Ike? What did you do with Ike?"

"I haven't killed him, if that's what you're asking. He's safely stored in the garage. I've already tried to get some information out of him, but that old boy has surely resisted. But, you know, Roy, he's not in good shape at all. An old man like that ought to be sitting on a porch somewhere with a glass of lemonade instead of traveling through galaxies. What we did do, however, was confiscate his two magical belts. I was then able to go back to 2002 and rescue Abel here. Look at me, Roy, I really do fit a lot more nicely in 1992 than when you interviewed me in 2002, don't you think?"

Allred Kosinski had spent billions of dollars developing travel to parallel worlds in parallel galaxies. If Allred and his fellow scientists had stayed up nights and asked themselves what could go wrong, they would go a million years before they could anticipate this scenario. But, this was the scenario that I was living. With minds that were evil, this scenario presented great opportunity. With Allred's technology, Abel Burrard could protect thousands of Abel Burrards.

Burrard continued, "After young Abel freed me, I took a little side trip. I went to 2003. My, I never realized that my life would become a best seller. You did a wonderful job on that book, if I must say so myself."

Burrard-2002 got up and pulled the kitchen curtain back so he could look outside. He didn't see anything that interested him and pulled the curtain closed.

"In fact, I bought three of your books and brought them back with me. I use them as tools."

"Tools?"

"Of course, *recruiting* tools," Burrard-2002 said. "Some of the Burrards that I meet in different parallel worlds don't believe me. They're in denial. I show them your book; I show them that they are going to die in the electric chair. It's an excellent piece of persuasion."

"How many of those other Burrards have you contacted?" I asked.

"That's why we need more of those magical belts," Burrard-2002 said. "We have three of those magical belts right now, and I want to save as many of my...er...brothers, if you will...that I can. We'd like more belts. But, it's not like we can go down to Rutter Hardware Store and buy a bunch. That's why you're still alive. That's why I'm talking to you. I'm willing to make a bargain with you."

"That is?"

"Beautiful Rachel downstairs," Burrard-2002 said. "I'll let her live. She's a little nicked up right now, but nothing permanent—maybe a slight scar, but there should only be one person that sees that scar, eh? I'll let you, Rachel, and your 1992 self live. Just tell me how to program those magical belts to go back 'home.' I want to go to the person who makes those belts."

"You want more belts? Well, there aren't any more. That's all there is," I said lying. "It's a secret government program and they made just three belts. You've got them all."

"Why do I feel that you are lying?" Burrard-2002 said. "Maybe I should cut off Rachel's right nipple and put it on a plate right in front of you. I bet you remember seeing her nipple in one of my jars downstairs, don't you? Beautiful nipple, that right one was. So, maybe when you have it on a plate in front of you then you'll start telling me the truth and be willing to work with me."

Burrard-2002 had all of the cards, of course. He had my 1992 self and me as captives. He had Ike a captive someplace else. He had Rachel locked up in the basement, ready to carve up at the slightest whim. I didn't have any cards in my hand. It was a complete bust. I knew that Burrard-2002 was fully capable of slicing off Rachel's nipple and using that as his opening bid.

"You'd let us free?" I asked. "If I tell you how to program 'home', you'll let us free?"

"Absolutely," Burrard-2002 said. He must have thought that I believed him.

"You'll let Rachel, and Roy here, go?"

"Yes, yes, of course."

"And, you'll let me go, but back to my own parallel world?"

"Ah, Roy," Burrard-2002 said, "I can't do that. You know too much about this technology to let you go back to your own parallel world. I'll let you go here—in 1992. Just think, instead of writing books, you could be the king of the stock market. You'd be rich, you'd have women. You gotta stay here."

Then, as if a brilliant idea had flashed in his brain, he said, "Or, Roy, I'll be a little more flexible just to show you goodwill in your cooperation. You can go back to *any* year from 1992 or earlier. You pick the spot, we'll send you. We'll accompany you, of course, so that we can get our magical belt back, but think of the adventures you'll have, Roy."

"Why not let me back to 2000?" I asked.

"Roy, look at me now. I know you think I'm crazy, but do you think I'm stupid? You know the people that have been working on this time travel. It's not like some tinkerer in his garage. It must have taken years and a fortune to invent this. In the year 2000, they were probably pretty close. They might even have been testing it. I don't want you to go back, introduce yourself to them, and then come back, if you will, to kill me. So, consider me cautious, but you can go back to any parallel world as long as it's earlier than 1992. And you can feel comfortable that this Roy and Rachel live happily ever after."

I heard somebody slowly clomping up the wood basement steps. Burrard heard it too and snapped to attention.

"Who's that coming up the stairs?" he asked the younger Burrard-1992.

"I don't know. The two women are locked up."

"Go see, *idiot*," Burrard-2002 said, "with these magical belts, it could be anybody."

Burrard-1992 jumped from his chair, knocking it over.

The clomping continued, one slow step at a time.

Burrard-1992 jumped into the basement doorway. As soon as his feet had touched the floor, a shot exploded from the stairwell. Burrard-1992 was propelled backward. He dropped his gun as he fell against the back door. There wasn't very much blood from the bullet wound. I could just see a small hole directly, and evenly, between his eyes.

Burrard-2002 was on his feet, aiming his gun at the stairwell.

Allred stepped into the kitchen from the basement, stooping a bit to get through the entranceway.

Burrard-2002 pointed his gun at Allred.

"I'm the inventor of traveling to parallel worlds," Allred said, evenly, almost conversationally, to Burrard. "I imagine that you want to talk."

Chapter Forty-Six

Allred and Burrard-2002 each held their stance with guns pointed at each other.

"You invented these magical belts?" Burrard-2002 said, breaking the ice.

"I did," Allred said. "We call them Wayfarer Commanders by the way, but calling them magical belts would suffice."

Allred's normal slumping Gyro Gearloose posture was gone; he was standing tall like John Wayne in the movie, *Rio Bravo*. He held his gun steadily pointed at Burrard; there were no nerves showing on this Allred.

"It looks like we have a Mexican standoff here," Burrard-2002 said.

"Not really," Allred said. "*You* might think this is a standoff, but *I* think you're at a clear disadvantage."

Burrard-2002 laughed. "You do, do you? Why would you say that?"

"Well, number one, you're not really a man of guns," Allred said. "From what I've read in Roy's book, you're a knife and saw guy. I'm not even sure that you could hit me from where you stand. You might be able to wing me, but to kill me, I'm not so sure."

Wing me, I thought, who was this Allred? He was even talking the talk. He's a completely different persona than I've ever seen before.

"I, however, am a crack shot," Allred said. "If you looked at dead Burrard-1992, you'd find a bullet hole exactly between his eyes. If you used a caliper to measure the bullet hole from the iris of each eye, you'd find that bullet hole is no more than a centimeter off-center. In other words, if you shot me, the best chance you would have would be to wound me; if I shot you, you'd be dead before you even started to fall down, end of story. But there is a greater reason why we are not at a Mexican standoff."

"And that is?" Burrard-2002 said. I could see his gun tremble a little. Allred had been right—Burrard-2002 was not a man of guns. I wasn't sure if Burrard-2002 had even held a gun before this instance. Clearly he was a power saw and surgical knife guy.

"Suppose you got lucky and shot me dead," Allred said. "I wouldn't be dead for long. I have told my associates where I am. If I was killed by you, they would merely time travel to a parallel world just one month back, contact the Allred Kosinski of that parallel world, bring him back to all the things that we discovered, and Allred Kosinski would be alive just as much as if you hadn't pulled the trigger. In effect, you would have just wasted a bullet. You, however, if I shot you dead here, you would be dead for evermore. You avoided the electric chair; you wouldn't be able to avoid oblivion."

I'm not sure if I followed that logic, but it seemed that Burrard-2002 had accepted it.

"How did you know I avoided the electric chair?" Burrard-2002 asked.

"I was at the bottom of the stairs for quite some time," Allred said. "It's only when I realized that you had no chance that I came upstairs."

"No chance? Hah!" Burrard-2002 swiveled the gun to my head. "You may be able to kill me, but I'll take Hobbs here with me."

"Be my guest," Allred said. Allred must have noticed the alarm in my eyes. "Don't worry, Roy, we'd go back to a parallel world and bring you back. You won't even know you were killed. It would be like taking a short nap."

That sounded good, but I thought it was a bluff. I seemed to have remembered that Allred had told me that they had somehow protected themselves from their work being replicated in other parallel worlds. Allred had somehow figured out the physics of it all so that this *one Earth* was the *only world* where his parallel worlds work was going on. Sure, there were Allred Kosinskis in thousands of parallel worlds, but there was *only one* Allred Kosinski working on time travel, and he was standing in this kitchen like Clint Eastwood. Burrard-2002 didn't know that, but that's what a bluff was all about. So, Allred had shown us his John Wayne persona and now he was showing bluffing talents that would have baffled any pro card player in a Texas Hold'em Poker tournament.

"Now you understand we aren't in a Mexican standoff," Allred said. "However, Burrard, even though I am clearly holding the upper hand, I am willing to negotiate. How many of our Wayfarer Commanders do you want?"

I felt like screaming to Allred, *don't negotiate with Burrard*, but I didn't know where Allred was going with this.

"I'd like to have five," Burrard-2002 said.

"And, what do I get in return?" Allred said.

"I'll spare these lives here," Burrard-2002 said, nodding toward younger Roy and me.

"I think I've already got that," Allred said. "I want your commitment that if I let you go that you will stop the killing."

"Stop the killing?" Burrard-2002 said. I could see that he was absolutely surprised by Allred's demand. It was such an easy lie to agree to.

"Yes, stop the killing," Allred said. "Can you do that?"

"Absolutely," Burrard-2002 said, clearly feeling that he could lie his way out of this. "I've known I've needed help. If I went to some parallel worlds in the 90s, I could make myself rich on the stock market and afford the help I need."

"You wouldn't kill Rachel Hobbs in any other parallel worlds?"

"Absolutely. I wouldn't kill anyone," Burrard-2002 said. Burrard-2002 almost looked saintly in trying to convince Allred that he had seen the light. "I need help. Through these parallel worlds I've seen what a monster I had become; I would get help."

"Why should I believe you?" Allred asked.

Burrard-2002 put his gun down on the table. "I'm at your mercy. You can shoot me now, or you can help me save my soul. I want to change the Burrards that I have known."

Allred walked across the room and picked up Burrard-2002's gun. He looked at it like it was a valued antique and then set it back on the kitchen table. Allred stared at Burrard-2002. "I tend to believe you," Allred said. "I believe you enough to at least give it a try. If you didn't change, we could always come after you and get you."

"That's right," Burrard-2002 said. "I can prove it to you. You can always check me out."

"There is a problem, however," Allred said, "I don't have five Wayfarer Commanders with me. You would have to accompany me back to my base."

"I would?"

"Yes, and while you are there, I'm sure that my fellow scientists would want to spend some time with you. That would be one of the conditions," Allred said.

"Why would they want to spend time with me?" Burrard-2002 asked.

"They're scientists, not psychiatrists, so their interest in you would be the time travels that you have made. They would not condone the needless violence that was part of your life, but they would be very much interested in the physics of your travels."

"How much time would I have to spend with the scientists?" Burrard-2002 asked.

"Maybe two or three days," Allred said. "No more than that."

I could tell on Burrard-2002's face that he didn't consider the scientists a threat to him. Two or three days weren't even a blip of time. I was sure that Burrard-2002 was thinking that he could con those scientists for a lifetime, let alone just two or three days.

"So, Mr. Burrard, for some reason, I believe you," Allred said. "We will help you in your quest to save your soul and the souls of other Abel Burrards. Do you want to go back now?"

"Now? Right now?"

"Yes, right now," Allred said. "You've already got on a Wayfarer Commander. I could program it for you to go back to our base. I, of course, would accompany you. We would leave Roy and Roy here, but they would be tied up for just *minutes*—once we get back to our base, I would send somebody to free Roy and Roy and the two women downstairs. And, Ike, he's in the garage?"

Burrard-2002 had forgotten about Ike. "Yes, he's in the garage. He will probably need medical attention."

Allred nodded. "I should look at him now, but I want to get you to the base and the scientists. As you know time travel is almost instant going from one parallel world to another. I could take you back to our base, introduce you to some of the scientists and then, like I said, send somebody to come back to fix the situation here. I would be leaving Roy and Roy here for what, ten minutes?"

"Okay," Burrard-2002 said quickly. "Let's go."

"Open up your belt," Allred said. Burrard-2002 fiddled with it until it popped open.

"Now type in the numbers as I recite them to you," Allred said. He then slowly gave Allred the coordinates that he would need to go back to Allred's barn. There were thirty-six letters involved.

"Hold the belt up to me so I can see that you've typed in the coordinates correctly," Allred said.

From a few feet away, Allred looked at each letter that had been typed in the Wayfarer Commander.

"Those are correct," Allred said. "I've already got mine programmed in. So, what we need to do is almost simultaneous. I trust you Burrard, but not unconditionally. I don't want you to arrive more than a second or two earlier than I do. You need to press that square button 'go' and the second that you disappear, I'll push my square button. I will arrive just seconds after you do. We will, of course, leave your weapon here. There are no weapons needed back at the base."

"That's all?" Burrard-2002 asked.

"That's all," Allred said. "Once you push that square button, I'll see you just a few seconds later."

Burrard-2002 smiled. It was interesting watching his face. At one point, it was that harmless altar boy, so innocent and pure, and then a wrinkle formed on his forehead that seemed to start a chain reaction of wrinkles and twitches that was transforming his face to evil. Just before he pushed the button, his face was wrapped with a maniacal grin that he had beaten the rap. In one swift motion he grabbed his gun from the kitchen table and pushed the square button 'go.'

I felt a slight movement of air. There were no sound effects like a whoosh. Burrard-2002 had just disappeared.

Chapter Forty-Seven

Allred didn't disappear. He had not pushed his square button as he said he would.

"What's going on, Allred?" I asked, struggling to get my hands out of the rope.

"Let me untie you," he said. He jumped behind me and started to work on the knots. He wasn't very adept with rope. I could tell that he had never been a Cub Scout or Boy Scout. He wouldn't know a square knot from the Gordian Knot. Finally, the knots became loosened and I shimmied my hands out of the rope.

"Allred, you've sent that maniac back to the barn and he grabbed his gun and you're still here?" I asked practically yelling.

"Untie the hands of young Roy there," Allred said calmly. "I need to sit down."

I untied Roy's hands much quicker than Allred had untied mine. I looked over at Allred. Allred's hands were shaking like he was in the latter stages of cerebral palsy. He looked like he was going to faint. I quickly got a glass and filled it with water and held it up to his lips.

"I need to lie down," Allred said.

There was no doubt about that. My 1992 self and I helped Allred to his feet and we walked him, step-by-tiny-uncertain-step to the living room. It was like we were helping a ninety-year-old man shuffle to the bathroom. We set him down on the couch that had the plastic coverings. Allred's eyes rolled up under his eyelids. I felt his forehead. He was burning.

"Put some ice in a rag," I told Roy. "We've got to cool him down." I thought about Gatorade Fierce, but I didn't think Allred's condition was because of travel and I knew there was no Gatorade Fierce for another decade or so.

"Burrard-2002 is back at the barn!" I said. "With a gun! Let me use your belt to stop him."

Allred waved his hand like I shouldn't bother him.

Roy-1992 had put the icepack on Allred's forehead. It seemed to be an elixir. His eyes fluttered open. His breathing started to regulate itself. Some color started to spread through his face. A few minutes after that, Allred said, "Help me sit up."

We got him sitting on the couch. He took deep breaths.

"What happened, Allred?" I asked.

"I just hyperventilated," he said. "I've never been in a situation like that before. I was so frightened."

"You were?" I asked. "You acted like a combination of John Wayne and Clint Eastwood."

A smile started to curl on Allred's mouth. "I did, didn't I? John Wayne. Clint Eastwood. Yes."

"Where'd you learn to shoot like that?"

Allred laughed. He was coming back to life. "I always liked western movies as a kid. Gene Autry, Roy Rogers, Lash Larue, all of them. When I first purchased the farm outside Astoria, I had plenty of time on my hands. I learned how to shoot a handgun. I had hours of practice. Hours and hours! I even practiced the quick draw. It's the only physical thing I ever got good at. Ask me to hit a baseball, and you'd wait for the rest of your life to see me hit it. But, shoot, yes, I found out I had a real talent."

"How'd you know where to find us?"

"Well, the scientists had quickly figured out the algorithms so we could trace where each Wayfarer Commander was. We saw quite a bit of movement with Charles' Wayfarer Commander. And we saw yours and Ike's. There seemed to be a lot of movement emanating from the basement of Burrard's house. So, when you and Ike—especially Ike— didn't come back, I decided to go looking for you. I must have arrived right after you had gone upstairs and the younger Burrard had put Rachel in that cell. She doesn't look good at all, by the way, we need to get her to a hospital quickly."

Young Roy had already gone downstairs.

"What about Burrard-2002?" I asked. "He's back at the barn; he's got a gun."

It was as if Allred hadn't heard me. "Roy, there's a small satchel downstairs. It's mine. Please find it and give it to me."

"*What about the barn*?" I said, grasping Allred's shoulders.

"Don't worry," Allred said. "They can take care of themselves. Get me the satchel."

"What's in it?"

"There are three Wayfarer Commanders in there. For some reason, I thought you and Ike and Charles might need them."

I left Allred on the couch and went downstairs. I figured that Allred must have his big brute security guys waiting at the barn.

Downstairs, young Roy was holding Rachel, cuddling her. The other woman in the cell, Melinda Uline, was awake. Young Roy had put his jacket around her. She looked like she was in deep shock or drugged or both.

"Roy, I need to speak to you," I said. He looked up, still holding Rachel.

"Obviously, both women need medical attention," I said, "but before we get it, we need to get our story straight. As you know, Allred and I come from a different parallel world. Ike, who is wounded in the garage, comes from where we come from. We can't be here when the police come. We need to go back home. You, however, have a huge story here. *HUGE!* This is *page one* above the fold for a week. It might be a Pulitzer. You've got to say that you got an anonymous tip—which you did, only you and I know it wasn't exactly anonymous, that it was from me. You were following it up. You found your wife and Melinda Uline downstairs. You shot Burrard-1992 with his own gun. I know you can't shoot any better than I can, so you got a lucky shot, right between the eyes. Write the story, Roy, write it big."

Roy nodded as I talked. Heck, I knew what he was thinking. He was indeed thinking front page, above the fold.

"So, just hold on for a few more minutes," I said. "I've got to see what type of condition Ike is in. Then I've got to get Allred and Ike out of here."

Roy nodded again. He was already writing his story in his head. When he finally would sit down at a typewriter and write the story, it would already have been written and stored in his brain—he would just be typing it out.

I picked up Allred's black satchel and went to find Ike. Sure enough, I found Ike trussed up in the garage. Burrard-2002 was right; Ike was not in good shape. It looked like he had taken a dangerous whack on the side of his head. It was probably a concussion. I got him untied and slowly walked him to the house. I sat him down on the couch with plastic covers next to Allred.

"Can you two guys travel?" I asked. What a pair; both looked like emergency room candidates. "I mean, I think Ike's got a concussion, and Allred, you look awful. Can you guys make it through the white hole okay?"

"We should be able to," Allred said. "We won't be doing cartwheels for the next few days, but we wouldn't have been doing any of those anyway, so let's get on our way."

"I want you guys to go back to the barn," I said. "I'm going to go pick up Charles. By the way, Allred, Charles is in 1978. But, I can wait on Charles if you need me back at the barn because of Burrard-2002. But, I assume you've got a few of your bigger security guys that have already snatched Burrard-2002 back at the barn, so I don't think you'll need me."

"Burrard's not back at the barn," Allred said.

"He's not? I thought that's where you sent him."

"That's where *he* thought I was sending him too. I didn't. I lied."

"So where did you send him?"

"Remember when I told you about inconsistencies?"

I nodded.

"Remember when I told you I once went to Chicago and it was nuclear rubble? It was after that trip that I invented the Red Button so we could get out of trouble with just the push of a button."

I nodded again.

"I sent Burrard-2002 there, to nuclear Chicago," Allred said, smiling. "I could have shot him, plugged him between the eyes, but I thought that would be too easy of a release for him. I sent him to nuclear Chicago."

"But, when he finds out what you did, he'll just push the Red Button and he'll be out of there," I said.

"He can push the Red Button all he wants," Allred said. "He can push it to doomsday—which for him will probably be in less than a year after breathing all that radiation—but I gave him code that disabled the Wayfarer Commander with the last command that he typed in. Because of the code I gave him, that Wayfarer Commander will never work again. Believe me, Mr. Burrard-2002 got a one-way ticket to nuclear Chicago, end of story."

I helped put the Wayfarer Commander on Ike. He really was in bad shape.

Allred and Ike stood together in the kitchen. They looked like they should lean on each other to provide stability.

"You're going to get Charles?" Ike asked weakly.

"Yes, you just go back to the barn and get better," I said.

"Okay, Ike," Allred said. "Let's go."

They both pushed the square button and like the rabbit in a magician's hat were gone in a blink.

I went back downstairs. I motioned young Roy over to me.

"Allred and Ike have gone back to where they came from," I said. "I'm going to be leaving in just a minute. I just wanted to say 'good bye' to you."

We embraced. As we embraced, I whispered to young Roy, "Now don't fuck up this marriage. I've been able to give you the benefit of my experience. You could consider this a do-over for yourself and Rachel."

"I appreciate it Roy," young Roy said. "I really do. It's so strange talking to yourself—a little bit older self—but I listened. Believe me, I listened. We won't get divorced."

We shook hands.

"I gotta go," I said. "I just have one last word for you. I don't want you to forget it."

"Yeah, what is it?"

"Microsoft," I said. "Buy all the Microsoft stock you can get."

Chapter Forty-Eight

From the lobby of the Marriott on Michigan Avenue in Chicago, I called Charles' room. I let the phone ring and ring. Finally, a hotel operator came on the line and told me that nobody was answering.

I said, "I probably would have figured that out if you would have let it ring fifty more times." I didn't need to ask the operator if I was being rude—I could feel it with every word I said. I was tired, my body was wracked from bouncing from one galaxy to another, and my mind was putty from being threatened by various incantations of Abel Burrard.

The operator must have been used to snotty guests and in a nice tone of voice asked if I wanted to leave a message. I caught myself before I said something crude. I just thanked her, and then hung up. I needed to go and get Rachel from South Bend, Indiana, but I was first committed to getting Charles back to Allred's barn. That shouldn't take too much time; just slap the Wayfarer Commander on him, push the square 'go' button and then wave him good-bye.

I took the elevator to the fifteenth floor. Charles had the suite at the end of the hall. The door to his suite still had the 'Do Not Disturb' sign hanging from the doorknob. I opened up the door with the Marriott key that I still had from checking in Charles. I walked into the suite.

It was a mess. It looked as if a tornado had swept through the room. My first thought was that a white hole had been unleashed and had gone wild. When looking at the wreckage, however, I realized it wasn't a white hole. A party had been going on. There were various liquor bottles on tables and the floor. All but one of them was drained dry. Empty beer cans filled the waste paper baskets. The ashtrays were filled with cigarette butts, more than half of them having a red ring of lipstick at the end.

I looked in the bedroom. I fully expected to see Charles passed out on the bed, with or without a couple of spare bodies for companionship. The bed was as messy as the room, but empty. There were two crusted condoms on the floor. The suite was a bigger mess than any party I had experienced in college.

The bathroom stunk. Whoever had used it last hadn't flushed. It looked like a cow had taken a crap in the toilet. I flushed the toilet twice.

I went back to the living room and found a chair that wasn't covered with bottles or cigarette butts. I sat there thinking. I couldn't go back to Allred's barn and tell them I couldn't find Charles because he was partying. Everybody knew that Charles wasn't the partying kind. Heck, he couldn't even look anybody in the face, let alone be a party animal. If he ever would fall in love he would fall in love with the tops of somebody's feet. That would probably be a whole new definition of foot fetish. So, I would have to track him down.

I couldn't ask the Marriott about any disturbances. It seemed that they didn't know what had gone on in this suite. If they did know, they would have cleaned these rooms up pronto. I would just have to play detective and try to track Charles down.

The first place I looked was for any notes on the pad of paper near the phone. There was one note on the top of the pad. It was a phone number. Maybe the person at that phone number could tell me where Charles was. I dialed the number.

"Gino's East," a person said.

I knew Gino's East. "Pizza?" I said.

"Yeah, we got pizza. What can I do for you?"

Across the room, I was staring at a stack of pizza boxes.

"Did you deliver a bunch of pizzas to a party at the Marriott last night?" I asked.

"Yeah, I heard it was really wild," the pizza guy said.

"Do you know anybody that went to it?" I asked.

"What are you the cops?"

"No, I'm just trying to track down a friend," I said.

"Can't help you, bub," the pizza guy said and then hung up.

In the ashtray there were several spent books of matches. All of them were from bars in the area. I now had my assignment: I would check out each bar, trying to find Charles. Once I found him, I'd pack him up with his Wayfarer Commander and send him home to Allred. Then I would go get Rachel.

I stacked the books of matches in the order I would go. The first book of matches was one block away from the Marriott—the bar at the Wrigley Building. A lot of young professionals would go to this bar after work. Heck, I had met Rachel there plenty of times for drinks after work.

It wasn't difficult in finding Charles. He was perched on a stool at the front of the bar at the Wrigley Building.

He waved to me when I walked in.

All of his partying didn't make him a better looking man. He was wearing what looked to be a new red-on-black checked leisure suit. With Charles' egg shaped body, he could have passed for a fire hydrant at a Halloween party. The tufts of his white hair spiked straight up as if he had put his hand in an electric socket.

"Roy!" Charles said, like we were long-lost buddies. "Let me buy you a drink." He slurred when he talked.

Charles wasn't a pretty sight when he was sober; he being drunk just made it ridiculous.

"Charles, we gotta go," I said. "We gotta go back to the barn. Allred needs you."

"Of course he does, of course he does," Charles said, "but let's have a drink first."

The bartender leaned over the bar and said to Charles, "Hey, Future, want a refill?"

Charles said, "Yeah, sure."

"What did he call you?" I asked.

"Future," Charles said. "That's my nickname."

"What have you been up to?"

"I've had more fun than I've ever had before in my life," Charles said. "I've just been talking about the future."

"So they call you 'Future'?"

"That's short for 'Future Man.'" Charles said.

"What are you *telling* these people?"

"Easy stuff, like who is going to be president, who's gonna win the World Series. Everybody wants me to tell them that the Cubs win the World Series, but I tell them that it's not in the cards."

"And these people listen to this gibberish?" I asked.

"Well, I think they believe I have some psychic powers," Charles said. "It's all in the delivery. I give copious details, so it really sounds real to them. Plus, Roy, look at me. I do look like I'm psychic. I don't look like a movie star, I just look strange, I look different. I've looked different all my life. This is the first time looking different made me feel special." He then lowered his voice and leaned toward me. "I even got laid last night. Twice."

"Yeah, I saw the evidence," I said. "But, you gotta go back. Once back at the barn, you can come here as often as you want. But, right now, I told Allred and Ike that I'd get you back to the barn. They're in pretty bad shape, you know."

"What happened to Allred and Ike?" Charles asked. I gave him a quick synopsis of our Abel Burrard adventures. Just as I was finishing, a woman came from the back of the bar and put her arms around Charles' shoulders. She kissed him on the cheek. I guessed that she had been the owner of those crusted condoms in Charles' suite. Charles would have never carried condoms; if he did, he would have never figured out how to use them. This woman was his tutor.

And what a tutor she was. She was a tall bottle-blond, probably five-ten or so, making her a half head taller than Charles. She was mid-forties, probably worked in ad sales for one of the rep firms in the Wrigley Building, she had big knockers. I couldn't tell about her, but I could clearly see that Charles was in love.

Charles introduced us. Lola. Her name fit. She seemed nice. She also had a body that looked like it could hurt you.

I excused Charles and myself to Lola and pulled him near the entrance of the bar. "Charles, you gotta go back to the barn right now.

Then you can come back." This was like trying to get a drunk out of a bar. "After you're back at the barn, you can come back here any time. This is serious shit that happened with Abel Burrard. You gotta go back."

Charles nodded. He finally agreed to go back. He walked over to Lola and said he had to go on a short trip with me. Once outside of the Wrigley Building, we walked toward the Marriott. Charles stopped. "You're not going with me right now, are you?"

"No, I'll be back there in a bit," I said. "I have to go get Rachel."

"Then let's part here," Charles said. "I'm having a little difficulty walking. I'd rather take the Wayfarer Commander here. You got it with you?"

I nodded. I took the Wayfarer Commander from my pocket and handed it to him. He flipped the cover of his belt, typed in a string of commands.

"Thanks," Charles said, offering to shake my hand. He looked me straight in the eye. Strangely, when he looked me square in the eyes his eyes weren't beady like a snake's. They were normal. Or maybe that was the after effects of Lola.

"Why thank me?" I asked.

"Well, in a sense, you were the one who brought me to 1978," Charles said, the whole time keeping eye contact. "I've never been happier." Charles wore a level of confidence—even in that silly leisure suit—that I had never seen in him before. If I had to bet on Charles' future, I would bet that Charles was going to return to 1978 and live the life of Future Man with Lola, the woman who knew the magic of condoms.

"See you back at the barn," Charles said, and then he was gone, just as quick as that. If somebody had been walking down the sidewalk on Michigan Avenue, they would have seen me talking to a weird looking guy. An instant later they would have seen me, alone, walking down the sidewalk toward the train station where I could catch the South Shore to South Bend, Indiana.

Chapter Forty-Nine

When I knocked on the door of Rachel's room at the Morris Inn on the Notre Dame campus I was nervous.

Somewhere submerged in my subconscious mind I feared that somehow Burrard had been able to figure out where Rachel was. I didn't really believe that he could have got to Rachel, but I did have an underlying fear.

Rachel opened the door to my knock. She peered out through the slim space that the chain on the door would allow. When she saw me, her eyes lit up like a pinball machine.

"Oh, my God!" she exclaimed. She quickly shut the door, and I could hear that she was fumbling with the chain.

She yanked open the door and jumped in my arms. That neutralized another reason that I had been nervous.

It had only been a couple of days, but it seemed like *light years* since we had been together. Maybe it was indeed light years. I'd have to ask Allred about that; I never did understand the physics of time travel and light years. The one physics I did understand was what exhibited between Rachel and me.

Rachel smothered my face with kisses. It's difficult to explain, but this was almost like an out-of-body experience. I could certainly *feel* her kisses, and I could *feel* my lips when I kissed her, but everything seemed so unreal. Here I was with the woman that I have always loved—but she had died a horrible death—and now I was with her again, in the flesh. Certainly this was a younger woman, and I was an older man, but these two people, through a strange and wonderful incarnation were together again. This time, I was better for Rachel.

This time, I wasn't obsessed with a career. This time, my love for her was allowed to manifest itself. I was bothered a bit by the age difference, but she didn't seem to be. Somehow she felt my love for her through the difference of ages.

I didn't know where this would lead. I did know one thing, however. That one thing was that I had accomplished what I had set out to do: I had saved Rachel from Abel Burrard in at least one world. Mission accomplished. I had *seen* the 1978 Burrard die; the shot that killed him had flown between my legs to end his life forever. And, Allred had sent Burrard-2002 to nuclear Chicago. Two Rachels were to live.

Rachel pulled me into the room. It was apparent that there had been no party going on there. The room was neat as if it were being prepared for a picture in a brochure. The only thing out of place—and even that could have been considered a prop—was the book that Rachel had been reading, *War and Remembrance* by Herman Wouk. The book was over a thousand pages and it looked like Rachel was close to finishing it.

"What, have you been a hermit?" I asked.

"You better believe it," Rachel said. "It's been mostly reading, worrying, walking, worrying, eating, worrying, mostly worrying. There are some pretty good looking studs walking around this campus, you know, but this is the stud that I've been waiting for."

I really never considered myself a stud before, but in this do-over, I was Rachel's stud. If that worked for her, it worked for me. Rachel started to unbutton my shirt, but I worked faster on her buttons, and as quick as our hands could get our clothes off we were in bed, on top of *War and Remembrance*.

Afterwards we took a stroll down by the lake on campus.

"Am I safe?" she asked. She didn't even want to say Burrard's name.

"Yes, absolutely," I said. "You're safe."

"Was he killed?" Rachel asked.

"Yes," I said, "but not by me."

"Will there be something in the paper about him killing my roommate Janet?"

"No," I said. "But you are safe."

She snuggled up to me as we walked.

We stayed overnight at the Morris Inn. After dinner, we made love again, and then I nodded off. We weren't exactly like newlyweds who could break bed springs. I was exhausted. I didn't wake until morning. By that time, Rachel had already showered, ordered coffee, and read both of the Chicago newspapers.

We took the South Shore train back to Chicago. I didn't say much on the train. I was thinking about the future. I knew I had to go back. Allred wanted a full meeting on everything that had happened with the various Abel Burrards that we had stirred up. The question I had wasn't about going back to Allred's barn; I had to do that. The biggest question was 1978. Would I come back to 1978 and try to live the rest of my life with Rachel?

I thought the right thing would be to re-introduce Rachel to my 1978 self. However, I wasn't confidant that my 1978 self would do things differently than I had in the first go-round. Yes, I was certain that my 1978 self would fall in love with Rachel, they would marry, they would pursue their careers, and they would get divorced. The one element missing in 1978 that was there before was Abel Burrard. Rachel, after divorcing my 1978 self, would not be murdered and mutilated. She would just pick up the pieces of her life and live on. Obviously, there was nothing wrong with that. But, there would be pain along the way. I could eliminate that pain. If I came back, I would be loving her with the consistency that I should have had when I was chasing a career. The biggest difference would, of course, be age. No matter how much I wanted to twist time, I couldn't twist away that I was fifty-one and she was twenty-three. I could give her ten good concentrated years, maybe twenty years or twenty-five tops. That was a lot more years than I had given her before, but was it enough?

If I came back to 1978 to live, I would, of course, be rich. I would bring a lot of cash with me and then play the stock market like a maniac. So, I wouldn't have to worry about a career or money. And, my competitive juices of getting on the front page—above the fold—

had long ago left me. I would be coming back for one reason—to be with Rachel for as long as I could.

The strange thing was that it looked like Charles would be coming back to 1978 also. It's not that 1978 was a great year. Heck, of all the years that I had lived, it was pretty humdrum. Jimmy Carter was the president. I think 1978 was the year that Carter had the Camp David Accords between Anwar Sadat of Egypt and Menachem Begin of Israel. That was a big deal at the time, but in the end meant nothing. I think the Jonestown mass suicides happened in 1978. I couldn't even remember who won the World Series or the Superbowl back then. The *only* reason I went back to 1978 in the first place was because I first met Rachel on Wednesday, May tenth, 1978. I sorta screwed that up the first time; if I came back I would have a truly inexplicable, but real, do-over.

Once the train arrived in Chicago, we cabbed it to her apartment. I walked her through it just to prove that there wasn't a bogeyman in the closet.

I knew she wanted to get to work, but I sensed she did not want me to leave. We made love one more time, softly, slowly, like we were floating in a breeze. I didn't know if this was going to be the last time, so in case it was, I tried to savor each touch, remember the feel of each caress. Did fingertips have internal memories? I wanted mine to remember each touch on each part of her body. Did lips have internal memories? I tried to will my lips to remember, to remember the sensation of kissing hers, of kissing her breasts, of kissing parts of her body that had never been kissed before.

Chapter Fifty

T he first person I saw when I returned to the silo was, as usual, Charles.

This Charles, however, wasn't standing there with a full jug of Gatorade Fierce. This Charles was slumped against the wall, one leg folded under his body in such a position that it would have hurt like hell. If he had been alive. Charles was clearly dead. There were five bullet holes in his body; blood had spilled out freely on his red-black leisure suit. There was a bullet hole in his face, or more accurately, that had torn off the right side of his face from his eye to his ear. Charles was missing his right hand. What remained was just a bloody stump of a wrist. I thought of the security system. Allred was so confidant about his security; I guess he didn't think of an attack starting from the *inside*.

This wasn't some random shooting. This was an act of an automatic weapon that could deliver hundreds of bullets in less than a breath. I immediately thought of Abel Burrard. But, I had seen the 1978 Burrard die from a bullet from Ike; I had seen the 1992 Burrard die from a bullet from Allred; I had seen the 2002 Burrard go on a one-way ticket to nuclear Chicago.

I didn't have any weapons with me. I didn't think I would need any coming back to the barn. I looked to see if Charles had a weapon. He didn't; all he had was a broken bottle of Gatorade Fierce. He must have thought he was greeting me. Instead, at least five bullets from an automatic weapon greeted him. I noticed that his Wayfarer Commander belt was not on his corpse.

The silo was on the seventh sub-floor. I ran to the elevator. The elevator door was closed. I pressed my thumb and palm print to the security pad. I thought of Charles' hand being pressed by the killer to the same security pad. The elevator door opened.

I took the elevator to the first sub-floor, where my suite was. Down the hall, there was a body on the floor. I ran to it. It was Doctor Wu. He must have been on site attending to Ike and Allred. He had probably been looking down at his feet and didn't even see the fusillade of bullets flying until they ripped open his chest.

Further down the hall was Leona, Allred's twin sister, who had run the Company Store. Her legs were splayed out as if she had tried pirouetting her way away from a barrage of bullets. The pirouette didn't work. There were at least three bullet holes in her, two that had entered her side, one which had hit her square in the chest. Her skirt had fallen above her knees; I reached down to tug the skirt in a more conservative position, but then stopped, thinking, *she would have liked her skirt to look like it was flying in the wind*, so I left it the way it was.

The first thing I thought of was the weapons in the Company Store. I ran back to the weapons table. It seemed that every weapon that had been there was still there. I grabbed the last Beretta. It was about the only gun that I felt comfortable with. I took a box of bullets and loaded the gun. The rest of the bullets I dropped in my pocket.

I ran to my suite. The door was open. I tiptoed inside. My panoramic view of a Maui beach had turned to a slab of cement. The wall had been shot up like it had been a duck at a carnival shooting gallery. At the base of the wall were scattered mounds of the great high-definition screen that had become my Maui refuge to the world. The cement wall was pockmarked with small chips where the bullets had hit.

My laptop computer was on the floor. It too had been shot.

I took the elevator up to ground level. The large work room was a mess. On the floor in front of the elevator was one of Ike's monster guards. He was in his uniform—black boots, black pants, black shirt, all with no insignia. His black beret was on the ground about a foot from his body. All that blackness was punctuated by spots of red. This guard had been shot several times, just like Charles, Leona, and my Maui wall. I couldn't tell if this was the handiwork of one man or a platoon, there was so much damage.

Robert McDougald, the scientist with the hair that looked like an unraveled beehive was dead at his computer workstation. It looked like he had never looked up when the shooting started—he had been concentrating so deeply that the last thing he would have seen was on the computer screen. He'd taken two bullets on his right side. His beehive hair had taken a couple of hits and even in this gory tableau I expected to be seeing bees heading for the hills. Two of the other scientists were dead at their workstations. Neither had looked like they were trying to escape. As much as they knew about physics—and they knew more about physics than any group of people in the history of the world—it didn't seem that they understood the physics of a barrage of bullets heading their way.

This whole scene reminded me of the movie *Apocalypse Now*, where Martin Sheen goes upriver to kill Captain Kurtz, Marlon Brando. Sheen was on a riverboat and when they emerged from a deep fog, they saw Kurtz's headquarters with dead bodies all over the place. There were more dead bodies in the movie than at Allred's barn, but *Apocalypse Now* was a movie, this was the real deal. "The horror," Captain Kurtz had said, "*the horror*," and I was now living it.

With a Beretta in my hand, I knew I wasn't equipped to fight. But, I hadn't seen anybody to fight. I was just seeing dead bodies; I was just seeing destruction.

I didn't see any more dead scientists, nor did I see a dead Ike. The death toll was now at five.

I left the barn. An instinct popped up that I should just take one of the cars parked in the barn and drive like a bat out of hell. Get help. That would be the safe thing to do. That would be the right thing to do. But, I had to find Allred. I might be able to save him if he wasn't already dead.

I crept up to the house.

I pushed open the back door. A shot exploded inside the house; I felt something whiz past my ear.

Chapter Fifty-One

"Get out!" a voice yelled.

It was a woman's voice. The only two women I had seen on the compound were Allred's sisters. Leona was dead. I wracked my brain to remember the name of Allred's other sister, the dumpy one who served us dinner.

Her name came to me. *"Anna! Don't shoot!* This is Roy Hobbs."

"Roy?" It was as if her voice had transformed itself from an old witch to a young, scared girl.

"Yes, Anna, Roy Hobbs," I said, "can I come in?"

"Yes, Roy, *come in."*

I stepped in the doorway. I was ready to dive either way. Anna placed her gun carefully on the floor as if she didn't want to dent the linoleum.

She came crabbing over to me as fast as her short heavy legs would carry her. She hugged me like a mother would. It's strange what dangerous times will do to people. Before all this violence, all she knew of me was to serve me some more meatloaf; now I was a returning and living member of the family.

"Allred? Is Allred okay?" I asked.

"Yes," Anna said, sniffling. "He's upstairs. First door on the right."

I quickly walked upstairs. I had never been in the upper level of this house. It was like walking through a house that was on the historical register. The hardwood steps creaked as they probably had for the past hundred years.

At the top of the stairs were four doors. I guessed that those doors would lead to three bedrooms and a bathroom. I stepped to the door at the right. The curtains had been pulled tight with only an open sliver allowing daylight to streak in. There were, however, a rack of fluorescent lights across the ceiling.

Allred was at a work table. Ike was there. Two of the scientists were there. They were looking at a large high-definition computer monitor.

"Allred," I said.

Allred looked up, surprised. I wondered if he had even heard the bang when Anna had shot her gun.

"Roy!" Allred said, smiling. He came over and embraced me.

"You've seen what happened?" he asked.

"Yes," I said, "what did happen?"

"Burrard," Allred said.

"*Burrard?* How can that be? We killed him! Ike, you killed the 1978 Burrard. Allred, you killed the 1992 Burrard at the top of the stairs of his basement. And then, Allred, you sent the 2002 Burrard to nuclear Chicago."

"There was one more," Ike said. He still hadn't regained the luster that he had showed when he was the boss of security, but he looked far better than when I untied him in Burrard's garage.

"Remember, I shot the Burrard of 1978," Ike said. "We were dragging him to the 'killing room.'"

"Right." I remembered the scene vividly. I remembered the bullet whizzing between my legs.

"I asked you to help drag the bastard," Ike said. "When you grabbed him around the waist and started pulling, you inadvertently hit his Red Button and he was gone."

"Yes, but he was dead," I said. "The Red Button wasn't going to rejuvenate a dead guy."

"The dead body went back to his last stop," Ike said. "Didn't he tell us that he had gone to 2000 to warn that Abel Burrard? Burrard at that time in 2000 had killed many times. When I shot 1978 Burrard and killed him, his dead body showed up in 2000, probably at the feet of that version of Abel Burrard. That version of Abel Burrard—the

2000 guy—figured out how to program the Wayfarer Commander to get back here."

"He came with weapons," Allred said. "We're just looking at the security tapes now. It looks like he shot Charles first. You know, in the control room, a light flashes when somebody is returning through the white hole. Charles was probably thinking it was you who was returning."

Shit. I had pushed Charles to return. If it hadn't been for my persistent insistence, Charles would have spent at least another day with Lola. That extra day would have saved his life. The life that Charles had wanted to live—a life that he had found long after he had gone to Stonehenge and Easter Island—was now snuffed.

"Burrard had two Uzis and gun belts strapped around his shoulders like he was Pancho Villa," Ike said. "He shot Doctor Wu, Leona, some security guys, and Robert McDougald. Fortunately, two of our scientists were in Astoria, seeing a movie, *Halloween*, of all things. I was upstairs recuperating from our last trip. Allred was here with me when all hell broke loose."

"Did you kill Burrard?" I asked.

"No we didn't," Ike said. "We just had one weapon here—Anna's gun—but we followed what was happening on the security cameras. Burrard gathered five Wayfarer Commanders, strapped them around his chest and then, poof, he was gone. He never came to the house. He probably didn't know we were here. But, he got what he came for—Wayfarer Commanders."

"Do you know where he went?" I asked.

"Absolutely," Allred said. "Our new algorithms can track him every step of the way through different parallel worlds. In the last two hours, he has already visited two different parallel worlds. On each trip he took a spare Wayfarer Commander with him. We surmise that he has given that belt to another Abel Burrard."

"Shouldn't we be going after him before he can do too much damage?" I said. "Let's go, I'm willing."

"Roy, look at us," Allred said. "Look at all four of us *and* yourself. I'm not John Wayne who can traipse after bad guys. I know, I know, I did it once, but that practically gave me a heart attack. Look at these two scientists. They're like me. They're *scientists*, not Rambo types. Look at Ike. Do you know how old Ike is? Well, he's in better shape than any eighty-two year old that I know, but he's *eighty-two*. Sure, Ike might have a body like a guy forty years old, but he isn't a forty year old. Lastly, look at yourself. Are *you* a Rambo type? I don't think so."

I didn't have to look at myself. I knew I wasn't a Rambo.

Allred stepped away from the computer monitor. He walked over to the window and opened the curtains. He looked out at the barn, and the field beyond it with the same winsome stare as when he wondered if he had seen whales from my high-definition window.

"No, Roy, we aren't fighters," Allred said. "We're *dreamers*. We're techies that could dream impossible dreams—and produce things that man has never been able to do before. What we didn't anticipate was *evil*, the *force* of evil."

"So let's hire some people who can go get the various Burrards" I said. "We might not be fighters, but we can *hire* them. We can hire soldier-of-fortune types. You know where each Burrard is; let's send killers after them."

Allred put up his hand as if it were a stop sign.

"Roy, we can't hire soldiers-of-fortune," Allred said. "Once we gave them the Wayfarer Commanders, how could we ever know that we could control *them*? They aren't family. They haven't been trained and reared by Ike. And, if you looked at the pure physics of it, by the time we hired some soldiers-of-fortune, there would be hundreds of Burrards that would have been warned. Or, even worse, five Burrards would come back here, armed to the teeth, before we've found our soldiers-of-fortune guys, to grab even more Wayfarer Commanders. No, Roy, all the kings horses and all the kings men couldn't put Humpty Dumpty back together again."

"What does that mean? Humpty Dumpty?"

"We've got to shut it down," Allred said. "We've got to shut the whole thing down."

"What do you mean?"

"We're going to turn it off," Allred said.

"What will that do?"

"That will stop those five Wayfarer Commanders that Burrard has as if they ran out of batteries. They won't be good for anything. We can't stop the Burrards that are out there, but we don't have to aid them. We'll turn off the switch. We've already achieved far more than we had ever imagined. We have proved that there are parallel universes and parallel worlds. We've already done a tremendous amount of research—as much as I could ever imagine. What we didn't know was how *evil* could inject itself into our research. We don't know how to handle that. There's only one solution: we're now going to pull the plug. We're going to shut down our experiment forever."

I sat down on one of the stools around the work table.

"When are you going to do this?" I asked.

"Within minutes," Allred said, still looking out the window. His old firing range must have been out there somewhere—the area where he had become a quick-draw crack shot. "We were concerned about you. If you hadn't come back when you did, I was about ready to go find you in 1978."

"Did Burrard go to 1978?" I asked. "Could you track him going back there?"

"No, he went back to 2000, where he had come from," Allred said. "From there, he reached out to various times of 2000 in different parallel worlds. It looks like he's tipping off his 'brothers' that were just about ready to be caught."

Allred turned to face me. "You can write that book I hired you to write," he said. "It will be shorter than what we had thought, but far more adventuresome than we thought. I'll still pay you, of course, what we agreed upon."

"I want to go back," I said.

"Go back? Where?" Allred said.

"To 1978," I said. "I want to go back to 1978. I can make a difference."

I didn't refer to what area I could make a difference. The difference wasn't to mankind. It was to one person. I had saved this one Rachel from being murdered and mutilated by Abel Burrard, now

298

I could give her a compressed lifetime of my love, the love that had been spotty in so many other parallel worlds.

"I'll write the book there, in 1978," I said.

Allred chuckled. "Once we shut it down, Roy, we're going to dismantle it piece by piece by piece. That's the Humpty Dumpty part. *Nobody* will ever be able to put this thing back together again. We had always worried a bit about governments trying to get our technology, but we didn't figure on *evil*. So, Roy, I won't be able to get back to you to retrieve the book. This place will be totally shut down, forever. If you write the book, you'll be the only one who reads it."

"I understand, but I will write the book," I said. "Can I go back?"

"Well, Roy, you have a Wayfarer Commander on you right now," Allred said, "and the system is purring like a kitten. You don't need my permission; we certainly won't stop you. I would rather that you stayed, you've earned a tidy sum, but I think I understand. It's Rachel isn't it?"

"Yes, it's Rachel," I said. "By the miracle of your genius, and the others here, I can do a *do-over*."

Allred nodded. I think he understood. "You'll need some things," he said. "Stop by the Company Store and take as much old cash as you can. In 1978 I was just a young code writer for Bill Gates and Paul Allen, so I'd recommend that you buy Microsoft when it eventually goes public. You'll become a very rich man. But, I'm afraid I can't give you much time to gather things. We *have* to shut this down before Burrard does some more recruiting; it's only fair that we do this for those poor souls in other parallel worlds. We can give you an hour." He looked at his watch. "Sixty minutes from now, we're pulling the plug."

I nodded. "Thank you, Allred." I went over and did something that was uncharacteristic of me. I hugged him. He seemed a little embarrassed by my show of emotion, but he hugged back.

I turned and started to walk out of the room.

I heard him say to one of the other scientists, "Do-over. Interesting concept. Yes, very interesting concept."

Epilogue

R achel and I got married in the same church on the same date, September fifth, 1981.

A lot of things were the same as when we first got married. Rachel was, of course, the same. I was the same with two small exceptions. My name was no longer Roy H. Hobbs. It was Homer Murphy. Instead of being twenty-seven years old as I was the first time I married Rachel, I was now fifty-three. I looked younger, but even if people thought I was in my mid-forties, it still could have looked like I was robbing the cradle. But, Rachel didn't mind; I didn't mind.

I was no longer, of course, the crime reporter for the *Chicago Sun-Times*. I was now plainly, an investor; a very brilliant investor. My brilliance came from several sources. I had cash. I had taken about one hundred thousand dollars in cash from the Company Store. That was my seed money. I also had taken my laptop computer. Inside a file on my computer was a list of hot stocks from the 1970s, 1980s, and 1990s. I bought fifty thousand dollars of a company called ChemFirst. I didn't even know what they did. It didn't matter. I knew the stock was going to explode. I eventually found out that they were originally a venture capital firm and in the 1960s bought a chemical company. ChemFirst eventually went up over two-thousand percent. I sold a lot of it along the way, but my net gain over the years was over twenty million dollars. This sure was a lot more fun than my first experience of buying pork bellies on the Chicago Board of Trade. Later on, I bought a ton of Microsoft when it first came out.

My laptop was, of course, my secret genie. The world wouldn't see a laptop computer like mine for another fifteen years or so, so I kept it locked in a vault in my home office closet. Inside its hard drive was everything I ever needed to know about the future.

Coming from the twenty-first century I was a lot more knowledgeable about health. No longer did I think that a Big Mac was a health food. I stopped eating junk, becoming a connoisseur of green vegetables, fruits, and fish. The last Big Mac I had was twenty years in the future on a different parallel world.

I developed a ritual of walking five miles a day, *every* day, three hundred and sixty five days a year. No only did I walk off a budding old man's gut, I think I walked myself into a younger appearance. All that walking and eating like a health guru sort of flash-froze my appearance. Rachel matured gracefully, of course, even after giving birth to two children. Yes, in this do-over, there were no miscarriages, no failed attempts. Our son was born in 1983; our daughter was born two years later.

Even though we could afford a lot more, we bought the very same house on Sherman Avenue in Evanston. I had always been comfortable there and I knew that Rachel had truly loved that house. It was interesting to see the pictures that Rachel added to the wall in the hallway. Before, the mosaic of pictures on the wall told a story of a relationship that would end in divorce; the pictures from this parallel world told a story of love and a relationship that deepened and blossomed a little more each year.

Over the years, I read every story that Roy Hobbs wrote. He was the star crime reporter for the *Chicago Sun-Times*. I helped him along a few times with tips on stories that I had broken in another parallel world. All that stuff was in my computer—like the Chicago alderman who had his hand wedged in to the political cookie jar—and I just had to write out where smoking guns were and send it to Roy. I was, in effect, Roy Hobbs' anonymous Deep Throat. I never talked to Roy, but I did check up on him occasionally. He had married, had two kids, was divorced. The chase for crime stories had not left him. He hadn't written a best-selling book, *The Monster Among Us*, nor would he since the monster had ended up on a different world.

I had stopped by Rutter Hardware Store every year until it was sold. Old man Rutter had never heard a peep from his erstwhile young worker Abel Burrard. It was as if Burrard had vanished from the face of the earth, which was exactly the case, his corpse going to a parallel world, never to come back.

After the Millennium, I took a trip out to Oregon. I told Rachel that I wanted to investigate a possible investment. That was the only lie I had told her. At that time, I had not told her about my do-over.

After arriving at the Portland Airport, I rented a car. I drove to Astoria. I drove past the Astoria Golf Club and found the left turn off of the highway. I drove up to Allred's farmhouse. In the driveway was a Chevy Caprice. Allred had told me that their great experiment in traveling to parallel worlds was *not* replicated in any other world. I never understood how he could defy nature like that, but he said it was all in the huge magnets that he had buried under his barn. I believed Allred at the time, but now that the year 2000 had rolled by his merry band of genius geeks could have been working feverishly on time travel, I thought I'd just take a look.

The Victorian farmhouse looked exactly the same. It needed paint. The lawn needed cutting. I knocked on the door.

There was no answer.

I knocked again.

Finally the door opened. Allred peered out. He looked exactly as I remembered him. I, of course, looked a lot different. When I first met Allred I was fifty-one. I was now seventy-four. If I say so myself, I was a very sprightly seventy-four, and I could easily pass for a sixty year old, but I was different looking than the last time Allred had seen me.

"Yes?" Allred said.

"I'm Roy Hobbs," I said. That was the first time I had used that name in over twenty years.

"Yes?" Allred said. "Do I know you?"

I could tell that my name wasn't familiar to him at all. And, I could tell that he didn't recognize me in the slightest. He wasn't acting; he just didn't know me.

And, he didn't ask me for the manuscript of the book I owed him.

"No, you don't know me," I said. "I just stopped to get driving directions. Do you know where the Astoria Golf Club is?"

Allred was polite and told me that it was just five minutes down the road.

I thanked him and went back to my car.

From a distance, I gazed at his red barn. His red barn did look different. It was old. It clearly needed paint. It looked like it was listing to the side. It seemed that a strong wind could blow it over. This wasn't the fortress barn that I had become so familiar with. So, Allred was probably right. His great experiment to parallel worlds was a one-time event. For some unknown reason, I felt sad. Those great brains had been so focused, so *alive*. Now, they were probably just rich brains that no longer had the immense passion to dream impossible dreams.

I flew back to Chicago the next day.

Eventually, I told Rachel all about Allred and my wild travels to parallel worlds. I think she initially thought I was going nuts. She probably wondered if Alzheimer's made old coots tell strange stories. I had no proof, of course. I had my old laptop, but it looked like I had bought it at a garage sale. I had my old Wayfarer Commander, but that looked like it could have been a cheap prop in a low-budget sci-fi movie. But, I did have her love and her trust of over twenty years. That meant a lot to Rachel.

Let me tell you, this do-over was wonderful for both Rachel and me, and the kids. I wasn't preoccupied with chasing crime stories like I had been in my other life. I was preoccupied with one thing: living my do-over to the fullest with Rachel and the kids.

So, Rachel believed me. At least she told me so, and she seemed sincere.

"Why don't you fulfill your agreement with Allred?" Rachel asked me.

"What do you mean?"

"You agreed to write a book about your experiences in these parallel worlds," Rachel said. "That was your deal with Allred."

I nodded. "But, this Allred doesn't even know me," I said.

"A deal is a deal," Rachel said. "And besides, parallel worlds have brought you and me such great joy. Homer, you saved my life from this Abel Burrard character you told me about. Without parallel worlds, I would be dead; you and I wouldn't have lived this wonderful life. Write the book for Allred. Write the book for me."

I dusted off my latent writing skills. It seemed a lifetime ago that writing was part of every one of my days as a reporter. There was supposed to be just one reader of this book—Allred Kosinski. But, in my will, I gave permission that this book be sold to a publisher, if any publisher wanted it. If you're reading this, it looks like a publisher did want it. It's a fantastic incredible story, of course. Nobody in their right mind could believe it, right? But, I hope there are some young physicists out there who will read *Do Overs* like Allred and Charles did with Jules Verne's *Time Machine* and be inspired to dream impossible dreams.

Albert Einstein believed in parallel worlds, but couldn't prove it.

Allred and Charles believed in parallel worlds and created the mechanism to make it all possible.

And I, I traveled to parallel worlds. Those travels created my do-over. If I could, I would do it all over again. Again and again.

From Jon Spoelstra
June, 2015

I've been a fan of time travel novels for a long time.

Two of my all-time time travel books are:

1. *Time on My Hands* by Peter Delacorte
2. *The Crucifixion Conspirators* by Jeffrey R. Jacobs

Both have been out of print for a long time, but you can still get them on Amazon.com.

So, is there time travel? I'm sure there are parallel worlds, and I'm sure that one day we'll discover how to reach those worlds. That's when we may find out that this book was written a long, long time ago and I just got around writing it in this parallel world. Yep, time travel is fun.

Jon

P.S. Every author loves to get good reviews. If you enjoyed *Do-Overs,* I certainly would appreciate a review of yours on Amazon. Click here for a shortcut: Amazon.com. Thank you.

P.P.S. I've got another novel that travels back in time. This time travel doesn't need a white hole or a time machine. It just places you in 1951 in Brooklyn where you'll experience the greatest pennant race in the history of baseball, and witness Tailgunner Joe McCarthy chase Commies all over the place. You'll have fun reading this.

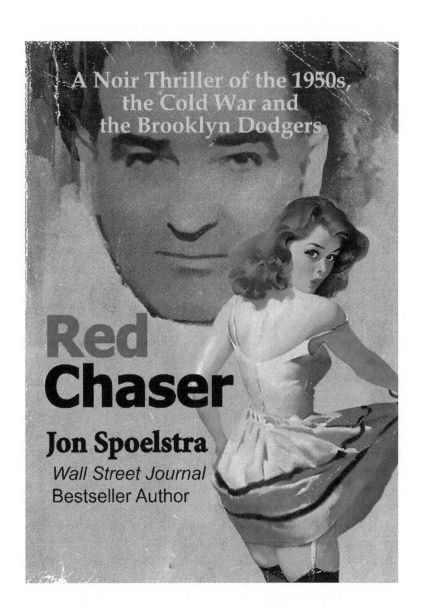

A Noir Thriller of the 1950s,
the Cold War and
the Brooklyn Dodgers

Red
Chaser

Jon Spoelstra

Wall Street Journal
Bestseller Author

The novel **Red Chaser** tosses you right into the 1950s. You'll meet the kinkiest and most beautiful spy this side of the Iron Curtain. You'll meet Joe McCarthy. Best of all, you'll live the life of Jake McHenry.

Jake seems to have a near-perfect life. After all, he spent five years in Germany after World War II and came back laden with ill-gotten Nazi riches. Being young and rich ain't bad.

Back home in Brooklyn, Jake became a private detective for the simple reason that he needed a pretend job to hide the source of his riches. Mostly, however, he went to Brooklyn Dodgers games at Ebbets Field and drank beer.

Then Joe McCarthy entered the picture. A childhood buddy introduced Jake to Tailgunner Joe. They wanted Jake to steal a secret list of celebrity communists from the Ice Queen, a rich high-society leftist named Arabella Van Dyck. The Ice Queen also happened to be the most beautiful--and most depraved--woman that Jake had ever seen.

The break-in of the Ice Queen's brownstone in Manhattan was easy, but it unleashed a flurry of Russians, North Koreans, J. Edgar Hoover and mobsters in a wild chase for the list.

The backdrop to all this is the greatest pennant race in the history of Major League Baseball. The New York Giants chased the Brooklyn Dodgers all summer long for the National League pennant. That's the year that Bobby Thomson hit the "shot heard 'round the world." The pennant—and Jake's life--comes down to the last inning and the last pitch at the Polo Grounds in New York City on Wednesday, October 3, 1951.

1.

Friday, September 14, 1951

I went to war poor. Nine years later, I came back rich.

Along the way, I became known as a Red Chaser. Now, I was going to meet the greatest Red Chaser of them all. Senator Joe McCarthy. Tailgunner Joe himself.

I was in Dowling's Oyster Bar, a small saloon in Brooklyn. It wasn't a fancy joint; it was a drinking place more akin to pubs in Ireland. Gray cigarette smoke formed a cloud over the room.

From the front door, three booths were wedged against the front window, and four booths went down the wall toward the toilet;. A long bar ran the length of the room, dominating it. Above the bar was a sign: *The food here is for the convenience of the drinkers.* Bill Dowling, the owner, didn't want people to think his joint was a restaurant, even though he had the best crab gumbo in the world.

This bar was just down the street from Ebbets Field, where the Brooklyn Dodgers play. Even though the Dodgers were playing a road game against the Pittsburgh Pirates, the bar was filled. The game blared over the large radios that Dowling had placed in each corner of the bar. It was hot in the middle of September of 1951. The drinkers didn't mind the heat: they had their beer and their Dodgers had a five and a half-game lead in the National League pennant race. It couldn't get any better than that. Ebbets Field and saloons like Dowling's were where I spent most of my time during the summer. Baseball and beer, that's this rich man's life.

Tailgunner Joe came barreling through the open front door like a fullback from the New York Giants football team. There was a New

York Giants baseball team, of course, but I don't talk about them much if I can help it. Sure, I had seen McCarthy's picture in the papers, and I'd seen him on the television in the bar, but this was the first time in real life. He was big and blocky—maybe a hair shorter than six feet—an offensive guard size. His pants were wrinkled as if he'd slept in them. His wrinkled white business shirt was soaked through with sweat in spots and matched the color of clam chowder. His tie had been loosened to where it looked like a colorful lasso.

As he lumbered toward me, my immediate thought was that he could take care of himself in any bar he walked into. He looked like he was born to a bar—the only thing better than a good dirty joke would be a good fight. A beer bottle smashed across the face would be considered hilarious.

He walked right over to the booth where I was sitting, stuck his meaty right hand in front of my face, took my hand, and shook it with a quick crunch. "You must be the Red Chaser," he said.

2.

Friday, September 14, 1951

Before I could answer Senator McCarthy, he slid into the booth across from me. Quick too, he was. My long-time friend, Nick Salzano, grabbed a chair and pulled it up to the booth. He was the matchmaker who had brought Tailgunner Joe and me together.

I had known Nick since we used to pop open fire hydrants, freeing gushers of water to cool us on those blistery summer days when we were kids. It was either the fire hydrant or grab a dime somewhere and go to an all-day Saturday matinee where the best feature was often the new air-cooled air. Heck, now we had cooled air in some bars.

Nick grew up to be a movie-star handsome guy—a tall, dark Italian movie star. He was an inch or so shorter than my six feet two, looked like he could go three rounds in the ring right now, hadn't seen any of his hair run off, and had a face that should have been on a male model.

The one flaw—and if he had been a male model, he would have had to have it fixed. You see, his broken nose had never been set correctly. Halfway up the bridge of his nose, there was the unmistakable bump of a long-ago broken nose. That was courtesy of me. We had not had a fight; it was basketball, and his nose got in the way of one of my elbows. Nick had always been a ladies' man, even when we were just twelve or thirteen. The broken nose added to his allure—a bit of testosterone plastered on his pretty face.

While Nick and I were like twins growing up, we weren't *identical* twins. One look at Nick and you knew he was Italian. One look at me and you knew I was Irish, even though I was half German, fair skin, some freckles. I didn't have carrot hair, but it was what some would call dirty blond. With the blue eyes and almost blond hair, I would have been a guy that Hitler would have waved on to the procreate line. Put Nick out in the sun for a while and he would bronze; put me in that same sun and I would blister.

We both went to college, which was something for our neighborhood. Nick went to Columbia; I went to Brooklyn College. Then I went off to the war; Nick went to law school. I guess Uncle Sam must've figured he needed lawyers more than just another grunt.

In college, Nick married his high school sweetheart, Gina Provenzano. Her father worked at the docks just like Nick's, but I think he was pretty high up in the mob. He went by the name of Tony Pro, and I don't think it was just a nickname that shortened his last name. Gina had huge tits, and Nick followed them around everywhere like a puppy dog. Being a good Italian Catholic girl, she would let him fondle them on occasion, but if he wanted to get into the honeypot, he'd have to make the big commitment as he had told me years ago. So, he made that commitment; he married her.

Nick and Gina now had a couple of kids. Gina, he had told me recently, had added some ample padding around that big bosom. Instead of the hourglass figure she had in high school, Nick said, she was looking more and more like a squash. "I think she's grown a third tit, and it's bigger than the first two," he had told me, laughing, "but it has no nipple, and she claims it's her stomach." He now worked for some law office in Washington, D.C. I had to figure that marriage hadn't slowed him down with the ladies. That would have been like swearing off air to him. I'd bet there wasn't a good-looking woman in DC within wooing distance that was safe from Nick. I wasn't a natural ladies man like Nick, even though I had matured into a rich, single guy. Any girl was safe with me—I had to make a considerable effort just to get to know the ones I wanted to know.

It was just two weeks ago that Nick had unexpectedly sat down next to me at a Dodgers game at Ebbets Field and said, handing me a beer, "Hey, Pal, you want a beer?"

"Whoa! What the hell are you doing here?" I asked. I was surprised to see him. It had been about a year since we had tossed back a few beers together. His movie-star face had started to age a bit—light crow's feet were stretching around his eyes, and a small puff had sprouted under each eye. All work and all play would age even Nick.

It was after a couple of beers, a couple of Nathan's dogs, a homer by Duke Snider, a great play at the plate when Roy Campanella threw down a tag that would dent a tree that Nick said, "I got a guy I want you to meet."

"Sure," I said, "who?"

"Joe McCarthy."

"What? The guy on TV?" I asked. "The senator chasing down Commies?"

Nick nodded his head as he plopped the tail end of his second hot dog in his mouth. "The one and the same. I'm working for him now. Great guy. You'll love him."

"What's this all about, Nick? When'd you start working for him?"

"Whoa," Nick said, "he just wants to meet a guy like you. You'll find out why when you meet him."

Nick wouldn't tell me anything about this mysterious meeting. No matter how many beers I bought, I couldn't pry his tongue loose to tell me. So, here we were, two weeks later, me—Jakob Finbar McHenry—and Tailgunner Joe.

Nick ordered a round. The waitress—a stout Irish lass named Betty who could probably munch on bits of glass like it was peanuts—brought a pitcher of Schaefer and a Scotch and soda for Joe. While Nick was pouring from the pitcher, Joe clanked his glass down on the table top. It was empty. He raised his hand above his head—the sweat ring under his arm was the circumference of a basketball—and waved to Betty for another.

"This was only half full when you delivered it," Tailgunner Joe said, grinning when Betty brought him a fresh one.

"Yeah, Sweetie, here's the other half," she said, handing him the new drink. "Hey! Aren't you that guy on TV?"

"Rocky Marciano?" Joe asked, referring to the heavyweight champion of the world.

"Nah, you ain't him," she said, "but I'll figger it out."

Joe took a sip of his drink. Now it was indeed half empty.

"So, Jake—I can call you Jake, right—you were a Red Chaser during the war?" Joe asked. No chit-chat here.

"We got that fancy name because of Wild Bill Donovan," I said. Wild Bill was the founder of the OSS during World War II. After the war, Truman changed its name to the Central

314

Intelligence Agency. "Red Chaser sounded good, but we didn't really *chase* any Reds."

"What did you do then?" Joe asked. He knocked down the second half of his drink. Another one was on its way.

"Well, we chased down Waffen SS officers who had been in Eastern Europe for the last few years of the war. After the war, these SS guys scattered all over the place, trying to blend in as if they were rank-and-file soldiers or citizens or anything but SS. We had to track them down."

"What's that got to do with Reds?" Joe asked. Betty placed his third tall Scotch and soda in front of him. My buddy Nick just sat drinking his beer; he knew this was Joe's show.

"These Waffen SS guys had spy networks in Eastern Europe during the war. It took them *years* to build those networks. These Eastern Europe spies had two missions: to rat on where any Jews were being hidden and, more importantly, to keep detailed lists on who the Commie sympathizers were. The Nazis had some great spy networks in Eastern Europe. The SS knew every Commie in Czechoslovakia, Bulgaria, Hungary, Yugoslavia, places like those. Wild Bill wanted those networks. He wanted the guys who spied for the SS to spy for us—not spying on Jews, of course, but spying on Communists. That was Wild Bill's plan. He knew way early that it was the Russkies that would come out of that war as our enemy—and he wanted an experienced, built-in spy network."

"Brilliant," Joe said, "genius. *Built-in spy network.* So how many networks did you corral?"

"You know, I've never really talked about it. I think it's confidential, but since it's you, I guess I can tell. I personally picked up seventeen networks. I had first to find the Waffen SS guy, turn him, and get all of his information about his spy network. I didn't go into the East to work the networks; Wild Bill had a different crew for that. That's why I say I really wasn't a Red Chaser. I guess you could say I was sorta a Red Spy Network *Finder*, but that didn't really sound so hot, and Wild Bill sure knew how to make things sound better."

Joe sipped his drink. This time it was just a sip. Almost ladylike.

"Interesting," he said and took another ladylike sip. I guess his drinking slowed down when he was thinking. I'd say a minute went by with nobody talking, though it seemed like an hour, just sitting there, not drinking, not smoking, just sitting.

"What'ya do for a living now? Private cop, Nick tells me," Joe asked and answered in the same breath. "What type of cases?"

I don't seriously consider myself much of a private detective. When I came back from Europe as a rich man, I didn't want anybody to know I was rich. Certainly not the OSS, definitely not the taxman, surely not my friends. But I *was* rich. To follow my passion for baseball and beer, I had to pretend at least to have a job.

What better than a private detective? I could work my own hours, be out all hours of the night and nobody really knew who my clients were or who was paying me. I certainly didn't need an office in an office building. When my folks bought the house out on Long Island in Levittown—my Mom had always wanted a backyard with trees and grass and maybe even a little tomato patch—I bought their brownstone in Brooklyn. There's plenty of room for me to live in and, of course, to have an office. The office is where I kept track of the baseball box scores. I also kept a few files of my detecting work there.

"Divorces," I said.

"Pay much?"

"About a hundred a week for each case. Sometimes I've got three cases in a week, and sometimes I don't have any."

"So you sneak around..." Joe said, holding up his big hand like it was a stop sign, "I don't mean to offend, Jake, it's just that you're *used* to sneaking around, being invisible, getting the goods on some guy."

"Or some woman." I said, "And I take no offense at your 'sneaking around' comment. Sure, when I'm working, I sneak around. I did that in Europe, too. The type of work I do isn't like a door-to-door Fuller Brush salesman. I *gotta* be sneaky. That's what I do."

Joe was back to sipping his Scotch, back to thinking.

"Nick," Joe said, "give Jake that envelope.

Nick propped up his briefcase. It was one of those slim jobs. It might hold a sandwich, but never a thermos. Nick extracted a plain brown envelope, the sort you could buy at the post office. He pulled out a picture and laid it down on the table in front of me, right next to my beer. The photo was a headshot of a woman.

She was the most beautiful woman I had ever seen in my life. When I say that, I'm not exaggerating. Heck, I had the pictures of Betty Grable and all the rest over in Germany. Betty was beautiful, and there must have been a million GIs that wanted to jump in her panties, but she was beautiful in a fake movie star way. You know, everything was posed and perfect and staged.

The woman in the picture in front of me was *real*. This wasn't some glamour magazine picture with hours of makeup and queers fussing over her hair; this was a woman with little or no makeup staring into the camera in such a way that it was a miracle that the camera hadn't melted. Now, this might have been a one-shot wonder in which the camera had just caught her perfectly and, if she twitched her head just a little, the picture would have lost its magic, but I don't think so. I got the feeling that you could take a warehouse full of Kodak film and snap pictures until your thumb fell off, and each picture of this woman would grab you and pull you into it.

I figured that she was all-day beautiful.

I imagine a professional fashion guy would say that she didn't have a perfect face. It was clearly asymmetrical. Maybe she didn't have the most beautiful nose you could find. Or the most stunning lips. Or the sultriest eyes or the best hair. But, there was no doubt about it; when it was all put

318

together, this was a face that could knock you on your ass. And even though the picture was in black-and-white, I could just tell that her hair was flaming volcano-hot red.

I just stared at the picture. It was as if somebody had turned off in the bar.

Finally, after a part of a lifetime, Joe said, "The Ice Queen."

"The Ice Queen?" I found it strange that it was difficult to find my voice.

"Diamonds, Jake, diamonds," Joe said. "She's the heir to one of those Dutch diamond merchants in New York. She wears them on her ears, her neck, her ankles, and for all I know on her little toes."

I looked at the picture again. I couldn't tell if there were diamonds on her ears. Her hair cascaded down, covering anything on her ears, whether it be diamonds or pickles.

"What's her name?" I asked, "I mean, she doesn't go by the Ice Queen, does she?"

"Arabella Van Dyck," Nick said.

"I want you to do the same thing that you did with those SS bastards—I want you to get her Commie network," Joe said.

"She's a Commie?" I asked.

Joe nodded his head. "She's got red hair, red toenails, a red heart and a deep dark-red soul. She's a Commie, all right. She's like the Queen Bee. Everything flows through her; she's got all the names that count; she knows everything. We've been told that the Ice Queen keeps a private list of celebrities that are Commies or lean so far left they walk around in a circle when they're trying to walk straight. These celebrities come from all different types of Commie front organizations. Arabella Van Dyck is so connected to so many Red organizations that she knows which celebrities are in which Commie organization. There's movie stars, there's TV people, there's newspaper columnists, there's magazine editors, all belonging to different groups, but the Ice Queen has put together her own personal master list. Hell, you said yourself that you're the Red *Finder*. This is right up your alley. I want you to find me a *lot* of Commies."

I had experience tracking down Nazis in all types of backwater towns in Eastern Europe, but the Ice Queen wasn't a Waffen SS, and this wasn't blown-out Europe. "Why not the FBI? Isn't this what they do for you? Track down Reds? Isn't that what gets Hoover going every morning?"

"This isn't a Hoover thing," Joe said. "Sure, Hoover has slipped me plenty enough files over the year, but most of them—*all* of them, let me say—were intended to embarrass Harry Truman. I certainly got no problem with embarrassing Truman, but this list ain't state department folks. This list is *celebrities* and *media types*.

"If the FBI grabbed the Ice Queen, she's Hoover's, her information is Hoover's. He's always sidled up to media people like Walter Winchell. He's always parceled out the information to his media favorites like penny candy, one here, one there, but rest assured, he's always got headlines every time he handed out a little sweet. So, if that kinky bastard got the Ice Queen's information, there are no guarantees he'd pass it along to *me*. Most likely, he'd use it as blackmail to get himself more ink. Nope, this is all off the books. This is my *private* venture. This is a big deal. You get me the Ice Queen's list, and this will be a bigger blow to Communism than if you put a bullet between Joe Stalin's eyes."

"How do you expect that I'm going to get this list?" I asked.

"That's what I don't want to know," Tailgunner Joe said. "You can talk to Nick about all the details, but me, I don't know. I will tell you this; it's not likely that she's going to mimeograph the list and hand it over to you." He laughed hard—a good barroom laugh.

Steal it, that's what Joe meant, but he didn't want to say it, nor did he really want to know if that's what I would do. All he wanted was the Ice Queen's list.

"Do we know where the list is *supposed* to be?" I asked.

"We've heard it's in a safe in her house—a brownstone on the Upper East Side," Nick said, speaking for just the second time since he sat down.

"Nick," Joe said, "give Jake the other envelope."

Nick reached into his briefcase and pulled out an envelope that was the size of the regular business envelope that I'd use to send my detecting bill. It wasn't glued shut; it didn't have a postage stamp on it; it had a rubber band around it.

"Expenses," Joe said, pointing at the envelope. "There's two grand in there. That's to get you started. There's no end to it—you need more, call Nick, we got an unlimited supply for this job."

I didn't reach for the envelope.

"Get us the list, Jake," Joe said. "I've got a young tiger on the committee—name's Bobby Kennedy—and he's chawing at the bit to get at that list. He's an intense little sonofabitch—a real pisser. Hell, he's more intense than Richard Nixon, but Nixon looks like a criminal; my little guy looks like a fucking altar boy. But he's an assassin, a real assassin. His old man, Joe Kennedy—a former bootlegger no less—wants to get rid of Commies as much as I do. Along with my boys back in Wisconsin, he'll fund whatever we need. Go on, pick up that envelope. The Ice Queen is waiting for you."

Before I could answer, Joe was out of the booth as if he had just sat on a thumbtack. "Got another meeting to go to," he said. He quickly turned to Betty and twirled his fist, signaling another drink. With his new drink in hand, he had

321

his roadie. He turned to me, tossed out that big hand, and shook mine. "Nick's got all the details," he said. Then he looked me square in the eyes so hard that it seemed that a few volts of electricity jumped from his eyeballs to mine, "This is important to me, Jake. Really important. Don't let me down."

He turned and barreled out of the bar, roadie in hand. If a guy with a beer in his hand had been standing in Joe's way, that guy would have been splattered like a cornerback facing a thundering fullback at the goal line. I thought at the time that the Commies better head for the hills because that guy was going after any and all of them with a maniac's fervor.

After Joe was out of the bar, I said to myself: Yeah, I'm going to do it, I'll chase that Ice Queen, I'll get all the things that she knows. It wasn't for the money; it wasn't because I hated Commies; it was for one reason and one reason only. I wanted to see that picture materialize into a real person. Yep, I wanted the Ice Queen.

3.
Monday, September 17, 1951

"When are you going to go in to get the list?" Nick had asked me Friday night at Dowling's Oyster Bar.

"In a week, probably," I had said.

Nick had shaken his head. "We don't want to wait. We want the Ice Queen's information now."

It seemed like every client wanted the goods right away. The cuckolded husband wanted evidence right away and didn't want to wait for me to get rock-solid evidence on his wife's next tryst with the tennis pro at the country club. I guess getting a list of Commies was no different.

"Well, usually I like to case the place," I had said. "I like to go into a house when I know nobody's there."

"Nobody'll be there," Nick had said. "I'm gonna give you a couple of shortcuts. The Ice Queen leaves her brownstone every Monday morning for most of the day. I guess that's her day to go down to Wall Street and visit her money and then go to Fifth Avenue and spend some of it. That's this coming *Monday*, pal. She lives alone in that big old brownstone, does not have a maid, doesn't have an alarm system, doesn't have a dog, doesn't even have a fucking cat. It's got locks. And a safe. You told me you could handle that, right?"

I nodded. "They taught me that stuff in OSS."

"The place will be just sitting there waiting for you. And, if you want to do some homework, study this." Nick reached into the briefcase and brought out a set of blueprints.

"That's her brownstone, right there," Nick had said, his finger stabbing at the blueprint. "Look at it over the weekend to get a feel where the rooms are, go in on Monday, snatch the list, and we'll have a few beers afterward. Easy as pie."

"Nick, you've got this job really scoped out," I said. I was amazed. "Why don't you guys do it? Why me?"

Nick stared at me. "Jake, for Christ's sake, we're the McCarthy Committee of Un-American Activities; we don't do such things. We don't have any B and E guys on our staff. Just lawyers. The FBI could do this, but then the list would end up in Hoover's mitts and not Joe's. So, I thought, we want the list, we know where it is, why not bring in an old buddy who knows how to do these things, who wouldn't mind making a pretty good chunk of change for a pretty easy B and E and do something patriotic in the process."

All those reasons made sense, but I wasn't feeling comfortable about it. I felt uncomfortable going in so quickly without being able to case the place to my own satisfaction. It's not as if I had a regular routine for breaking and entering. Heck, I'm the good guy, not a crook. There have been *occasions* where I've had to break in to get some evidence in a divorce case, but no way breaking and entering could be considered as one of my usual activities. Still, with all the background stuff that Nick already had, it did seem to be easy as pie.

So, today was the easy as pie day. Monday, September 17, 1951.

The break-in would be a three-man job. The first man was me, of course. Then I needed a lookout in case the Ice Queen came back unexpectedly. That would be Rafael Ordonez.

Rafael was a Puerto Rican kid who lived in Red Hook, the neighborhood bordering Brooklyn Heights, where I lived. Many Puerto Ricans tended to live close to where they worked, and many worked at the rope manufacturer in the

Brooklyn Navy Yard in Red Hook. I had met him, however, not in Red Hook but at a Dodger game. I caught him trying to pick my pocket. I offered him alternative employment, and I used him occasionally on jobs like this. This beat working in the rope factory.

Rafael had spent most of his young life dodging the police, so he was a world-class lookout. He was thin, a little bit shorter than me, and looked as innocent as a choir boy. The cops in Brooklyn knew that he would steal something in a blink of an eye, but he was a portrait of honesty here in Manhattan. He was even carrying a small shoulder satchel that made him look like a delivery boy.

The third man wasn't just critical—the safecracker—but essential. I was accurate when I had told Nick that the OSS had taught me how to get into locked safes. Easy, just blow it open with dynamite. But, this job was *stealth*. My resident safecracker was a person nobody would ever suspect. It was my secret weapon from Japan. And she wasn't a man; she was a *she*.

Hiromi Kitahara could pick a lock almost faster than I could open it with a key. She could crack a safe faster than I could memorize the combination. She developed these skills, oddly, after her family had left Hiroshima.

It's a long story, but her family had immigrated to the United States two years *before* Pearl Harbor. Hiromi's father came to help his younger brother in his business. Consider this move a gift from God since the United States literally blew Hiroshima off the map just a few years later. That gift, however, wasn't free. Just two years after Hiromi and her parents had arrived in the United States, they had been tossed into an American prison in Tule Lake, California. Of course, our government didn't call them prisons; we called them Internment Camps. Welcome to the good old U.S. of A.

In the Internment Camp, Hiromi refined two skills: painting and locks. The locks were a family thing. Her father was a locksmith, as was her uncle and her grandfather. While in Internment, Hiromi learned the family locksmith trade. She practiced on the locks on the doors. With the painting, I'm not talking about painting a wall or something. I'm talking about *art*. Hiromi's painting brought her a scholarship at Pratt Institute in Brooklyn after the war.

Halfway through her first year at Pratt, she found my house. Our family house in Brooklyn was massive, a classic three-story brownstone on Middagh Street in Brooklyn Heights.

We had been taking boarders since I left for the war. When my folks bought the house out on Long Island in Levittown—tomato patch and all—I bought their brownstone in Brooklyn. Hiromi became my third boarder on my third floor.

She was nothing close to the buck-toothed slit-eyed thick-eyeglassed Jap that the movies had stereotyped the Japanese to be in the 1940s. Her eyes were much rounder than a movie-goer would expect. She had black hair that was so shiny that it seemed that it was wet. She didn't wear glasses. She was taller than the women I would see down in Chinatown—I would imagine she was about five-six or so. She had a smile that Pepsodent could use in a magazine ad. She was thin, of course, but instead of frail-looking, she looked athletic. I don't think she was beautiful in the sense that we Americans understand—not knock-down beautiful like the Ice Queen was or the big tits like Marilyn Monroe—but there was a certain radiance about her that made her pleasing to look at.

Like any college kid, Hiromi needed money. When I found out that she had this unusual skill with locks, I made her a part-time employee. Cash didn't exchange hands exactly. We worked on the barter system. For every lock she picked, she'd get a free month's rent. She just had one rule for me: she would not use her skill to *steal*. However, getting evidence about a wayward husband was, as she would say, hunky-dory. So, working part-time for me was a heck of a lot better than working in a Chinese laundry.

That was my team: a Puerto Rican, a Jap and me. And today, our United Nations-like forces were going to invade the Ice Queen's castle. Easy as pie.

4.

Monday, September 17, 1951

I found a parking spot on the Ice Queen's street, a few houses down from her brownstone. She lived in a large brownstone on 72nd Street, between Second and Third Avenue in the Upper East Side. Three-story brownstones lined the street. Nick had told me that the Ice Queen lived alone. No relatives, no live-in maid, no caretaker, no nothing.

Hiromi and I were in my parked Ford when the Ice Queen stepped out of her brownstone. Positioned down the street, Rafael stood like a lamppost.

I savored what I was seeing: the Ice Queen was tall, I'd say about five-eight or so; she had long and shapely legs that looked strong and feminine at the same time. She walked with a certain bounce that spilled off supreme confidence. Her hair was indeed flaming red. You could tell from a mile away that her hair was no dye job. It bounced and flowed as she walked, leaving a lightly luminous trail.

She was wearing a dark green suit that made her look like a million dollars, which being the Ice Queen, was probably worth at least that. You don't see too many women with that presence; I would bet that most men who met her would be instantly intimidated. Nick had given me files that said she was thirty-one—the same age as me—but she had a bearing that practically made her timeless. And, somehow, she had become a Commie and was under the microscope of Tailgunner Joe McCarthy. What a waste.

From his position at the end of the block, Rafael could see the Ice Queen walking toward him. He would stand by a payphone, giving the impression that he was waiting for instructions for his next delivery or pick up. Rafael would stay near the phone after the Ice Queen caught a cab. If the Ice Queen came back earlier than he expected, he could see that from his position near the payphone. He would then drop a nickel into the phone box and call the Ice Queen's home, allowing the phone to ring just once. He would then hang up and quickly redial the same number and allow it to ring twice. That one-two rings sequence would give us the warning that the Ice Queen had changed her patterns and was coming back to the brownstone earlier than expected.

After the Ice Queen started to walk toward Third Avenue, I pulled out of the parking spot and found a spot on the street behind the Ice Queen's. I liked to break into a house through the back door. Exits were better too at the back door.

331

Hiromi and I walked toward the Ice Queen's street and turned in to the alley. We ducked through the gate to the Ice Queen's backyard and walked up to the back door. A deadbolt lock stared us in the face.

"Easy to crack," Hiromi said as she nimbly worked her tools to pop open the lock.

"That goes for safes, Hiromi," I said, "Not for deadbolts."

"What you say for deadbolts then?" She whispered.

I said, "Pick." She looked quizzically at me, not knowing if I had tried to make a joke. After about ten seconds of fiddling with the lock with her kit of bobby pins, she opened the door. She led me to the foyer at the front of the house as if she had been born there. Hiromi walked with a certain familiarity through the house; she had studied the blueprints better than I had.

The blueprints showed that the Ice Queen's safe was in a small office off of her bedroom on the second floor. Hiromi knew the path better than I did; she was a woman on a mission, all business-like, heading up the stairs moving as quietly as a ghost. I followed.

I walked up the stairs slower. There was art lining both walls of the staircase. It was marvelous art, including a Pablo Picasso. I touched the frame and jiggled it. Picasso wasn't screwed to the wall; it would have been easy to swipe. It seemed strange to me to have works of art like Picasso and not have some type of protection against thievery. Maybe the Ice Queen had so much money that she didn't give a fuck.

"This way," Hiromi whispered with some urgency underscoring her words. She moved so quietly that she had already found the bedroom and had floated back to me admiring Picasso.

At the second level of the brownstone, there were six doors that branched off the hallway. Hiromi pointed to the first door on the right. It was open.

"Ice Queen's bedroom," Hiromi whispered.

She motioned for me to follow her. We walked into a very large room. On the far wall was the most oversized bed that I had ever seen. It looked to be the size of three queen-sized beds. Above it was a huge mirror bolted into the ceiling.

"Funny times," Hiromi said, smiling, pointing at the ceiling. That was the first time she had ever said something to me that had a hint of a sexual connotation. It looked like she blushed, but it wasn't easy to tell with Orientals.

Hiromi skittered ahead while I gave the bed a closer inspection. I wondered where the Ice Queen had got sheets big enough to cover this monster.

I walked to a large Hieronymus Bosch painting on the wall. With all of its demons, half-human animals and tortured souls, I found a Bosch to be a strange painting to have on your bedroom wall, but what the hell, I wasn't the Ice Queen. I jiggled it. Like the Picasso, the Bosch wasn't screwed to the wall, and I could have easily lifted it. The Picasso might have worked in my house, but the Bosch I would have donated to Dowling's. Let those drunks there figure out what the hell Hell was all about.

Hiromi hissed a 'pssssst' at me. She moved around as quickly as a dragonfly over water; she had probably cased the whole upstairs while I was looking for myself in the Bosch painting.

She motioned me to follow her. She led me to a bathroom. Some bathroom! There was a large bathtub that could pass for a swimming pool in some neighborhoods. There was also a walk-in stall shower. This bathroom was larger than most people's living rooms.

"Funny times here, too," Hiromi said, this time not blushing.

She then pivoted and led me across the bedroom to two open French doors leading to a small office. On the opposite side of the small office was another door leading to who knows where.

"Safe," Hiromi said, pointing at another Picasso on the wall just left of the desk. This Picasso, like the one on the stairwell, wasn't a print. It was the real McCoy. Hiromi pulled the Picasso frame from the left side, and it pivoted like a door. On the wall was the safe.

"Excuse me now, Jake, I must listen. You be quiet." Hiromi twisted the combination dial a few times and put her ear to the lock. I wandered back into the Ice Queen's bedroom.

I had never seen a bed so large. It had to have been custom made, along with the dust ruffles, the sheets, everything about it including the mirror above it. I leaned over and looked at myself in the mirror.

Before I could fantasize about the different movie sequences running in my head, I heard Hiromi say, "Okay."

It had been just a minute—two at the most—and Hiromi had cracked the safe. When I walked into the office, I just saw the open safe in the wall. "It's all yours," Hiromi said.

I carefully pulled out of the safe a large bundle of papers. They were held together with a rubber band. The papers were of various sizes, with some longer with their ends sticking out of the pile. I put the papers down on the desk and began to sift through them, looking for a list. Hiromi had the small camera ready to take photos of any of the pages.

Hiromi pointed at the safe. I looked in the deep recess. This was a very large safe. I peered in. Cash. I pulled out one bundle. It was all hundred-dollar bills. Probably about fifty of them. There were at least ten more bundles. I put the money back. We were there to get The List, not steal. No Picassos, no Bosch, no cash for us—we had *honor*.

I pulled the rubber band off of another pile of papers and started to shuffle through them. Halfway through the documents, I ran into something surprising. It wasn't the list; it was a bundle of folded papers that looked like they were written in Japanese.

"What do these say?" I asked Hiromi.

She looked at the papers. "I don't know," she said. "That is Korean." She said it with a very slight sneer; if she had been raised in Brooklyn, she would have said, "I don't read that shit." I guessed that she didn't like Koreans. That stumped me; I'd ask her about it later.

"I don't read Korean. But, look at this," she said, pointing to a page full of diagrams. I stared at the diagrams. I couldn't figure out what the drawings represented. I did know they didn't represent a bike or a baseball diamond; it looked like they depicted some type of bomb.

"Take a picture of this page," I said, handing it to her. I found five more pages of drawings to be photographed. She snapped off pictures as quickly as she turned the pages.

The phone rang, and Hiromi and I both jolted up straight. It rang only once. We froze. After a three count, the phone rang again. This time it rang twice.

"Let's go," I said. I folded the Korean sheets of paper back into the bundle and put them back into the safe as we had found them. Hiromi closed the safe door and repositioned the dial to be at the same number that she had found it.

We padded back through the massive bedroom. In the hallway, we heard the lock open and somebody walk across the hardwood vestibule. Rafael must have been asleep at the switch, I thought. There was no way the Ice Queen could have walked down from Third Avenue to her brownstone in the time between the phone call warning and the opening of the front door.

"This way," Hiromi whispered. We tiptoed through the master bedroom again, tiptoed through the office, and Hiromi opened the door on the far side. It led to another bathroom.

This was a more conventional bathroom. Next to the bathtub was another door, and Hiromi was through it like an expert tour guide. It led to a smaller bedroom. There were two beds, a large wardrobe dresser, a sitting area with two oversized chairs and a love seat. Across the way was another door—a closet.

Hiromi whispered, "We can hide in here until she leaves again."

"What if she doesn't leave?" I asked.

"We wait," Hiromi said, separating the hanging clothes with her hands as she burrowed into the back of the large closet. There must have been a hundred dresses hanging in the closet and maybe two hundred pairs of shoes. We had burrowed to the back; for the Ice Queen to find us, she would have to decline to wear the ninety-nine dresses in front of the last one that was hiding us.

We were in pitch darkness and feeling like we were suspended in a vast void. Through the closet door, we heard the voices of a woman and at least two men. Both of the men were speaking with Asian accents.

Hiromi touched my face with her fingers and then positioned her mouth over my ear and whispered in the darkness, "Korean." The word didn't titillate me, but her whisper sure did.

We stood there in the back of the closet; I held her shoulders in my hands. We heard a tinkling sound—one of the men was taking a piss. He said something, and both men laughed. He didn't flush. Then we heard nothing. It seemed like they had left the bathroom.

About ten minutes later, what we heard confused us. It came muted through the Ice Queen's office, the bathroom, and finally to us in the closet. It was a woman's squeal, then a laugh, then a scream, then another squeal. I tiptoed toward the door of the closet. A moment later, I peered out. Nobody was there. I heard the woman squeal again and then some Korean words that sounded very harsh.

I whispered back to Hiromi, "Stay here."

I tiptoed out of the closet, then through the bathroom, stopped for a moment, and heard a squeal that turned into a scream. I tiptoed through the small office and held my breath. There were grunts. I peered around the door to look into the Ice Queen's bedroom.

There she was on that football-field-sized bed. She was naked. The two Korean men were naked. They were squirming around in that vast bed like pigs in mud.

I felt pressure on my arm. Hiromi had ducked under my armpit to see what I was seeing. I don't know if she zeroed in on the same thing that I saw, but I noticed that the Ice Queen's flaming red hair was indeed natural, and something glittered from her navel. It looked like a huge diamond. The Ice Queen, you betcha.

The Koreans faces were contorted. They looked strong, their muscles extending. It looked like they were on the brink of a rousing finish. They twisted the Ice Queen around. I saw a tattoo on the small of her back. It looked like a *snake*.

Hiromi pulled my arm, and I followed her through the bathroom to the office.

"I found a backstairs," she whispered, "I think it comes down into the kitchen. It is locked. I think I'll have a few seconds to pick it. Should we try?"

"Yes," I whispered. "Let's get out of here. She might be here all day."

From the guest bedroom where we had been hiding in the closet, Hiromi opened the door to the hallway. It sounded like the Koreans and the Ice Queen were still going strong. We tiptoed down the hallway. At the end was another door, and Hiromi knelt down, her lock picks in her hand, and manipulated the lock. She opened the door, stepped through

337

it, and down the stairs. I gently closed the door and followed her.

Within a minute, we were out the back door and in the alley. The fresh air felt to us like the air must feel to a released prisoner. Both of our faces were sweaty; both of us had sweated through our shirts; both of us just wanted to get back to the car.

I had never seen an orgy before. A ménage-de-la-whatever hadn't been one of my experiences in life. I'm sure that it hadn't been one of Hiromi's life experiences either. As a voyeur, it was shocking. It wasn't appealing. It seemed so violent. I had never seen a rape before either—even in all my post-war days in Berlin—but the orgy we had witnessed had to be a cousin to rape. That could be the Catholic upbringing in me censoring my feelings, but I knew that that type of sexual exercise wasn't going to be a part of my lifestyle.

I did, however, still feel the sensuality of Hiromi's whisper in my ear when we were in the closet. I still felt the touch of her hand on my face and my neck. When I looked over to her as we walked down the alley, I noticed her sweaty shirt clinging to her and saw a different Hiromi than the one I'd known as a boarder.

Back at the car, Rafael was waiting for us, leaning against the fender. He started explaining right away. "She didn't come walking down the street," he said, "she was dropped off in front of her home in a black Cadillac. Two Oriental guys got out of the car with her. That's when I called. Are you okay?"

I mumbled that we were. We didn't say much on our drive back to Brooklyn. I think Rafael was feeling so guilty about the close call that he didn't ask any questions, and he slumped in the back seat, taking a quick siesta.

When I pulled the Ford onto the Brooklyn Bridge, Hiromi finally spoke. "Did you see the diamond on her stomach?" she asked.

I nodded. Then I asked a dumb question, "How does it stick? How does it stay there?"

"I think it was attached to her skin," Hiromi said, "like those African natives that we see in *National Geographic* that have different things sticking through their bodies. It's probably like an earring that is stuck through an earlobe, but this is her belly button instead."

I winced. The Ice Queen was really weird. She had a body that didn't need any adornments, so why in the world let something be jabbed through her belly button?

"Yakuza," Hiromi said.

"Yock what?"

"Ice Queen have tattoo, you see? Only gangsters in Japan have tattoos," Hiromi said. "Gangsters. Yakuza. Gangsters."

Just click on this link to order Red Chaser at Amazon.com.

339

Made in United States
Troutdale, OR
10/04/2023

13415426R00210